SILVER OR LEAD

James Cox

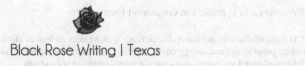

Black Rose Writing | Texas

The author grants the final approval for this literary material.

First printing

This is a work of fiction. Names, characters, businesses, places, events, and incidents are either the products of the author's imagination or used in a fictitious manner. Any resemblance to actual persons, living or dead, or actual events is purely coincidental.

ISBN: 978-1-68433-921-1
PUBLISHED BY BLACK ROSE WRITING
www.blackrosewriting.com

Printed in the United States of America
Suggested Retail Price (SRP) $20.95

Silver or Lead is printed in Garamond Premier Pro

*As a planet-friendly publisher, Black Rose Writing does its best to eliminate unnecessary waste to reduce paper usage and energy costs, while never compromising the reading experience. As a result, the final word count vs. page count may not meet common expectations.

For my Mom, Lucille

SILVER OR LEAD

"Always do what is right. It will gratify half of mankind and astound the other."
–Mark Twain

"Plata O Plomo ... silver or lead?"
–Pablo Escobar

CHAPTER 1

August 2019

I never thought that dying would be this complicated. What is it with this guy? Is he ever going to stop pissing?

I digress.

I am getting ahead of myself. Let me go back to the beginning if you don't mind.

May 2019

I'm Ben Rooker. I'm 48 years old. I'm a Scorpio. I like long walks on the beach... Well, forget about that for now. That's another story. I'm a widower. Rita, my heart, love of my life died of breast cancer a few years back. On second thought, let's not talk about that right now either. Anyway, I was sitting there at the Bard Café in Old Town Pasadena with my buddy Teddy Dabrowski. Teddy's one of those "vertically challenged" types, Polish guy with a chip on his shoulder. You don't really want to get into it with Teddy with those short jokes or the Polish ones, if you know what I mean. Very sensitive. Tough childhood growing up in an Irish, Italian, Polish neighborhood on the south side of Chicago. Mother at church every morning and father worshipping at the altar of John Barleycorn, lifting bourbon and beers to fight off the guilt of a failed life. He blamed Teddy for it, of course. Came home and beat him up while Mom prayed in the next room. Teddy took it until his 16th birthday. That was a memorable day. Teddy blew out the candles on the NY cheesecake and his dad punched him in the mouth and knocked Mom across the kitchen. No particular reason. Teddy walked/staggered into his room and grabbed the butcher knife from under his bed, the one he had lifted from Sal Durante's old man's shop. He took the knife and walked back into the kitchen calm as could be. His father was on another one of his pathetic, alcoholic crying jags, apologizing to his mom. His back was to Teddy. While old Dad was bent over Mom, crying his pathetic tears, Teddy lunged at his father. His mother caught his wrist just before the blade found the old man's hind quarters. Teddy looked at his mother and dropped the knife. No charges were ever filed. Mom told the old bastard she'd cut his balls off if he did, while he was sleeping. One thing that brought me and Teddy together. Our fathers. Hate. It's a motherfucker.

Anyway, like I said, Teddy and I were in Pasadena, CA on an unusually hot day in May at a little coffee shop/book store. Teddy and I, despite what some would call "Right Wing Neanderthal" leanings were passionate supporters of the arts and of independent bookstores. Go figure. Think that's kind of weird? I don't. We were there for our weekly coffee klatch where we talked about the movies, books and theater, but we always seemed to get waylaid on politics. It never failed to happen, me and Teddy being of a slightly different persuasion politically than probably 95% of the people in the LA Metro area, not to mention Hollywood. Just the two of us in the outside area of The Bard in what used to be the Smoking Area. That's funny now. Smoking in LA is right there with pedophilia or being a registered Republican. A guy who weighed at least 300 pounds was in front of us and a couple of senior citizens to our right. We were seated next to a garbage bin. I only bring this up since it's important later. An integral part of the story, you might say.

Well, we were talking low, so Big Brother doesn't hear us. Don't remember what we were talking about. Maybe Hillary or Bill or Trump. That would be as good a guess as any. Teddy raised his voice to a level that broke the zone of what we call the New McCarthyism. Sure enough, this woman wearing a "Frida Kahlo" T-shirt who had been sitting across from us chattering with an older guy darted her head up like a prairie dog on mescaline and gave us a glare that would have melted glass. Looked right at Teddy and stared him down. A moment of clarity struck me. This wasn't the first time she had been here. It dawned on me then that she had been here at least two or three times before. Teddy looked right back at her as if to say, "Give me a reason you bit...," well now we don't want to get crude here. Lots of chances for that later on. I got to tell you though, it was disconcerting. I could see that Teddy was fed up. So, there they were. Teddy and crazed prairie dog lady looking like Mayweather and Pacquiao at the pre-fight weigh-in. They're doing the dance macabre and Teddy gets up. "Jesus Christ," I was thinking. She's 60 if she's a day, Good skin, though. Latina, I would say. Attractive. Oh God in heaven, Teddy, do not get into it with this woman. I thought that because that's exactly what it looked like old Teddy was going to do. He got up and walked straight at her and then like the ex-marine, sorry former marine that he was... there are no ex-marines, did a right face that Chesty Puller would have been proud of and disappeared into the bookstore. It would have been the perfect exit if it weren't for the 300 pound barista guy pulling the aforementioned big ass garbage receptacle across the entrance, cutting Teddy off, albeit just for a moment, as the dumpster guy then proceeded to trip over my foot as well in the process and I was all set to give him a few colorful metaphors when all hell broke loose and my life and Teddy's changed forever.

CHAPTER 2

April 2019
Pasadena, CA
A Few Weeks Earlier.

"Look, Teddy, you got to get out there. Meet somebody. You're not dead yet."

I was talking to my good friend. Yea, you already met him, Teddy Dabrowski. Anyway, I'm trying to go back so the story will make some kind of sense. You know, so maybe you can form your own opinion about this whole shit show.

"Who's going to date a short Polack on a fixed income who hates Hillary here on the border of 'Holly weird'?"

"You're taking a very negative view here, my friend. You don't need to bring up politics all the time. Plus, you don't hate anyone. Under that gruff exterior lives the heart of a compassionate renaissance man."

"Fuck you."

The 35er Club in Old Town was just up the street from The Bard. It was what my old man used to call an upholstered sewer, only now this dive bar was considered "In" by the millennial crowd. A place where college kids, computer techs, and even the editor of the Pasadena Weekly could mingle with the real alcoholics and various Runyon-esque characters who had spawned the bar years ago.

A change of pace this day. Teddy drinking boilermakers and me pulling back Diet Cokes as we shot the breeze and talked Shakespeare.

"What really was the deal with Ophelia and Hamlet? I saw a bit of sexual tension."

Teddy wanted no part of it.

"She was his sister for Christ's sake."

The 35er added to its "If the Algonquin Table was a shithole out West" vibe by having a large bookcase that lined the walls in the backroom next to the pool table. There was everything from Louis L'Amour to Virginia Woolf; and yes, there was Shakespeare as well. Supposedly, Ray Bradbury, a Pasadena native, would drink here occasionally and, after downing a few bottles of Kolsch's, would proceed to secretly autograph copies of *Fahrenheit 451* and *The Martian Chronicles* which he kept in his tweed jacket and would place discretely in the bookcase for some lucky, literary drunk to find.

Okay, enough meandering for now. Let's move on with the story.

Teddy and I were at the 35er because he had something on his mind. Teddy was not what you would call a guy who wears his heart on his sleeve, so when he said he needed to talk, I took it seriously. Very seriously.

"How'd you like to take a road trip, my man?"

"Is that why you wanted to talk to me? Ask me if I wanted to drop everything and just leave?"

The look on Teddy's face made me pull back a bit. He was serious. Not some small talk bullshit between two old friends. Two middle-aged old friends at that.

"Okay, yea ok. So where? When? Why?"

"Tomorrow. Texas. El Paso. I can't tell you the 'Why' yet. I'm not sure myself."

"Okay, I'll just cancel everything and jump in the car and haul us down to Texas tomorrow. I mean, I assume we are taking my car, the CR-V. I mean, I seriously doubt your '94 Honda, with respect, will get us past San Bernardino. Christ, Teddy, what's going on? This is Ben here. You haven't been yourself the last few weeks. What's eating you?"

I half expected him to laugh, but he didn't. Instead, he looked me straight in the eye.

"You ever kill somebody, Ben? I mean cause somebody to die. Like, have you ever been in a situation where you could save someone, but you had to risk your own life to do it?"

"Hey, man... Jesus, I..."

"That's where I'm at. I was there. And I failed, I fucking failed, Jesus, God help me, Ben. Help me!"

Nobody was near us at the bar. It was still early, even for a professional day drinker's paradise like the 35er. A chilly day in April. Teddy was bawling like a baby. A different Teddy Dabrowski. He calmed down after a bit. I gave him some space. Then he told me.

Everything.

Looking back at that day later, after everything that has happened, I realize I should have acted then, at that moment. But I didn't and that, my friends, is something I will regret until my dying day—which will probably be shortly after this guy next to me finishes pissing.

CHAPTER 3

The Bard Café
May 2019
RINGING
DARKNESS

The middle of the god damn day.

That's what I remember.

The darkness, ringing, screams and then the sirens.

Smoke, burnt flesh, glass.

Teddy had just gone into the bookstore after his stare down with crazed prairie dog lady. He was going to the head; or rest room, for you civilian types. Maybe a few minutes or seconds had gone by. I remember feeling kind of relieved. I didn't want the tension to escalate. I'd seen it happen before. So, when Teddy did his exit stage right and headed into the bookstore, I relaxed. Until the explosion.

I came to and the first thing on my mind was how many pieces I might be in. Then I thought about the prairie dog lady. Lots of smoke, so I didn't see her at first. Then I did. Right away I thought a department store mannequin had flown across the street from the Target with its wig hanging half off and nose askew. Not the case. Upon further review, I realized I was peering at the source of Teddy's recent resentment. This woman had been an animated, vital, arguably obnoxious human being just a few moments ago. Now, well, she, it, whatever, was a torso; a head and a bad wig. I didn't want to know where the rest of her was.

The ride to the hospital was bumpy. I imagined it was like that car in the "mea culpa" story Teddy had relayed to me a few months ago at the 35er. Funny what comes to mind after one gets blown up.

He had been in another one of his vulnerable moods. He talked about the time he got drunk in Juarez on his way across country to Los Angeles. He would have gone farther, but he couldn't swim, he used to say. He was on a well-deserved 30 days leave and was riding in the back of a beat up Toyota. Eileen, he says, was driving and Veronica was in the passenger seat. The banter at the Juarez strip joint with these two coeds from Las Cruces had turned into a drunken early Christmas for Teddy. He was in his early thirties then. Not exactly a virgin, but let's just say Teddy had nothing on George Clooney, hell he had nothing on Benny Clooney, the one-armed waiter that Teddy's dad used to drink with back in the South Side. Anyway, Teddy was fondling Eileen's ample boob (his term) with visions of what was to come and then... the car hit something. A god damn school bus! Right in the middle of some Saint's fiesta day in Juarez. Well, more like side-swiped it. Eileen decided it was a good idea to leave the car and walk into a nearby shoe store. Like they owned the place. Nothing to see here, right? Wrong.

He liked that about her. The chick had balls. I mean all about booze and lust, but the other one, Veronica, was all about being a stuck-up diva. She was all about being a stuck-up diva, like she was the daughter of royalty or something. Teddy liked this Eileen though. Good prospects. Maybe he'd settle down with her. Oh yea, the fantasy world of the practicing drunk. Anyway, Teddy said that the whole town became central casting background actors from *The Good, the Bad, and the Ugly* and Teddy, Eileen and Veronica, well they were the ugly Americans. That shoe store thing worked for about 30 seconds. Long enough for the local policia/cartel to show up and throw Teddy and friends into the back of a squad car. They drove out to what looked like the middle of the desert to Teddy and then just stopped.

"Senor, I am very sorry, but you were driving drunk."

"Yes, I know officer, oh great, you speak English, but I wasn't driving."

"Yes, but the young lady was driving. It does not matter. You will all have to spend the night or perhaps the week in our jail. And the young ladies, well I cannot vouch for their safety. So many "accidents", is that the word... happening these days. A shame."

What happened next changed my dear friend Teddy forever. One of those life affirming things, I could say, except there wasn't anything affirming about it.

Teddy took the C-Note out of his pocket. The Little Voice days ago urging him to take hundreds rather than twenties at the credit union on Parris Island for the trip. He always took twenties, but not this time. The Little Voice. His Mom always said it. "Follow the Little Voice, Teddy. God works in mysterious ways. It won't steer you wrong. It's Jesus talking to you."

Mysterious ways indeed.

Minutes later Teddy said that Eileen was driving the banged up car back towards the border.

She was still shit-faced so Teddy asked to drive.

"No chance. I'm good."

Veronica was passed out, so she was no help.

They reached the border and of course were picked for a "random" search.

"We're good right?" Teddy asked/pleaded.

No answer from Veronica, who was now wide awake.

Veronica mentioned amphetamines in a rushed tete a tete with Eileen. Teddy was calculating how old he'd be when he got out of federal prison when the border guards waved them back into the car.

Thank you, Jesus, or whoever is running the show, he thought.

A mile or so from the border on the outskirts of downtown El Paso, Veronica lifted 1000 amphetamines out of a hidden compartment next to the steering wheel and Teddy puked. And then they went back to his motel room and had teenage fantasy threesome sex.

Well, I'd like to tell you that, anyway. I mean, that's what Teddy kept telling himself. Figured if he told that part of the story enough, well, it would magically become true. Fact was, he told it that spring day in the 35er and years before and in every saloon and with anyone who would listen. Killed the guilt. Not for long, though. It's a nice story. But it's not true. And since I'd like you here for the entire ride, I need to be straight with you. I'll tell you the real story. The one Teddy told me after he had drunk himself sober.

They managed to talk the Mexican cops into letting them go. Well, Teddy did. I mean, he was the one that was let go. You see, the C-Note only covered the release of one person and since in those days he was a self-centered, self-pitying piece a shit, well, I guess you can figure out that person was Teddy. He would always hear the cries of Eileen and Veronica as they were being dragged away (until the third or fourth shot of Jack Daniels anyway). He was thrown into the girls' car and driven to the border. He told himself he would get word to the authorities as soon as he got across the border and rescue both of them.

The story about amphetamines was true as well. After the policia/cartel guy dropped him at the checkpoint, he drove the girls' car across the border. He was searched at the checkpoint. They found nothing. Then when he got to his Best Western in El Paso and looked for the registration in the glove compartment, the bag of bennies magically dropped to the floorboard. They had been in a compartment hanging by a thread from all the bouncing in the car. He did puke as well. That part was also true. He lived with the look on their terrified faces. He told me how he had nightmares where they were being raped repeatedly, begging for their lives before they were shot and thrown into a lonely grave in the middle of the desert. He never told the authorities. You see, Teddy never knew their real names... Never knew what happened to them. Well, I mean he knew they called themselves Veronica and Eileen and they said they were from Las Cruces but how was he to know if that was true or not? And besides, he didn't have last names. The car was a rental and since it was all beaten up, he didn't want to take it back to the Budget or Avis or whatever the fuck it was. There was no paperwork in the glove compartment either. Policia must have taken it or one of the girls had it. It was probably decomposing at this moment right next to their stinking, rotting bodies. He just left the car in the motel parking lot, got in his own vehicle, and drove to Los Angeles. Teddy was drunk as soon as he hit the first bar in LALA land. Stayed drunk for years. Of course he made up stories in his head, rationalizations that the girls got released, that their parents or whoever paid a ransom. Truth be told, I got a good idea where they are. Probably right where he left them that dark day. Six feet under. I never told Teddy that. Didn't have to. Best to forget it. Move on. The drink helped Teddy for a while but was not a permanent solution.

He went back there a few years later. He had originally told me he was going to Chicago to visit what was left of his family. Turned out he went to Las Cruces. The place the girls said they were from. When I asked him how it went, he just changed the subject.

CHAPTER 4

I didn't require any major medical work. You might ask, "How does a person 10 feet from me have their head removed from the rest of their body while I end up with a few cuts and a minor concussion?"

Luck. Pure luck. And a timely interest in Shakespeare. It was unseasonably hot that day at The Bard. The sun had just got to the level where it was a royal pain in my ass. Shining just above my eyes. Just as the thought occurred to me to investigate whether prairie dog lady and Teddy were going to go at it, the sun momentarily blinded me. In a reflex action, I picked up my thick as a bullet-proof vest copy of *Arden Complete Works of Shakespeare* to shield my eyes to get a better look of what I perceived as a pending physical altercation when the god damn bomb went off. Glass and pieces of wood and metal were impaled in the damn volume. It pays to have a bit of culture. Also, it helps to have a large container full of garbage being pushed by an enormous barista that is directly between you and the bomb blast trajectory. We both survived. The barista and me. Sadly, the garbage container was recycled forever.

Teddy ended up in the Neurology section of Huntington Hospital. Beautiful place. It's been around since 1892. Pasadena itself is only six years older. Stunning Spanish architecture. In the 1930s Henry Huntington, your basic railroad gazillionaire gave the hospital millions of dollars to bring it into the modern era. Thus the name Huntington Hospital. I found Teddy sitting upright, finishing what looked like a fruit cup and watching ESPN.

"You know I'm liking these women sportscasters," he said to the guy in the next bed who appeared to be in a coma.

"I mean, they know their sports and that should be all that matters. That and being built like the proverbial "brick shit house'."

Teddy was happy to take on both parts of a conversation if need be. It's a Chicago thing, I believe.

"Ben!"

We exchanged pleasantries. He was happy to see me. He looked okay except for a bit of a lazy eye that I never noticed before and a slight tremor in his left hand. He told me he remembered nothing after he walked into the bookstore. He opened the door. BOOM. Then everything went black. He woke up with the *National Women's Day* promo bookcase on top of him. Probably saved his life.

"You remember nothing after that?"

"No."

"Nothing at all. You didn't see anybody, anything that might have been suspicious."

"Nothing. I just remember that crazy broad glaring at me as I opened the door. Then a blast of light. I woke up with this fucking bunch of books all over me."

I told my good buddy that he might want to defer from the "B" word while he was recuperating here. I felt it was a good safety tip considering the gender demographic of most of the people responsible for his care here. I gave him a bit of a pass considering what he had just gone through.

"You never saw that woman before or the guy she was with?"

"Believe me, I was trying to place her. Nothing."

There was a bit of a hesitation. Teddy and I went way back. Long enough that my internal bullshit meter registered, but I chalked it up again to the ordeal.

Well, maybe after his head cleared... "What about the eye and the shaking?"

"I don't know. The docs aren't telling me a lot. They don't know, I guess. Dr. Mancuso, have you seen her yet? The hot little Italian number. She was just here. You probably walked past her on the way in. She says it's probably collateral damage from the concussion and the shock. MRI showed nothing weird. They think it will go away. I just want to get the hell out of here."

We talked a bit more about him taking it easy. Well, I did most of the talking on that subject. He just wanted to get out. I said to rest up. I thought the road trip to Texas he had mentioned might be a good idea after all but only after he was all patched up and healthy. But first I needed to speak to Dr. Mancuso.

Teddy was right. Very attractive. She looked like a young Marisa Tomei. Not that Marisa isn't still attractive at her current age. But, again, I digress.

"He's had none of his current tremors before now? You noticed nothing? The lazy eye?"

"No. Nothing."

I told her that Teddy had no family left that I knew of so I couldn't go down the ancestry route for the history of various genetic maladies or any of that jazz. I left her with that and told Teddy I'd be back to visit soon and we would talk more about the trip.

"Yea, sure. We'll talk about it."

****

The Pasadena Police station is located next to the Pasadena City Hall which is another magical example of Spanish architecture. I know you've seen the city hall before. You just didn't know what it was. A shot of the structure is on every TV show or movie that needs a classical looking government building. The cupola-like rotunda echoing the 16th century Italian architecture probably because John Bakewell and Arthur Brown, the architects were influenced by renaissance artisan Andrea Palladio when they built it in 1927. The Pasadena Police Station also on Garfield avenue is decidedly less impressive but still a distinct upgrade from, say, the Waukegan Police Station, a place that Teddy Dabrowski, recuperating in Huntington Hospital, was patently familiar with. All that mattered to me though was that on this May day the Starbucks was right around the corner.

As I sat listening to Detective Samuel Jackson Jr., "I am no relation to the brother from *Pulp Fiction* so let's not even talk about it," it was nice to have that vente drip even though the temperature outside was in the mid-seventies and the coffee was twice as hot.

It was all about the caffeine. Since I had given up the booze three years ago, it was indeed only about that buzz. Filling the void in A.A-speak. I rationalized it of course and said it helped me creatively, but of course that was bullshit. Oh yes, indeed. And women. Yes, they were another way to fill the void left by the removal of the booze.

"So, let me try to understand this. You and your buddy, Lenny, were…"

"Teddy, his name is Teddy."

I had told him that twice already. He wasn't stupid. I get a feeling about people. Intuition. This cop, try as he might to play some street-wise heavy from Compton with a Martin Lawrence smile was not what he seemed. No, this guy needed to be watched and listened to closely.

"So, run it by me again. What did you see and hear from the time you and Teddy got to the coffee shop till the time the bomb went off?"

I went through it again. How I picked up Teddy at his apartment in South Pasadena and we drove the ten minute drive to The Bard. How we were immersed in our weekly discussion about the arts and religion. I didn't mention the politics. How the middle aged Latina had seemingly stalked Teddy several times at our coffee shop rendezvous. How Teddy almost got run over by the barista pushing the trash bin and then made his way through the bookstore entrance. A few moments went by and then the explosion and darkness.

"What was Teddy's mood on the way to the bookstore? Was he happy, sad, angry?"

Teddy seemed to be contemplative when I picked him up. That was Teddy though. He could go from sad to happy to whatever faster than Lindsay Lohan leaving a rehab. Remember that *Sybil* movie? The one with the woman with a thousand personalities. That was Teddy. Well, maybe not that many personalities but the truth be told, Teddy was moody.

"He seemed fine."

"Had you ever seen Rose Vasquez at the book store before?"

"Who?"

"The woman that was apparently seated only a few feet from you and Teddy. You mean to say you didn't know who she was?"

And then it hit me. She was wearing glasses. Her hair was different in the newspaper pics and the ones on TMZ. "Rosey V." The estranged wife of "Roy Boy, the Tire Guy" Vasquez. The head of the Venganza cartel. The biggest, most powerful cartel in Mexico. "Roy Boy, the Tire Guy," so called because of the way he would execute the poor bastards who he believed had narc'd on his cartel.

In a typical scenario, he'd put two of them together, bound by rope about six feet away from each other. Then he'd have a tire doused with gasoline fitted over one of their heads. Standard stuff, right? Well, here's where Roy Boy got creative and separated himself from the status quo. Roy would tell the guy who had the gas doused tire over his head to give him something on the guy next to him. If Roy liked the info, he would release the guy. He told them that anyway. Well, invariably the guy with the petrol shampoo job would rat the other guy as everything from the Lindberg baby killer to the man on the grassy knoll. Roy Boy would laugh his ass off and then light his head, anyway. Let the guy next to him see the poor SOB's head boil and then fucking explode all over him. By the time the fire was out the surviving guy was a whimpering mass of jelly. Roy would let him go to tell his story, well as much as he could communicate through his screams and pathetic incoherent sobs. Few people narc'd on the Venganza Cartel when Roy Boy was the boss.

I realized Teddy had talked about Roy once. It seems he had become very interested in cartels in the last few years. Particularly, in recent days when he talked incoherently of Eileen and Veronica during a Jack Daniels fueled binge. How the hell didn't he know that was Rosey?

Or did he?

"I know who she is but only from what I saw on the news. Are you telling me that was Rose Vasquez the ex-wife of the biggest cartel boss in Mexico sitting across from me and Teddy? But why the fuck would she be giving Teddy the evil eye?"

"Yes, it was, and as to your second question, I was hoping you would answer that."

"Maybe you should ask Teddy."

"Oh, I will. I will."

CHAPTER 5

I let Teddy rest and recuperate for a few more days before I asked him about Rosey or Roy Boy or any of that shit. Truth be told I needed a meeting. I'd been sober a little over three years thanks to Alcoholics Anonymous and a God of my understanding. Not yours. Mine. You get that? Ok. I don't want any bitching about God and his or her existence. My God is my God. He is a God of my understanding that I do not understand. I went into the abyss big time after life with *Father Knows Best* and weekly "wrestling" after altar boy practice. Drinking to forget is cliché but it hits the target or comes fairly close. You see, I was a piece of shit. I still am on bad days. The difference is that today I own that piece of shit status. I don't blame my father or my mother. No. Today, I own it. Well, most of the time.

Now, Father Chuck, well, he is a different story. Going to take a helluva a lot more work.

Father Chuck Castenato. Young priest at St. Brigid's. That's where I went to elementary school on Long Island. St. Brigid's. St. Brigid of Ireland. Beautiful Irish girl. Patron saint of babies. Evidently her patron saint duties were limited to the infant years. Once you were walking and talking, well, old Brigid apparently clocked out.

Yes, I was an altar boy. You already think you know where this is going and you're right. Well mostly. Father Chuck was about 28 when he came to St. Brigid's He stood out not just because he was Italian in an Irish church but because he was younger than the other priests. Much younger. He was a good-looking guy and the girls loved him. The boys looked up to him. Especially yours truly, the boy who suffered a daily litany at home of, "You're not my son. Nothing but a zero," etc.

Yes, that would be me. Guilty as charged. I was first in to altar boy practice and last out. He was not just a priest. He was the older brother I never had and the surrogate father. I adored the guy.

And then one day everything came tumbling down, like an alky without a drink on the day after.

All the other boys had left. Father Chuck asked me to stay. He had some fried chicken from KFC and we ate it after I helped clean up. I felt a real need to talk on this afternoon. Dad had returned the other night in "Bad Alky" form. Slapped me around a bit and tried out some colorful metaphors on Mom like "syphilitic whore"(a new one) and "cheating bitch" (recycled).

"I really enjoy being an altar boy, Father. I really appreciate you being my friend. I can't really talk to Dad or Mom and I have these fears. I mean I don't even know what they are. What's that Father? Oh yea, that's right, ... *irrational fears*, yea that's right. My dad, he drinks too much and then he takes it out on my mom. It's my fault I know. If I was a better son, he wouldn't drink so much. Well, I guess, I better be going now. I'll be late for supper... The chairs?

"I almost forgot. Oh sure, I can help you with the chairs It's the least I can do, You're a great listener. Okay, that looks like the last chair. What's that. Wrestle? You were a wrestler in college, Father Chuck? Wow. Yea, I suppose. Just for a little while...Father, you're getting kind of red, sweaty... are you okay, my pants... please Father!"

Father Chuck is dead now. I found out a few years ago. It seems he suffered a massive stroke while in retirement, playing golf in Florida. Apparently, the church had hidden him away by giving him an "early retirement." His last church was a rich parish full of celebrities. You see aside from being charming and good looking and being responsible for several bath house rapes in New York after his encounter with me (I was what you would call in the vernacular, the tip of the iceberg) Father Chuck could raise money. Oh yes. The Cardinal would not let a valuable guy like this waste away in prison. No killing of the golden goose. I rehearsed so many times what I would say to him if I ever met him on his deathbed. I even had dreams about it.

Father Chuck! Damn, it's been a long time. Don't get up. Oh, I don't suppose you can. Don't talk. If you recognize me just nod or drool. Whatever. Yes, it's Ben, the altar boy.

Ben Rooker. That's right. Oh, let me wipe that for you. Getting red now, are you? No need to get excited. There will be no wrestling today. Some boys that you preyed on

after me became priests themselves and carried on where you left off by wrestling with
other little kids. Children. Innocents. Well, no I didn't go that route. I suppose I should
be thankful. No, I just tried to drown myself in Jack Daniels and sex. Meaningless sex.
No relationships for me! A normal relationship? A loving, nurturing no. Oh, God, I
tried. But you see Father Chuck every time I got close to the intimacy, the caring, the
need for trust, well, there you were with your red face, your desperate hands pawing at
me. How could I have any kind of bond with another human being without guilt?
Without shame? No, God no. God fucking no.

Jesus, I don't know what happened there. Sorry about that. I guess I got
"triggered," isn't that what they call it these days? Well, like I said earlier, I needed
a meeting.

****

"My name is Ben and I'm an alcoholic."

"Hi, Ben."

I was at my Tuesday Night Men's A.A. Meeting. It's in a beautiful old
monastery in Sierra Madre, an all American, main street town to the north east end
of Pasadena nestled in the foothills. The meeting was called "Monks and Drunks"
which explains a lot about the sense of humor of recovering alcoholics. One more
thing about Sierra Madre, remember the original *Invasion of the Body Snatchers*
movie? The one made in the 50s? Well, the "pod delivery scene" was shot right in
the Sierra Madre town square. There's a Starbucks there now. Appropriate.

"I've been sober a little over three years now. Some days are better than others.
I know they say there are no 'Big Deals' here but I've got to disagree with that one.
Some of you may have heard that I was having coffee with a buddy of mine at the
Bard Café in Old Town last month when somebody blew it up. Resentments can
be a terrible thing."

Lots of laughter on that one. Alkies are sick bastards indeed.

"I just had a few cuts and bruises. My buddy, who is a candidate for these
rooms, was seriously hurt but he's going to be okay. I'll be picking him up tomorrow
to take him home. Anyway, the reason I mentioned all this is if there was ever a
reason to drink it was after that. What an excuse to drink, right? Not that we ever
need one, but shit, in the bad old days I would have been downing them at the 35er
before the fire was even out. I didn't mention that three people are dead from the
blast and there is a fourth in 'grave condition.' A woman about six feet from me

ended up in pieces. Don't ask me how I'm here. Grace of God, I guess. Anyway, I just wanted to tell you how grateful I was for you guys and this program."

There was clapping and assorted chants of "Keep coming back." I stepped down off the podium and my phone vibrated. I don't normally answer at A.A. meetings but we were on a break. As soon as I did though, I regretted it. It was a familiar voice. You ever hear a voice and you know that person from somewhere but they are out of context from the place you are in at the time? Well, that's how I felt when the voice of Detective Sam Jackson of the Pasadena Police Department reverberated on my phone.

"Sorry to call you after hours. What's all that noise? You at a party or something?"

"I'm at an A.A. meeting."

At that point I didn't give a shit about anonymity. I just wanted to get off the god damn phone.

"Damn! How long have you been sober?"

"Almost three years."

"Good for you there, Rooker. Yea, we got lots of cops with booze problems. A.A. is a damn good program."

The last thing I wanted to talk to this guy about was the program.

"Can I help you, Detective?"

"Oh yea, sure. Yes indeed. I saw our man, Teddy, today at the hospital. He looks good."

I didn't know if Jackson knew I was picking up Teddy tomorrow. He was being released. I didn't feel in the mood to volunteer anything new even though I had just told him I was a recovering alcoholic.

"Great. So you haven't arrested him."

"Shit, now why would I want to do that? Just trying to solve a case. He said nothing about that Rose Vasquez to you? You know the cartel lady?"

"Yea, I remember. No. I mean we saw her at the coffee shop but that was it. I just thought maybe she heard Teddy make one of his comments specifically designed to annoy thin skinned types. . He never gave me any sign he knew who Rose was if that's what you're getting at."

It was of course, but Jackson was locked in on something else right now.

"Okay, well look, this can probably wait until we see each other officially again."

"Christ, I've been at the station; I told you everything I know."

"Yea, sure, well see, things have gotten a bit more interesting lately. When I saw Teddy today, he was kind of edgy, you know, irritable. Like he had something on his mind."

"And your point? The man was almost killed recently."

"Oh yes, sure. Understood. Thing is, I believe Mr. Dabrowski knows more than he is saying."

"How so?"

"Rose Vasquez for starters."

CHAPTER 6

I had always thought of Pasadena as a miniature New York City. Especially the Old Town area. It was founded in 1874 and incorporated in 1886 specifically so the town's only saloon could be shut down. Classic. A city created solely to close a bar. Then, of course, came the Tournament of Roses parade which has brought billions into the city. The Tournament of Roses' Queen was "white only" for many years, one of the last bastions of the WASP class but recently had been integrated to the point where the last five Tournament of Roses Queens were women of color.

One of the reasons Pasadena made me think of New York is because it is one of the few areas in southern California where people walk rather than drive. There was also a briskness to the city. It's not laid back like, say, Venice. I imagined this has something to do with the pedestrian ethic. Teddy hated it when I used that term by the way. "Of color? What the hell does that mean?" I could hear him saying it right then as I made a left off Fair Oaks and headed towards the visitors parking lot at Huntington Hospital.

I was there to pick up Teddy. He had called the night before to say he had a clean bill of health. He would have a limp for a while. Maybe permanently but what the hell. He survived. Detective Jackson kept calling me. Wanted me to come in when I "have a chance. Tie up some loose ends," he said.

Well, fuck! I didn't have time for this shit. I needed to go on auditions. Did I tell you I was an actor? Yea, got into it after the Navy. Acting, my escape from my childhood of nightmares. What I also was in need of was an agent. But Christ, I'm a 48-year-old guy, 49 in a month with not much in the way of credits. It is tough. But ever since I did *The Crucible* on stage a few years back, I had been addicted. You think booze or drugs are an addiction? Get on stage in front of a packed house one time. It's terrifying. The kind of terror you feel when you're about to jump out of an airplane. With a parachute of course but still; that feeling of the unknown. Then you jump or step out on stage and you connect with another actor. You don't even know the audience is there anymore. Like you don't realize you're 10,000 feet above the earth free-falling. You are present! Focused. As close to the pure NOW than you will ever be. Then you take your final bow or landing and you are hooked, my friend. You don't sleep maybe the rest of the night. It's a good thing though. You did it. You overcame the terror. You communicated a story to a group of strangers and you connected. Sober. Life. This is living.

Speaking of "free-falling," caught up in my artistic reverie I almost didn't notice the airborne body. I had just parked my car and gotten out and began my walk to the hospital visitor entrance. I thought it was a bird at first glance. A blue flash out of the corner of my eyes. Then I saw the gown flapping. A hospital gown. It was a clear day. You could see the foothills. No pollution. Still though, at this point reality had not set in. I'd figured the flapping object was a kite. A very weird, awkward kite. Like a kite that was coming apart. It was falling like a missile or one of those cliff divers I used to watch on *Wide World of Sports*. Yea, in Acapulco, before that gorgeous city was taken over by the cartels. But why was it falling that way? And then I saw it. I mean I really saw it. A human body in a gown. You would expect arms to be extended or flailing like I remember them doing on one of those videos I saw in my college days called *Faces of Death*. An 8 -track video collection some sick fuck or fucks had put together about all the various ways people died. There was one where some poor bastard's parachute had not opened and he was spreading his arms out like he was trying to swim. Swim through the air. No, this wasn't like that, though. This body seemed to be plummeting straight down. It's amazing what you can see in a flash. The human missile disappeared behind a pillar (A disadvantage of Spanish architecture, the pillars) and then I heard it. That sound. The sound I never thought I would ever hear again. The sound I last heard on that September morning in New York, a lifetime ago.

Standing outside the World Trade Center. In those days I wanted to be a volunteer fireman. Another thing that didn't work out because of old John Barleycorn, the old English name for booze. It only lasted a month but enough time to witness 9/11 up-close and personal. Just a small town fire department on Long Island but, as fate would have it, I was in the city for training. Hung over like a son of a bitch. Stayed up drinking, watching my NY Football Giants lose to the Broncos the night before. I will always remember that game even though the Giants sucked that year and the game was meaningless but it was where I was the night before 9/11.

So long ago, a few blocks from the WTC watching a body, a human body plummet towards the earth and then... THUD SPLAT. I imagined that the body had only minutes before been a human being, A guy who had probably just been talking about the game an hour ago in the coffee room. How his oldest son might be good enough for the Giants one of these days, now falling to oblivion and then THUD SPLAT. That's exactly the sound.

Now years later, again THUD SPLAT. Like when you are patting hamburger meat vigorously with your bare hands to form it into patties. I looked up in time to see the blue hospital gown with a figure inside. THUD SPLAT right off the visitor's entry structure of Huntington Hospital.

But this was different from 9/11. Apparently, there was a temporary canopy there. I found out later it was for a makeshift blood drive. Anyway, the gowned hamburger/figure hit the side of the building but slipped off and bounced off the canopy before finally landing. THUD SPLAT.

I thought of Olga Korbut doing a dismount from an uneven bar routine only this was not a 10.0 dismount. More like a 5.5 as Hamburger Gown just laid there. No more bouncing. No arms outstretched in victory. THUD.

I began running towards the landing point. From a distance of about twenty yards I noticed the gown was almost completely off. (Always tie the back of your hospital gown securely.) I stopped. A kind of foreboding enveloped me. I stepped towards the obliterated mass when every part of me said don't look. Run away.

"Dispatch, We have a possible 10-55. Send ambulance and coroner. Huntington Hospital entrance."

"What the hell does that mean? Speak English."

"What!? Shit I thought that was you. What the hell are you doing here, Rooker?"

Somehow Detective Sam Jackson had made his way to the "Landing Site" ahead of me and was now calling in what I would learn later was the code for apparent suicide and a dead body.

I was in no mood to shoot the breeze with the good detective. I didn't see clearly who that bloodied thing was, but I knew. God help me, I knew.

I took a knee and cried. Cried like a baby. For New York, The Hamburger Guy, for Teddy.

To Jackson's credit he gave me a few moments. I got it all out, well most of it. Still in shock, I sat on a bench well away from the scene of the crime. If that's what it was. After a while Jackson sauntered up next to me. He was smoking a cigarette (illegally).

"I was here to pick Teddy up. He was going to be released today," I said.

"I was here to arrest him, I'm afraid. Looks like I won't have to do that right now."

I got about two feet before a couple of uniforms grabbed me.

"Let him go, officers. It's okay. Sit, Rooker. We'll have to wait for a positive ID but someone saw him. The plant manager says he saw Teddy Dabrowski leaving his room in a rush and heading towards the point up there where the John Doe jumped. As for why I was here to arrest him; the bombing of The Bard, domestic terrorism, three counts of murder and various counts of attempted murder, mayhem, etc. Look, I know you're in shock. He was your friend and all that. I'd like to..."

I was already running across the parking lot to my car and out of earshot before he could finish the sentence. The uniforms started after me but stopped no doubt on orders from Jackson. I wasn't going anywhere, and he knew that.

Teddy dead?! A terrorist. Fuck no. He was to the right of Genghis Khan, but Teddy wouldn't hurt a fly. Well, as long as the fly didn't hurt anyone he cared about. In my view there were very few people Teddy cared about. There was his mom, Lenore, who had lived in Waukegan but had died a few years ago. His father died long ago of cirrhosis. He begged Teddy to visit him in the hospital, but Teddy told me he got drunk on the way there. Made a wrong turn or something. He had stayed close with his mom, one of the few people he would talk about at any length from his past. She had worked at the Naval base at Great Lakes about 20 miles outside of Chicago. No brothers or sisters. No girl friends or ex-wives that I knew of. As I raced out of the parking lot, my thoughts were broken up by Joe Jackson's *Steppin Out* on my iPhone.

"Hello? Yes, this is he. Paula Garcia? I don't think I... a friend, an associate of Teddy's? Oh, well Ms. Garcia, Paula, yes, I'm afraid this is not a good time."

I hung up. After a moment *Steppin Out* was back. Surreal. For some ungodly reason, I answered again. The Little Voice.

It was Paula again. I told her what I'd just witnessed. After a long pause in response to the sharing of Teddy's death and some sniffling no doubt brought about by the attempt to stifle tears, Paula Garcia was able to speak again.

"Ben, I know this is a horrible time, but I'd like you to come by Children's Hospital when you're not busy and you have time to process everything. I'd like to talk to you in person. There are some things... things that I can't share over the phone."

"I see."

"Just come anytime but call ahead so I can have a visitor pass for you. You don't have a cold or anything like that... I mean you're healthy, right?"

"No, no colds, no diseases... that I know of."

Nervous laugh. Silence.

"Bad joke. No, I am very healthy."

"Great. There's someone I want you to meet as well."

"Sure. Yea, I'll be there."

Then it dawned on me. I had just seen my best friend in the world fall to his death. What the fuck was I having a conversation with a complete stranger for?!

"Yea, actually, look, ah, Paula this is not a good time right now. Let me call you back."

I hung up again. My first instinct was to get the hell out of town. There was nothing holding me. Teddy was really the only friend I had. He had a lot of faults but he would never kill himself or anybody else. I mean anyone that was innocent. The guilty? Now that was another story.

Why the fuck did the estranged wife of one of the world's biggest cartel bosses just happen to be at the Bard Café every time Teddy was there over the last few weeks? Who blew up Bard Café? Why? Where the hell should I start?

All these thoughts swirled through my head in a matter of seconds. Then it hit me. The Little Voice. Again. Like seeing "11:11" on my car radio clock. I would head over to Children's Hospital. Speak to the mysterious Ms. Garcia. And just like that in the rear view it was red light symphony time. I pulled over and if it wasn't Det. Sam Jackson, at your service. The best laid plans. Shit.

CHAPTER 7

Pasadena Police Station

"I just wanted to have a little chit chat. I turn around to call the coroner and the forensic people and you're doing Starsky and Hutch out the dang parking lot. A hospital parking lot, I'll remind you, dumbass."

I was sitting in an interview room of the Pasadena Police Station on Garfield. My only friend in the world was dead. It was about ten in the morning and I had not had my first venti drip Starbucks. This was a major issue. I knew Jackson knew it. Evil bastard.

"Oh, and I am sorry for your loss."

"Am I under arrest? If you have a problem with my driving, then just give me a damn ticket. Okay?

"Rooker?" he said, ignoring my question.

"Wasn't there a pitcher by that name a few years back.? Yea, Jim Rooker, now I remember. White boy. Pitched for a bunch of teams. What you'd call a 'Journeyman.' Pittsburgh Pirates was one of them. I remember because I had just graduated from high school and I went with the fellas to see the Dodgers play the Pirates at Dodger Stadium. Chavez Ravine, most beautiful park in baseball. Anyway, it was the early 80s, and it was September. The Dodgers really needed a win. This Rooker who had a lifetime record of under .500 comes in and pitches like Sandy F'n Koufax. Shuts us out 1-0, I think it was. No wonder you're on my bad side already, Rooker, I hate that fucker. Nothin personal."

"I grew up in New York. Long Island. Mets fan. I hate the Dodgers and the Pirates. What do you need, Detective? I lost my best friend a few hours ago. Do you fucking understand that, you ignorant bozo? I'm still in a bit of shock. You think I killed him or maybe used my telekinetic powers to fly him out the window?"

Maybe it was Jackson kicking the table on its side, his look, or a combination of both, but I could tell right away that this tact was the wrong one. Any chance I had of getting a coffee was gone. The way things were going, I probably wouldn't be able to take any fluids for a good while anyway. Frankly though, I didn't give a fuck. Teddy was dead. Nothing else mattered.

"Do you dislike black people, Reeker?"

"Its 'Rooker' actually, and no I do not. I dislike a lot of people. Some of them may happen to be black, but I find the question…"

There goes the table again, this time sliding on its side after another swift kick from the detective, followed by his still lit cigarette (did I tell you he was smoking?) It whizzed past my head like a firefly on meth.

"I am supposed to retire in a year's time, Rooker! I would like to do it with full benefits and not with the reduced pay that I would be stuck with if I violated physics lesson number 35."

I bit.

"And what would that be, Sir, ah Lieutenant, ah Detective?"

"That would be 'A 3 by 5 table cannot fit up the anal orifice of a 6'2" white boy.'"

"Yes, Detective that is a tough one to break. Old physics lesson number 35. Love the humor, Sir, with just a dash of irony."

"Who killed Dabrowski!?"

I don't know if it was the coffee, withdrawal, the loss of my best friend or just this Jackson asshole inferring that I was a racist. In any case everything started to clear up.

Like Lee Remick says in *Days of Wine and Roses*, "This is the way I look when I'm sober. It's enough to make a person drink, wouldn't you say? You see, the world looks so dirty to me, when I'm not drinking…. Remember Fisherman's Wharf? The water when you looked too close? That's the way the world looks to me when I'm not drinking."

Anyway I was "coming to" and I was hurt and mad. Angry as hell.

" I love black people. Most of them anyway. I spent twenty god damn years in the Navy. I lived, slept, ate, fought together with black sailors. They were good people. Damn good shipmates. There are exceptions to everything of course and one of them is standing right in front of me. I have no idea how Teddy died, and why he was killed. What do you know detective? I sure as hell don't believe he would kill himself. I am frankly lost. You're the detective. You find out. Anyway, he said a lot of shit. Posted some of it on Facebook which I warned him against but he never told me he wanted to actually kill someone let alone blow up our favorite coffee shop and murder innocent people. Does that satisfy you? Now if you want to keep me here, I'm going to need someone to keep me company. Someone with a law degree. And I'll need them now."

Jackson's response was a statement. Just two words, "Rose Vasquez."

"Yea, yea, I know, we had this discussion."

"Why the fuck was she there?"

"Look, like I said, I now know who she was. I had no idea, though, who we were sitting next to all those times we had coffee there. I mean it just seemed like she just started showing up there every time we were there. Two, three times, I guess. I didn't think much of it. I just thought it was some woman that Teddy had pissed off. I swear. I never knew her name and as far as I know, Teddy didn't either. I mean we weren't properly introduced. Like I said, I just assumed she was just another snowflake, (Teddy's word) who was reacting to his distinctly non-PC rhetoric of the day. Happened every place we went. Teddy was not low key and LA is not a bastion of Trumpism. So that combination got him and by extension me into issues. Nobody wanted to kill him for it though."

I said this with no small amount of uncertainty. My acting skills were in full Daniel Day-Lewis mode now. I did not remember Teddy mentioning Rose Vasquez to me. As far as I knew Teddy didn't know her. I was sure that nobody would have thrown Teddy out a hospital window for his politics either. Well, I was pretty sure. Oh, Christ! Who the fuck knows these days?

"So, are you going to tell me why you were about to arrest Teddy for blowing up The Bard?"

Jackson looked at me for a good minute. No words. No change of expression. Just looked. And then he farted. A soft, yet distinctive blast, and then left the room, shutting the door to make sure his self-made atmospheric disturbance was kept in this confined space.

Maybe it was the shock of Teddy's death but it made me think of Navy boot camp years ago. We were all placed in an enclosed space with gas masks on. Our company commander made us take our masks off and turned on the tear gas. He then explained to us that we would stay in the tear gas chamber until we answered one simple question: "What are the last two words of the National Anthem?" After several vomit filled screams of "the brave," the sadistic bastard finally turned the gas off and revealed the answer: "Play Ball."

I was about to puke myself when Jackson opened the door.

"Ongoing investigation, Rooker. I cannot share anything that has to do with what is still an open investigation."

"Now wait just a fucking minute. You can't just accuse a dead man and then..."

"You can go, Rooker. But stay close."

I could have sworn that was a smile on his face.

CHAPTER 8

Teddy Dabrowski's Memorial Service
The Women's Club
South Pasadena, CA

I was told that Teddy's body was shipped to Chicago for burial. It seemed a Last Will and Testament had been found and it was his wish to be buried next to his mother at St. Mary's Cemetery in Waukegan. Teddy had never mentioned this to me but apparently it was in his will. The more I thought about it though, the more it made sense. Teddy's mother was the one person he loved in this world. He talked about her whenever family came up, which was often, especially after a few Jameson's. Teddy looked at her as his hero. The one who had saved him from his father. I was sure Mrs. Dabrowski felt the same way about her son, a point I tried to convey to Teddy many times but one in which he never seemed to concur. The Irish Catholics were not the only ones with guilt.

I decided to set up a makeshift memorial for Teddy. I rented out the Woman's Club in South Pasadena, a historical landmark built in 1899. To my surprise, Detective Jackson came by along with a few of my A.A. buddies for support. Teddy never admitted to being an alcoholic unless he was hungover, and even at those times, it was tough to get him to a meeting due to his fondness for the "Hair of the Dog that bit him." It seemed like every time I turned my back to take him to the car and a meeting he would take a quick belt of any alcohol based product that was in the vicinity.

One other visitor showed up. Another person I didn't expect but in some odd way was not surprised to see. Ms. Paula Garcia of Children's Hospital, Los Angeles.

"I'm sorry I called you at such a, well, I don't..."

"Hey, it's okay. How were you to know?"

I could tell right away that Paula Garcia had had more than a passing interest in my dear friend Teddy.

"Look I just wanted to come by and pay my respects. He was such a dear, dear human being. He was our most valued volunteer. The kids loved him. I'm sorry, this is, well look, here's my card. I'd still like you to drop by the hospital. I need to go now. Some work to do and I'll make a scene if I stay. Please understand."

She hugged me and walked out of the room before I could say a word.

Jesus Christ, Teddy.

I was about to make a scene myself.

"Damn fine looking senorita there, Rooker."

What's that? Oh yes, yes, she is. "

"Who is she?"

"I have no idea. No idea at all, Detective."

The kids loved him.

You think you know a guy.

Damn, I missed my friend.

31

CHAPTER 9

The 35er Bar
Pasadena, CA

I needed a drink. For the first time in three years of sobriety I really felt like I was going to drink. Throw it all away. The pain and suffering of the early days of white knuckle sobriety forgotten. The stuff I had to go through before my body was finished with its physical withdrawal of the alcohol conveniently disregarded. The truth be told when an alcoholic of my type is about to drink there is no reason. No sane reason anyway. I didn't care.

You see my best friend in the world, my only friend if the truth be told, was gone. I wanted to pick up the phone and call him. I had actually done just that in the few days it had been since he fell or was pushed to his death. "Well, what are you waiting for... Talk!" his classic Teddy voice mail message. I wanted to just sit with him at The Bard, hear his voice, even if it meant listening to some of his right wing nut job stuff. Of course I never really believed that he thought most of it was true. Teddy was a conservative, and yes, he said he supported Trump but only because he looked at principles rather than personalities. Apologies to Bill Wilson, the co-founder of Alcoholics Anonymous for paraphrasing an A.A. saying to make a political point. I won't do it again. In any case, most of what Teddy said was for effect. He wanted to get a rise out of people, and as I stood outside the 35er on this hot June day, I wondered if he may have been too good at affecting people's emotions. The aforementioned prairie dog lady, Rose, a case in point.

The regrets were pounding down on me like a freak hailstorm in mid-summer.

Why didn't you take that road trip to Texas with him? Why weren't you at his hospital room earlier to pick him up? You could have saved him.

All of this burning through my conscious until I was either going to take a drink, call someone or blow my fucking head off.

I walked into the 35er and ordered a shot of Jack Daniels and a beer. The hand on my shoulder pissed me off. I was deciding whether to turn and stream a few epitaphs or just do the convenient sucker elbow. Both solutions seemed perfectly acceptable in the Wild West confines of the 35er. I chose the former.

"Hey asshole, what the fuck are..."

"Bartender, yea this gentleman ordered that by mistake. I'm buying anyway. We'll both have a couple of diet cokes."

Then glancing at me like we were old friends, Sam Jackson, Detective, Pasadena Police Department says, "You want a lime or a lemon in yours?"

I was having none of this.

"I need a drink. I will have my drink. Now please get your black ass away from this bar and let me order my drink."

This was a decidedly bad time to go racist on my part even if I was mourning the sudden and violent loss of my dear friend. The bartender who was waiting patiently to take first my order and then Sam's revision of said order was about 280 pounds with zero body fat and, as my dear racist grandmother would say, "Black as the ace of spades."

Sam took me by the shoulder and before I knew what was happening, grabbed my right wrist while sliding his other hand to hook my thumb. I was helpless to do anything as he walked me out of the 35er while the enraged bartender glared at me all the way out. I found out later this technique that Sam had used was called "Farbairn's Thumb Hold," a standard part of training at most police academies.

"Let me go, god damn it. Look I'm sorry for the 'black bastard' thing. I'm not a racist."

"Shit, I've heard lots worse my pasty, honky friend. Oh, shit, a yogurt place. Damn I have not had a yogurt in way too damn long."

So we went into the 24 Flavors Yogurt on Colorado Blvd, and next thing you know, I was eating like five pounds of banana, pineapple, orange yogurt with gummy bears on top and skittles, not to mention chocolate syrup. The last thing I wanted then was a shot of whiskey. Sam Jackson knew what he was doing.

"How are you feeling now, Ben?"

"How did you know that sugar is what the alcoholic really craves?"

Sam reached into his pocket and took out a medallion. Not just any medallion. A circular coin with a triangle and the number "20" in the middle. Detective Samuel Jackson was a member of Alcoholics Anonymous with 20 years sober.

"That's the last time I do that, Rooker. The very last time. If my sponsor knew I forcibly stopped another alcoholic from taking a drink he would have my ass. You want to drink, that's your business from now on. You want to stay sober, well that's my business. You got my number. Call me anytime."

"I already got a sponsor."

"Oh, you do? Where is he and why didn't you call him?"

"Hawaii, and I didn't call him because I wanted a fucking drink. I just lost my best friend. My wife died of breast cancer only a few years ago. It seems like yesterday."

"I'm very sorry for all of that, Ben, but you know that sure as a coke whore will sell her body for another hit, well an alcoholic will drink because he or she is a god damn alcoholic. It can be a rainy day or a sunny day. You can have a million dollars or be homeless. In the end, you will drink for one reason and one reason only and that is because you are a real alcoholic. Now finish your god damn yogurt. We're going to a meeting."

CHAPTER 10

Children's Hospital, Los Angeles
Literally Healing Office

I had gone online to the Children's Hospital site and found that it was located just around the corner from the Church of Scientology, among other things. It began operation in 1901 in a small house on the corner of Alpine and Castellar Streets which was now Hill St. in Chinatown. Now it had more than 350 pediatric specialty programs. Most of the kids were minorities, nobody is turned away for lack of money. This day I was deep in the bowels of the hospital. Men and women walking around with crimson shirts and blue aprons, most young but a few from my era. I had beat the traffic from Pasadena; well one never really beats Los Angeles traffic, but I got there within the same 24-hour period that I left in, so that was a good thing. A forty-something Latina was sitting across from me in an office filled with children's books and puppets. She was wearing khaki pants (no jeans were allowed in Literally Healing), a white shirt and a photo badge that said *Paula Garcia, Director, Literally Healing*. She was attractive in a younger Patti LuPone kind of way. Short, skin like brown butter, a strong roman nose, puffy lips and brown eyes that seemed to be watering as we spoke. Or maybe she had just been crying. Her thick brown hair was pulled back to reveal some aquamarine earring bling.

"Mia menso."

"I'm sorry?"

Paula Garcia had been muttering to herself. I hadn't noticed right away though. I was locked in to her eyes. There was something alluring and yet dark in those eyes. Something hiding. In the shadows.

"I'm sorry, Mr. Rooker..."

"Call me Ben. "

"Yes. Okay. Sure. I'm sorry I was not able to speak with you more at the memorial. So, you were with Teddy when the coffee shop explosion happened and also at Huntington Hospital when he, ah, fell to his death?"

"Well, yes. I mean not quite accurate on the Huntington Hospital thing. I was on my way to pick him up. I had just parked in the lot when I saw...when I saw him fall."

"Yes, of course. Right. Still it must have been terrible for you. Teddy was a good man. A very good man. A little crazy. In a good way. No filter, is that the right ..."

"Oh yes, most definitely that was Teddy. *Menso*?"

"Sorry, yes it means a bit eccentric, crazy, but in a good way."

"Nailed it again, Ms. Garcia."

"Paula"

"Paula, yes, of course."

"When I heard about the explosion at the bookstore and realized he was one of the victims, I was shocked and then so grateful to God when I found out he was recuperating. Then the hospital. Teddy would never have killed himself. Is that what the police are saying?"

"Well, honestly the police aren't really saying anything at this point. Well, not to me anyway. Shit, I'm sorry, I don't believe he killed himself either. I don't see how he could. But there's also supposedly somebody at the hospital that saw a person resembling Teddy leave his room before... Christ, I don't know. But I will find out. I'll get the bastard who is responsible. Oh, there I go again, I'm sorry."

I left out what Jackson had told me about the plant manager. The fact that he had seen Teddy running with a limp from his room right before the suicide or murder or whatever. This plant manager, a guy who would know every nook and cranny of the hospital telling Detective Sam Jackson that he saw Teddy heading towards the spot where he, Teddy, allegedly jumped or was pushed.

"No need, Ben."

"Can I ask you a question?"

Yes, I do date white guys. Oh, Dios Mio! I am sorry. It's been a week.

Well, that's not what she said. It's what was in my mind though.

"Sure."

Those eyes.

What are the words? "Pregnant pause?" I was a bit uncomfortable but at the same time exhilarated. A bit of a tingle in the nether regions, even. It had been a "minute" as the kids might say. Onward.

"Did Teddy ever mention the name 'Rose Vasquez'?"

The look on her face told me what her answer was. You know like when you catch somebody unawares. Not ready for a particular question. When you kind of come out of nowhere. They freeze. Just for a nanosecond, but it's there. The pause. And then they seem to have all the answers.

Paula just looked at me for a moment. Like she forgot who I was and why she was talking to me.

"No. I mean well, I'm not... Well not to me anyway. Why?"

Here I was in Children's Hospital, a couple of blocks from the hospital my Rita died in. I was talking to a woman who had apparently known Teddy for a good while unbeknownst to me. I was coming off one of the worst couple of weeks of my life. Anyway, that's my excuse. It's why I made the decision right there and then to tell a hitherto, at least up to a week ago, total stranger everything that happened at The Bard that day up to the moment the bomb went off and, perhaps most importantly, my feelings about the mysterious relationship, if that's what you'd call it, that may or may not have existed between Teddy and the woman named Rose Vasquez.

When I was finished, Paula still seemed unsure but there was something there. That little light flickering way in the back of her eyes. Just a speck of understanding, but it was there. Or was it something else?

"You remember why I asked you to come here in person?"

"Sure, you wanted to talk to me about Teddy."

"Did you know that Teddy volunteered here?"

My look told the whole story. I would never have thought that Teddy Dabrowski would volunteer to work with children, let alone at a Children's Hospital. But then, like other knee-jerk reactions we human beings have about people we think we know but really don't, I had another thought, and that was— of course. It made perfect sense. Yet another thing that should be filed under the "You think you know a guy" category. Another side of Teddy. Perhaps of the redemptive variety.

"I had no idea."

"As I told you, I am the director of the Literally Healing program here at Children's Hospital, Los Angeles..."

I listened at first in a state of shock but then as one who was now hearing something that made perfect sense. Paula Garcia told me the story of Teddy Dabrowski, savior of the children.

How did Paula know Teddy you ask? Teddy Dabrowski, Right Wing loon and now alleged domestic terrorist was a volunteer at Children's Hospital for the last four years. He worked for Paula Garcia. He read books to kids with pediatric cancers, Cystic Fibrosis and those that had been battered. Kids who got beat on by fathers and boyfriends. Sometimes they were just babies. Apparently, he was not just a volunteer. To hear Ms. Garcia tell it, Teddy was a frigging angel. She told me about the day she was leading a tour of city officials around the hospital and they came upon Teddy reading to a little girl in the respiratory disease ward. The girl was Asian and had Cystic Fibrosis. She was on a donor list for a lung transplant which would not come in time.

"You really want me to read you this? A book about cemeteries?"

"Yes, c'mon, Teddy. It's funny. You know it's my favorite book. Start with the part where the body jumps right out of the coffin and scares the shit out..."

"Angelica, geez. You're going to get me fired."

Teddy laughed though. The little girl did as well.

Neither one of them had noticed the tour group just behind them. Teddy and Angelica were both immersed in the story. A story about graves and dead people. The favorite book of a terminally ill little girl. A human being that Teddy had connected with.

Paula wanted to talk more, and I wanted to know more. More about this side of my friend that I never would have guessed could have existed. I thought about Teddy's upbringing. The father that beat him. Teddy protecting his mother. And then there was the more recent Juarez story (a story I still was not sure I believed). The desertion of two young girls named Veronica and Eileen who may or may not have existed.

"Are you okay, Ben? Can I get you some water?"

"I'm okay. It's just, well it's a lot. It's amazing how he kept it to himself, for what, four years?"

"He swore me to secrecy. I got the impression that this was something he wanted to be completely anonymous about."

"It all makes sense now. The moodiness. I thought it was just... well... you said on the phone you had someone you wanted me to meet?"

"Yes, Ben. I'd like you to go with me to the 4th floor."

"What's on the 4th floor?"

"The Pediatric Cancer Unit and Miss Lexy Perez."

"I see, and who would Lexy Perez be?"

"An eight-year-old girl with terminal cancer and Teddy's best friend in the world."

CHAPTER 11

Four Years Earlier
Children's Hospital Los Angeles
Literally Healing Volunteer Orientation
"Is it Theodore?"

"What?"

"Theodore? Is that your name or do you use Teddy on your official documents?"

"Oh, no, yea, Teddy is fine. That's how I sign my checks, anyway. Teddy Dabrowski."

The sign-in sheet for the orientation. Teddy was a bit nervous. The background investigation had been a bear. Christ, lucky his buddy Jake Witkowski, later Alderman Witkowski was able to get his record expunged. I mean most of it was stuff he did as a kid: a few shoplifting charges, vandalization of Suzy Harrigan's house—he broke her bedroom window with a handful of pebbles when she stood him up for a bowling date, that kind of stuff.

The main thing was that Teddy was really doing it. Volunteering to help kids. Kids who had been fucked over just like he had been. Black, brown, yellow, white, it didn't matter. Teddy Dabrowski was going to make things right starting today.

After the paperwork was filled out and everyone was seated, a lanky old guy, eighty if he was a day, shuffled to the podium and addressed Teddy and the ten other volunteers seated in the auditorium.

"I'm Bill Leftwich. I've been with the Literally Healing Program for about ten years, since its inception really. I'll be answering any questions you may have and taking you on a short tour of the areas you will be working in. I'll be retiring this year as I am a bit long in the tooth, as they say. That's not why the tour will be short though. You will be given everything you need to know but in a small dose. You will understand when you see the presentation and meet some of the children. This place has been a big part of my life, and I hope that it will become part of yours as well."

Bill clicked an unseen switch below the dais and a screen appeared from the ceiling. A moment later a picture of a little girl in a hospital bed with a pink ribbon around her head appeared. She was smiling. Bill was seated next to her holding an open book.

"I need to interject something before we go any further, though. I would feel that I was being unfair to you if I did not. A month from now, maybe less than that, half of you will be gone. In three months' time, out of the eleven of you here now maybe two or three at the most will still be in the Literally Healing Program. You will be what in the vernacular are called 'Keepers.' Whoever you are, 'Thank You' in advance. There will be various reasons for this attrition but the most prevalent will be the pain. The loss. The helplessness. The grieving parents. The empty bed that was occupied by a five-year-old just the day before. You might have just read *Cloudy with a Chance of Meatballs* to her. She had smiled through the nausea of the chemo. You did your damn job. You created a respite from the horror called pediatric cancer and yet she had died. Know this though: the majority of the children you work with will survive. They will leave here at some point and live normal lives. You will be part of this."

There was a slight disturbance in the audience. A low weeping sound followed by whispers.

"Oh, God no, I'm sorry, I can't, I'm..."

The young man was consoled by one of the staff and gently led out of the auditorium.

After a brief silence, "And now, if there are no questions we'll start our tour."

Bill led Teddy and the group to the elevator. They all piled in as he hit the "4" button. He gave Teddy a smile as he did. Reassuring. The elevator stopped, and the doors opened.

"The 4th floor is the Bone Marrow Cancer unit as well as the Blood Disease area. I usually start at the nurse's station and ask which kids need to be read to or just need a visitor. Some of these kids have nobody. In a few cases, isolated but still tragic, their parents, because of economics, fear of deportation and other reasons, leave them here and never come back. The age group I deal with is from infant to about ten years old although the ward does have teens from time to time. I'll also visit the Pediatric Intensive Care Unit if I have time. We have kids who have very serious ailments from cancer to respiratory issues to heart disease…"

There was movement in the hallway to Teddy's left. No one else noticed. Teddy almost missed him. A tall black man wearing a roman collar down the corridor from Bill Leftwich's tour. A priest, Teddy guessed. He was holding a young boy who looked to be about two years old. Teddy walked away from the group as Bill Leftwich continued his talk. He was mesmerized. No one noticed. As he got closer, the priest acknowledged him with a smile. It was a smile of comfort and reassurance.

No danger here.

"Oh, hi, sorry to disturb, ah, I'm Teddy, Teddy Dabrowski. I'm a new volunteer. I'm with the Literally Healing Program. I'm here for the orientation. I hope you don't mind me bothering you. I don't really know why…"

"Oh, no bother at all. And I know who you are. I'm Father Jim O'Brian. Call me Jim. This is Joey. He's not really able, I mean wanting to talk right now. You'll have to excuse him. He's had a tough, short time here. His mom's boyfriend got drunk one night and decided to smash Joey's head against the wall. The damage may never be repaired. For some reason, though, when he is holding on to me, he is okay. He is at peace. The kid has never had love in his short life. All it takes is for me to hold him and whisper that he is loved and somehow he is okay. Oh, I'm sorry. I am sorry. I'm afraid I'm on my soapbox again. Here, why don't you hold him."

Teddy was overcome for a moment. He lowered his head. He was fighting to keep himself together. He was staring at the roman collar. He wanted to say something to him. Then. There. To confess. Get it all out. Juarez. The screams.

"Father, I mean, Jim, I…"

Father Jim touched Teddy on the shoulder. The priest did not speak but Teddy 'heard' him say, "It's going to be okay. Another time."

Father Jim moved down the hallway, Joey clutching him, cooing. Teddy heard the sound of Bill Leftwich's voice and walked back to the group at the other end of the hallway.

Teddy rejoined the group as Bill Leftwich was speaking to a little boy. The boy was about five years old. Bill was speaking to him in a gentle voice.

"Looking good, Ricky. Is that your race car?"

"Yup. I made it. You helped me, 'member?"

"I sure do. But you did the hard parts. How about a story?"

Bill took a book from his bag, sat down next to Ricky and began to read a story. The boy was smiling as he held Bill's arm subconsciously. Ricky raised his head from the book and he and Teddy's eyes met. Ricky had an angelic smile. Teddy returned the smile but looked away after a brief moment.

Later that evening Teddy was seated, holding his head in his hands in the lobby of Children's Hospital, waiting for an Uber. Paula Garcia was seated across from him.

"Everyone in Literally Healing is not just a volunteer. They are family. My family. I'm the volunteer coordinator and I will not have it any other way. These kids are too damn important. I don't know what happened to you as a kid. I don't need to know anything about your scars. I can see them. Clear as day. We screen you. Did you know that it's tougher to be a volunteer here than it is to be an LAPD cop? I think there is more to your story. Something you need to let out. Maybe something more recent than your childhood. Know that you can tell me anything. My door is always open."

Teddy was about to do just that. He knew he needed to talk about Juarez. Somehow Paula knew that as well.

Life is full of decisions. Many of them of the instantaneous variety. These decisions can change one's life.

In some cases, they can end it.

Maybe it was the change in Paula's voice. The subtle almost imperceptible tension in her manner. Just for a second, but it was enough.

Teddy raised his head and looked at Paula without speaking. The silence conveyed his decision to pass on her invitation. For the moment.

The tension passed in the blink of an eye. Teddy wondered if he had even seen it in her.

She continued, "Bill told me how you transformed at the orientation when you saw those kids for the first time. Here's the deal though, Teddy. The bottom line. You need to want to be here. If you don't, then we can't use you. It's that simple. I need to know now, Teddy. Do you want to be here?"

"Yes."

CHAPTER 12

Children's Hospital
Teddy's First Week

"Hello, Teddy. May I call you that? I mean if you want me to call you Mr. Dabrowski, I'm good with that. I'm Alexandria. My friends call me Lexy though. I'm almost five years old and they say I won't be around for much longer. I know better, though"

Teddy's first official day at Children's. He was on the 4th floor and the first kid he met was Lexy Perez, the child that Paula wanted him to meet. She never told him why. He made a mental note to find out who told her his name. In the orientation they were directed only to use first names and not get into the patient's family situation, history and especially, most especially, do not discuss the patient's prognosis. Well, so much for that.

Lexy was lying in her bed hooked up to what Teddy figured was a chemo bag and some saline to keep her hydrated. The other bag was probably an anti-nausea drug. She was bald, of course. Probably had her head shaved when the hair started coming out in clumps. Teddy knew about that from the few times Ben talked about his late wife Rita's bout with breast cancer. Better to just shave your head rather than be left with patches. Lexy was a cutie, Teddy thought. Big brown eyes, light brown skin, although a bit pale right now. She was wearing a Jennifer Lopez tee shirt and there was a signed photo of J-Lo next to her bed. Teddy grimaced a bit when he saw that. He recalled his experience with Paula Garcia in her office the night before. Teddy was there to go over some last minute procedural things before his first day as a volunteer. Paula noticed him looking at the stack of J-Lo pictures on her desk. They were unsigned.

"You a Jennifer Lopez fan?"

"Oh, hell, yes. And I like her singing as well."

"Okay, of course, the booty. Men."

She thought for a moment and then looked him straight in the eye.

"How's your handwriting?"

"Second to Mary Otterbein in my second grade cursive writing class."

"You don't obsess much on the past, do you Teddy?"

"I was robbed. The teacher liked her better."

"Terrific. Take this pen and autograph as many of those headshots as you can."

"You want me to forge J-Lo's signature? Isn't there some kind of law?"

"Look, she visited the kids today. They loved her. Her people forgot to bring signed headshots, so she left these here. The kids won't know the difference. Okay?"

"Okay. But when I get a butt the size of Texas, I'm going to blame you."

Paula laughed and Teddy felt something swell up in him. That feeling he had when he first met Paula. A feeling not so much of excitement but of peace. A good thing. A true thing.

He had dutifully signed the headshots.

"Did you meet J-Lo yesterday, Lexy?"

"Of course. I call her Jennifer though. She appreciates that. I'm not just one of the other fan girls. I'm sorry you had to go through so much pain. You had to, though. To get here. To get to this place right now, here with me."

"Wha...Lexy, you don't know me. What are you talking about? Who are you? Have the nurses or Paula...Has Paula been talking about me?"

"Nonsense."

"Nonsense?"

"There is a reason for everything. That's all I'm saying."

"But how do you know...?"

"Can you read me my book? I mean I can read a little but it helps me sleep if someone else does. And anyway, I like you."

She handed him a hard bound volume.

"C. S. Lewis? Look I'm not much of a reader but this is pretty heavy stuff."

Chronicles of Narnia. It has a talking lion in it. Come on, get with the program, Teddy, my boy. There's not a lot of time."

"Hey, look Lexy, don't say that."

Teddy hesitated. Shaky territory. No talking about the patient's medical prognosis; under any circumstances.

Fuck it.

"You have tons of time. You're a young kid."

"Teddy, can we talk? In my office?"

He thought he spelled the perfume. Paula had been right behind him. She would have been a great sniper.

"Don't blame Teddy, Ms. Garcia. I kind of roped him in. Anyway, Teddy, I wasn't talking about me."

Sitting in Paula's office later.

"Who is this kid?"

"That's not important right now, you broke the..."

"Hell it isn't important. She knew my entire name. She knew about my childhood. Well not specific things but she knew. I could feel it. I could feel her inside my brain, my fucking soul... Christ, sorry."

"One of the things you have to understand is that the children here are not really children."

"What?"

"I don't mean they're not children. They are. In the chronological sense anyway. The longer you're here the more you'll realize that most of these kids are old souls. The cancer doesn't just take their hair. It takes their childhood. Don't look so sad. It may actually be a good thing. These kids are facing death every day, every moment. A child in the true sense of the word could not deal with this. Christ, lots of adults can't either, but at least they have a chance."

"What do you want from me?"

"I just want you to be you. You have dealt with a lot of the same things these kids have. Not the cancer but other things. I can sense it."

"What's Lexy's story?"

"We don't know."

Once again Teddy sensed something lurking somewhere behind Paula's eyes. She was holding back. He filed it for further evaluation. Another time.

"You don't know? What about the screening? The checks. I mean I thought these kids' parents went through the same stuff we went through as volunteers."

"They do. Normally. We don't know who Lexy's parents are. We don't know where's she's from. A security guard found her in a basket covered with newspapers in front of the entrance to the hospital."

"My God. So, she was dropped here right after she was born?"

"Yes, it appears that way."

"So, she would have no idea who her parents are."

Teddy appeared to be muttering to himself.

Paula continued, "Yes, but there is someone, I don't…"

"Who? But how could she…?"

"A priest. 'Father Jim, my African hero' she calls him. She says he brought her here. He watches over her. Right here in the hospital."

"Hell yea, of course, Father Jim. Father Jim O'Brian. I met him."

A nerve had been struck. "You met him? When? Where?"

"Well, here of course. Why are you looking at me like I'm bat shit crazy, Paula? Here in the hospital. A few days ago. During orientation."

Paula was looking at Teddy the way Ben used to look at him when he was telling one of his bizarre Polish ghost stories that his grandma would recount to him when he was a kid. The only difference was Ben would smile and laugh eventually after shaking his head.

"Teddy, Lexy is a child. A special child. With all she has been through we let her have her fantasies."

"Fantasies, what the fuck?"

"Yes, fantasies. We let her tell stories. We even act as if we believe her. She has a very serious form of cancer. We want her to be happy and if anything comforts her, whether it's real or …, how do I say this, ah, surreal, well we give her that."

"What the hell are you talking about? Sorry, but I just don't get…"

"Father Jim O'Brian was the chaplain here until about four years ago when he was found hung from a stanchion in the boiler room. It was ruled a suicide. He had been under a lot of pressure due to the fact he was facing charges of child molestation. He insisted till the end that they were untrue. The fact that he was a black man did not help. Many otherwise God-fearing parents rushed to judgement in the case. He was found guilty in the court of public opinion even before a trial simply because of his skin color. Lots of folks prejudged him. Many in the Latino community, I am ashamed to say. He was a wonderful man but sometimes accusations are enough to destroy one. Now tell me about this priest you met."

Teddy told her about the tour and catching Father Jim standing with the baby down a side hallway.

"So, you actually talked to this person?"

"Of course. He had the baby with him as well. I wasn't hallucinating either. I think I even touched the baby's arm. The kid was really in bad shape. Physically and emotionally."

"Was the baby's name Joey?"

"Yes, yes... how did you know? Joey was alive. I saw him. He was abused by his mother and her boyfriend, right?"

"I'm sure that was the case, but the mother, 18 years old and terrified, accused, Father Jim. He was innocent, of course. All of us who knew him realized that, but it destroyed Jim none the less. He hung himself shortly after the accusation. Little Joey died the next day."

"Oh, my Jesus."

"It's okay. You're not crazy, Teddy."

"Why do you say that? I mean, you don't know me aside from the background investigation. Maybe I am crazy. Maybe this is punishment for Juarez."

"Juarez?"

"Look, I have to go now."

"Tell me about it. I'm listening. You know how we Latinas love to gossip."

"No different from us Poles. Another time. I should go."

"Rest, Teddy. Some things are better left unexplained. In any case, don't hate yourself. I would like you to read with Lexy as much as you can. She likes you. You're good for each other."

"How do you know that?"

"It's my business to know. And besides, you have a mutual friend."

"The bartender at the 35er? The kid's too young to drink."

"Father Jim. Lexy says he reads to her every night. When it's quiet and the volunteers all go home and the nurses are doing their rounds at the other end of the wing."

"You believe that?"

"Like I said, some things are better left unexplained. I will say that I don't disbelieve anything. Teddy, when I was a little girl, probably the same age as Lexy, I got my own room. I felt like a grown-up. Away from my younger brothers. The first night in my own bed I was just about to fall off to sleep and I felt, sensed someone or something standing over me. Watching. I didn't see anyone, but I knew there was someone there. Here's the crazy part. I wasn't scared. I felt at peace. Completely unafraid. Like there was love in my room. Pure love. Years later when I grew up, I told my Mama that story. She shuddered at first but then smiled and said, 'Tu Abuela.' There was a hint of a tear in her eye. A happy tear. In those days, hospice care was at home. My grandmother had lung cancer and was cared for in the bedroom that I would inherit. She died in my bed. My mother's tears were those of joy. My grandmother loved me and was watching over me. I don't think you or Lexy are crazy. Just don't tell anyone else about Father Jim. We'll both end up in the casa del loco."

CHAPTER 13

Downtown Pasadena
May 2019

I didn't really have time to watch the news, so I hadn't kept up on the latest as far as how many people were killed or injured in the bomb blast or any other updates. They weren't saying that Teddy did it. Not yet anyway. I was sitting in my humble two-bedroom apartment in Pasadena just a few short blocks from Old Town. I was trying to catch up by watching the local news. Four people were dead now. A 65-year-old retired history professor at Pasadena City College named Meredith Brock had been in an induced coma for a couple of weeks and could not be brought back. Her family pulled the plug that morning. A security systems business owner named David Baxter from San Marino. Unnamed sources hinted that his company was involved in some Black Ops work in the Middle East and more recently in Mexico and Central America. Next was Joe Florio, 22, a clerk at The Bard. It was his first day. He was to enter Harvard Law in the Fall. His parents saved every dime they could to get him through college at USC. Graduated top of his class. Valedictorian. Dead.

And then there was Rose Vasquez, of San Marino, who was identified in all news reports as "the estranged wife of prominent Mexican Cartel figure Roy Vasquez. Witnesses believe she was seated with David Baxter. The police have neither confirmed nor denied a connection. The investigation is ongoing."

Figures, Christ he is the boss of the Venganza Cartel for the love of God.

Strangely enough, the injuries of the survivors were not of the horrific type. A few concussions like Teddy had, and some broken limbs and burns. One guy had blurred vision, but he was expected to make a full recovery. The 300 pound Barista was unscathed and may even still play for USC. Could have been a helluva lot worse.

Lexy had rented space in my head. There was no denying it. There was a life-force emitting from her that I couldn't quite understand but somehow knew I would if I was patient. Perhaps it was because I felt in my very soul that "more would be revealed," as they say in A.A.

My cell vibrated. It was Jackson. He was on the scent again.

"You heard the latest? Another 'critical condition' changed to 'deceased.' That's four murders now."

"Yes, I saw it on the news, Detective. Why do you continue to harass me, I mean..."

"Oh, don't worry, Ben, if I was harassing you, you would sure as hell know it. Just make believe I'm your A.A. sponsor. Anyway, I got new info that I'd like to share with you. I need you to come in."

"First of all, Detective, I already have a sponsor and second, I got an audition. I can't."

"Audition! Damn. I checked your IMDB, is that what you call it? You haven't worked in like three years. Your rating is like 10 billion or something and..."

"Are we done?"

"I need you to come down to the station. We got new forensics."

"Detective!"

"You're late buddy, Dabrowski is cleared."

"What the fuck. What about all the evidence you said you had on him?"

"Call it 'police tactics.' Nothing is ever true until it's out in the media and shit then, well, anyway, he's cleared. Just come in when you get a chance. Within the next 48 hours."

"I'm sure he's real happy about being cleared, Detective. I mean he's dead now and everything. But hell, he appreciates it. What about his death? Who the fuck killed Teddy? Do you have any clue about that?"

"I'm not at liberty to say anything over the phone. Just come in and we'll go over all of this. I'll update you on what we have."

"Christ, don't tell me you're calling it a suicide? You are, aren't you?! Jesus H Christ, I don't know what to..."

"I'm going to say this one time only, Rooker. Come in. The sooner the better. I am not going to threaten you with sending a squad car to haul your scraggly ass in, bound like a Christmas goose or whatever the fuck you white boys eat during Thanksgiving, Christmas or whatever. No, I don't do shit like that. That would be illegal."

"I'll be there but after my audition. Its right here in LA, near the station. God damn it, Detective, it's not like I get these every day."

"Yes, like it mentioned earlier, I saw your IMDB and the thing you call a reel. I understand completely."

"Asshole."

Did I tell you that being an actor is tough? Anybody that says otherwise is probably named Leo or Robert or Meryl. Once you make it, though, it's the greatest job in the world. But here is the deal, two percent of the members of the Screen Actors Guild are making 98 percent of the money. Think about that. Now think about trying to make it as a man of a certain age actor, new to the business going up against respected character actors like Richard Jenkins, BD Wong, C. Thomas Howell, JK Simmons and, oh, you haven't heard of these guys? Well, they work ALL the time and one of them has won an Oscar. Okay, you say, "Nobody forced you into this." You are absolutely right. I did have a choice. I could have continued to sell irrigation landscape services to cities, working with contractors who had the morals of Michael Avenatti and made a decent living until I hit sixty-five and then retire to Leisure World in Seal Beach and live in a trailer for a few years playing bocce ball and getting hit on by seventy-somethings until one day I wake up and realize that my life was over and I had not even tried to be what I wanted to be when I grew up. Do you know what it's like when you are a man of a certain age and you run into your 22-year-old self at three in the morning in a bed all alone in your trailer at "Seizure" World and he asks you "Why? Why did you give up on the Dream?" If you don't have an answer, then it's time to eat the .38 that you have kept next to your bed since your lovely wife Rita died, Rita the one who said, "Follow your god damn dreams, Ben. Why else live?"

Anyway, I digress. There I was at the Space Station. I have no idea why it's called that but it's one of the places where actors go for auditions. One of the many in the Los Angeles area. I was going in for a crazy comedy role. I was playing an eccentric lab technician. The role was perfect for me. It was a pilot for a Netflix series produced by Ben Stiller. If I got this, I'd be made. That's all it takes. One break. One role. I did a read through with one of the writers before I went in. It was a scene with me and two other actors, a young guy and girl. The writer was pissing on himself laughing at my take. I asked him if I needed to tone it down, He said, "No, the bigger the better for this piece."

Great. So I was all set. I got to the audition room. There was just one guy there. It turns out he was the guy who would direct the pilot. He looked at me and said, "Start whenever you're ready."

We did the scene just like outside. He stopped me three times just to give me notes. Each time he told me, "Tone it down. You're too big. We want subtle. Do you understand?"

Like I was a fucking moron. We did it one more time. Same shit. I walked out knowing that it was a wasted hour. I glared at the writer as I was leaving. He avoided eye contact. A day in the life of an actor of a certain age. Hell, A day in the life of an actor, period. Next. Onward.

CHAPTER 14

May 2019

The Morning of the Bard Café Bombing

Nestled in the foothills just beside Pasadena is the richest area in the United States. No, it's not Beverly Hills. The city of San Marino was created in 1913 after a few ranches along with the Shorb estate owned by Henry Huntington, yes that guy again, were incorporated. It was modeled after the European municipality of San Marino. Mean home price is right around two million dollars. You would have seen many Latinos in San Marino in 1970 but most were caring for rather than living in estates which were then 99 percent white owned. Due to an influx of Chinese immigrants, the city now boasts 40 percent residents of Asian ancestry.

San Marino is five percent Latino now, and they are not gardening for someone else. No, they own some two million dollar plus properties. In the words of Teddy Dabrowski, "It's a great country, isn't it?" In one of these estates just up the road from the Huntington Library, Ms. Rose Vasquez was planning her day. A woman who would be called striking rather than pretty, probably due to a perpetual stern visage caused by years of internal conflict rather than bad dieting. She was 58 years old, thick brown hair, flawless skin with no aid from any doctors in the Rodeo Drive area of Beverly Hills. Big hats, genetics, and hydration were her secret. No Botox. At least that anyone would speak of.

Rose grew up in Tijuana the youngest of four kids born to a failed jack of all trades and master of none named Felipe Ramirez and his wife Margarita. Felipe tried his hand at everything from bullfighting promotions to smuggling older Mexicans into the United States who dreamed of living with their children in Chula Vista and adjacent border towns in the San Diego area. Unfortunately, his bullfighting business failed due to promotions like "Ninos Day" where children were brought onto the bullfighting grounds and allowed to witness up close "The Kill," a grotesque spectacle at the end of the bullfight wherein the bull is essentially slaughtered. This could last up to six minutes. As for the smuggling operation, it went under after numerous seniors had to be rushed to the emergency room after being pulled out screaming and coughing from the trunk of Felipe's 1958 Buick Roadmaster Sedan due to exposure to CO_2.

Rose was named after her maternal great-grandmother who it was whispered knew General Antonio Lopez de Santa Anna in the "Biblical Sense." One day after learning of Santa Anna in class, a young Rose brought up the general at dinner. She was summarily beaten by her mother and then sent to her room while her father and siblings silently continued to eat. Santa Anna was never discussed again. Years later, Rose, a new bride, innocently recounted this story to her husband Roy Vasquez, a budding cartel boss, in the presence of his new mother-in-law, Margarita. Later that night when Rose was asleep, poor Margarita was escorted off the Vasquez compound, stripped of all possessions and left in the street, homeless. A year or so later she died penniless in an Ensenada gutter despite several entreaties on her behalf from her daughter, Rose. Roy would not suffer his wife, or any of the people close to him for that matter, to be humiliated no matter what the reason. Margarita was posthumously redeemed to a certain extent when the man Rose married ended up making Santa Anna look like a choir boy.

Today, Rose had things to do.

"Dave, we need to hurry. I want to do some shopping and then have coffee at that nice cafe. You know, the one we like."

Dave Baxter was San Marino new money. Late sixties, bushy white hair, a bit of a belly but in decent shape. A lot better than most of those "millennial assholes" in Dave's words. After serving in Vietnam in Black Ops, another way of saying "Murder without Consequences," Dave was called back to service to Iraq during Desert Shield where he became enamored with a company called Halliburton. Yes, that Halliburton. Dick Cheney's company. Technically described as "one of the world's largest oil field service companies," it operated in more than 70 countries. Some might have further described it as an appendage of the Bush White House. It all depended on one's point of view and what one chose to see.

After leaving Halliburton, Dave built a security company from the ground up in Altadena, California. He started with a Chevy van and walkie talkies and strobe lights. Baxter Security and Alarms became the biggest independently owned home security firm in Southern California. Dave's company had another side, something not promoted on his Facebook ads or on his business card. This dark underbelly was how Rose was extricated from the clutches of Senor Roy Vasquez and his cartel and placed in Dave Baxter's bed.

In order to find this "alternative" side of Dave's company, one had to search the Dark Web. Networks with names like *Tor*, *Freenet*, *I2P* and *Riffle*. Imagine if Amazon had a bomb making section or a kidnapping service. This would be found on *Tor* and company.

Dave and Rose had been what some would call an item for the last ten years. Dave, an old school military guy would call it "Fuck Buddies." Rose grimaced when he used the term but inside she had to admit it was true. Her days of *Harlequin* romance love had ended after her psychotic tryst with Roy Vasquez. The truth be told, if Dave had not rescued her, she would have probably put a bullet between her eyes rather than spend another minute with that cabron.

"Please, Rose, I know I'm getting old but give me some credit for a semblance of god damn clarity. We're going to the Bard Café for one reason and one reason only—so you can glare at a guy, a guy you don't even remember but hate anyway. Am I right?"

"Chingada madre! I do not stare at him. I am just, what is the word, 'assessing' him. Yes, that is the word."

"Well, you could at least tell me why."

"I told you, baby, there is a good reason. It will come to me. I'm going to talk to him today. I promise. I know if I see him one more time it will bring everything back. All I can say for sure is that it's been years, perhaps many. Something about Mexico. That's all I can say. For now, it's enough to hate his guts for what he says about Hillary. Please trust me."

She fluttered her big brown eyes and kissed him. She was 58 going on 25. Dave instantly lost any recollection of what the conversation had even been about.

"Okay, Andiamo!"

When they got to the bookstore after two hours of shopping in Old Pasadena, at Tiffany's and Saks 5th Ave, yes, there is one in Pasadena, they entered the Bard Café from the back parking lot. Dave was interested in some Tom Clancy while Rose searched for *It Takes a Village*. She loved Hillary Clinton and prayed every night that she would somehow still become the first female President of the United States. Their backgrounds were similar. Well, maybe Rose's upbringing was closer to Bill's than Hillary's, but the cheating husband she could definitely relate to.

56

Roy Vasquez was a cartel boss, of course, and all that went with it. Rose had fallen madly in love with Roy the moment she set eyes on him. It was at a bullring, of all places. Rose hated to go but her fiancé, the guy her father had set her up with, insisted.

He was her father's client and Rose was about to be stuck in an arranged marriage. She had spotted Roy as he walked down the aisle with his entourage. Dark hair slicked back. Armani suit. Ten thousand dollar cowboy boots. That was all fine but when Roy took his dark glasses off and looked her way, actually right into her 18-year-old eyes, she was in the words of a guy named Dickens "smitten." It was mutual.

The boyfriend was encouraged to find another evening pursuit and Rose spent the night with Roy. Lost her virginity. A couple of weeks later she started getting sick every morning. Roy made her father, Felipe, a "Don Corleone" offer for Rose's hand. He also paid him a nice sum and made sure he had tires for the rest of his life which wasn't that long. The baby girl, Alvina, was born nine months later. Alvy, the love and the tragedy of Rose Vasquez' life.

The last Rose had heard of her daughter she was living in New Mexico. Dave's security people had been searching for her and actually had found her in Las Cruces. Then they lost her. She just disappeared. This was highly unusual for Dave. He always got his man or woman. If they were alive that is. Dave never mentioned this last part to Rose. Better to let her hold on to her hope.

Alvina would have been in her late thirties. Rose was confident she would find her and they would all live happily in San Marino. A *Harlequin* novel ending after all.

Roy Vasquez loved animals as it turned out. He hated bullfights. Detested witnessing the slaughter of an innocent animal. The cartel, under the name of "Roy's Wheel and Tires Inc" gave a substantial sum to PETA each year. You think you know somebody. Their marriage was really over after the second year or so when Roy realized that Rose couldn't or perhaps wouldn't give him a son. In truth Rose had become pregnant a second time but had a miscarriage, probably due to the stress caused by his increased drinking and drugging. Something she didn't dare tell Roy. Soon there were separate bedrooms, Roy's constant travelling and of course when he started using more and more of his product, he went from wanting to bang every five minutes to "Droopy" from the Seven Dwarves.

At least she got the money though. One thing her dear departed Mama taught her was to provide for one's self. Don't count on the man. Rose followed that advice to the letter. Opened an offshore account in the Caymans right after the first of the many of Roy's cheerleader sleepovers. She met Dave at the bar in the Beverly Hills Hotel during a break from her monthly shopping trips to Estados Unidos. He was much older than her but in better shape than Roy and easy on the eyes. He treated her nice too. Rose liked that. She wasn't used to it but acclimated quickly. After a few discrete dates and then some not so discrete, one afternoon they moved from the bar to a bedroom suite and Dave told her about the bull market on real estate in San Marino. What better place to clean some cartel money then in a mansion in conservative, law and order San Marino? Rose was set. She just had to leave Roy without ending up with her head inside a burning tire. No easy task. The key was Dave Baxter. He bought the mansion under his name and then signed it over to Rose after she filed for divorce in Tijuana from Roy. It had been 20 years now since all of this had happened. Dave wanted her to get a makeover. He knew people who could make her look like anybody she wanted. Rose was adamant. She wasn't going to give up herself, her identity for that prick. She would trust in God... and Baxter Security Systems. Strangely enough after numerous death threats and a very suspicious incident where Rose's Benz was driven off the road coming back from 4th of July at the Rose Bowl, Rose the newly minted American citizen had not heard or even seen any news about Roy for years. She figured he had moved on. I mean, after all, she wasn't suing him for alimony or anything like that. Unfortunately, she had lost touch with Alvina as well. Despite several attempts to contact her, it seems Alvina was her father's daughter in respect to addiction. Alvina disappeared one night after a night of drinking and drugging in Juarez. There were rumors that she was with her father but Rose couldn't or wouldn't believe them. The truth be told, Rose had dreams of her daughter. In every one she was in danger from some unseen force. At the end of each nightmare, there was a picture, albeit a blurry one. It was a man. A gringo. Rose knew him but never knew from where. It was maddening. He was somehow the key to finding out what happened to her precious Alvina.

****

Dave spotted the white van with the Kansas plates as he and Rose were exiting the car and walking through the parking lot towards the back entrance of the Bard Café. The dark skinned Hispanic guy looked straight at Rose and jabbered something to the driver. Dave found it unusual that there were plenty of parking spaces near the various stores yet the van parked at the farthest one away. He jotted the plate number and some other info into his phone and then sent a message before putting the phone away.

"It is amazing how many books Clancy has come out with since he died," Dave remarked as they took their coffees to a table near the door at the outside patio of The Bard.

"Dave, Clancy is dead. He's been dead for years. His son or somebody else writes them. They use his name. He's a brand. It's all about the brand."

In discussions like this Dave truly wondered whether his girlfriend wasn't born in the basement of the old J.R. Thompson Advertising Company rather than a hovel in Tijuana.

"I mean he has a formula, a template for the books and anyway... Fuck!"

Rose sat up abruptly while Dave glanced at the apparent cause of her colorful metaphor. Two guys seated across from them. A tall guy wearing a Mets hat (these god damn New York transplants) and the other guy short and stocky wearing a "Don't Tread on Me" tee shirt. He caught him, just for a brief moment glaring back at Rose.

Then the short one went back to his conversation.

"What may I ask was that all about?" Dave asked.

"God damn right wing storm trooper. 'Don't Tread on Me,' my ass! I thought we were rid of those Tea Party locos."

Was it him? The guy from the dreams. The man she believed raped her daughter.

Perhaps if Rose had more than the minute or so she had left on Earth and had some time to talk with him she would have liked Teddy Dabrowski. Maybe not his politics but she would have realized that her pain and anger had been focused on the wrong person. That was not to be though.

She turned her attention to Dave. He was fiddling with his phone.

"You're running the info on the white van with the three latinos in it?"

"Christ, I've taught you too well. Yea, the Kansas plates stood out. Maybe nothing but can't be too careful. Plus, they kept driving around the lot looking for a space when there were plenty of them. They ended up parking on the god damn north forty."

Dave was at once proud and a bit wary of the way Rose's keen mind seemed to devour everything about his business. Also the way she embraced American politics so quickly. He wasn't surprised, though, as she went one hundred and fifty percent all in with anything she developed an interest in. He finished with his phone.

"That's done. Should get something back pretty quick."

Rose had already moved on from the white van and its occupants and was now looking at Teddy.

"Look, it's a free country honey, I mean…"

"No. I have to remember who he is. I just can't put my finger on where or when. It will come to me though."

Rose was still mulling this over as Teddy got up and started to walk to her table as if to finally confront her only to turn abruptly causing a crash into a rather large barista who was at that moment taking out the trash. At almost the same instant, Dave Baxter's phone alarmed. Dave looked at the message. A message that had come too late. He instinctively touched the ring in his pocket. The one he was going to propose to Rose with at dinner later that evening. Rose Vasquez was oblivious to all of this. The newly made millionaire and American citizen, ex-wife of the head of a cartel, had one thought on her mind seconds before her head was removed from her body by a bomb planted in the *Welcome to Old Pasadena* book display that had been recently placed in the Bard Café storeroom;

"How can that enormous gringo find his 'pene'?"

The bomb was remotely detonated by a Mexican national sitting in a white van at the farthest corner of the Bard parking lot. He had delivered the display a day before. The man's name was Pedro and he and his two cohorts would be killed execution style as they stopped for gas at a remote service station outside Tijuana. Their bodies were incinerated at a cartel owned morgue.

A sound of thunder and then silence as the neurons and whatever was making up Rose's last thought were dispersed throughout the patio and out onto Colorado Blvd itself to be trampled on by firefighters and then later by some school children and finally a homeless man.

What would Vonnegut say?

For a nanosecond Rose's remaining eye "saw" Teddy Dabrowski and she realized who he was. The dream. The picture. Then eternal darkness.

CHAPTER 15

Pasadena Police Station

"Here I am, Detective. Rushed on over from my audition. Just for you."

"So, you really did have an audition? Shit, maybe you're an actor after all. That was a little of me havin' fun with you Rooker. Don't be lookin' all sensitive and shit. Look I know you and Dabrowski were tight. I'm sorry for your loss and all that but..."

"Are you any closer to finding out who threw him out that Huntington Hospital window? How about who blew us up at the Bard Café or are you just sitting around holding your Johnson thinking of ways to demean me and my acting career?"

"Damn, wait a second, hold that thought."

Detective Jackson turned to the one-way mirror behind him and waved someone in. A second later one of the largest white men I had ever seen sidled through the door. A buzz cut worthy of any drill instructor, gut hanging over his belt like a Northridge porch after the earthquake. And a pink bowtie.

"Larue, you ever meet any movie stars or actor types?"

"Talk about! Mais J mais. Can't say I ever did."

"Ben Rooker, allow me to introduce FBI Special Agent Larue Belmont. Don't let the Cajun bullshit bother you. This now being a terrorist related case, the Feds are involved and on the scene."

Larue just stared at me like he was trying to figure out how to clean up a nasty spot on the wall. Then as if he was coming out of a blackout, he blinked, walked towards me and shook my hand so hard I felt like Hulk Hogan's bum of the week about to be hurled across the ring and into a crowd of Trump supporters.

"Damn nice to make your acquaintance."

And just like that he walked to the corner of the room and just stood there but not before, "Oh, very sorry about your friend."

Jackson's eyes followed him for a moment and then came back to me.

"Well, Larue is impressed. Anyway, thanks Larue, just wanted you to meet Mr. Ben Rooker, just in case he becomes a movie star one day, you can say you knew him when."

Larue pulled a bag of banana chips out of his pocket and started to eat them absentmindedly. I should say "chomped." He peered up at me between the inhaling of the chips and gave me a look that said, "Don't fuck up, boy" or well, you get the gist.

Meanwhile Jackson was continuing to stare back and forth between me and Belmont. Finally, Larue put the chips back in his pocket but not before spilling a few on the floor and proceeded to take a seat next to Jackson and across from me. As he began to speak, he spit part of a chip in my direction.

"I understand your concern for your friend."

I looked in the direction of the spent spittle/chip with disgust.

"Wait, what in the 'Dukes of Fucking Hazard' was that shit?!"

"'Dukes of Hazard'. Love the reference. No good anymore though. Confederate flag and all. Now don't get me wrong. I understand all that historical significance bullshit but you got to look at it...."

"Who is this clown?"

Jackson was looking away now.

Larue continued.

"Mr. Rooker, this is now a federal case with the terrorist angle. A new set of eyes and ears, that's all."

"You're playing with my head, both of you. That's what this is. Some *Law and Order* bullshit. For the love of God, Detective, just tell me what's happening here. Am I a suspect? Is Teddy really cleared? Let's do this. Now."

Jackson finally looked at me.

"Okay, look, chill, oh, I hate that word, calm the fuck down. We have had some forensics come back on the Bard Café bombing. Fingerprint analysis, DNA, hair comparisons, photo imaging, all kinds of technical shit. Everything we have clears Dabrowski. I can't go into how we know this, so don't ask me."

"But how, who?"

Larue gave Jackson a look which stopped him in his tracks. This was the FBI's show clearly.

"We don't know yet. We have some leads though. We do know, and if I hear this outside this room I will, well let's just say it won't be good for your acting career or Detective Jackson's promotion chances... We believe the bomb was what they call a 'pressure cooker' type. First ones were used in India. Remember that incident in Mumbai? A very sophisticated operation. They are also used by Islamic radicals, Central American drug operations, etc..."

I must have flinched or did something that caught both their investigative minds.

"You got something you want to add, Rooker?"

"Nothing, well, I mean you mentioned 'Central America.' It might be nothing but Teddy, shit, no its nothing."

"No, no, it is something. Your body language pretty much confirmed that. Look, Rooker, Ben, your buddy is dead and he ain't coming back. That bomb was not set off by somebody who was pissed that the latest Harry Potter wasn't in stock. We believe whoever did this was targeting someone specifically. Someone that was at that café on that day. Now, that is a very small sample size with your friend being a big piece of the damn sample. He's dead. We need you to tell us anything, whether you think it's important or not... Ok?"

So I proceeded to tell Special Agent Larue Belmont and Detective Samuel Jackson everything I knew about my dear friend Teddy Dabrowski.

"So this guy comes out here from Chicago, but first he stops in Juarez long enough to get involved with two college girls from Las Cruces partying in Juarez who are then kidnapped by the local 'Policia' no less?"

"The Juarez cartel, Teddy was sure of it. Like I said, he saw the cops there and the cartel as one and the same."

"Of course. Sorry. Forgive me for that oversight."

Jackson glares at me but moves on.

"So these girls, Veronica and Eleanor..."

"Eileen... and Teddy was never sure if those were their real names."

"Of course. Eileen. He leaves them there because a hundred bucks will only cover one person and Teddy decides that that person will be him?"

"Yes"

"Okay, so Teddy drives out in their car and leaves them both to be raped and killed by the evil cartel cops?"

"He never said that. He believes that's probably what happened. He... We were going to take a road trip, go down to Juarez and check it ourselves but we never went."

"Why?"

This was a tough one. I had accepted the fact that I would tell Jackson and Belmont everything, well almost everything, but this one... oh fuck....

"I had an audition."

Jackson paused, thought about it, then moved on. All my recent animosity towards the man vanished right then. Well, most of it.

"Okay, so you had an audition. I mean that's only a one day thing right?"

"It went straight to callback."

"What the fuck does that mean?"

Larue broke his silence.

"If I may? Normally an actor will have an audition and if they like you, they will 'call you back' a 'callback.' This can be anywhere from a few days to, in some cases, a month or even longer. 'Straight to callback' is when you either had an amazing audition and are exactly what they are looking for or they are in a hurry. Maybe over-budget and they need to cast right away. Usually, it's a combination of both of these things. My apologies. I did a bit of summer stock in my younger days. *Stanley* in *Streetcar*, 'Off- Off Bourbon Street' you might say."

I'm amazed at how seamless Belmont is with his transition from Cajun to Midwest news anchor accent and then back.

"Well, you summed it up perfectly there Special Agent."

You think you know someone.

Jackson was shaking his head.

"Right. I get the feeling that this is not a regular, what you call 'occurrence' for you, Rooker. I mean we're not talking Denzel here, with all due respect."

Animosity returned.

"Yes, sure. Well, anyway I did the callback later that day and they called me the next day saying I booked the god damn thing."

"Shit, I am impressed."

"Have I seen this movie?"

"Not a movie. A commercial for Mountain Dew. My co-star was a goat, and no, you have not seen it."

"What do you mean, I..."

"The commercial never aired. The goat beats the shit out of a waitress in the spot. It was supposed to be satirical but no matter, the director was ridiculed for his 'glamorization of abuse against women.' Plus he was also hit by PETA for infringing upon the rights of a working mother."

"The waitress?"

"The goat. It was alleged that 'Billi' was not allowed sufficient nursing breaks with her baby 'JoJo' who was three months old and on set every day."

"That is one fucked up business you're in Rooker. Damn."

"Can we move on?"

Belmont nodded.

"Teddy was pissed at me at first but then, being the friend he was, told me how happy he was for me. Life happened. Some other things came up. We never made it to Juarez. Never left Pasadena. Then this woman, the one who turned out to be Rose Vasquez, starts showing up at the Bard Café. Teddy and me loved meeting there. It was kind of a compromise from meeting at the bar. I've been off the booze for over three years and Teddy was trying to stop, but he just couldn't deal with the A.A. meetings. Said the men were pussies, and the women were drama queens. Teddy wasn't a big one to show his feelings. At least not till recently."

"What was the connection with Rose Vasquez?"

"I thought you'd tell me."

"In the course of our investigation we found out that Teddy volunteered at Children's Hospital for a few years. Worked in some reading thing for the cancer kids."

I tried my best to ignore the decidedly un-PC commentary. I had gotten used to it, though.

"Pediatric cancer. Literally Healing."

"So, you knew about that."

"Teddy was my best friend in the world but there were things I didn't know about him. His volunteer work was one of them. Until recently anyway."

Jackson was fishing for info on how Teddy knew Rose Vasquez. More specifically, what he knew. I could have told him the "what" but then I would have had to tell him the 'how' and that would have involve a little girl named Lexy and a "ghost" she called "Father Jim". I decided to hold on to that info just a bit longer. I don't know why. Maybe because I realized Jackson would put me in a psych wing of Cedars Sinai or probably, and this was closer to the truth, I needed to decide whether I believed everything I heard and saw at Children's Hospital Los Angeles.

CHAPTER 16

Larue Belmont

That whole Cajun accent thing was all bullshit. Let's get that out of the way. Larue Stonewall Belmont was born on November 14, 1972 with possibly the worst middle name a southern gay man could be cursed with. It is true that Larue was born in New Orleans. Well not entirely. More accurately, he was born in Belle Chasse, Louisiana, a suburb of New Orleans which Wikipedia says is the largest town in Plaquemines Parish. Larue was what you'd call a Navy brat. His father, Andrew Belmont, was a Second Class Aviation Electronics Warfare Technician when Larue was born. Larue, his father and mother, Gladys Loveless Archambault, a middle name which unfortunately suited her to a tee, were stationed at Naval Air Station Joint Reserve Base when Larue was born. He was named after his paternal grandfather who was killed in Korea when the jeep he was using to try to outrun the military police after a first date went terribly wrong and he attempted to rape the base commander's daughter, flipped several times decapitating Larue Senior. The junior Larue wondered for years why he was named after a rapist and was never given a clear answer. Finally, dying of cancer caused by exposure to the asbestos the Navy denied existed, Larue's father told him. It seems his mother had had a very difficult time giving birth. This was indeed true as she would never be able to have another child as a result of the ordeal. In any case, Gladys, who could hold a grudge with the best of them, decided that since giving birth to "that boy" had felt like a violation anyway, well why not name him after the family rapist. And there you have it.

By the time Larue's father died, Gladys was on her third boyfriend, this one a marine. She put on an academy award-winning performance with Larue and the

Navy officials long enough so she could get Andrew's pension and then promptly married the marine, a sadist even by marine standards named Werner who proceeded to beat Larue every time he acted like a "sugar britches."

The happy family moved to Virginia when Werner was transferred to Marine Corps Base Quantico when Larue was 16. The base happens to be home to the FBI Academy. It was also where Larue fell in love for the first time. The object of his attentions happened to be the son of a FBI Special Agent who was teaching at Quantico. At the age of 18 Larue's life was changed when his boyfriend, the love of his life up to that point anyway, Chas Burke, was hit by a city bus after he had fallen into traffic while doing handstands. Booze was involved. Larue's isolation was complete. By this time his mom was divorced from Werner and working at a bar on base. Larue escaped his pain by going to movies. On one particular night he went to see *Silence of the Lambs* where he fell in love with the FBI and Jodie Foster, in no particular order. As Larue had not yet read up on the man who created the Federal Bureau of Investigation, the irony was lost on him. He transferred his credits to Virginia Tech and received a BA from there with a minor in Criminology. He applied to the FBI shortly after graduation and was accepted. He finished the academy at the top of his class and was sent to the Chicago field office for his first assignment. Larue loved Chicago. The Cubs, the Bears, the Blackhawks, Opera, the museums, Lake Shore Drive. Hell, he even liked the 'Lake- Effect', the brutal cold that came off Lake Michigan during the winter. Since the 90s were still not without homophobia in most institutions, including the FBI, Larue kept a low profile. That is until one day he met a short, gruff, totally un-PC guy with panda bear brown eyes by the name of Teddy Dabrowski and everything changed.

CHAPTER 17

Children's Hospital
Paula Garcia's Office
May 2019

"So, did Teddy believe the Father Jim story? What else did Lexy talk to him about?"

Paula looked tired. I almost just got up and told her I could come back but she wanted to talk. I could sense it. There was something more I needed to know about Teddy. I had the feeling that the key was Lexy.

"He never saw Father Jim again. I think he believed in him, though. He believed in Lexy. They had a connection. He wanted to find out where Lexy came from. I'm not sure if he ever found out. I do know that Teddy was happy, if that's the word, after his visits with Lexy."

"How much time did he spend with her?"

"He volunteered three nights a week. He was here on Tuesday, Wednesday and Friday from 4 till 9PM. He was responsible for visits to the other kids as well, but he always managed to see Lexy when he first arrived and on his way out. Can I ask you a question, Ben? You must promise to tell me the truth no matter how crazy it may sound."

"Fire away. I don't think anything you ask me will surprise me, though."

"Did Teddy ever mention seeing, how do you say it, 'spirits,' maybe you call them. 'Ghosts,' 'creatures from the other side'?"

"Ghosts? Not that I can think of, and I believe that's something I would remember."

"Why do you ask?"

"Have you ever heard him mention the names Veronica and Eileen?"

"Juarez."

"Juarez? What are you saying?"

"When he was drunk or going through a depression, he had a lot of those bouts, he talked about two college girls from Las Cruces that he met in Juarez."

"He left them in the desert to die?"

"How the hell did you know?"

"Lexy. She talks with Eileen. She thinks maybe the other one is too afraid to speak or..."

"Or what? What are you saying, Paula?"

"The one you call 'Veronica' may still be alive. Apparently Lexy was helping Teddy come to terms with his guilt. Through Lexy, Teddy was beginning to make amends to Eileen. Then he died."

I was, needless to say, having a very difficult time with this. I mean I believe that some part of us lives on after the physical body dies but this idea of an eight-year-old *Oracle of Delphi* was a bit too much. I needed to see Lexy again.

"Come back tomorrow. I'll get you another visitor's badge. They're having the quarterly orientation for new volunteers. You can tag along."

"That's fine. I'll be here. Oh, all this talk about Lexy—how is she, I mean health wise?"

"It's hard to say. Some days are better than others. She has leukemia. A particular pediatric strain that may or may not respond to a bone marrow transplant. She's been in and out of Children's Hospital for years; ever since she was brought here. It's a stubborn disease. The nuns over at the archdiocese take care of her. Friends of Father Jim. All under the table so to speak. She has no relatives that we know of that we could test for a match."

"Why not test me? I'm O negative blood type. I read somewhere that that was the universal donor. If I'm a match, I will have more of a legitimate reason to see her and talk."

I really didn't know why the hell I volunteered for this. One of those things that just comes out. In any case Paula wasn't ready for it. She paused, looked at me with those luscious brown eyes, leaned forward as if to... and then back to reality.

"Are you sure? It can be a painful process. Also it's not just about blood type. It's a bit more complex but yes, a matching blood type is a good starting point. Yes, of course it would make more sense for you to be visiting her, but what more information could you hope to get? She's a child who needs people who care not some random person looking for answers."

I thought about my answer for a moment. How much could I trust Paula? Who was this Lexy child after all? Teddy's savior or just another broken kid... There was something going on with Paula. Something at once beautifully mystifying while also a bit threatening.

"I would never have even thought of saying this even a week ago but so many things have happened—some real, some surreal. I'm probably crazy but I think Lexy may know who killed Teddy and what happened to Eileen and Veronica. I believe the answers to those questions will tell us who blew up Bard Café. Everything is connected."

Paula just nodded her head and walked me to the door and then said something which further complicated the puzzle that was Paula Garcia.

"Be careful."

She gave me a look which I had not seen up to this point and closed the door.

CHAPTER 18

Juarez, Mexico
July 2005

"Jesus Christ, Teddy or whatever the fuck your name is, you can't leave us here. What the fuck are you doing? Stop god damn it! You can't just leave us here with these scumbags!"

Teddy rolled up the windows in the beat up sedan, the rental that belonged to the two college kids calling themselves Eileen and Veronica. A day of fantasy turned into one of horror. *Drive god damn it. Drive. Don't look back.*

And just like that, Teddy was gone.

"Don't worry, Senorita, you and your friend are safe with us. Just a couple of days and..."

"No, god damn it, I know what you do. I've seen it on the news. I..."

The Policia Federal named Juan had had enough. He was a good Catholic. His mother had favored him among all her five boys. He had studied hard to get into the Federal Police. At first he was an honorable man. A good cop if you will. But things happen. The salary was peanuts. Juan wanted to marry his sweetheart Felicia and have babies. A strong son perhaps. Impossible on his paltry salary. So, when his friend Sancho, his best friend and the policia who had helped in the arrest of the gringas and gringo, introduced him to the man from the cartel, he was ready and willing. The idealism of youth vanquished by the reality of life. And so here they were, he and Sancho holding the women because the cartel had sent word to do just that. Hold them. They were not human beings to Juan or Sancho. That was how he rationalized everything these days.

He gagged and bound Veronica and Eileen, even though the latter, appeared to be in a catatonic state. He then dragged them both, one at a time into the filthy holding cell. It was the only one in the abandoned jail twenty miles outside the El Paso-Juarez border. No one was ever taken to a "real" police station in those days. Not since the cartel anyway. They would be arriving soon.

The two black heavily armored SUVs arrived out of nowhere almost on cue. Doors opened, and armed men from both vehicles jumped out to take up tactical positions. Policia Juan Santos and Sancho Davila stood at perfect military attention as the front door of the rear vehicle opened and Roy "Tire Boy" Vasquez, head of the Juarez cartel himself, soon to be boss of all of Venganza stepped out.

"Who is in charge here?"

"Officer Juan Santos, Senor. At your service."

"We were told that there were three of them. A man as well. Where is he?"

Juan looked at Sancho who failed to meet his eyes.

"Are you telling me he is not here?"

"Well, Senor, I, we thought you were just interested in the girls. We..."

"Who told you that? I never said that. Did my associates say that? Why would you think that? Why would you think, period?"

"I am sorry, Senor. Very sorry. But wait, we, I mean, I took a picture of the gringo. Standard procedure, senor."

Juan said a silent prayer that the Polaroid he had taken was still in his pocket. A moment later his divine plea was answered as he fished it out and handed it to Roy.

"Here you are, Senor. Again, I am sorry. So sorry."

Roy ripped the photo from his hand, glanced at it and placed it in his jean pocket.

"You should be. You will be. A 'morbido' I suppose? Come now you can tell me. I was not always so wealthy. I started as a poor, humble boy like yourselves. It's okay. Tell me."

The cartel chief's smile disarmed Juan. He smiled himself. He started to nod his head and then realized that he has made the worst mistake, the final mistake in his young life.

The Cartel boss motioned ever so slightly, imperceptive to the untrained eye and a hail of gunfire erupted from his henchmen. Sancho Davila was dead before he hit the ground.

"Oh God no! Senor, I beg of you!"

Juan Santos began groveling on the ground. Suddenly he was a ten-year-old child begging his mother to come in his room and turn on the light.

"Make the monster go away, Mama. Mama, please help me, Mama. I'm scared."

"Your mama cannot help you now."

A look from Vasquez and one of his men tied Santos to a nearby post and removed his clothes. Santos saw the knife. A butcher knife.

"We saw foxes and rabbits on the road on the way here. Dead. Bullet holes through their heads. You were having a bit of target practice?"

Again the disarming smile from Roy.

"Well, yes, Senor. Of course we want to keep our skills up while we are out here. One can never be too careful."

A sense of relief from the doomed man. Short lived.

"Yes, you never know when a band of kit fox and Jack rabbit will attack."

Roy was no longer smiling. He took the knife from his soldier.

"You like massacring innocent animals, do you!?"

"No Mio Jesus Cristo!"

Santos screamed one last time as he felt the blade between his legs. He would bleed out but not till the sun had gone down and the desert creatures had taken notice of his ravaged flesh.

There would be no military funeral. Their families would be dead by morning. The price for a mistake. A fatal lapse in judgement.

A noise came from the holding cell. Veronica had managed to remove her gag. Screaming incoherently. She and Eileen were dragged out of the cell and thrown at the feet of Roy Vasquez. Veronica's screams stopped as she looked up at the figure in front of her. A flash. A remembrance of younger days.

She was 13 years old. Still, her Daddy's girl. At least her young naïve self had still believed it to be true. The nightly visits from her father. Roy telling his teenage daughter that he was lonely. Her mother you see was torturing him. He needed love. So Alvy gave it to him. She took the drugs from him to blot out the shame. Eventually she stopped feeling anything. Everything a blur. The cocaine and the other drugs became a regular part of her life. She stopped associating with her girlfriends. They were doing the things normal 13-year-old's do. She could not explain to them or herself that she had died, at least her soul had. The body would not be far behind, everything a blur to her. Booze, drugs, sex, anything to stop the pain of a sexually abusive, sadistic father and a mother who looked the other way. Alvy was 17 when he took her for the last time. She used her wiles on one of her father's soldiers and got him to smuggle her

73

to the border. From there she got across with money wired from her guilt-ridden mother and eventually settled in Los Cruces and changed her name to "Veronica."

Alvina did not know that her mother was only allowed to escape by letting Roy keep her. Yet another bit of collateral damage that would be bestowed on Alvy from the evil/tormented genius that was her father.

Betrayal, one thing that Roy "Tire Boy" would never forgive. The fact that he had stolen his little girl's childhood while in his now permanent drug-induced haze never dawned on Roy. In his warped mind, he had been betrayed. First by his wife and then by his daughter. Never would he forgive this. Never.

"Hello, Amada Nina, my eternal love. My dearest Alvina. Why did you leave me? Why?"

Veronica/Alvina struggled to her feet and embraced this man who had just called her "Alvina," her birth name. Her baptismal name. All these years but she was sure about who this was holding her tightly. Her protector. She detested him with a hate all-encompassing, but her mother had taught her well. To show this hate would mean instant death.

Wait and live. Wait and live.

"Mi Padre!"

She cried with the tears of one who only moments before had resigned herself to certain death and now will do anything to stay alive, even if it meant the embracing of this monster, her father, before her. The monster continued to hug her as he reached around his back and ever so slowly found the knife. With a snake like action Alvina felt the knife graze her hands as the rope binding her was cut. She looked up to see her father's dark brown eyes, the ones she remembered as a baby. They were staring through her as if waiting for something, and then there was only darkness as she passed out.

"Take a nice picture please. Send it to the address in ..., where the fuck does the whore live?"

"San Marino, Senor."

"Yes, Yes. Make sure she gets some good copies. Now put my beautiful Alvina in the car. Make sure she is comfortable. She has suffered so much. She must be exhausted."

Roy got into the SUV next to his unconscious daughter as his entourage readied its departure, but not before Eileen was visited one last time. Her only fault in life was meeting the daughter of a cartel boss at a party in Juarez. A man who would do anything to hurt his estranged wife, the mother of his daughter, beyond any human revenge. A fling in Juarez. Eileen punishing her boyfriend because she thought he had cheated on her (He had not) back in Las Cruces. She was thinking about how much she missed him as she lay on the filthy desert floor when behind her she felt the cold metal barrel as it came to rest just below her ear. A click. Almost imperceptible and then... nothing. Emptiness. Peace.

Eileen was buried in an unmarked grave. The policia were left to rot in the midday sun. A message sent. The motorcade traveled into the gorgeous sunset. Roy remembered for a moment how much Rose loved those sunsets. He looked over at his daughter who was sleeping peacefully.

Better days were coming. He had let Rose go before. That was a mistake, Roy's paranoid, drug addled mind told him. Now it was time for retribution.

CHAPTER 19

Huntington Hospital
Pasadena

Teddy's roommate in the hospital room at Huntington was interviewed and released. The guy was a 75-year-old Vietnam vet with PTSD and prostate cancer. The kind that is treatable where the doctor tells you in a jocular manner, "Hey, you'll die of old age before the cancer gets you." Anyway, the roommate was having an MRI when Teddy was launched or jumped to his death. The nurses and doctors were all cleared as well. Teddy had just been delivered a lunch of cheeseburgers and fries, a dish that he loved. It was left untouched. There were no signs of a struggle. The window in Teddy's room which is locked from the inside was closed with no sign of tampering. Maintenance told Jackson that the windows could be opened from the inside but one needed a special key which only the plant manager, the person in charge of the energy plant for the hospital had access to. Jackson decided to pay him a visit.

"Steve Radcliffe, is that you?"

"That would be me. I bet you're the detective that's been calling every day. I told that FBI guy everything I know already.

"Special Agent Belmont?"

"Belmont, yes, that's the name. Big guy."

Jackson and Radcliffe were sitting in the plant manager's office at Huntington Hospital. Jackson thought it reminded him of his old man's place in the cellar of their house in Compton when he was a kid. Before the days of "man caves." Anyway, black people like him never had "man caves." That was strictly a white man thing, he thought as he looked over Radcliffe's office. Posters of Jesus, the white one with blue eyes all over the walls. Jackson was glad he was raised a Baptist and didn't have to deal with that Brad Pitt looking Jesus growing up.

"So, Mr. Radcliffe, I..."

"Call me Steve or Reverend. Because I'm so close to Jesus, you understand? That's what my friends call me."

"I see, okay... Reverend, how in God's name could Teddy Dabrowski have opened that window without a key and without any sign of it being tampered with?"

"Exactly."

"Reverend" sent a gob of tobacco juice into the coffee can on his desk. A pinch of tobacco mixed with saliva alighted on Jackson's lower chin. In an act that required the self-restraint of Jeffrey Epstein during an open house at an all-girl college, Jackson ignored it and continued talking with Radcliffe.

"Exactly?"

"God works in mysterious ways. Nobody opened that window."

"God? And so how did he fall to his death if he couldn't get out his room window?"

"Or Satan. The Dark One. Beelzebub. It happens, you know. We think we know the answers to everything in this world with our book smarts and our technology. Well, the truth is we don't know squat."

Another tobacco/saliva projectile was launched, this time missing Jackson and the can.

"Did anyone do any work in that room, you know maintenance, painting, before Mr. Dabrowski checked in."

"Yea, that FBI guy Belmont already asked me that. Didn't he tell you what I told him? I saw the guy Dabrowski run up the stairs that go to the roof right before he fell."

"Fell? And wait a minute we got witnesses saying they saw him in the room."

"Well, you're the detective. Jumped, fell, whatever. All I can tell you is what I saw. I saw him run towards the roof. Don't the Feds and the cops talk to each other? Damn. Some fucked up country we got. Lot a weird shit. I was just listening to George Noory last night. He's got that show called *Coast to Coast*. He's always talking about people disappearing or dying in these really mysterious ways. You know, like Mr. Dabrowski. You should give it a listen sometime."

"Yes, sure, yea, maybe I will. Does your position require any kind of psych...? Never mind. Thank you for your help, Mr. Radcliffe."

"Reverend."

"Of course, yea, Reverend. Crazy ass cracker fuck wad."

"What's that?"

"Oh nuthin... God Bless you."

"One thing. Why did he have to go out his window?"

"What are you saying, Radcliffe, I mean Reverend?"

"Only one way to fall all that way down."

"How's that?"

"The roof, the smoking roof. Only place to smoke in the hospital. Not really allowed of course but hey, some folks believe rules are made to be broken. I already told all this to that FBI guy, Belmont. Maybe you should talk to him."

Jackson departed in a rush but not before kicking the can of tobacco juice over.

"Now why'd you go and do that?!"

Well, the redneck bastard didn't change his story, anyway. A good thing, Jackson thought.

He smiled on his way out as the man's screams of protest echoed behind him.

CHAPTER 20

Huntington Hospital – Later that same day
Nurse's Station–Neurological Section

"I'd use another word other than 'Character,' Dr. Mancuso," said an exasperated Jackson.

"Well, I'm sorry you weren't alerted before you talked to Steve. He is a top rate plant manager though."

"Sure. Sure. I take your word for it, Doc. So, I know we talked before but I figured I'd drop in one more time since I had already visited 'Gort' in the basement."

"I'm sorry, I...?"

"*The Day the Earth Stood Still*? The original? Michael Rennie? The alien humanoid or whatever was named Gort. Another one of those sci-fi films that came out during what they used to call the Cold War. No?"

"Sorry. I was never much on movies. Med school and all that."

Jackson made a mental note not to assume that all white people watch old science fiction films.

"Sure. Understood. I know you're just starting your rounds but, one more time. Dabrowski had no visitors the day he died?"

Mancuso was about to answer when –

"The priest visited him. I'm sorry, Doctor, I didn't mean to interrupt. Couldn't help but hear you."

A young black girl. RN about thirty, easy on the eyes, thought Jackson.

"Not a problem. A priest?"

"Yes, he would come once a week. He visited Mr. Dabrowski a few times while he was here."

"Ms. Ah...?"

"Desmond, Dory. Dory Desmond. I just started here about a month ago."

"Of course. Yea, I'm Detective Sam Jackson. So did Teddy, Mr. Dabrowski, seem happy to see the Father? Do you know his name?"

"Well, that's the thing. I never saw Father Jim. That's what Teddy called him. Nobody saw him it seemed, except Teddy. Teddy would just say that he was happy to talk with him. It seemed like I always came in right after Teddy told me that Father Jim had just left."

"So, were you on duty the day Teddy died?"

"Yes, earlier in the morning. I was just getting off my shift. I was on my way out and I just stopped to say hello."

"How did he seem to you? I mean was he happy, sad?"

"I wouldn't use either of those words. I would say he seemed like he had something on his mind. I can't really put my finger on it. Also, like he had been up for a while. You know, not drowsy at all."

"Yes. Sure. Any of you know anything about the smoking roof?"

Desmond had the look of a fourth grader caught while passing a drawing of her math teacher with a giant breast in his mouth.

"Well, I mean yea, I heard that some people may from time to time go..."

Mancuso had heard enough.

"Yes, Detective, there is a smoking roof. It is off limits. No one is allowed on the roof to smoke or otherwise, except maintenance but..."

"Rules are made to be broken."

"Well yes. The nicotine addiction is not something unique to patients. Unfortunately, doctors and nurses have succumbed to it as well."

Mancuso was staring at Desmond who was decidedly nervous.

"Well, time for my rounds. Doctor, Detective."

"One more question if you don't mind, Nurse Desmond?"

"Yea, sure."

"Did Mr. Dabrowski say anything else to you? I mean anything out of the ordinary?"

"No... well, wait, yea, now that I'm thinking about it. The other night when I came in to update his vitals and check his IV. The assistants normally do that but I was a bit bored and..."

Mancuso cleared her throat. Wrong thing to say in front of Huntington Hospital's version of Nurse Cratchit. Desmond would no longer be "bored."

"Well anyway, I went in and he looked happy. I asked him if it was because he was getting out soon. He told me that was part of it."

"Part of it?"

'Yes, he said he was not so much happy but felt like a heavy burden had been lifted. He told me he had been forgiven."

"By Father Jim you mean...?"

"No, no, that was what was weird. He said "She. She forgave me". Those were his words."

Dory thought about telling them about that Ratcliffe guy, the plant manager. How she saw him walking, actually running towards the elevator. It was just after she realized that Dabrowski wasn't in his room. She was just about to in fact when the glare from Dr. Mancuso sent her on her way.

CHAPTER 21

Las Cruces, New Mexico
August 2005

The day she saw the pictures, Rose Vasquez was at a Denny's about two blocks from her daughter Alvina's Las Cruces apartment building. She and Dave had moved there a week before to search for her daughter who had ran away from her and Roy Vasquez, her father and drug cartel boss extraordinaire. Alvina was only 17 at the time she made her way to Las Cruces. She was now 22 and her father was so far gone that he had periods where he was unaware she had left. That would change, though. Despite Roy's increased descent into drugs and his maniacal attempt to control Rose and Alvina, he failed to take one thing into account; social media. Aside from her mother's help, Alvina had several contacts on Facebook and on Craig's List that aided her in her escape and in finding shelter and a job in Las Cruces. Amazingly she had lived in Las Cruces for almost six years now.

The thing that Rose or Dave, especially the latter did not understand is why they could not find Alvina in Las Cruces. It seemed all of a sudden her social media activity had stopped. Dave's state-of-the art spying techniques had told him that Alvina was living there in an apartment just a few miles away. The problem is no one had seen her in months and the trail had dried up. What Dave did not know was that even with state-of-the-art technology, the weakness of any business is its human factor. Alvina had indeed been here in Las Cruces. One of Dave's top men had found her and was tracking her up until one morning about four months before. That's when Alvina's best friend, Misty, a vixen with powers of seduction that would make Lolita look like a Mormon salt festival queen, knocked on the back of the van across the street from Alvina's abode. Misty was wearing a rain coat with nothing but "Oh my Jesus" underneath. The employee of Baxter Home Alarms and Security who opened the door found himself on his back with two breasts and, with apologies to Miller, "a gorgeous mound of Venus" pinning him down. Twenty minutes later when he removed himself from Misty, Alvina was already on a plane to El Paso enroot to Juarez.

Rose was at the moment deciding whether to get the All American Breakfast or just some scrambled eggs. Dave Baxter, the man in her life, her Salvador redeemer was sitting across from her smoking a cigarette and waiting patiently. He had already ordered what he always did. Two eggs over medium, ham, hash browns and coffee, light and sweet. Just the way Dave's father back in Baltimore where he grew up would have had him order it when he sent him to pick up coffee and cigarettes from the *Krauts*, his father's endearing name for the German Delicatessen down the block from the family's duplex. The coffee preference, if not the racism, stayed with Dave as well as the simple needs where food was involved. He could be at Denny's or Sardis', it didn't matter. Dave had no problem with ordering the basics. It was fast and efficient. Rose, who would go into a major depression if she ate the same thing within a one-week period was beside herself.

"Jesus, Dave, you make things so stressed."

"Stressful."

Rose was doing amazingly well with her English but she was never happy with anything less than perfection. She had been in the States for ten years after all so she insisted that Dave correct her.

"Mierda!"

"It's okay, baby. You're doing great. I know you don't want to hear this but if we are going to get to your post office box soon enough so we don't hit heavy traffic on the way home, we better eat quick."

"Oh, it's okay, Dave. Probably just bills."

Rose was trying to act the calm, stable parent who it just so happened had not seen her daughter for all these years and was terrified that her ex-hubby, the insane, sadistic cartel boss would find her first. A good performance. Only one problem. Dave could see right through it.

"Look, would you mind very much if we just got yours to go and left now?"

Intuition. It had been nagging her since she got up a few hours ago.

Go to the post office.

That Little Voice again.

Dave had agreed of course. They had left and arrived at the post office in plenty of time.

It was a yellow legal envelope postmarked El Paso, TX and marked "Photos—Do Not Bend."

Dave offered to open it but Rose would have none of it. She grabbed the letter opener from her desk and cut the top of the envelope off. A picture fell out. Face up. Alvina.

"My baby. Oh, my dear baby girl. Why? Why?"

The Cartel was very prompt in sending important pieces of mail. This was no exception. Alvina's fingerprints were all over the picture so there would be no doubt. Roy knew Rose would check. He even left a little note. Roy still had moments of lucidness even as he descended further into an drug addicted stupor.

"My Dearest Rose, Know that this hurts me probably more than you but I have learned to live with the suffering. You will too. You see, I could not let you take away my precious Alvina. A child should be with her father. You should have never taken her from me. Good bye, Mi Amore. I will see you again. Maybe tomorrow. Maybe ten more years. Know this. I will come for you."

Rose went to her bedroom and shut the door. When she came out two days later she looked like her old self. As if nothing had happened. Dave knew better.

CHAPTER 22

Children's Hospital
Blood Bank

Twenty years in the Navy had made me immune to shots. I had so many of them I couldn't even guess the number. When I joined in the early 90s, they still had this kind of air shot. It would just shoot the antibiotic or whatever into your arm. This was great in one way because it took away the needle which many people had a problem with including old Snuffy Perry, a good old boy shipmate of mine.

"I hate the god damn needles worse than an outhouse on a hot summas day. Besides, they's just injectin us wit microchips or sum such thing to keep track a us foreva."

As time went by, I actually thought Snuffy might have had a point. But, again, I digress.

The big problem with the air shots was that if one flinched at the moment the air was shooting into your arm you could get a hell of a gash. Not as bad as Snuffy's belief that he had heard tell "sum po bastard had his arm cut clean right off when the dumass moved," but pretty bad in any case.

The needles at the quarterly blood drive at Children's Hospital were of the conventional variety. I gave blood which would also be tested to see if I was a match for a bone marrow transplant for little Ms. Alexandria Perez AKA Lexy.

"How are you today, Lexy? I'm Ben, a friend of Teddy's."

"I know who you are."

A bit disconcerting but I let it go. Another time.

"What are you reading right now? I heard you like C. S. Lewis."

"I finished it."

"Oh, okay. Well, I live near a nice library or I could pick up something at the bookstore for you. Just let me know."

"I'm done reading. Thank you anyway."

I started to get up on my soapbox and talk about the wonders of reading but then remembered one of Paula's rules: Never get into a discussion with a patient/client that could turn into an argument. Stress is never an option for the children. Never.

Of course the fact that I was not even an authorized volunteer, and I had used a bit of stealth to go from the blood donation area to Lexy's ward, added to my somewhat cautious attitude as well. I continued.

"So, Teddy and you were good friends I hear."

"We still are. I just talked to him last night. He visited me right after the girl from Las Croooses left. Is that the right way to say it?"

"Yes, that's right, Lexy. Can I call you Lexy? Wait, you said that Teddy came to visit you last night?"

"I said I talked to him last night. Him and Eileen. Do you know, Eileen? Mr. Ben, are you okay? You look kind of wobbly."

One thing about giving blood—it's a shock to the system. I mean even if it's only a relatively small amount. Always drink the juice and eat the brownie they give you, unless you're diabetic of course, but then I don't know if you'd be allowed to give blood in that case. Oh, whatever, you get my gist. Anyway, if you are going to pass out like I just did, a hospital is as good a place as any. Whether it was the dehydration, low sugar or the fact that this child had just told me she had spoken with my dear, departed friend Teddy and the more than likely dead Eileen is not really important. I was coming to via smelling salts with Paula's beatified face looming over me, the fluorescent lights just about creating a perfect halo effect. If this was heaven, I wanted in.

"Mr. Rooker. Can you hear me?"

The Ernest Borgnine look alike EMT with the breath of a three-day-old dead harbor seal (For you kids out there and I mean you millennials, please look up Mr. Borgnine on IMDB. An amazing actor. I recommend *Marty* as an introduction to his wonderful work) slapped me albeit not real hard, but god damn, he was slapping.

"Okay, okay, I'm up, Mom!"

"What's his name?"

"Ben... Ben Rooker."

"Mr. Rooker! Ben! You had an event. You're okay now though. Just breathe now. Breathe for me. Stay still."

Yea, that's great. *Marty* had been beating me like a frozen piece of beef in a Chicago slaughterhouse but now he wanted me to breathe easily and stay still. Christ.

"I'm good. I just was dehydrated or something. See, I can say that word so I'm good. I got things to do. I'm just going to get up."

"Ben?"

It's Paula. I think I'm in love with her. Bending over me with those beautiful lips. Wait a minute, did they inject me with something? Oh, who gives a fuck.

"Paula, marry me."

"Sure, Ben. Sure. Just rest. Stay still. We'll talk about it later."

What a wonderful feeling. A thought hit me that I was no longer sober because of these drugs, but then I realized they were given to me involuntarily so I got, ladies and gentleman, what is called in the lexicon of Alcoholics Anonymous, a "Free Pass."

"How many kids do you want, Paula?"

And then I passed out again.

CHAPTER 23

Roy Vasquez killed his first human being when he was 12 years old. He was, interestingly enough on a hunting trip with his best friend, Jorge Valdez. It might be a bit of a stretch to call Jorge, Roy's best friend. It would perhaps be more correct to call him his only friend. They were hunting desert mule deer in the Sonora desert area of Mexico. Again a clarification. Jorge was hunting. Roy was praying it would be over without the loss of any animals and he could just go home and watch *Bonanza* on TV. Roy was an only child who never missed an episode of the show that featured the love between a father and his three sons. He even started calling himself "Little Joe" to the chagrin of his own father who beat him when he caught him doing his fantasy role play that included talking to two imaginary brothers and an imaginary father. Frank Vasquez took it all as a personal affront.

He missed his mother, Angelica. His only memories were of her hugging him when he was ten years old after his father had screamed at him for knocking something over or wetting his pants. This happened frequently to Roy. His father's screaming did something to his little psyche that made urinating impossible to stop. His mother was always there though until that horrible day.

She wanted to take Roy with her to the store in Ensenada. Frank had told her not to go. The gang war between his cartel and a small time but vicious rival, even by cartel standards out of Tijuana, had calmed down but Frank wanted to wait another week at least before they left the compound. In the middle of an argument, Angelica ran to the car and told Roy to follow. He tripped on his way and Frank grabbed him but not before Angelica sped off. She made it about a mile down the road before a group of soldiers from the rival gang saw her coming as they were preparing to leave the area. It was like shooting ducks in a row. Angelica was killed instantly. The men cut her breasts off her already mutilated body and left them on top of her car for Frank to see. He went crazy. He made Roy look at the grisly scene. Told him it was his fault. Took it out on Roy till the day he died. It was all Roy's fault.

He had killed his mother. Of course he had. That day something happened to Roy. He stopped pissing in his pants. From this day on everyone that crossed him was somehow involved in the massacre of his mother. He would see her butchered breasts on that car. Was it any wonder that he became a killer equal to the Borgias in his brutality and lack of mercy? But also, like the Borgias there was a genius behind it albeit touched with insanity. Every act, however grotesque, was done for a reason. Machiavelli would be proud.

Now on this day, Frank was in an insane asylum. Rumors of syphilis. Jorge a few years older than Roy had become a kind of surrogate brother. So Jorge thought anyway.

The deer had appeared out of nowhere. One moment Roy was admiring the picturesque desert and the next moment there it was. Standing ten yards from him. The most beautiful thing Roy had ever seen. The eyes boring through him as if to say, "We are one. I understand. Brothers."

An explosion came from his right ear as the majestic beast's leg flew off. Obliterated. Jorge cursed himself as a sound came from the animal that Roy would never forget. A pleading half groan and then almost a laugh. A panting. Jorge fired again and the animal's face was blown off. But he was still alive. A piece of meat writhing on the ground.

No, my god, no. This cannot be!

Roy raise his rifle to fire it for the first time. One round into the base of the wounded animal's skull. He died instantly.

"Well done, amigo!"

The last words that Jorge Valdez would ever utter as Roy Vasquez soon to be Roy 'Tire Boy' Vasquez raised his rifle again and pulled the trigger blasting a wide eyed Jorge's head off of his body.

Roy never killed another animal. As for human beings, well I don't have to tell you the answer to that one. Stories were created. Policia were paid off. Jorge's family, including his mother, father and sister, despite being too young to comprehend entirely what had happened, were given a choice: Bury your son and brother and forget. Move on. Or... well the other option need not be explained here I trust.

****

Roy lived with his father and an aunt and worked in the car repair business before building the tire empire he now ruled. Roy was a good student. He read everything he could on business and had a natural affinity for numbers. Numbers, tires and settling scores. No half-measures with Roy. And it was never "just business." When he felt betrayed, his mind immediately flashed to his mother's massacre and the grisly aftermath his father forced him to observe. Oh no, with Roy, if you crossed him it was personal and "personal" invariably meant a death not unlike the death of his mother or the mule deer that Roy had witnessed so many years ago. It was all about vengeance. Whether it be real or imagined did not enter into the equation.

Roy lost his virginity with a 19-year-old whore named Cherry. His father took him to the brothel in Tijuana himself. Frank had fucked her first. In front of Roy. He then made Roy go next. It was of course a disaster. Roy had finally completed the act, miraculously. A combination of Cherry's prowess and divine intervention saving him. No matter, Frank laughed at Roy all the way home. Roy wept softly. This made his father taunt him even more. Eventually he stopped crying. Indeed, that was the last time Roy Vasquez ever cried.

Frank got out of the asylum even though he was still quite crazy. No matter. The old man got diagnosed with lung cancer at the age of 60. Roy was 29 and had become adept at the tire business. His numerical prowess amazed everyone. Frank even admitted it himself.

"The boy can count."

Of course Roy wasn't just taking over a tire business. He was expected to run an ever expanding cartel. Frank had now become the boss of the entire Juarez Cartel. He hadn't done this merely by selling tires.

One day it came time for Roy to have his baptism in blood, so to speak. He was already getting a reputation with the ladies, the boyhood clumsiness with his father's whore erased from memory. Indeed he was called *El Caballo*. A nickname he pretended to detest but inwardly loved. He wore the most expensive boots in Mexico. Roy had them handmade from a place in Spain. Frank was getting sicker though. The cancer had metastasized and had gone to his stomach and his bones. It was only a matter of time. The day had arrived for Roy to prove himself.

The poor soul was named Pablo. He had been running the cocaine deliveries between Culiacan and Los Mochis. There had been rumors recently that he had been skimming. No real evidence but not to worry. Frank needed someone to test Roy. Pablo was the one. God save him.

Pablo was brought to an abandoned warehouse outside Mazatlán. Shaking under a black hood, he was seated in a chair in the middle of the empty warehouse. The hood was removed as Frank entered in his wheelchair pushed by Roy along with four soldiers.

Frank spoke gruffly, the pain from his rotting body was overwhelming. The stink as well.

"Pablo my friend. You are shaking like we are in fucking Alaska. Don't be upset. We are all friends here. You know my son, Roy?"

Pablo fell to his knees.

"Please Senor, I am a good and honest worker. Five years I have made the run. No problems. I do not know what happened."

Frank signaled Roy to push him towards Pablo. He was just inches above him. He looked down. A benevolent, kindly look on his face. He put his hand on Pablo's cheek.

"Now Pablo, I told you we are all friends here. You are making my son upset. He wants to meet you."

Frank started to cough. First a small irritation and then a hack that continued for a full minute. He spit a huge gob of blood on the floor next to Pablo. Speckles of the rancid, crimson yellow mix descended on Pablo's face. He was in terror.

Roy took a handkerchief out of his pocket and cleaned his father up as best he could. Finally, Frank's coughing subsided. He sat silently for a moment and then while in deep thought pulled a box cutter from his pocket and stuck it into Pablo's eye. Blood shot across the warehouse like a Tijuana fire hydrant in the middle of summer. Frank tried to remove the cutter but it wouldn't come out. Pablo's screams were deafening. One of the soldiers handed Roy a .357 Magnum. He looked at the gun and then at Pablo. Pablo was in another world. Pure horror on his face. Roy leveled the gun and shoved it down Pablo's throat breaking all of his front teeth. Pablo was gurgling blood now. Roy held the gun in place for a full minute at least, staring into Pablo's one eye. Finally, he pulled the trigger sending brain matter and blood all over his face and upper body, ruining his suit.

For the first and only time in his life, Frank Vasquez looked on his son with what could be an expression of pride. A gesture another father would give his boy for finishing first in his college class or taking a pretty girl to the prom. Roy nodded to his father. No smile. Just a nod. The transfer of power with the brutal murder of an innocent man had been completed.

A week later, Roy's father lay dying in the master bedroom of his palatial estate on the island of Palmita Verde.

"Papa, I am sorry to see you like this. What can I do?"

Frank was mumbling incoherently. Soaked with sweat and the blood from his incessant coughing. In an act of excruciating pain, he managed an intelligible sentence.

"I love you, Miho. Kiss your padre before I die."

Roy took a handkerchief out and cleaned some dust off his Zara boots. He then wiped his father's face and tossed the handkerchief into a nearby basket.

"Don't be foolish, Papa. You have a good journey. I must go now. I know you want me to continue the work you started. Adios"

"Miho, no, please..."

The coughing started again but Roy was already out the door, the clean taps of his boot heels resonating throughout the house. An hour later, Frank was dead.

His last words, "Miho, Miho, my son."

CHAPTER 24

Roy and Rose

Roy Vasquez knew that Rose Ramirez would be his wife the moment he set eyes on her. He had been watching her for at least an hour from his private box at the Plaza de Toros in Mazatlán. He knew her entire family history as well as that of her soon to be "ex-fiancé" well before Roy introduced himself. Roy was an important man. A man who did not have time for the "social niceties." He wanted a son and the only way to do that in his culture was to marry a woman who would give him one. He had to be discrete as well. In his business idle gossip would not just ruin a reputation it could put one in the desert six feet under or in prison for a hundred years. For this reason, Rose had been carefully picked. Her father had been a jack of all trades and a failure at all. Her mother was still alive. Rose did not have any brothers or sisters. Another positive for her in Roy's eyes. Lastly but not the least important, she was beautiful. The only problem, and it was easily dealt with, was her aforementioned fiancé, Nacho Alvarez, 28 years old and the heir to a trucking empire. A trucking empire that it so happened Roy was very interested in acquiring.

It was time for 'The Kill." The matador was beginning his dance of death with the bloodied bull. In a matter of minutes, the bull would be massacred. Roy detested this "sport." He loved all animals and was repulsed when he saw one hurt in any way, let alone tortured and killed. Human beings were, alas, a different story. This was the part of the spectacle that Roy refused to watch. His only reason for being there was standing below his private suite two hundred feet away. He raised himself out of his chair which instantly alerted his entourage of eight bodyguards to surround him as he made his way downstairs and to Rose.

"Buenas noches, Preciosa."

"I'm sorry, you must be mistaken. This lady is my fiancé."

Roy never took his eyes off Rose as he addressed the trucking magnate heir.

"Oh, forgive me my friend. I am Roy Vasquez and you are?"

"I'm Nacho Alvarez and what can I do..."

Ole!

Uproar from the crowd as the bull was close to death. The slight wince from Roy was barely perceptible.

"What can you do for me, senor? You can bid the lady goodnight. Go out to your limousine and go home. One of my associates will call you tomorrow with details of the acquisition."

"Wait! What? This is ridiculous. I am not..."

In the flick of an eye the trucking magnate was lifted off his feet just a couple of inches and transported like a wounded ant being taken back to the colony by his worker brothers. Throughout this whole spectacle, Rose had not taken her eyes off Roy. Now, as if awakened from a dream, "Wait, what did you do with Nacho, he's my..."

"Ex-Fiancé? Yes. He is fine. No worries. He must have been tired. You must be hungry. I know a wonderful place. Please follow me."

Rose started to protest but realized it was fruitless. This was Roy Vasquez, the most powerful man for a thousand miles in any direction. She should have been offended. She should have been scared. She was neither. Truth be told, she was delirious. She had become engaged to Nacho, a bland and ignorant boy purely because her family had ordered it. This turn of events was a relief. A commutation of a life sentence of boredom. Nacho did not recognize Roy. A blunder that would normally have cost him his life. Luckily for him, Roy's interests were not limited to Rose.

She came twice in the car on the way to Roy's villa. Just a touch from Roy had awakened a delirious, erotic carnival-like lust. They ate oysters and drank tequila naked on his veranda. Roy offered cocaine but Rose wouldn't have it. This did not stop Roy, though. A sense of alarm hit Rose but only for a moment. They made love into the next morning. Rose could not seem to get enough of this man. In turn she felt his need. An animal-like urge that enveloped both of them. Wondrous and toxic at the same time.

"Orange juice, my dear?"

"What in the name of God has happened. How? I am not this kind of girl, Senor...I..."

"With respect, if I may, Rose, you have sucked my balls, and I have licked your beautiful asshole. Social etiquette has long ago become unnecessary and is at this point, frankly absurd."

He handed her a glass of tequila with a curious gleam in it.

"You know I can't go back to my mama like this."

"There is no problem."

"Oh, yes there is. I…"

She had put the glass of tequila to her lips and now saw the source of the light. A ring with a diamond as big as her fist.

"Oh my God. I can't believe this."

"Just listen to me very carefully. Can you do that?"

Roy was on bended knee now. He had taken the ring out of the tequila glass and had put in on her finger. Looking directly into her eyes. She was mesmerized again.

"Are you listening?"

"Yes."

"Rose Ramirez, will you marry me?"

"Yes."

The wedding was a lavish but civilized one (by cartel standards) in a beautiful church on the outskirts of Mazatlán. Rose's former fiancé was at the reception. He seemed nervous and had a distinct limp. He spoke to her only briefly and did not make eye contact. He had sold his share in the family business to Roy Vasquez Tires LTD and was moving to Spain permanently, he quickly explained. He was relocating his entire family there. Rose found this strange. She always thought that Nacho was in love with the family trucking business. Nacho limped away, though, and soon she was in Roy's embrace and never gave Nacho Alvarez a second thought. She didn't even notice it when a few months later the news reported that Nacho had been killed in a freak skydiving accident and thus did not have a chance to wonder what he was doing jumping out of a plane when he was terrified of heights.

The honeymoon was brief but passionate. Roy had business to attend to.

Nine months later Rose gave birth to Alvina Lourdes Vasquez. Roy loved the little girl more than life itself, until that is, his subtle mistress Lady Cocaine joined by Queen Heroin courted and imprisoned him in a mountain of snowy false promises and fruitless expectations. The *White Rabbit* that had "given him wings to fly" had now "taken away the sky."

Rose and Roy's intimacy became less and less frequent as the beatings of Rose and Alvina increased. When Rose, by then free herself, learned that 17 year-old Alvina had somehow got out of the country, Rose helped set her up in Los Cruces with money from what she thought was an untraceable off shore account. Still Alvina was able to build a life and even managed to stop the drugs for a while until that fateful day she and her new American friend Eileen met a gringo named Teddy at a bar in Juarez.

CHAPTER 25

Hollywood Presbyterian Hospital

"What the hell happened to you, Rooker? Are you really that scared to meet with me that you'll go and put yourself in the damn hospital?"

"Hospital? I am in Children's...?"

"Hell no, you're in Hollywood Presbyterian. Practically next door. It's..."

"Yea, yea, I know where it is."

"Oh, so you were here before."

"You might say that. My wife died here."

"Shit, okay, yea right, the cancer. Okay, so anyway, you passed out after giving blood at Children's."

I sat up. I needed to get the hell out of there. The last place I wanted to be was the scene of so much torture and grief from just a few years ago. The place where Rita got her chemo. The place she got her mastectomy. The place she died.

"Mr. Rooker, how are you doing?"

Doctor Yousef. Rita's surgeon. Old home week.

"Hey, Doc. What brings you here?"

"Oh, I was in the area. Just thought I'd drop by."

Yousef picked up my chart and read it. He looked over at Jackson.

"Oh, yes this is a, ah, a friend of mine. Yes, Sam Jackson."

"Nice to meet you, Mr. Jackson."

"My pleasure, Doc. So, how's old Ben doing? Is he going to live?"

"Oh, sure. Hey would you excuse me for a moment. I need to talk with Ben's doctor."

"Hey, Doc, what's going on?"

97

Yousef left the room before I could say anything else. Unlike him.

"Isn't that the shit? Christ."

"What was that all about?"

"Oh, Probably nothing. Just precautions maybe."

"Yea sure. Precautions. So, Rooker, if you feel up to it, I wanted to share something with you. I was just at Huntington. Figured you might be at Children's so I dropped in over there and they pointed me here."

"Share something? Is it about Teddy?"

"Yea, he ah..."

Doctor Yousef returned with an Asian doctor. They both looked to be a bit anxious.

"Mr. Rooker, Hello, I'm Doctor Jung. I'm a resident here at Hollywood Presbyterian. I'm an oncologist. Specifically, I deal with blood cancers. How are you feeling?"

"Great. What's going on Doc? I'm over at Children's Hospital giving blood and next thing I know I wake up at the hospital next door. A hospital that I don't have the most wonderful memories of. Why the hell do I need a cancer doctor?"

"Let me try to explain. We can understand your confusion. When your medical records were checked due to the fact you were giving blood, a normal procedure, the staff at Children's Hospital saw that you had been in Scotland and..."

"What does that have to do with anything?

"Ben, have you ever heard of mad cow disease'?"

"No, oh wait yea, back in the late eighties. There was a big thing about tainted meat. I think it was mainly in Europe. I happened to be in Scotland at the time on a school trip when... Oh shit."

"You were in Scotland at that time which means you may or may not have been exposed to the disease. There is actually no way of telling, which is why no one who lived in the United Kingdom during the eighties is allowed to donate blood."

"So, what are you saying? Do I have mad cow disease?"

"Like I said, there is no way of saying. We do know you were exposed. Which also ruled out your bone marrow for use in a transplant. Anyway, in the course of all this record searching we found that you had not had a blood test since you left the Navy. Due to the fact you passed out and we didn't know why, we decided to run a few tests."

"So why am I here Why did I pass out?"

"We need to get some tests back first but…"

"But what?"

The doctors looked over at Jackson.

"Hey, I got to go. No worries. Just give me a call when you get a chance. Anything you need."

"Wait, what about Teddy?"

"No worries. Plenty of time for that. Just get your crazy self better now, okay?"

Jackson was out the door before I could say another word to him.

I went back to 2019's version of Dr. Kildare.

"Like I said we need to get a few more tests back but we believe you have a very common type of Leukemia. It is treatable. That is the good news. It's called acute myeloid leukemia. We are waiting for one more important test to come back but…"

"What the fuck!?"

"It's lucky we were screening you for a possible bone marrow transplant or we may not have found it."

"Yea, buy me a lottery ticket. I mean I can't lose today."

"While there is no cure for AML, we believe we may have caught it early. With aggressive treatment, you have a very good chance of living a normal life. I took the liberty of sending your records over to Doctor Moise Solomon, I believe he was your wife's oncologist?"

"Yes, yea, fine. Define 'aggressive treatment' and 'good chance' please."

"Chemotherapy and 50-50."

"Christ. This is not happening."

I bet you never saw that coming. I sure as hell didn't. No history of cancer in my family. I mean my wife died of it but of course she wasn't "blood." Well, the good news was maybe Sam Jackson wouldn't bother me so much. I could get my head shaved after chemo started and do a reboot of *Kojak*. For you millennials and others, *Kojak* was a popular TV show in the seventies about a bald headed Greek NY City cop who had an affinity for lollipops and said "Who loves ya baby?" About fourteen times an episode. That's what we call in the business, a "tag line." Telly Savalas starred in it. Remember I told you about IMDB? Look him up.

Anyway, as an old Navy shipmate of mine would say, "Fuck me to tears."

CHAPTER 26

Mazatlán
May 2019

"I want another fucking drink. Do you know who the fuck I am?"

"Senorita, please. You have had many drinks. The policia may come soon. I am sorry but this is a nice place. Families come here, you see."

"Oh, fuck your mother. Families."

"Ms. Vasquez you will come with us now. Do not cause any further disturbance. Your father is worried about you."

Alvina Vásquez was in her mid-thirties now. A full blown drunk and addict. On her sixth tequila, an English language newspaper was in front of her. The source of her latest alcoholic binge. Not that she had needed a reason but the headline on the "Mazatlán Messenger" screaming at her from the lemon and alcohol scented bar was enough.

Estranged Wife of Cartel Boss Dead in Café Bombing.

Her father's soldiers were careful but nonetheless serious about the task in front of them. The directions were clear from Roy Vasquez himself.

"Get my daughter out of that bar before she is all over the fucking television and social media."

Roy Vasquez had had it with his only child. He had to deal with her, though. His beautiful, tortured Alvina. He would have to tell her about her mother's death. It needed to be done with the utmost delicacy. Anything less would mean any chance of a reconciliation would be gone. Alvy was all he had. The women, the drugs had ceased to fix him long ago. He was an empty shell. He would have put a bullet in his brain long ago if not for his daughter. In his sick twisted mind, she was his life.

****

"She is outside, Senor."

"Has she rested, been fed?"

"I'm sorry, senor, but the guards report she would not sleep, and we found her food on the floor of her room this morning."

"Very well. Bring her in."

The soldier left and a moment later Roy turned to see Alvina standing in front of him. Somehow she had kept her beauty, in spite of the drugs, the booze, the men; indeed the women. She was shaking. Crying softly. Head bowed. He went to her and embraced her. She exploded in rage.

"Keep your hands off me. You murderer. You fucking piece of shit. You killed my mama. You killed her. Blew her up. Nothing left to even bury."

Alvina let loose with a fusillade of punches. He stood letting the blows fall. The door opened, and a soldier started for her. Roy dismissed him with a look.

Minutes went by. Finally, she collapsed from exhaustion at his feet.

"Why did you kill her? I want my mama. I want her back. Why?"

"Mijita, you do not understand. I mourn the death of your mama. I did not kill her. I would never hurt you that way."

"You are lying! I saw it on the television, in the newspapers."

"It is all a hoax. It is the fake news they talk about. The Americans and my enemies here in Mexico. They are trying to frame me so they can justify killing me. This was done by the Americans. You must believe me."

"Believe you? You kidnapped me when I tried to get away from you. Do you not find it somehow absurd, even tragic that a father has to kidnap his own daughter to get her back?"

"You had no discipline in America. Your mother didn't care. She just wanted to punish me."

"Don't you understand? Mama did not help me get away from you. How many people have you killed? Tortured. All in name of the Holy White Powder. You killed that girl I was with in Juarez all those years ago, didn't you?"

This took him aback. He was not ready. After all those years and the drugs and alcohol he thought she would forget about the gringa Puta, Eileen. He went to his safe, opened it and took something out. Two old Polaroid's. He handed them to his daughter.

"This is the source of all your pain. This is who killed Eileen."

Alvina stared at the picture of the young American. Despite everything, she recognized him immediately. The guy she and Eileen had met in the strip club in Juarez. The one who called himself "Teddy." All those years gone by.

"He came back after we took you. He raped and killed her."

He showed her the picture of Eileen's bloodied corpse.

She fell to the ground and began to vomit. Roy leaned over and tried to console her. She spit at him. He went to the bar and got a bottle of water and handed it to her. She took it and drank and then dropped the bottle on the ground.

"But why? Why would he kill Eileen? He liked her. I could tell. She liked him. They were going to get together. He was going to take her to Los Angeles. I remember now. Yes."

"I don't know, my beauty. We know he took the drugs that were in the car. The amphetamines that you hid in the car. We know that this "Teddy" was a drunk and an addict. Your mother knew as well. Why do you think she was following him?"

"Following him. Why?"

"Because he raped you."

"What are you talking about? He would never..."

"You were unconscious most of the time. You told the policia who picked you up. Before you passed out."

"What are you saying? I don't remember anything."

"Your mother wanted to avenge you. She was going to kill the gringo bastard. Unfortunately for her, he got to her first."

"Bullshit! Fucking bullshit! You are telling me that he would blow himself and innocent people up just to kill Mama?"

"Yes, and I have proof."

CHAPTER 27

Cadavers Inc.

Steve Radcliffe, plant manager at Huntington Hospital liked to walk home from work when it was nice out. This was one of those evenings. He lived alone in a tidy colonial in South Pasadena which was only about a mile and a half from the hospital. Sometimes he'd stop in at his favorite Thai spot but tonight he wasn't very hungry. That detective's visit, the black guy, Jackson had disturbed him a bit. Steve was a law-abiding citizen. He'd done a tour in the Gulf. Sure, he'd been in the Air Force, and though he'd seen lots of dead bodies working in the morgue, he hadn't really seen any action. He had been there though, and that was all that mattered. Serving his country and keeping it safe. Lately however Steve had had some doubts about all of that. It seemed to him that there was more of a threat from inside the country than there was from those camel fuckers thousands of miles away. Oh, now he didn't like to think that way; he was a good Christian man but those Muslims, they just weren't like real Americans. They just wouldn't jump into the old melting pot. They still wanted to cover their women from top to bottom and were even trying to get that Sharia law shit as part of the Constitution. Over his dead body he thought. And what was going on with this new generation, anyway? Christ they just had that new play called *Hamilton* breaking all kinds of records for people going to see it. I mean he had read the book. It was written by that guy Chernow. Steve thought he was kind of a lefty, of course all of these intellectuals were these days, but what was the idea of having a black actor play George Washington?! I mean George Washington, for the love of God. All the actors were black! The only damn one who was white was King George, and he was a nut job in Steve's opinion, not to mention a damn homo.

He decided to stop off at the warehouse. It was on the way. One of the best moves he ever made was using his Air Force bonus money to buy that old building next to the power company. Set way back away from everything. The punk kids from the high school would throw rocks through the windows sometimes but most of them were scared to come close let alone come inside. Who wanted to see a bunch of cadavers, anyway?

The morgue duty really ended up being a gift for Steve. Watching Staff Sergeant Renko put that makeup on those bodies. He made them look like they were alive, almost. One secret that not too many people knew was that some bodies brought to the morgue were so badly maimed that they couldn't be viewed. The problem was that the loved ones wanted to see their son or their daughter. They wanted a proper wake. They were in denial about what an IED or a rocket attack could do to the human body. That's where Renko came in and later, Steve. Renko was a real artist. Steve spent every extra moment watching him. He even took notes. Some guys thought he was a little weird. Hanging around the morgue even during his off time. It all worked out, though. He started his side hustle, Cadavers Inc. and did a good business selling fake dead bodies to the movie studios and to theatrical companies. Well, not completely fake. But nobody had asked. A tribute to his art, Steve thought. Business was so good that he was just about to put in his retirement papers at Huntington Hospital. All set until that day about a month ago when that big guy with the weird name, "Larue", came into his office and made that offer. The most bizarre thing he was ever asked to do. But, hey, it was for homeland security, Larue had said. The money was damn good as well. Steve Radcliffe was a patriot, but he was also a capitalist. As his dear departed father used to say, "You can buy as many flags as you want when you're rich, son."

E Pluribus Unum.

CHAPTER 28

Pasadena Police Station

"What the hell you doing here, Rooker. Shouldn't you be on chemo or something about now?"

"Don't start till next week, Lieutenant. Frankly, I'm not in a hurry to be bald."

Sam Jackson stopped going through his paperwork and rubbed his smooth head.

"What are you talking about? Don't you know that bald is beautiful?"

"Yeah, yeah, whatever. Actually, the reason I came over to visit was not to admire your Nubian cranium. I need to talk to Special Agent Belmont. Any idea where I can find him?"

"Why you want to see Larue? I thought he would be the last person you would want to see."

"I got nothing to hide. You know that, Sam."

I had been in a few meetings with the detective. He wasn't a bad guy. He had been helping a few of the newcomers at the Monks and Drunks meeting. The guys who only have a few days sober. I took a chance. I decided to level with him. Just a bit.

"Look, Ben, I wouldn't mess with the Feds."

"That is not my intention. I just want to find out where he is as far as the terrorist angle on the bombing and also about Teddy's death. I think the feds know more than they're telling. I got a week before I start chemo. I want to put it to good use."

"Leave the detective work to me, okay? I know Teddy and you were tight, Ben, but he's a dead man. Nothing is going to change that."

"Did you see his body?"

"Of course I did."

"What about an autopsy?"

"Belmont was involved in that. That was requested by the FBI. Nothing unusual. Cause of death was, wait a minute, I'll even get the file they sent over."

Jackson looked through his file cabinet and pulled out a manila folder. He opened it, found what he was looking for and read from it.

"Cause of death: sub...what the fuck is this word, subarachnoid hemorrhage and subdural hematoma. Oh, right, yes; It means his head exploded like a watermelon when he landed. Sorry, that was pretty crude. Anyway that's it. Official cause of death from the god damn FBI no less."

"I'd still like to talk to him. Where does he hang out when he's off duty?"

"Larue is never off duty but even if he was and I knew, I am not allowed to give you that information. Why don't you just leave a message with me, and I'll have him contact you?"

"Yea, whatever."

"And get some god damn rest."

I started to leave and then I realized that I had almost forgotten the real reason I had come to see Jackson. Pre-chemo brain maybe.

"Oh, yes, Detective, you started to tell me something when you visited me at Hollywood Presbyterian. Do you remember what it was? As I remember, it was something about Teddy."

Jackson never turned to look at me. Odd.

"Teddy? Oh, yeah, it was about his mom. Larue wanted to send his ashes to her."

I could have called Jackson on his bullshit right then but, yes, a little voice told me not to. I needed to get out of here. Process all of it.

"Yea, well, you probably forgot that I told you that she was dead."

I didn't let him answer. I just walked out the door.

I didn't believe anything Jackson told me at that point. I mean as far as the program was concerned, A.A., oh yea he was a saint but outside the rooms as it were, a different story. Jackson was a cop and, as far as I was concerned, Belmont was as well. Birds of a feather. I needed to find out what they both knew about Teddy, the cartel, everything. I was beginning to think that what I knew now was clearly just the tip of the iceberg. I needed to get to the truth. However complicated it was. I was also beginning to think that I didn't have the luxury of time.

CHAPTER 29

FBI Headquarters
Quantico, Virginia
July 2019

"Larue, thanks for taking the time to come out here."

"No problem, Sir. Anything I can do to help. So, you said that you had more information on the Venganza Cartel?"

Special Agent Larue Belmont was at FBI Headquarters on Pennsylvania Ave. Seated in front of him was the Deputy Director of the Bureau, Joseph McManus, rarified air indeed. The bombing of a café in Pasadena, California had taken on national security implications.

"Right to the meat. Haven't changed since the Academy. Commendable, Larue. So how are things going? Still single? Any special lady on the horizon?"

McManus knew he was gay. Most of the department did. No big thing these days of course. J. Edgar himself used to wear a dress at home. It was common knowledge. For some reason, Joe McManus, an old friend of Larue's father liked to continue to play the game. Larue humored him.

"You know how it is, Deputy Director. The Bureau is my family. No time for any outside social activities. One of these days, maybe."

"Yes, of course. 'All work and no play,' though...anyway, okay. Let's get to it. Our intelligence in the Mexican government has confirmed what we thought all along. The bombing of the Bard Café in Pasadena was a hit on Rose Vasquez, Roy Vasquez's estranged wife, now widower."

"But Sir, if I may, that seems to be a bit of 'High risk, low payback' for Vasquez. I mean we know that he hated his wife for leaving him and what he perceived was the kidnapping of his daughter but by killing her and other innocent people on American soil no less, well, with respect, it makes no sense."

"Yes, well of course you are right, Larue. But there is more to all of this. The bombing was just the beginning we believe."

McManus had a bit of the showman in him. He paused to let it sink in with Larue.

"Roy Vasquez is not the same man he was even a few years ago. He's making mistakes he would never make. Taking things personally. Last month he torched a house, burning an entire family alive because he thought the father was cheating him in his monthly payments. A revenge killing of his wife on American soil is just another example of his recklessness. He is no longer respected by the people in and around Venganza. It's the drugs. He's graduated from coke to heroin. He's become the slave of his product. Add to that the fact that his father was bipolar. It appears that Roy inherited the disease. Our sources say he has stopped taking his Lithium. He is susceptible to periods of elation and creativity. Non-stop work and then a black depression that he tries to quell with the coke and heroin or anything mind-altering. A vicious cycle. We believe he is ripe to be taken down."

"By who?"

"Not us, if that's what you're asking. Our days, shall I say 'assisting' in the affairs of our neighbors to the South are over."

Larue cleared his throat which McManus judiciously ignored. He continued.

"Of course. A rival cartel. But who?"

McManus picked up a manila folder marked "SECRET – eyes only". He handed it to Belmont.

"Our sources or should I say 'source,' indicates this will be an inside job."

"It would have to be someone he trusts. If he's as addicted to his product as the intelligence says and he is bipolar, he's only going to trust someone who has been loyal, who has been close, someone..."

Belmont had opened the file that the Deputy Director has handed him and viewed the picture inside.

He actually had a dizzy spell. A bit of vertigo. He was not ready for this. Never in his wildest dreams. This changed everything. He composed himself. Years of training kicking in.

"But I don't understand, sir. All evidence had pointed to his daughter. Revenge for the death of her mother. This woman here? Why would she want to kill Roy Vasquez? How could she? This can't be."

Belmont turned the page. Another picture. The caption "Known Associate." The FBI not known for flowery description.

"Teddy Dabrowski? What the fuck?"

Special Agent Larue Belmont thought for a moment about whether to tell his superior about his relationship with Teddy Dabrowski. A relationship that the bureau believed was purely one of the "normal" kind and had begun this year after the Bard Café bombing but in reality had started much earlier. If he did, of course, he would have to reveal his own breaking of departmental rules and protocol and explain to McManus why he knew that Teddy Dabrowski was alive and well and safely stashed in a safe house in South Pasadena.

"A problem, Agent Belmont? Of course, Dabrowski is dead and of therefore no help to us now, but I thought you should know where our investigation has gotten us thus far."

"Not at all, sir. Not at all. Of course. Interesting information indeed."

On the flight back to Los Angeles, Special Agent Belmont now realized that all the planning, the coverup of the fake death of Teddy Dabrowski to fool the cartel and Roy Vasquez was all for naught. Had he been played by Dabrowski? And if so, why? The other picture, the woman. Her picture in the file was burned into his brain now. Paula Garcia RN. Head of the Literal Healing department at Children's Hospital. Co-Conspirator in a plot to assassinate the head of the Venganza Cartel.

He ordered a Bacardi and coke, and closed his eyes as the captain announced preparations for landing in Los Angeles.

CHAPTER 30

Las Cruces, New Mexico
June, 2017

June was not the right time to be in Las Cruces. Teddy figured it had to be 110 degrees in the shade, not that there was any. Believe it or not, according to good old Wikipedia, Las Cruces, New Mexico is the second largest city in New Mexico. It's called the "City of the Crosses." What better place for Teddy Dabrowski to make amends. He knew that "Veronica" and "Eileen" had said they were from here. He also knew that the car that sideswiped the school bus in Juarez all those years ago was from a Budget Rent a Car in El Paso. Teddy had gone to the office which was miraculously still in existence. He rented a car himself so he had a good reason for being there. The manager, a woman of a certain age by the name of Penny reminded him of an aunt on his father's side who could start a conversation based on the clearing of one's throat.

"So, Penny, I have kind of a hypothetical situation for you, well hell, you don't look to me like the type of person that believes BS. I mean I'm sure that you've heard more than your share around here."

Teddy had hit a nerve here. Penny brightened up like a sparkler on the 4th of July on a summer's night in Chicago.

"Well, damn, thank you for noticing that, Teddy. People do a lot of assuming sometimes. They think that a woman of my age, maybe one who hasn't had a lot of formal education, well I might be easy to get over on."

"Exactly. They underestimate you and therefore you have the upper hand."

A couple came in and started to approach Penny but she was not having it. Not when she was about to go into her zone.

"Hi, welcome to Budget, Las Cruces, folks. If you could just take a seat, Billy will be back from Denny's shortly and he will take care of your vehicular needs."

She returned to Teddy. He had her undivided attention.

"Okay, now so this is not a hypothetical; am I correct?"

"Damn, Penny, you have got me. You sure you didn't grow up in the city? Maybe Chicago or New York? Okay, so yes, this is about yours truly. You see, I am looking for a couple of young women who may know where my long-lost sister is. Amy ran away twelve years back and it broke our family's heart especially my dear Mom's; she has the cancer and we don't know how long she has left. All that chemo, of course, drains her. It would mean the world to her if Amy came back into her life."

Penny was locked in now. The couple seeking transport would have a better chance selling their asses in downtown Las Cruces than renting a car from Penny that morning.

"You poor thing. Can I get you a coffee?"

"No, I'm fine, Penny. Thanks though. I need to find Amy. The last we heard from her she was in El Paso. She said she was with these two college girls who were from Las Cruces. That was over a decade ago. She said their names were Veronica and Eileen. They rented a Toyota."

Penny had already started typing away on her computer keyboard.

"You don't have any last names? How about the make and model of the car?"

"Damn, all I remember is that it was a Toyota. Not new."

"Okay, let me run a search then. That might be enough."

"I think it was Veronica that actually rented it."

Penny typed away for like 10 or 20 minutes. It was of course pointless. Teddy found out later when he talked with Detective Jackson of all people that it would be impossible for a rental company to trace a car going back that long and with so little information. It was one of the things that Teddy had said to him that had made Jackson suspicious.

"Excuse me."

"Now I told you, sir, that we will get to you as soon as..."

"No, It's not about the car."

The male portion of the couple was looking at Teddy.

"Did you say Eileen? Eileen Palestrena?"

"Eileen who...? Oh yes Palestrena, yes Eileen Palestrena. You know her?"

"Our daughter went to school with her. Grammar school through High School. What do you know about Eileen? She's been missing for a while now. Ever since she went partying in El Paso."

"Vern, honey, maybe you should call the police?"

The female half.

Teddy moved towards the couple but not too far away from Penny. She might still be needed.

"No listen here for a second. Like I was saying to Penny here, I'm trying to find my sister, Amy. She's been gone for a long time as well, around ten years or so. My family has reason to believe that she was with a couple of young women named Veronica and Eileen. I'm trying to find out what happened to Amy. I don't know anything more than you do about the other woman. Maybe we could pool our resources? By the way, I'm Teddy Dabrowski."

"Vern Lattimore. This is my wife, Francine. We've lived here in Las Cruces all our lives. We were real close with Eileen Palestrena. Don't know anything about the Veronica girl."

"Well, hey, why don't I let you folks rent your car. You got plans for the weekend? Got time for a coffee?"

Vern shot a glance at Francine.

"Yea, well, we do but nothing that can't wait a bit. Anyplace but Starbucks though."

CHAPTER 31

Cadavers Inc.
South Pasadena

"Hello, Steve. I wouldn't do that"

Special Agent Larue Belmont was always the quickest draw during "cowboys and Indians" in kindergarten. Some things just didn't change.

"Put the gun down, Steve."

Radcliffe placed the shotgun he kept at the Cadavers Inc. warehouse on the workbench right next to a severed head. He used it mostly to scare the punk kids away. Lately though its use had been of a more urgent nature.

"You don't need to be comin' up on me like that. Scarin' the devil out of me."

"Just keeping an eye on you, Mr. Radcliffe. You are a very important investment to me, the FBI and your country. We want to make sure you stay safe and don't do anything crazy."

"Look, I told you, you could trust me. I haven't talked to anybody about Dabrowski since..."

"Christ , now there you go mentioning top secret information. How do you know there's not someone behind me? How do you know this chamber of horrors isn't bugged aside from being haunted?"

"I'm sorry. Just anxious. I need to haul ass. You know that. It's not safe for me. With the spics and..."

"There you go again. And can we please keep the blatant racism to a minimum? A certain Detective whose assistance we are counting on might not appreciate it."

From the first time this Larue fellow came into his shop, Reverend Radcliffe had him pegged as a weird one. I mean an FBI Special Agent who wore pink bow ties on duty and was more interested in how he, Radcliffe, got his different facial shades on the stand-in mannequins he made for the studio than any other part of the craft. It was as if he was interested in that information for his own make-up needs. Shit, that first day he even tried the ghost blue powder on himself.

"You are a modern day Leonardo da Vinci, Reverend," he had told him.

Then Steve found out that DaVinci was a fag. Christ. If it wasn't for the money, and of course the chance to help out his country, well Steve Radcliffe never would have gotten involved in that thing at Huntington Hospital.

"Look, I need to get paid. That cop, the black one has been asking me too many damn questions about the Dabrowski thing. I just want to get my money and get the hell out of Dodge."

"Steve, sit down please. Relax. 'Paid?!' You realize how many years you'd get in federal prison if the government found out you were using real dead bodies in this movie 'stand-in' scam you've been running."

Radcliffe looked towards the rifle. Special Agent Larue Belmont pulled out a taser and gave him two doses. Big time tases. Not like one of those tases you saw on *Law and Order* or even *Cops*. No, this was the real shit. Radcliffe was paralyzed. He couldn't breathe for a few moments that seemed like eternity. Then he could. But not before Belmont had handcuffed him to the work bench chair.

"Breathe. Feel better? Good. Don't say a word. Listen. Listen and learn."

Radcliffe started to speak and Belmont slapped him with enough force that his lip started bleeding profusely.

"God damn it now I got blood on my suit. Do you know how hard it is to get this shit out?"

Radcliffe was weeping now. He was terrified.

"I just need to know if anyone else knows about what happened at Huntington Hospital."

"I swear, nobody knows. Just me and you. That's it. I didn't tell Jackson anything."

"Good man."

Belmont leaned over and licked the blood off his mouth and then kissed Radcliffe on the cheek. Radcliffe was beside himself. He started to scream. Belmont took the shotgun from the bench and proceeded to jam the stock end into Radcliffe's nose. Pieces of bone splatted on the floor. Radcliffe passed out. Belmont began humming Samuel Barber's *Adagio for Strings* as he walked out to his car, opened the trunk and grabbed the old tire he had picked up at a junkyard and the gas can he had recently filled at the nearby Chevron station. He walked back into the warehouse still humming the dirge like tune as he placed the tire over the head of a conscious and alert Radcliffe and soaked it with gasoline. He poured the rest of the contents of the gas can on the highly flammable paint cans lying nearby before he stopped in front of the life-size replica of Mr. Teddy Dabrowski, a bit the worse for wear after it had been launched off the roof of the Huntington Hospital by the currently gas doused Mr./Reverend Steve Radcliffe.

Radcliffe was a born artiste. That much Belmont had to admit despite the disdain he had for the man personally. A real piece of art thought Larue. All that time it took just getting a John Doe from the morgue who was the same height and weight as Teddy as well as gender and ethnicity. Belmont had been lucky enough to find a recently deceased homeless guy that fit the specs at a morgue in Tennessee. Had him FedExed to Pasadena just in time for Radcliffe to do his magic. After he was done, the body was no longer a John Doe. No this was Teddy Dabrowski.

Radcliffe had double crossed him though. He had somehow replaced the "Teddy" cadaver with another one before it was incinerated. Actually, it was easy for the Reverend. He had a long standing symbiotic relationship with a guy at the city morgue. His supplier, so to speak. Radcliffe paid him 100 bucks a head for any homeless bodies that were brought in. He took advantage of this relationship and switched out the "Teddy" cadaver with a John Doe. The John Doe was incinerated and placed in an urn forever to be labeled "Teddy Dabrowski" while Radcliffe was able to keep the original "Teddy," his masterpiece. Over his dead body would this "Nancy boy" Belmont destroy his piece of art. Unfortunately for Radcliffe, his demise may well have been the price to keep his art "alive."

Special Agent Larue, a devout Baptist, said a short prayer before dropping the lit match on the "Teddy" cadaver. Belmont felt a momentary pang of regret as Radcliffe's screams over the demise of the work he had labored over with such love and care, resonated through the warehouse. A beautiful piece of art. He hated to destroy it. Of course this redneck racist, homophobic shit stain, Radcliffe should have destroyed it already. A lesson needed to be taught. Just like Belmont's father would have done. He watched the faux "Teddy" cadaver burn. It took a while, but it was eventually unrecognizable. The floor started to catch on fire as well and the flames were heading towards the poor "Reverend." Belmont had spotted the fire extinguisher on the way in and grabbed it just in time to douse the flames that were barking at Radcliffe's legs. He then threw some sand on the floor and removed his tire from Radcliffe's head.

"Why did you do that you crazy bastard? I could have burned alive."

"Next time I tell you to do something like destroy incriminating evidence, do it or next time there won't be a fire extinguisher or sand or whatever. It just might be the cartel who pays you a visit and not the Federal Bureau of Investigation. You have a safe day, Mr. Radcliffe."

Belmont exited the warehouse with the sound of Radcliffe's mourning over the pile of ashes that had been his *David* resonating in his ears. Larue didn't know whether to go back and shoot the man or kiss him.

CHAPTER 32

Children's Hospital Los Angeles

"Where is Ben? I want to see Ben."

Paula pondered this for a moment.

"I'm not going to lie to you, Lexy. He's sick."

"He won't be able to visit me?"

"Not for a while. I can read to you, though."

Lexy thought about pouting some more but finally accepted the fact that Ben would not be coming, at least not on this day.

"It's okay. Father Jim reads to me at night."

"How is Father Jim?"

"He's sad."

"Why is he sad?"

"He wants people to believe him. That he was a good person. That he would never hurt the children. He knows that other priests have caused pain. He hears them. Hears their screams."

"Lexy. Maybe you shouldn't see Father Jim for a while."

"I'll be lonely without Father Jim. Anyway, I think he needs me."

"What about the girls? Veronica and Eileen, do you see them?"

"Eileen says that's not her real name."

"Whose real name?"

"Veronica's name. Eileen visits me but not Veronica. Eileen says Veronica told her a fake name when they met in Juarez."

"Did she say what Veronica's real name was?"

"No. I don't think she knows. Even though she says she's on the other side now, she can't talk to Veronica or whatever her name is."

"What do you mean, the other side?"

"C'mon Paula you know."

"No, I don't know. What do you mean?"

"Eileen is dead. Just like I'm going to be. Soon. Don't worry about me, Paula. I'll be okay. Eileen is still a little scared, but Father Jim has been helping her."

Paula wanted to protest. To shake this little angel who has seen so much pain and darkness.

Another part of her, the part that governed her anger, resentment and hate, her dark side wanted to question this Lexy more. Indeed, needed to know what Father Jim was telling her. Paula didn't really believe this little girl was in communication with the man Paula herself had helped drive to his death but she needed to be sure. There was too much at stake.

She stopped herself, though. Deep down in some place in her soul, perhaps the place that felt the presence of her grandfather, she knew that Lexy was speaking the truth. Her only reconciliation was that she would soon have her vengeance against the man who was responsible for so much pain in so many lives, including Paula's. She would tread softly.

"Do you ever talk to Teddy?"

Lexy started to answer but then thought better of it.

"It's okay. You can tell me. Teddy is on the other side now."

"He's not on the other side. He's alive. Please, Paula, I'm not supposed to tell. Teddy asked me not to tell."

"What? How?"

"I saw him last night. He was here. He has a beard now. He was wearing a funny hat. He told me not to tell anyone. Now he's going to hate me."

"Teddy could never hate you, Lexy. Of course I won't tell. You can trust me, Lexy. I realize that there are certain things that we do not understand. With all our science and all the progress we have made we still do not understand the spiritual side of our lives. It's okay if you 'talked' with Teddy, Lexy, even though he is on the other side. You are a special little girl. A beautiful, gifted little girl."

"But he's alive, Paula."

"Of course. Yes."

"I love you, Paula."

"I love you too."

"So, what did you and Teddy talk about?"

"Well, we didn't have much time. Teddy was jumpy. You know running around and always in a hurry. He said he had things to do. Things to fix."

"Things to fix?"

"Paula, Teddy says that people are in danger. Alvina is in danger. Other people as well. There is an evil man out there, Teddy says."

"In danger? Who is Alvina? Oh my God, Veronica is Alvina. Alvina is Veronica. Christ...I'm sorry baby. I shouldn't have cursed. But she, Alvina/Veronica is on the other side. She died with Eileen, I thought?"

"Alvina is alive."

"How do you know?"

"Teddy told me, and..."

"What my love?"

"He's coming back tonight."

Teddy is alive. How could that be? A game-changer, thinks Paula. A phrase she got from watching CNN.

Yes, the plan can still go forward. Just a few minor changes.

Retribution is still at hand.

But what if Lexy was wrong? Well, tonight would come soon enough.

She smiled and fixed her hair.

Tonight.

CHAPTER 33

Samuel Jackson had grown up in the Compton of the sixties. The real Compton. Not the Williams' sisters, faux ghetto Compton that is put out there by the mainstream media looking to exploit every black kid from Los Angeles that makes it either in rap or sports or, shit social media. Sam never could understand this Instagram or Twitter or Facebook shit. All about "Likes." Sam never had to be liked. His father Amos left when was about five and his mom, Clarice, worked seven days a week. Every job from working at the Salvation Army picking lice filled stuffed toys out of donation bins to "under the table" caregiving jobs cleaning up after 90-year-old men and women after they had shit themselves. She loved "Little Sam" and his older brother, Andre. Loved and cared for them till the day she slumped over dead at the dinner table at the ripe old age of forty-nine. Little Sam and Andre were placed in the care of their Aunt Livy. Livy was a good person and did the best she could, but she had three kids of her own and liked her Thunderbird and Mad Dog 20 20.

In a situation like that, kids can go one way or another. Andre took the hard road, held up his first 7-11 at the age of twelve. Sam studied all the time which made him feel isolated. Neighbor kids made fun of him. Called him "Sammy the pole smoker" because that's just what kids do. If they don't understand you, then you are an aberration in their world. Pure and simple. Sam was 22 and going to Pasadena City College taking criminal law classes when he got the call to go to the county morgue to identify his brother's body. One 7-11 too many, actually an AM PM but who really cares? This time, when Andre came in brandishing his nine-millimeter, the Korean owner's wife came out of the storeroom with a .357. Took Andre's leg almost off with the first shot. She probably would have left it at that if this hadn't been the fifth robbery this month at the Inglewood store. A message needed to be sent. She stood over Andre's bloodied leg, stepped on it for good measure and then blew the side of his face clean off. Resentment is a terrible thing.

Sam was able to ID his brother by the *Malcolm X* tattoo on his back. He walked out of the morgue not feeling anything. That night he cried like a baby. The next morning, he took the test for the Pasadena Police. He scored in the top five percentile and became a patrolman at the age of 24. He never looked back.

Sam went into A.A. shortly after becoming a cop. He had thought he could handle the booze and do his job. One mid shift he was half drunk when he and his partner were called to a domestic dispute with shots fired. Sam jumped out of the patrol car as soon it stopped and ran to the duplex, police special drawn. He got to the house just as a kid who couldn't have been more than four years old opened the door. Sam started shaking from tremors. His gun went off, missing the kid by a centimeter. The next morning he called A.A. Central office and asked for help. He'd been sober ever since. Even managed to help his dear Aunt Livy get off the booze. She died with three years sober.

He was seated at his desk at the Pasadena Police Station and thinking about this Belmont, Larue Belmont. Jesus H. Christ. Something about the guy. A southerner but not a redneck. Not a racist bone in his body either. Sam had run into his share of racists in the department. Most of them were of the type whose "best friends were black." Who would overtly give to United Negro College Fund and the NAACP, who would push for a black chief of police but wouldn't want a black partner. All very much under the radar. The types who called you "Nigger" to your face, now Sam could deal with them. It was this other kind of racism. The subconscious type. That was the difficult one. You know the person that doesn't even realize they're a racist kind of thing. That's the toughest nut to crack, and that's why Samuel Jackson believed that despite being the greatest country in the world, racism in some form or another would always exist in these United States.

Belmont didn't care for the ladies either. Jackson picked that up pretty early. That was okay though. He knew his shit. Sam, and most of the black community, had changed significantly when it came to gays. A lot different from when he grew up. Sam remembered a kid from the neighborhood, Levon Washington. Lived a few blocks away. Kept to himself. Then one day one of the kids heard that he had been playing with dolls. That was enough. This was 6th grade. Old enough for kids to hate. Sam was out sick that day. Flu or something but he heard what happened. Bunch of kids jumped poor Levon in a back alley. He had his dolls out. He was role playing with them. They pounced on him and beat him so bad he was never the same. Cognitive Damage the Doc said. Had to ride the Special Bus after that. Sam felt bad about that. He didn't feel bad enough to report the kids who did it, though. One of them was his brother. Maybe one of the reasons he tolerated all the craziness this Larue Belmont, Special Agent FBI brought to the table. That pink bowtie another thing. What kind of G-Man wore a god damn pink tie? A bow tie for that matter?

The man knew his job, though. A bit unorthodox but hey, he got the god damn job done.

The staging of Teddy Dabrowski's death was brilliant. Lucky the mannequin that whack job preacher made was the real deal. Who the fuck could have expected Teddy's best friend, Ben Rooker, to show up right as the "Teddy" impersonator was being tossed off the roof of Huntington Hospital by the "Reverend" Steve Radcliffe?

Anyway, it was all fixable. That's what his dear Mom would say or words to that effect. "When you get lemons, just make lemonade." Sam Jackson felt he needed another saying. That one was a bit worn out. Maybe something like Larue Belmont had mentioned one day. Just when they were getting Teddy Dabrowski set up in that safe house he was currently residing at in South Pasadena. The War Memorial, that's what it was called, with a statue of John "Black Jack" Pershing sitting out front. He was the General Patton of World War I. God who even knew about these guys anymore. The heroes. The Greatest Generation they were called, at least the ones from World War II. Now those guys from the first World War, the so called "War to end all wars," now they were pretty damn impressive as well. Sam had read his history, particularly his American history. He knew about the Tuskegee Airmen, a bunch of black guys in the Army in World War II. Now at that time there was no Air Force. It was called the Army Air Force. The U.S. Air Force didn't start till after World War II. They flew escort duty for American bombers over Italy. All black pilots. Jackson wondered how many white guys that they saved had ended up going back to the South after the war and lynching black men. Maybe the very men who had saved their lily white asses. He thought like this in his resentful moments. Not so much anymore. Being sober in A.A. taught him that for an alcoholic having a resentment was like "drinking poison and expecting the other guy to die."

Anyway, Teddy Dabrowski was at the War Memorial right at this moment and was not happy about it. The day they brought Teddy there was also the same day Larue Belmont had told him his version of the lemonade story. It came from his Navy father. It went something like this: A guy wakes up in the hospital. The doctor tells him, "I got good news and bad news for you son." Guy says "Give me the bad news first." Doctor says "We have to amputate your legs." Guy says, "Damn Doc, but what's the good news?" Doc says, "The guy in the next bed wants to buy your slippers."

Jackson was thinking about how that little story didn't really have the effect of cheering Teddy up that Belmont wanted; or shit, maybe Belmont didn't give a fuck how Teddy felt.

Jackson was proud of himself. He was a pretty damn good actor as well. Ben Rooker had no idea that Teddy was still alive. A way to protect him. Ignorance can be a good thing, was Sam Jackson's reasoning. If Roy Vasquez thought that Teddy Dabrowski was dead then Roy would let his guard down. Teddy knew enough to bring down Vasquez. Better for "Tire Boy" to think Teddy was out of the picture. Larue had a plan you see. If it all worked out the Venganza cartel would be finished, scores of addicts would be saved, not to mention the huge reduction in gun violence. Of course, if the plan didn't work Sam, Larue, probably Teddy and Ben would all be dead, more than likely wearing burning tire necklaces.

"Ain't life a bitch," Sam thought as he headed out to an A.A. meeting.

CHAPTER 34

Las Cruces, New Mexico
June 2017

Teddy Dabrowski believed in loyalty. He was loyal to the 35er bar in Pasadena when he was drinking and he was loyal to his "greasy spoons" when he was in a period of dryness—not sobriety mind you. That would entail working a program and going to A.A. meetings. Teddy did not want any of that. That's why Teddy was happy when the Lattimore's, Vern and Francine, agreed to let him buy them a late breakfast at the Denny's on Bataan Memorial road.

Teddy liked Las Cruces already. A main road named after an important event in World War II. People needed to remember the Greatest Generation, especially those god damn millennials. Teddy liked Francine and Vern as well. He figured them as the kind of folks that would have fit nicely in the south side of Chicago. Although Francine would have to get used to what Ben called colorful metaphors, F- bombs and such.

"So, Mr. Dabrowski, you think that you might be able to find Eileen?"

"Please, Francine, call me Teddy. The only time I get called Mr. Dabrowski is when I'm being addressed by someone in uniform."

Francine chuckled at this.

"Of course, I won't let it happen again, Teddy."

Teddy noticed the gleam in Francine's eye. He glanced over at Vern but there was nothing there. Marriage will do that, Teddy thought. And then he felt Francine's foot. At first, he thought it was just an accidental touch under the table.

"I'm going to drain the main vein if you don't mind."

"Now, Vern. You are embarrassing me."

"Damn, Francine, Teddy has heard that and more."

Vern left the booth and headed to the rest room. No sooner had he exited when Teddy felt Francine's foot. Her bare foot was now rubbing on his crotch. He looked across at her and she was reading the menu. Rubbing harder now. The beginnings of a "Woody" was in evidence.

"What do you think of the sausage? I like their sausage here because it's hard and moist. Not like those limp pieces of meat you get other places. And the eggs. How about sunny side up and when you cut through them the juice just comes dripping down?"

She was licking her lips now and Teddy was rock hard. She still hadn't looked at him. Rubbing like a Thai whore in a massage parlor two minutes from closing time.

"Now honey, move your fool leg will you please? How am I supposed to get in here? You're probably kicking old Teddy as well."

Christ that was fast. Vern had returned. Teddy thought he had been given a reprieve or at least a "Stay of Ejaculation." He was mistaken.

"What's good? Teddy, you look a little flushed."

Francine's foot was right back in place. Never missing a beat.

Oh, yea, no, no...Jesus!

Christ that's going to take more than two Tide pods to get out.

Francine looked up and gave Teddy a quick smile. She removed her foot from his drenched crotch area.

"I think it's my turn now."

He placed his table towel in a strategic manner and went off to the rest room.

Teddy washed the stain in the rest room and tried to figure out the Lattimore's.

What is their deal? Do they really know Eileen Palestrena, if that's her name?

Teddy fixed the "water damage" as best he could and headed back to the booth.

"Everything come out all right?"

"Oh yea, thanks"

"Wow, looks like you had a little accident?"

Francine loved this game.

"Yea, those water faucets just go off on their own sometimes. Just water. No harm done. So, this 'Eileen' girl. What can you tell me about her?"

Francine hesitated for a moment and then, "Good girl. Attractive in an All American girl kind of way, if that makes sense. She would have been about your age right now. Not a slut like some others if you get my meaning."

Oh, Teddy got her meaning. Yes, indeed.

"Very sad when she disappeared. They never did find her. Last anybody heard from her was when she called from Juarez."

"Juarez?"

"Yes, I mean we assumed it was Juarez. Her parents, God Bless them, both dead now. Ron, the father, committed suicide a couple of years after she went missing and Nancy, her mom, got dementia and died a few years after."

"I'm so sorry."

"Francine and I were good friends with the Palestrena's. When Eileen went, well it kind of ended everything. Her being an only child made it especially hard."

Francine was staring right at Teddy now.

"Yes, without any real friends we've really had to use our imagination to keep life interesting and exciting, haven't we Vern?"

"Oh, yes, darlin'. Oh, we most definitely have done that."

Teddy wondered what the fuck he had gotten himself into. The way things were going the next thing he'd be doing would be banging old Vern in the parking lot.

"What did Eileen say?"

Francine looked confused.

"On the call?"

"Yes."

"Oh, she didn't say anything. Nancy answered the phone and there was no one on the line. They traced it to Juarez through phone records. This was a couple of days after they hadn't checked in."

"They?"

"Oh, when I spoke to Eileen on the phone, she had said that she had met a Mexican girl in El Paso. A guy as well."

"I see."

"You know, young kids. Crazy. Booze and sex. You remember that stuff, don't you, Teddy?"

Teddy instinctively covered his still wet crotch with his hands.

"What about the Mexican girl? Did anyone ever hear from her. Any clue from Eileen before she disappeared?"

"Oh, you mean, Alvina?"

"Alvina?"

"Yes, or I guess she called herself 'Veronica' back then."

"She's alive? I mean you've seen her?"

"Well, she was. I mean that was the weird thing," Vern chimed in.

Francine cut him off. She was enjoying this.

"She lived here in Las Cruces for a few years. We found out later. Las Cruces cops told us. We bowl with Stan Hornbeck, the Chief of Police and his wife. A weird coincidence. Eileen had never met her till El Paso. I mean Veronica or Alvina being Mexican and all. I mean we're not prejudiced. We voted for Trump because we wanted to get our god damn country back, not 'cause we hate Mexicans. I mean there are some bad ones but..."

Teddy was getting a bit frustrated.

"Okay, I get it. You're preaching to the choir. Where is Veronica, I mean Alvina now?"

"Well, that was a long time ago now. They both disappeared, I mean them and that young guy they were with."

Francine and Vern both stared daggers at Teddy now. The games were over.

"Yes, 'Teddy,' that was his name, right, Vern?"

He nodded without taking his eye off Teddy.

"We knew it was you the second we heard you talking about Eileen. Now I've got a .357 magnum pointed right at that pecker that Francine gave such a sexy massage to a bit ago. If you want to use that little guy again you best come with us out to the car. We're all going to take a drive out to the police station."

"Don't worry Teddy, Vern's just jealous."

"Damn you woman."

Their laugh reminded Teddy of the movie Ben Rooker made him watch a few years ago when they were both drunk. *Virginia Wolf* or something like that. He was sitting with a cartoon version of Albee's play.

Vern was still looking at Teddy.

"She does know how to keep the excitement going in a marriage though. You keep that in mind if you ever get hitched. You got to constantly work on a marriage or it will just disappear. Like poor Eileen."

"I love you, dear heart."

"I love you too, Butter Titties."

And with that Teddy, Vern and Francine headed for the parking lot.

CHAPTER 35

The Medical Offices of Dr. Moise Solomon
West Los Angeles, CA
July 2019

Anybody that tells you that chemo is easy, well, they've never undergone chemo. I was puking constantly and looked like Billy Bob Thornton after a bad day as *Sling Blade*. I was in the offices of Dr. Moise Solomon, my erstwhile oncologist. Solomon was wearing camouflage hospital scrubs. Yes, you heard me correctly. It seems that the good doctor could not forget his years in the Israeli Defense Forces. He didn't let his nurses forget either as they were in "cammy" attire as well. A good guy, though. A renaissance man. He was a doctor, a soldier, an artist and, as I had just recently discovered, a stand-up comic. We were both watching one of his open mic sets on his iPhone while I was sitting in a Lazy Boy waiting for the various drips to finish. I will say, though, it did take my mind off the nausea.

"You have not remarried yet, my gentile friend? You know Rita would have wanted you to find someone by now."

Oh yes, one other tidbit. Not only had the good doctor Solomon been my dear Rita's oncologist but he was her trusted confidante as well. He took her side when she was alive and continued to after she had passed on. Frustrating.

"I don't have time, Colonel, with the acting career and everything else."

I called him "Colonel" when I wanted to butter him up, AKA "Kiss his ass." He was a First Lieutenant in the Israeli Defense Forces (IDF) . Of course, since he was a doctor, he entered the Army at this rank automatically but no matter. Moises Solomon exulted in being an officer.

"Of course, of course. Well, you won't be doing any acting for a while unless they make a reality show about an out of work actor with cancer. It's important to have someone, especially when one is getting older. I'm sorry about your friend, Teddy."

"Thanks, Doc. Yes, Teddy was a good man. That's another reason you got to get me cured and out of here. I need to find his killer and the murderer of the others massacred and wounded in that café. You got to make that happen, Doc. Promise me, okay?"

"I don't trust Trump with Israel. He talks a good talk but I don't believe him. And that 'Groz' gutless Kushner, the son-in-law from hell."

This was one of the good doctor's ploys when he did not want to deal with the matter at hand. I recognized it right away from Rita's last days, when we asked him what her prognosis was. Yes, Solomon talked a lot of politics during dear Rita's last days.

"I don't give a flying fuck about Mr. Trump or Israel right now, with respect, Doc. What are my chances?"

This got the attention of the rest of the room. Oh yes, no private facility for me. Tricare was good but unless I wanted to go to the VA, Dr. Moise Solomon's clinic on Olympic Blvd in West Los Angeles was the closest I could come to private care. Seven other cancer patients were in for treatment today including a young black kid, Dennis, I believe that was his name. I actually had seen him at Children's Hospital a few times. He was about 16. The rest were ancient. They were all connected to their IVs watching Turner Classic Movies on the two old monitors suspended from the east and west ceilings and chatting with the nurses who were at turns adjusting their drip and hawking the various handmade jewelry and bracelets that Dr. Solomon had made.

"I'm not a rich Beverly Hills Jew practicing dermatology on the stars. I am a poor man."

This was his standard afternoon speech. How many times had I heard it?

Rita, dear Rita, God I miss you.

She knew how to handle him, flattering him whether it be his looks or his art work or even his comedy. I know Moise missed her.

"Ben, it's still early. You've had three chemotherapy sessions. You are scheduled for at least 4 more. We'll need to see how your body is reacting to your chemo and whether it is killing the cancer. The police and the FBI are working on the case. I'm sure they can do without your services right now. Please be patient. I have to go now. Mrs. Shapiro needs my bedside manner, and I think she is in a jewelry buying mood."

A wink and a smile and he was off singing "If I were a Rich Man" to the adoring throng of older women, all dying, but all happy at least for today because Moise Solomon would have it no other way.

"You know he was in the Mossad, right?"

"What?"

"Don't let that bedside manner, Poconos shtick throw you. Colonel Moise Solomon was one lethal killer."

Doris Bilstein. I had forgotten Doris was there. She of the colorful menagerie of wigs, and the adoration of Sharon Stone.

"I love that woman. Whatever you think of her. If you think she's a slut because she spread her legs in that Michael Douglas movie, well I don't care. Her and that actress from *Law and Order*, the daughter of that bimbo Jayne Mansfield, both saints. I get all my wigs from them. Free. Because I have breast cancer. They have a foundation."

Yes, breast cancer, the sexy cancer. Lots of resentment in the competitive charity field.

"I mean why isn't there as much sentiment for ass cancer," Mrs. Friedman, not here today, would say. Of course, Mrs. Friedman had rectal cancer "Same as Farrah," and so had a bit of a vested interest. When Rita was dying of breast cancer, the last thing I thought of was sexy, but now fighting this AML shit which no one in the public had heard of, well, I had a touch of a resentment. Yes, a tad.

"Good Morning, Mrs. Bilstein."

"Call me Doris please, Ben, you doll you."

"Of course, Doris. Mossad? The Doc was in Mossad?"

"Two years. I'm surprised you don't know. Rita knew. He told all of us. Well, except for that Polly McManus. That Mick would tell the Pope's confession. We're all sworn to secrecy."

"Interesting. What did he do?"

"I can't really say. I've said too much already. Promise you won't breathe a word?"

"Hey, you forget that I was in the Navy, Doris."

"Sure, sure but we all know that the squids aren't really a part of the military."

And then I remembered that Doris' dearly departed husband had been a marine. It would be of no use to argue on this point.

"When was he in Mossad?"

"About 10 years ago, I think. He was down in Central America, if you can believe it."

"He told you this?"

"No, of course not. Rebekah did. You know his main squeeze. The worst kept secret on the planet aside from Dave Roberts being the most terrible manager in baseball."

Doris's tirades against the Los Angeles Dodgers' manager were legend and were best not engaged. Rebekah was Dr. Solomon's assistant and a RN. The personal relationship part was something Rita had talked to me about when she wanted to forget that she was dying and just gossip.

"What the hell would he be doing in Central America?"

"Beats me. She wouldn't say any more other than he didn't like to talk about it. Something about things that he saw."

CHAPTER 36

The War Memorial
South Pasadena, CA

The War Memorial Building has been around since 1921. Originally built as a way to remember Pasadena area serviceman and later women who gave their lives in all the wars up to that point including the "war to end all wars," World War I. Well, of course, that didn't work out very well, so not only are there markers for WW I but also WW II, Korea and Vietnam. They haven't put any of the various Gulf War dead in as yet. A beautiful, staid old structure that held square dances on Friday evenings and A.A. meetings on Sunday afternoon. Nothing going on that Tuesday morning as Teddy Dabrowski lay on an old couch in the basement pondering his next move. Special Agent Larue Belmont entered with a couple of Starbucks coffees from the place across Fair Oaks Blvd. Belmont handed him the venti drip, light and sweet, and kissed him on the cheek.

"You know those sons of a bitch South Pasadena cops give you a ticket for not having your wheels at a 45-degree angle towards the curb?"

"There's an incline. Cars could roll down the hill."

"Bullshit. Incline my Cajun ass."

"And a nice one it is. There is a hill, the signs are posted very clearly and you are not Cajun. Thanks for the coffee. Two Sweet and Lows and heavy on the Half and Half, right?"

"Yes, yes, mien commandant."

"Hey, I got to have some of life's pleasures while I'm cooped up here. You keep kissing me like that and I may need a few more. There are cameras in here, right? This place is haunted, you know."

"I am a disciplined individual. A little peck on the cheek can do no harm. Anyway, no cameras. Just outside. If you want to see haunted, come to New Orleans, I could show..."

"Alright, again, enough with the Cajun shit. You had spent like five minutes in Louisiana before you met me as I recall from our last conversation. The one where you came to my hospital room and talked me into this god damn scheme.'

"Yes, and this scheme will save countless lives and will have a much better chance of working if you would keep your lovely ass in this basement. I know you were out for at least a few hours the other night. Christ, Dabrowski, it won't be much longer. What if someone sees you? You know your buddy, Detective Jackson, wanted to put you in the Witness Protection Program. You would be shoveling ice in Anchorage right about now if it wasn't for my intervention."

"Yea, yea... I love you, damn it. You could be Cajun or Cochise, I don't give a fuck. I'd still feel that way. I am indebted to you, Larue."

Larue turned away 'til the redness that he could not see but most definitely felt, passed. Teddy for his part decided not to engage his lover any further at this particularly moment. In any case his sexuality was about as clear as a "soup sandwich with a side of dumbass" as his old man used to say. There would be time to figure it all out, if it turned out that anything needed figuring, he thought.

The fact that Larue had come back into his life and at the time he most needed him was enough to give him hope that there would be light at the end of the nightmare. The matter of leaving his hideaway to visit Lexy Perez at Children's Hospital was not really the brightest idea when cartel confederates and police were still in the area.

"Damn well you are. You aren't supposed to know this, but if I hadn't come up with that brilliant plan to fake your nose dive off the roof of the Huntington Hospital, well let's just say, there were a few unsavory types waiting in line to have you do the dive personally, without a stand-in, as it were."

"I am grateful. But like I said when I agreed to this bat shit crazy plan of yours, I told you I'm only doing it for one reason and that is, as god damn corny as it seems, redemption. If there is any way to get things right, to make up for Juarez and..."

Teddy started to get a bit misty.

"Look, Dabrowski, this thing is going to work. It will be worth it. Larue hugged him but only for a moment. There was work to be done.

Teddy got himself together. He thought about that night a couple months ago. Teddy and Ben were in the hospital room. He was happy that he was going to get discharged. Ditto for Ben who promised to pick him up the next morning. Smiles for everyone.

Teddy figured it must have been around eight in the morning when Radcliffe came into his room. He was the plant manager of the place so none of the nurses on duty found it suspicious that he was on the floor. He'd purveyed a cart with a large equipment box on it. He had to trouble shoot something on the wing. Some kind of electrical problem. That was his story. The staff all knew that Radcliffe or the "Reverend" was a bit eccentric, to put it kindly. This was not unusual. He was known to keep strange hours. Anyway, he'd always been a damn good plant manager. That's why nobody took much notice when he rolled the cart past the nurse's station with just a nod to the head nurse as he continued on towards a connection he said he had to check which just so happened to be outside Teddy's room. The nurses were deep in discussion about the rumor of hospital cutbacks and all agreed that Trump was pure evil although that Biden guy seemed a bit slow. Meanwhile Radcliffe had entered Teddy's room and had come out about 10 minutes later pushing the cart with the big damn box marked 'Electrical Supplies'. Teddy was inside the box wondering how he got himself into all this while Radcliffe rolled the cart into the service elevator, hit the "basement parking" button and then headed back out to the nurse's station. Teddy was thinking that he owed the Reverend or whoever he was a swift kick in the ass at the very least for ripping his IV out like a first year med student jonesing the morning after. He felt the elevator descending until it stopped and he heard the doors open. A loud knock on the outside. "God damn it, I'm in here for Christ's sakes."

"Sorry my friend, can't be too careful."

The cart started rolling again. It passed over the smooth floor and then transitioned to the coarse cement. He was in the parking lot. A few minutes later he was liberated just long enough to have a blanket tossed over his head, one that smelled like it had formerly been part of a homeless encampment on Los Angeles Street, before he was helped/shoved into a van by Special Agent Larue Belmont.

At just about the time the Fashion Dry Cleaners van was exiting the Huntington Hospital parking structure, piloted by Larue Belmont, Steve Radcliffe was on the roof gingerly tossing the body of the recently arrived John Doe, now a remarkable duplicate of one Teddy Dabrowski over the roof's edge. This task completed, the Reverend rushed down the stairs to the 4th floor making his way to the Nurse's Station just as Dorie Desmond, RN stormed out of the room previously containing Teddy Dabrowski.

"Dabrowski's not in his room. Christ it looks like his IV and monitor were disabled before it was pulled off. I need a code..."

Ratcliffe ignored her and continued towards the elevator.

Teddy remembered the whole story just the way Belmont and Radcliffe had recounted it in bits and pieces over the last few days.

"Hey, are you with me?"

Larue was seated across from Teddy in the sound proof basement of the War Memorial. Teddy thought the damn place was probably haunted. Like that Lexy Perez.

"Yea, yea, I'm here. It's been a stressful few weeks, Agent, Special Agent, or whatever. So, what the hell do I call you in public, anyway?"

"Like I told you when we brought you in here, Larue will do just fine. No need to overdo it. Most people could give a flying Huey Long turd what our relationship is. They're too busy thinking about themselves. Now we know you left here the other night and you went to Children's Hospital."

Teddy figured Larue had connected with Paula. Paula and Larue. Nice. Of course no threat from Mr. Bowtie. He wondered if Larue had any idea that he, Teddy, "played for both teams," at least as far as Paula was concerned. Damn, love could be confusing, he thought. Still it bothered him that Larue had Paula's confidence. That could complicate things.

"So, you were talking to Paula Garcia over at the hospital?"

"Shit, we could use you at the bureau. You got some fine investigative senses."

"Cut the bullshit. I don't want her involved in any of this. We clear?"

"Is a bit of romance in the air? Is that what I smell? Hey, nothing to worry about, Dabrowski. Just stick to the plan...and don't trust anyone. Our friend in Mexico thinks you're dead. We need to keep him thinking that for just awhile longer. You go visiting Children's Hospital every night, well that will fuck up our plan like an armadillo with a bum leg in the middle of a Texas highway."

"Why haven't you told Jackson about your wonderful plan? Does he even know I'm alive?"

"Why are you so sure Detective Jackson doesn't know? And in any case why would you even care? If I remember right, you have some amends to make, and we, the good old U.S. Justice system, are the ones helping you do that. Sam Jackson doesn't care one way or the other as long as he can close the Bard Café case."

He ignored this for the moment.

Teddy at once envied and hated Larue for the way he was able to compartmentalize their relationship and his day job.

"Look, I have a connection with that kid over at the hospital. She doesn't even know it's me with this scraggly old beard and these glasses and the god damn earing. This earing, that was your idea, wasn't it? Holy mother of Christ!"

"It's a beautiful touch. Bohemian. Kerouac."

"'Kerafuc', I don't give a rat's ass. Look, I talk to Lexy because she knows some things. I can't really explain it. She sees things. Sometimes before they happen."

"She sees dead people? Saw the movie. Well done. Excellent script. Willis miscast. The child actor hasn't worked since and he's like 35 now. Let's move on. Enough."

There was a sound of a door opening and footsteps coming down the stairs.

Belmont and Dabrowski looked towards the stairway in unison, like a couple of bloodhounds on the scent.

"God damn, Larue! Why are you letting the homeless come in for? Damn Salvation Army is down the street."

"Detective Jackson, nice to see you. I wasn't expecting..."

Teddy saw it coming before Belmont did. Maybe it was because Teddy hung out with Sam Jackson outside of work so to speak. Got to know the man and his resentments. Well, the right cross that connected directly under Special Agent Larue Belmont's chin was known as a product of resentment in the rooms of Alcoholics Anonymous. Belmont crashed into the wall knocking down the portrait of General George S. Patton. Jackson stood over him and reached down to help him up.

"Okay, we're good now. Maybe next time you'll try keeping me informed...thoroughly."

Belmont's 12 inch boot cut the detective off as it landed mid solar plexus. Jackson sprawled on the floor gasping for air just inches from Teddy. Using the reflexes of a bobcat the detective pulled Teddy off the couch and into a Belmont left hook that had just been launched. It found Teddy's nose instead of the skull of Sam Jackson and caused a geyser of blood to shoot out of Teddy's nose like one of the amputation scenes from an old Tarantino movie. *Kill Bill* rushed through Teddy's brain for just a nanosecond.

"God damn, Dabrowski, what the hell are you doing blocking punches? I thought you had more sense being from the south side of Chicago and all."

Larue lunged towards Jackson and...

Boom! The report of a Glock 17 filled the room as Jackson fired a round into the couch.

Teddy looked at Jackson as he holstered his piece.

"Now we are done here, Larue. Jesus Christ! Thanks to your dumb ass I got to do all that god damn 'expelling a round' paperwork shit now. I had a date scheduled tonight with the wife. The problem with you crackers is you don't know when to quit. More than a hundred and fifty years since you got your asses kicked in the Civil War, and you're still actin' up."

The FBI agent and the Pasadena detective stood nose to nose. Both had their respective hands on their service weapons. Teddy closed his eyes and waited for the stray bullet and then ... "'Chocolate thunder'! Damn you throw a nasty sucker punch!"

Laughter. The basement was filled with it. Like in that insane asylum where an 8-year-old Teddy went to visit his crazy Aunt Gina. Surreal laughter. Cackles. Yes, cackles. Only this wasn't an insane asylum. It was the basement of a government safe house in South Pasadena and the two men responsible for the cachinnation were a Special Agent of the FBI and a police Detective Lieutenant. The two people who Teddy Dabrowski was relying on to keep him alive.

CHAPTER 37

Children's Hospital, Los Angeles
I arrived at Children's Hospital at about 6PM. Visiting hours were still open. Dr. Solomon had told me to stay home and rest but I grabbed a venti drip, put on a mask so I wouldn't catch any germs that might kill me and went over to the hospital. I decided I would worry about being allowed on the pediatric cancer floor later. I found it ironic that I, a person with cancer, would not be allowed on a cancer ward. But what did I know? It turned out I had nothing to worry about on that score.

The first thing I noticed was that the parking lot was pretty full. It took me awhile to find a space. After a few minutes of searching, I finally parked on the roof and took the elevator down to street level before crossing Sunset and walking to the main entrance. I opened the door, walked in, and my world changed.

The entire waiting area was empty. All the lights were on but there was no living thing in view as far as my eye could see. Nobody at the check-in desk. Then the elevator opened. I instinctively walked in. Later I wondered whether I had actually been beckoned by some unseen force to enter the elevator. The doors closed behind me and before I could select a floor number, 4 lit up and I rose 1, 2, 3, and finally to 4. The doors opened to a sight that I wish on no one. It was the pediatric cancer ward. I knew that from the sign on the wall. I had been here before, of course, but all other familiarity vanished when I saw it. Where the nurse's station had been, there now was a stage. It looked like a replica of the one at Theatre West, my old theatre company, only this stage was larger. It was enormous. As I walked off the elevator (I don't know where I got the courage. Perhaps I was "helped.") I saw them. The children, countless children. Hundreds, no thousands. How could this be?

The voices started off as a whisper and then built up to a veritable cacophony of words, sobbing, laughter. Pleading.

"Read to us, Ben. Read to us. Please read to us. We want a story just like Teddy used to read. Please, Ben."

Enough!

I couldn't take anymore. I turned to go back to the elevator but was stopped by the hand on my shoulder. I knew that hand. Teddy. Teddy Dabrowski. Alive. But how?

"Take it easy now, sailor. It's all good. I know it's a lot of shit to get used to."

"Teddy, Paula will be mad."

The din had begun to abate and now had become a whisper just as the throng opened up ever so slightly to reveal the source of the admonition, Lexy Perez.

"Hi, Ben. I don't think you have met Father Jim."

"A pleasure to meet you, my son. God Bless You."

"Please tell Ben, Father."

"Well, now, I don't know..."

"You're going to be okay, Ben. Father Jim told me. You are going to go into 'mission.'"

An awkward chuckle came from the priest and then, "'Remission,' that would be remission. Well, yes you will get well, my son."

This was all too much.

"Jesus, Mary and Joseph and all the saints, Teddy, what the fuck is going on?"

But Teddy no longer had my attention. He was watching as if under hypnosis as now some kind of celestial music had started to play while as if on cue, Lexy and Father Jim were rising above the stage, levitating for Christ sakes. Up, up they went. Floating as if they were statues at St. Patrick's Cathedral and had become detached from their base and were being carried towards—towards what?

"Teddy."

It was a soft sound. The voice of a young woman to my left. I searched the figures rising above me to no avail and then I saw Teddy. He was on his knees. He was crying. The woman standing in front of him was brushing the back of his head as his cries become more anguished. He was groveling at her feet now.

"Oh, Eileen please forgive me. Please. Oh Jesus I never wanted you to be hurt. I'm a coward. A gutless piece of shit. I was scared. Oh Jesus God, Eileen, make my pain stop. Make it stop. I am so sorry!"

The young woman was dressed all in white. She had her back to me but only for a moment. She turned. There was bruising on her face and a bullet sized exit hole in her forehead. She had an angelic look of empathy on her face as she bent over to help Teddy up. She was not of this earth. Not anymore, anyway.

It all became clear to me. This was the "Eileen" Teddy had talked about, cried about during all those countless drunken jags at the 35er bar. This was the woman he had left to die. Here now, somehow, she was forgiving Teddy. Releasing him from his pain. If only he would let her. But if Eileen was dead, then maybe Teddy was as well. Lexy, as if hearing my thoughts, responded but did so through Father Jim.

"It's all right to be afraid. It is quite normal to fear the unknown, Ben. Eileen is on the other side now, as am I. As is Lexy. It's all right though. Your friend Teddy is with you. He is alive. Lexy is a very special child. She has opened a portal for you and Teddy so you can both understand. So Teddy can receive the forgiveness he so desperately needs."

I didn't understand all of this. I didn't believe it. I thought it must have been a dream. In any case, why was this happening?

And then I heard the voice of Lexy again. Inside my head but clear.

"Save her."

CHAPTER 38

Children's Hospital
Los Angeles

This time it was Aldo Ray. Another great character actor. The same generation as Ernest Borgnine. What was it with these EMTs that look like 1950s character actors?

"You took quite a spill there, sir. Can you hear me?"

"Save who? Who am I supposed to save? Please tell me, Teddy? Where are you?"

"Mr. Rooker, Teddy is not here. This is Children's Hospital. You apparently walked in here about a half hour ago, announced yourself to the admittance desk and asked to see Lexy Perez. You were, I have to say, a bit rude about it when you were told you could not get in without a badge."

"Where's Paula? I need to see Paula Garcia."

"Ben, what the hell..."

And just like magic, a common theme lately, Paula was bending over me with those killer brown eyes. I didn't propose this time. I just asked where Lexy was.

"Ben, you need to stay still."

"I'm good. Please, just help me up."

Aldo Ray grabbed my arm, and I started to get to my feet. The smelling salts he administered earlier were taking full effect.

"Easy now. Okay one, two and..."

I was up. It seemed I had caused quite a commotion. The guest admittance area at Children's Hospital was packed. Kids and parents all were ogling for a view of the crazy white guy who just moments before had some kind of fit and was thrashing about on the floor.

"What the hell is going on? No stage. No Lexy. No Teddy. Christ, no Eileen. What just happened to me?"

"Here, Ben, take this bottled water and follow me. Go slow. I don't want any god damn lawsuits. And take this."

Paula handed me a surgical mask and guided me to the elevator.

The clock in Paula's office said it was 7:30 PM.

"What are you doing here, Ben? You know you can't visit the patients in your condition."

"Temporary problem."

"What? You have cancer. A form of leukemia. Not necessarily fatal but Jesu Cristo! It's not the common cold. You need to take this shit seriously, Ben."

"Did I hear something other than professional concern there, Ms. Garcia?"

"Maybe. Wait, do not kiss me."

"I was just going in for a hug."

"No contact. Not till you clear this thing and then ...what the hell am I saying? Ben, we don't even know each other, I can't..."

"I'm going into remission."

"What?! I think we need to get you checked for a concussion. Remission?"

"Yes, look I'll explain later. I need to see Lexy."

"That's not going to be possible, Ben."

"I know, I can't go see her in person, but I was thinking I could just wave or something. I know I'm being crazy."

"No, Ben, it's not about quarantine or anything like that. Lexy left us this morning. She's gone."

"Wait, I don't understand. She's cured? She's out of the hospital, she's..."

"She's gone, Ben."

CHAPTER 39

Mexico
Cartel Compound
August 2019

Alvina Vasquez could not sleep. It had been months since the news of her mother's death. A death her father blamed on Teddy Dabrowski and insisted he himself had nothing to do with. Of course Alvina did not believe her father. It was too convenient to blame her mother's death and that of the poor Yankee girl Eileen on a man who had just been pushed or jumped off the roof of a hospital building. There was no evidence of his involvement. At least not in the papers or the internet, television, etc. Only rumors, most spread by loco conspiracy theory sites like QAnon and others. She had known the truth in her heart almost immediately. Now she knew it in her brain as well. She would kill her father. Of this she was certain. But this would not be the end. Travel arrangements to America would have to be made. Visits to certain individuals. The first would be the friend of Teddy's . The one who was at the café with him when the explosion came, wiping her dear mama from the face of the earth.

The memory of that day in the desert with the policia. The screams of the Yankee girl Eileen in her ears most nights. Especially lately. She had seen Teddy drive off before her father and his soldiers arrived. Eileen had still been alive when he left. Sure, Teddy left them to die but what else could he do? As for her mother, why would Teddy put himself and his friend in danger of almost certain death just to kill Rose in the café? Of course, if he had not been pushed and jumped of his own accord then a case could be made for him trying to kill Rose and not caring if he went with her. But what about his friend? No, it didn't make sense. And still, why would he want to kill Rose in the first place?

Alvina had spent the last weeks steeling herself for what was to come. She had managed to stay off the cocaine despite her father's efforts to make her use with him, to join the Caligula like parties. The debauchery had reached epic proportions even by Roy Vasquez standards. Alvina remembered reading a book called *Fear and Loathing in Las Vegas* when she was in high school. The author, Hunter S. Thompson, had painted a picture of drugs and alcohol that Alvina thought was mind boggling at the time. She had heard a professor say that the story was autobiographical. She refused to believe it. How could anyone do that amount of drugs and alcohol and still be alive? Well, years later she realized that one could but not without a price. She had witnessed the consequences herself one early morning when she was watching a YouTube of the Letterman show and had seen Hunter S. Thompson himself. Once a brilliant author and raconteur, now a babbling, incontinent buffoon brandishing a whiskey in one hand and a cigarette in the other. The old cool gone now replaced by the visage of a pitiful, bald old man whose soul had died years ago and would be followed by the physical form very soon. She vowed that morning that she would not follow his path or indeed that of her besotted father. But, of course, she had. Alvina Vasquez the shy, scared daughter of an international criminal. A killer. A sadist. A beast. Alvina, once unable to live in the world her father had created now not only living but flourishing with the aid of the coke and a few shots of Jack Daniels. But just like it did with the great author, it had ceased working, leaving Alvina to follow the oft repeated odyssey of the addict. The journey to reach that first magnificent high just one more time. A journey that led to insanity and death.

Alvina looked at her cell phone and saw 11:11 blinking. A good sign. "A sign from the angels," her mother used to say. In better days when Alvina was a young school girl, before she escaped to the States, before her father had not quite revealed himself, before his soul had left him, her mother and she would wander the malls of Mazatlán. Rose would look up and scream, "There it is, Muneca," as she pointed to the large mall clock flashing 11:11. Rose could never really explain why 11:11 was a good thing to see other than that the number 11 had a positive meaning as far as one's instinct was concerned. In any case, every time Rose saw 11:11 with Alvina she made her daughter stop whatever she was doing and make a wish.

Alvina felt at once sad and full of hope at this happy remembrance of her mom. She made a wish immediately and then made the sign of the cross as she silently prayed she would never take another drink or drug.

The party would be tomorrow night. Her birthday. She would be in her mid-thirties. Jesu Christo. A lot of life. *Whatever doesn't kill you...* Her father would be at her party of course. His body guards present as always but maybe not as vigilant as normal. In any case, their guard had not been up to snuff in the last few months. An assassination attempt on Roy had come very close to succeeding just in the last week.

Two men from the Juarez cartel had made it onto the compound. Roy no longer venturing outside. The cartel had not been making the money that was needed to insure loyalty. There were whispers now getting louder about Roy's drug use and cruelty. Unnecessary cruelty. It is one thing to rule with fear but one must remember that in the end it is all about the business. Pure and simple.

The would-be assassins looked out of place from the start. Dressed in tuxedos for a Roy Vasquez party. Roy's parties a few years ago used to at least attempt, albeit in vain, to be civilized but inevitably ended up as lessons in abject debauchery. Now there was no pretense. No attempts to hide what they were. Guests sometimes arrived half-naked with coke in every orifice. In any case, the frequent trips to the bathroom caught the eye of security almost immediately. As all guests had to enter through a metal detector, the would be killers had hidden the gun in the back of the toilet. Pre-staged it by paying off the janitor who had now disappeared. Shot and buried in the desert of course. No loose ends. In any case a janitor would not be missed.

"Mr. Vince," formerly Vincent Valenzuela was head of security for the Vasquez cartel and also an avid Pacino fan. Vince had seen *The Godfather* probably a thousand times. The bullets were carried in from the outside. What many people didn't realize including "Big Vince" is that most bullets were made up of a combination of lead and copper that will not even set off an airport metal detector. As a result, despite the fact that they had caused suspicion by frequent trips to the rest room to check the gun and load it, they still may have succeeded in their mission with a bit of luck. Alas, that was not to be the case.

You see there was a soldier named Paco Mendez who made Roy Vasquez look like a choir boy, if you believe that. Anyway, Paco was in the men's room stall snorting his lines off the breasts of a young woman whose name escaped him when he experienced the sensation of a truck parked on top of his chest. A heart attack.

His last act on this earth was to discard the remains of the wonderful buffet provided by Roy's kitchen staff onto the poor girl's gasping face.

Her screams eventually brought several people into the stall including Roy Vasquez's inept would-be assassins. You see, the toilet where Paco had chosen to get to know the anonymous young lady in the biblical sense also housed the gun that the aforementioned killers would use to do away with Roy. That was the plan anyway. When Paco collapsed onto Buffet Faced Lady he knocked the top of the toilet basin off revealing the 9 millimeter for all to see. It gets crazier though. One of the would-be killers saw the exposed gun and instinctively reached for it. Just then Roy Vasquez stumbled in.

"What the fuck are you doing with a gun at my party. That is very discourteous."

"No, this is not mine. I was getting it for you, senor. I believe it was this man's gun."

The poor bastard threw his buddy under the bus thereby sentencing them both to death.

The doomed saps tried to run but were grabbed immediately.

"If you tell me who sent you, I'll have you shot. One behind the ear. You won't feel a thing and I'll let your family live. If you choose not to and do what a fool would call the honorable thing, then I will cut your balls off and feed them to my dogs. I'm waiting."

They stumbled over each other trying to confess.

"We come from the Juarez Cartel, senor. We were forced to do this. They have our families."

"Ah yes. Of course. I wondered why the caliber of assassin has gone down so. It is actually very insulting."

He looked towards his head of security.

"Take them both to the kennel. Use a dull knife. Now, back to the party"

Alvina knew that she would suffer the same fate if she failed in her attempt to kill her father. What small particle of humanity he might have had was gone. He was a monster. A snow beast you might say. The cocaine, now free based, had overwhelmed any feeling he may have had. Family was nothing to him. He served his masters, King Cocaine and Queen Heroin along with their Court Jester, John Barleycorn.

It then occurred to Alvina that it might not be a good idea to kill her father after all. He would die shortly on his own, Alvina thought as she remembered the screams and the guttural growls of the starved pit bulls from last week.

Maybe she should just get out of Mexico. Find Teddy. If he was still alive. She used to think he was dead but now didn't know what to believe. Everything muddled lately. She needed to stay sober she thought. But, yes, that would be revenge enough. She would look him in the eyes with a dagger to his throat. She was sure that her father engineered her mother's death but she needed confirmation. There could be no doubt. Even if the gringo wasn't responsible for her mother's death, he had been with her in her last moments. She wanted to know that her mother was happy, and that she did not feel pain at the end.

She decided then and there that that was what she would do. She replaced the screams of the men in her memory with the beginnings of a plan. A plan to go to America, find the gringo, and get answers. The responses determining whether he lived or died. In any case, she didn't care. Most importantly, though, she would meet with her dear friend, the one who had protected her Little Angel.

No longer a baby now of course, maybe seven or eight years old. Alvina would start a new life. A brand new beginning with her Alexandria, her "Lexy." The miracle who was at once her daughter and her sister. This spawn of evil that Alvina, in her new found sobriety, had now realized was a beautiful gift.

She took out the burner phone she had hidden from Roy and called Paula Garcia.

CHAPTER 40

Las Cruces, New Mexico
2017

On the Road with Vern and Francine

The trip to the police station had been uneventful except for Vern running the poor bicyclist off the road. Vern did not believe that highways were meant for anyone other than people in automobiles. He felt, and he would tell you if you asked, that one of the reasons this country was going to shit was because people were getting too god damn entitled.

"Oh, I just gave him a scare that's all, Francine. He'll be all right."

Francine wasn't really concerned. Teddy was watching her as she tried to stifle a giggle. She lost the battle and then went into major guffaws. Vern was doing 80 if he was doing 10 while Teddy was seated terrified in the back seat more for himself, if the truth be told, than the poor millennial who had just gone airborne over the little ridge, along with his bike.

"Bicycles and skateboards. That is the millennial disease explained in three words."

"You got that right, my darling."

"Not to be a backseat driver but the guy was in the bike lane, and don't you think we should maybe go back and see if he's okay?"

"Oh now, Vern, did you hear that? Teddy here is a very caring and compassionate person. Isn't that sweet?"

Francine's hand sneaked not so stealthily into the back seat and onto Teddy's knee as it made its way due north.

"He's okay, son. Not to worry."

Teddy couldn't remember the last time he'd been called "Son."

"As for that god damn 'bike lane' you are talking about, well, I'll tell you, the worst thing that was ever created except maybe for those god damn skate parks that they have for the 30-year-old white kids to waste their lives in. They're nothin' but havens now for drugs and such. All part of what's wrong with this country. Oh yes, indeed."

Vern made a sharp left into a residential area and immediately slowed to twenty-five. A few blocks later the car was parked in a driveway at the end of a cul-de-sac in front of a craftsman style house that Teddy guessed was built in the fifties.

"Why did you decide not to take me to the police station?"

"Okay, let's get inside. More will be revealed."

Vern opened the front door to the house and sent Teddy in first where he was immediately attacked by a English mastiff as big as a grizzly.

"Now, Cujo, you be a good boy. This is our guest."

Teddy got up off the floor and wiped the saliva off his face.

Francine put her arm around him and guided him to the couch.

"Damn, sweetheart, you always shake this much? Vern, make Teddy a nice stiff drink, would you?"

"Already on it, dear."

"Look, maybe I should go now. I really appreciate the hospitality."

Teddy started to get up and Cujo stormed out of the kitchen like he was just told by some canine god that Teddy was made of solid dog bone.

"*Stay!* Sorry Teddy. You can't just get up and leave. Cujo finds it rude. Don't know how he got that way. Just sensitive, I guess. Anyway, we are going to let you go on your way so you can do a bit of sight-seeing. Well, we want to do that, anyway. I mean we really do. If you answer our questions then we will."

"And if I don't?"

Vern's look towards the other room needed no further explanation. The beast awaited.

"Francine why don't you start."

"Thanks, darlin. You see, Teddy, when we first saw you at the Budget and heard you talking about the girls in Mexico, well, it was like a divine intervention of some kind. Almost like Jesus himself was there guiding us to you. We were so close to Eileen. She was like a daughter to us, you see. We had given up hope of ever seeing her again or at least finding out what happened to her, right, Vern?"

"Yup. Most definitely. I decided right away to get your ass to the cops."

"Vern!"

"Sorry Francine. Like Francine said, we want justice, and it's been so long."

"Then why didn't you take me to the police station?"

"Well, it was something you said or more like how you said it. You care for those girls don't you? I mean you want to make things right? I mean I had a friend named Abner when I was growing up."

Francine shook her head. "God rest his soul."

"Yes. Now Abner got drunk with us fellas at the Tipsy Cow, that's an old joint just outside of town. Abner was getting ready to go in the service, the Army and was having his last big blowout so to speak. Problem was, he kept talking about his mom. Abner felt real bad about Ethel, that was his Mom. She died young of the cancer. Abner was about sixteen and he was wild, and the day his mom died all the family was there to say goodbye, except for Abner. You see, he was out doing that speed, that crystal meth stuff."

"The Devil's Drug."

"You got that right, Francine. Francine and I never do any drugs. Booze is enough and, of course, our bedroom antics fill in any more voids as they say, that we might have."

"Now Vern, you're embarrassing me!"

Teddy started to pray that Cujo would come back and rip his throat out. Make it quick, please God. But no, there would be no quick respite this day. Vern continued. "So as I'm sure you guessed, Abner never did make it to the hospital and his mom died crying his name."

"That's why you didn't take me to the police station?"

"I'm getting there, Teddy. Anyway, Abner had been trying to forgive himself or at least get some absolution for what he did to his mom. You see, he loved her. He really did. He just made a mistake. Now I figure you were young when you were in Juarez with those girls and maybe did some things you might not be proud of. We, Francine and me, want to help you get those things off your chest. We got to thinking that maybe the police station might not be the best place to do that."

Francine put her arm around her husband. They both were smiling at Teddy now. The smile of the truly insane, Teddy thought.

"So anytime you're ready, just start talking. Confession is good for the soul and we got all the time in the world."

So, Teddy told it. The whole story. He recounted it sober so there was nothing left out or colored with too much emotion. He talked about meeting "Veronica" and "Eileen" in the strip joint. Apparently "Eileen" was her real name, after all. The poor girl had nothing to hide, unlike Veronica/Alvina. He bypassed the making out with Eileen, the sloppy drunk kisses and such, though he believed Francine wouldn't have minded at all. He told of them leaving the bar in the car and crashing into the bus. Their arrest and transport to what had looked to Teddy like the middle of the desert, and finally Teddy's cowardly escape with the girls' cries for help in his ears. He lowered his head and waited for what he believed would be the final unleashing of Cujo and the end of his torment. At least in this world.

After a moment Vern got up and went over to Teddy. He put his hand on his shoulder. Francine was crying softly.

"Teddy we want to help you."

"Help me? Why?"

Francine had come over to sit with him. No more sexual advances. Just pure emotion.

"We loved Eileen, you see. What we didn't tell you earlier is that Eileen didn't have the easiest of lives. There were rumors of relatives, well, acting in untoward ways so to speak..."

"Francine, just say it. The poor girl was used and abused her whole short life."

"Yes, no, you're right, Vern. After listening to your story, Teddy, we believe her trip to El Paso and Juarez was just what they call an 'acting out.' Nothing more, nothing less. Unfortunately for her, tragically, she got involved with the wrong girl. A girl who was just as damaged, in different ways, but damaged nonetheless. Alvina came from a family of horrors as well, but hers was of the powerful and monstrous type. From what you've told us, once Eileen went to Juarez, she had unwittingly signed her death certificate. Eileen died because of Alvina, pure and simple."

This was all too much for Teddy. He began to weep, first softly and then out of nowhere, all the years of sorrow and guilt came pouring out. It was a good cry. Not the phony crying jags of a drunk. Real emotion. Real remorse. The amends process had started. He finally finished when no more tears were left and looked at Vern. Vern and Francine, two of the most unlikely saviors one could imagine. So with a feeling of resolve he hadn't had in years, Teddy said, "Tell me what you want me to do."

CHAPTER 41

July 2019
War Memorial Basement
South Pasadena

"It only takes two alcoholics to make a meeting. You should be happy to see me and benefit from my experience, strength and hope as they say."

Teddy was not happy. It had been three weeks since he had been stuck in "protective custody" with only one quick visit to Children's Hospital that Special Agent Larue Belmont unfortunately found out about. Well, two if he counted the "visit" with Lexy and Father Jim. So here he was now jittery from too much coffee and pissed off that Detective Sam Jackson of the Pasadena Police along with Belmont were putting a major kink in his plan to save Alvina Vasquez. Time was indeed running out. He was especially concerned because he had suddenly lost contact with Vern and Francine Lattimore of Las Cruces, New Mexico. Two years of sharing information and leads on the whereabouts of Alvina had been lost in the ether.

The Lattimore's were somehow sure that Eileen was dead. He hadn't had a chance to ask why they believed it. Teddy of course believed it as well but his sources were of the supernatural variety and so he had decided to withhold that from the Lattimore's even if he was able to contact them. To tell them that he believed Eileen Palestrena was dead because an eight-year-old cancer patient, now sadly passed away herself had seen her "on the other side" might stretch his credibility. In any case, there had been no word from Vern or Francine since Teddy's faux plunge to death from the roof of Huntington Hospital.

"Listen to the detective now, son. You just stay here awhile longer. No little soirees to hospitals or your girlfriend."

Belmont was now getting on his last nerve. The "girlfriend" comment was classic Larue. Larue the boyfriend.

"Okay, first off, you, Jackson, you rent a cop fucker, let's get something straight. I am not a god damn alcoholic. You want an alcoholic, talk to Ben. So, fuck you and your A.A. meetings."

Jackson was laughing uncontrollably now.

"Denial is not just a river in Egypt."

Teddy stared at him just long enough to take it all in and then turned his attention to Belmont.

"What do you know about my girlfriend, you inbred Cajun rooster fucker?"

Teddy was having a bit of fun now too. Two could play this game, he thought.

"You know, I have had enough of this. All of it. I am leaving here now and you cannot stop me. Nothing has happened on this case since the god damn FBI got involved. I'm leaving here. I'm going to find my friend Ben and we'll figure this thing out. There is a girl, a woman, out there and she is in danger. I let one die already. I will not let it happen again. So, you are going to let me walk out of here now or are we going to 'throw down' as we say on the South Side?"

Jackson started to walk between Belmont and Teddy but the gesture was moot. Belmont had taken on the demeanor of Buddy Ebsen on the old *Beverly Hillbillies* show. Teddy at first was stunned but then couldn't help laughing himself. Jackson, satisfied that there wouldn't be another wrestling match like the one he and Larue had just finished, sat down himself. The last thing Teddy remembered about Detective Samuel Jackson (no relation to that god damn actor), the policeman, the pain in the ass, the complex but good man was the wry smile he had as he looked at him for the last time.

"You white boys kill me."

And then his head exploded.

Belmont instinctively went for his service Glock just as the second shotgun round plowed into his leg.

The voice from outside the shattered window was unmistakable to Teddy and the wounded Belmont lying behind Teddy's coach.

"Mine eyes have seen the glory of the coming of the Lord. His truth goes marching on."

It was the Reverend. Teddy knew there was something crazy about that bastard the moment he was recruited to stage Teddy's fake death. An "I told you so moment" but Teddy looking at Belmont's shattered leg spurting blood knew this was neither the time nor place to bring that up.

Belmont whispered to Teddy from behind the couch. He was temporarily hidden. Calm as a cucumber. Teddy at first thought that Larue must be in shock but then realized it was his training.

"Look when he comes in just listen to him. For God's sake don't get him riled up anymore."

"Yea, good safety tip."

Belmont checked his weapon.

"Just keep him occupied. Tell him I crawled out back. He's not after you. I'm the one he's pissed at. Just give me a chance to get a shot."

"Why, Mr. Dabrowski, how are you? Risen from the dead. Well, looks like this black devil is gone to his judgement day. I'm truly sorry, Detective, but I was aiming for the FBI scum. It seems my shooting eye is a bit off. All that time spent creating beautiful works of art from dead bodies only to have them destroyed. My work laughed at by defilers like Larue Belmont. Where are you, Mr. Belmont? Time to meet your Maker."

The Reverend had seen the blood and had followed it towards the back of the coach. In another few seconds, Belmont would be finished. Teddy knew he may well be next.

"Reverend, how did you pull it off?"

"What's that? How did I pull what off?"

"Well, you make this cadaver thing or whatever you call it that's supposed to be me. I mean, it's no better than a department store dummy but at least those have nice tits. I mean, how the hell did anyone believe that was my corpse that hit the parking lot concrete?"

The Reverend had stopped now. He was no longer intent on reaching Belmont. There would be ample time for that. The Reverend had been insulted. His life's work, his craft desecrated by this little punk's mouth. Perdition was at hand. Steve Radcliffe, plant manager for Huntington Hospital, most recently corpse artisan extraordinaire, AKA "The Reverend" pointed the shotgun at Teddy's head and prepared to pull the trigger.

"Well, what kind of Reverend are you now. Aren't you going to say a few words for my..."

Six rounds from Special Agent Larue Belmont's Glock 22 took part of the Reverend's arm. Another three in the gut effectively disemboweled him.

Teddy Dabrowski power puked onto the intestines that had formerly resided inside Steve Radcliffe, now streaming onto the floor of the War Memorial.

Black Jack Pershing would have been proud.

CHAPTER 42

Moise Solomon's Office
West Los Angeles
A few days later

The shootings at the War Memorial were all over the news. Local and national. You got to understand, the Pasadena area is not normally this exciting. You may have heard of the Jan and Dean song from the 60s "Little Old Lady from Pasadena." Well, it was true then and still true 60 years later. Of course the area north of the 210 as the locals call it, referring to the other side of the 210 freeway, had over the last ten tears been known for crime, mostly drug related, and the Old Town area just twenty or so years ago was a real shithole. I had never experienced it as I had arrived after the area was gentrified, to use the vernacular of today. The 35er was actually a real dive bar not the millennial faux shit kicker place it now was. Ah, the good old days. I learned all of this on the Internet and on CNN. Seems an FBI agent was seriously wounded, and a cop was killed. Name unknown at the time due to notification of next of kin. Someone else was there apparently. The shooter and another civilian. The shooter apparently was a disgruntled employee of an area hospital. Again, all the info was sketchy. Unusual in this day of "Breaking News." The masses' appetite for instant gratification must be sated.

All of this was not really as important as it normally would have been had I not been waiting for the results of my latest markers in the good Doctor Solomon's office. It was unusual to get my markers checked this soon but Rebekah sounded excited when she called and asked me to come in.

Colonel Solomon entered. He had a look that I can only explain as a combination of "dumfounded" and "ecstatic." Think Melania on her first date with the Donald.

"Your cancer is gone. I have absolutely no explanation as to why. Yes, we have treated you with fairly aggressive chemotherapy, and although it is true that this type of Leukemia is by no means a death sentence, it is very unusual for you to be now cancer free."

"Doc, Colonel, can you double check?"

"Believe me, we have quadruple checked, and as I said before, you are completely free of any cancer. An act of God, that's all I can say."

It's not that I had thought I was going to die, but the fact was that five minutes before I had cancer. A very serious form of cancer and then, I didn't. And then my phone rang. If you believe in the yin and the yang, well, this was the latter.

"Excuse me, Doc, I have to take this."

"Rooker. Can I help you?"

"Is this Ben Rooker?"

"Yes, it is. Who are you?"

"Mr. Rooker, this is the switchboard of Huntington Hospital. I have a Special Agent Larue Belmont, a patient here who would like to talk to you."

"Oh, Christ."

"I'm sorry, Mr. Rooker, do you...?"

"I mean, sure. Put him on."

And then the yang took full effect as Belmont recounted the attack at the War Memorial by a crazed worker at Huntington Hospital and owner of a company that, from what I could discern, sold dead bodies to the movies.

"Jackson had no chance. I think the rounds were meant for me. He took them full on though. If it's any solace, I don't believe he even knew what hit him. Died instantly."

The strangest thought came to me. I wondered who would bring the cookies to the next Monks and Drunks A.A. meeting. Sam Jackson had that commitment for the month. We would have to find someone else. Have a discussion, what in AA parlance is called a Group Conscious at the next meeting. Yes, most definitely.

"Are you still there?"

"Yes, yes, sorry. He was a good guy. I mean we had our differences, but he kind of grew on me after a while."

Belmont was silent for a moment and then: "Look, Jackson's funeral is going to be Friday over at Forest Lawn, the one in Glendale."

I smiled remembering that Michael Jackson, the King of Pop was interred at Forest Lawn as well. I wondered how Sam would feel about that.

"Yea, I know it. I'll be there."

"Great. Listen, I have a few things to share with you. My leg is pretty busted up. I'm looking at a few more days in here at least and then desk duty. That is if I can dodge medical retirement, which I don't think is likely. Do you mind visiting me here in my room after the funeral?"

"Sure. I mean I don't have anything to add to the investigation. I've been kind of locked up myself the last few months."

"That's fine. I understand. I'm the one who will be filling you in. Also, there's someone I'd like you to meet."

The Special Agent was a bit cryptic, but with all I had taken in that day, my cancer pardon as it were and the death of Sam Jackson, I guess I just wanted to get off the phone. The fact that the internet story about Sam's death had reported another unidentified person at the War Memorial never came to mind. All I wanted was a long nap. But before that I needed to do one more thing. On the way home, I stopped in front of Children's Hospital and looked up in the direction of the 4th floor. The former home of a little girl who came into this world innocent and left the same way. A little girl that I knew had somehow saved my life.

"Fair winds and following seas my little warrior. See you in the next life. I love you, Lexy."

CHAPTER 43

Culiacan, Sinaloa, Mexico
June, 2011

St. Columban was Ireland's sixth century missionary to Europe. After he died, the Columban Fathers were founded to spread the word of Jesus Christ throughout the world. The missionary society had a special influence in Mexico, dealing as they did with the poorest of the poor where, on this scorching day in one of the most dangerous cities in the world, Father Jim O'Brian was conducting his weekly rounds which included a visit to Saint Innocent, the local orphanage. Father Jim loved all children but had developed a particular affinity for the six-month-old girl who had been left here just a little over a month ago. The little girl was very weak and would not eat. The local physician, a competent woman, had diagnosed her with a type of blood cancer that she believed could not be treated in Mexico without millions of pesos. If the baby did not get medical attention soon, she would die. The only answer would be treatment in the United States by a pro bono medical facility. The good Father believed this and realized that today's visit might be the last time he saw this beautiful little child alive.

"Father, so good to see you! Our little flower will be so happy you are here."

Sister Angela Joseph, an American Nun who grew up in a nouveau rich family on the east coast. Father Jim thought that if there ever was a picture that one could put next to the word "Vocation" it would be Sister Angela Joseph's nee Patty Fitzgibbon formerly of Germantown, Philadelphia, USA. What an amazing world where a black man from the Cabrini Projects of Chicago can meet a young white woman who in a different world would be a debutante. Yes, amazing, thought Father Jim.

"Lead the way, Sister."

The little one was dying. She should have been in the ICU of a hospital. An American hospital. Father Jim had been able to petition the highest levels of the former Bush administration for an emergency medivac flight because of an old friend from seminary who found secular politics more exciting than canon law. Indeed, the former President's sister-in-law, a Mexican national, had been instrumental in getting Bush's ear on this. It needed to happen immediately, though. There was no time. As of this morning, Father Jim had heard nothing from the embassy. There was a medivac flying out tonight. If the little miracle was not on it, she would surely die.

It was a Friday when Father Jim had found her. He heard the dogs first, the vicious wails of animals that are so hungry they will eat anything and everything. Even a precious baby. The baby's crying was what got his attention though. He changed direction and crossed the street so quickly he missed being run over by a garbage truck by a matter of inches. He was running so fast as he approached the entrance to the St. Innocent Orphanage that he did not notice that the barking and the crying had stopped. As he rounded the corner he spotted the three dogs, probably rabies infested. Most definitely emaciated. It was the figure wrapped in newspaper that made him forget about any threat from the dogs. There was a small face peeking out from behind a full-page ad for a rock concert, inches from the dogs. Father Jim reached the baby, ignoring the dogs. A strange and wonderful thing had occurred though. The dogs were now seated on their haunches. They were staring at the baby who had, *oh holy mother of God,* a smile on her face.

A smile that Father Jim believed would light up the entire city if it had not been the middle of the day. He gathered himself long enough to pick the child up, the dogs still motionless, and carried her into the orphanage. As he ran in with her, a piece of paper almost fell out of the bundle. He caught it and read it as he put the baby down on a table in the foyer. It contained two words. A name.

"Alexandria Perez."

A search for the baby's mother came up empty. "Perez" was, of course, as common a last name in Mexico as "Smith" was in the United States. In any case, "Alexandria" had been left at the orphanage because more than likely whatever tragic soul gave birth to her could not feed and clothe her. The poverty level in this part of the of Mexico was the lowest in the country.

All of this was coming back to Father Jim as he looked at this little angel smiling up at him. As sickly as she was, there was still that smile. Glorious.

The vibration in his pocket jarred the priest back to the secular world. He took out his iPhone 4 and looked at the screen. It was the American Embassy.

"Yes, this is Father Jim O'Brian."

"Father, this is Peter Ostertag, I'm the embassy's conduit between Mexico Child Services and our emergency Medivac program. Do you believe in miracles, Father?"

And just like that Father Jim O'Brian and Alexandria Perez were on the 2100 Medivac flight to LAX enroot to their final destination of Children's Hospital, Los Angeles and the Pediatric Intensive Care Unit.

CHAPTER 44

Las Cruces, New Mexico
2017
At Home with Vern and Francine

"You sure you don't want a drink, honey?"

Francine was going into maternal mode with Teddy. His crying jag had ended. Teddy thought she was one complicated woman. Vern was not far behind. In the complication area anyway. Before Teddy could answer, the landline rang.

"I got it, honey."

Vern in the kitchen now speaking to the caller. His voice was low and subdued. Francine stared at Teddy not paying attention. Like she knew who it was. She reassured Teddy again as Vern hung up and returned from the kitchen.

"It's going to be okay. All in God's time."

"Teddy, we are going to have a visitor here in just a few moments. You don't mind waiting around now do you?"

Teddy looked at Vern with just a bit of impatience.

"Look, I thought we were going to figure how to save Veronica or Alvina and Eileen or whatever their names are. I don't have time for any social calls."

Teddy's look indicated what he meant by "social."

Vern started laughing. Just like earlier. Francine jumped in. Before Teddy could start breaking windows and throwing furniture, Vern clarified things.

"There is a man coming over. He's with the Federal Bureau of Investigation. You might say he has a vested interest in helping us and also eliminating a certain cartel boss."

Teddy was shaking his head.

"How the hell is the FBI involved? Great, now I'm going to federal prison. Maybe I will have that drink. Do you have any Jack Daniels? Christ this gets more fucked up by the minute."

"Settle down, Teddy. The FBI is not involved. At least not officially."

Before Teddy could respond to Vern's curious comment, the doorbell rang. Moments later a burly white guy in a grey suit with a pink tie entered.

"Hello, Francine, Vern; and you must be Teddy. Nice to meet you. FBI Special Agent Larue Belmont but for our purposes, Larue will do."

Francine missed the look of mutual recognition between Teddy and the visitor. Only a second but it spoke volumes.

"Teddy's a good man Larue. He was with Alvina and Eileen down in Juarez. He managed to escape before Vasquez's men got there."

This was new and very unwelcome information for Teddy.

"How do you know this? We were just picked up by the 'Federals.' There were no cartel people there... at least that I saw. Oh, God!"

It was Belmont's turn. He made an ever so slight move to embrace Teddy but then thought better of. Again, unnoticed.

"Look, Teddy, can I call you that? Nobody is blaming you for anything. For all you knew, you were just having a wild, drunken party with a couple of hot college girls. Perfectly normal red blooded American, ah, heterosexual activity. You could not have any idea that Veronica, real name Alvina was the daughter of Roy "Tire Boy" Vasquez, the head of the Juarez cartel then and now the boss of the Venganza, the biggest cartel in Mexico."

Teddy had his head in his hands now. All of this had become clearer and more horrific.

"Christ! What about Eileen, if that was her real name?"

He waited with decidedly bated breath for the answer he knew would come but dreaded, nonetheless.

Larue drew a chair up and faced Teddy.

"An innocent young girl, who just ended up in the wrong place at the wrong time. Yes her name was Eileen. Eileen Palestrena. She was from Las Cruces. We believe she was raped and then executed shortly after Vasquez and his men arrived to 'rescue' Veronica AKA Alvina Vasquez."

Teddy reacted to the news that he had known all these years but had only at that moment accepted. Hearing it in the cold light of day brought it all home. Like the time he was staying at the YMCA in Chicago when he was just seventeen. A couple of years after he had left home. Talking to some drunks in the cafeteria till around midnight. One guy had been talking about the pain of losing his wife through divorce. She had taken his kids as well. The guy's name was Dave he remembered. Red-haired guy with glasses. He was about forty. Seemed old then. The next morning Teddy was having breakfast and Dirty Dotty, the manager of the cafeteria, a dark haired Armenian broad who had fucked anything and everything breathing in the South Side was cackling away and pointing towards the lobby. Teddy had looked out just in time to see the elevator door open and a stretcher with a body bag exit.

It was Dave, of course. Teddy heard later that he had hung himself from his closet door. Used his belt. The poor maid, a Guatemalan woman named Louisa, found him thrashing around and ran down three flights to get old Ed the janitor. By the time poor Ed got in the room, Dave's tongue was hanging out and he had shit himself. Dead as the proverbial doornail.

Yes, this was like that. The reality. Alive one moment and gone the next.

Teddy pushed Francine's arm away gently and looked at Larue.

"So, what am I here for? Is there some kind of plan?"

"We believe that Veronica, henceforth called 'Alvina Vásquez,' her given name, is alive and either in Las Cruces or back in Mexico with her father. Roy Vasquez's drug cartel is responsible for the torture and murder of thousands who have died of overdose or been killed in the commission of a crime while under the influence."

"All good, but why do you need me?"

Larue locked eyes with Teddy before speaking. It passed, but this time Francine noticed.

"We know from..." Looking at Francine and Vern not so subtlety, he continued.

"We have it under the most verifiable of sources, that Roy knows you were with Alvina. He can and will make you a scapegoat for any atrocity, real or imagined, if he hasn't already. We believe that at some time in the very near future there will be an attempt on your life."

Teddy was up now pacing. He glared at Francine and Vern.

"So, you're telling me that Ms. Foot Fetish of 1939 and her husband, The Skateboard Assassin are not just a couple of down home hicks living the American dream here in beautiful Las Cruces?"

Francine volunteered first, raising her hand.

"I work as an accountant in the Las Cruces FBI Field office. I have been there for two years. Before that I was at the El Paso Office."

"Christ."

Vern's turn.

"Las Cruces PD. Retired. You might say I like to keep my hand in, as it were."

"While Francine keeps her foot in." Teddy couldn't resist.

Fran and Vern both started to laugh.

"What a shit show."

Before Teddy could respond further, Belmont continued.

"I recruited Francine and Vern because they knew Eileen and were devoted to finding out what happened to her. Vern is a great investigator on his own. He had actually found the picture of you and with Francine's help, made the connection."

"What picture? What connection?"

"Francine, would you like to explain further?"

"Everything Vern and I told you, Teddy, at the Budget at the diner and on the road about Eileen was and is true."

"With just a few, what you might call, 'deceits by omission.'"

"What Vern says... We didn't actually run into you by mistake. You have been tracked since you left Pasadena."

Teddy's libertarian side exposed itself in all of its clarity.

"Is that even legal? Christ, what kind of police state do we live in?"

"To be clear," Belmont joined the fray, "none of our actions, mine, Vern and Francine's, have been approved by the Agency."

"Wonderful. So, what you are telling me is that because a friend of theirs was killed by a scumbag cartel and I was known to be with this poor girl on or about the time of her death, you three rent-a-cops have..."

Vern would not have any of this.

"Now, Dabrowski, that is hurtful and unfair. We are, I believe, after the same thing and I'll have you know, that I am also trying to save your ignorant ass."

Belmont attempted to regain control of the room. He locked in on Teddy.

"Look, you self-centered toy boy son a bitch, listen to me and listen good."

Francine looked at Vern with a look that said, *Where did this come from?* but nonetheless they held their collective tongue. They liked this "John Wayne" version of Larue Belmont.

"Do you know what a cartel is?"

Teddy, with a moment to grab a bit of composure...failing and then, "Of course I do. It's like one of those, what they hell was that movie a few years back?"

"*Scarface,* Teddy. Great movie. Vern and I saw it twice and..."

Francine was stopped by Larue's serial killer glare.

"CDS, Pacific Cartel, The Federation, The Blood Alliance, all names for one of the most evil organizations on the face of the earth, the Venganza Cartel. The Mexican and United States governments call it the 'most powerful drug cartel of all time.' It has more than 10,000 members. Most of them vicious killers called, 'soldiers.' Venganza Cartel has imported over 200 tons of cocaine and heroin into the United States. Recently they started dealing with large amounts of Fentanyl. Fentanyl is an opioid and is the number one cause of death by drugs in America today. But let's forget about these dry and boring statistics. Venganza has destroyed thousands of families in America and around the world. I'm talking about kids. Mostly white kids if that makes it closer to your heart."

Teddy was nonplussed.

"Look, I get all that. I've seen it on *Sixty Minutes* a thousand times. It sucks. I feel bad for those kids and their families. But, what the fuck, Larue. You've become a god damn vigilante, risking whatever career you got left with the FBI. I can understand, a little anyway, why Vern and Francine are in this. I mean Eileen was like their own daughter and she was raped and murdered by those scumbags. But why you, Larue? Why the fuck you?"

Something in Belmont started to crack. Just a very small part of him, but there it was. The treble of his voice gave it away in his response, if only for a second.

"Let's get back to the point of this whole discussion, if you all don't mind. Teddy, the reason we have been tracking you is that we have reason to believe that the cartel and possibly other elements will be coming to Pasadena."

"Right... to kill me. I believe that was mentioned earlier. Makes me feel kind of special. And what other 'elements' might you be talking about?"

Belmont doesn't hesitate.

"Rose and Alvina Vasquez."

Teddy was not entirely surprised by this. His only response was an affirmative nodding of his head with a brief commentary.

"So, what am I supposed to do or maybe I should ask 'What do you want me to do?'"

Belmont looked at Vern who got up as if on cue and walked to an adjoining desk, opened a drawer and took out a Glock 17. He gave it to Teddy without a word.

Belmont continued.

"I assume you know how to use that? We want you to return to Pasadena and just act like nothing has happened. Continue to meet with your friend Ben Rooker."

"Christ, is there anything you don't know?"

Francine tried to break the tension.

"Oh, you don't know the whole of it darling. He has a whole file on my foot fetish."

Belmont closed his eyes for a moment and then was back on point. He didn't want Vern and Francine to know that Teddy and he did in fact know each other and that Teddy had already been recruited in a sense. It would complicate things. This was the second stage. He appreciated the fact that it appeared that Teddy understood this as well.

"We need information. If we are going to do major damage to the cartel and save your life along with saving Rose and Alvina we need intel. If you have any feeling left for Eileen and Alvina, and I believe you do, you need to stay under the radar, continue to go to your same haunts, keep your ears and eyes open and practice with that Glock at the range at least once a week. Any questions?"

Teddy shook his head and laughed a bit maniacally.

"Hold on. Do you think I'm a total moron? I mean, I know you probably think I'm just another slug from the south side of Chicago but it is obvious to anyone with an IQ above that of a urinal cake that I am the bait. The worm you are going to use to get Roy Vasquez. Am I right?"

The silence from Larue, Vern and Francine told the story. No need for an answer.

Teddy had stopped laughing now. He looked directly at Special Agent Larue Belmont. His eyes told the story. He was all in.

"Yea, I suppose if I say anything, the director will disavow any knowledge and burn up the tape," said Belmont.

Francine and Vern laughed at the old *Mission Impossible* TV show reference.

The FBI man handed Teddy a set of keys and motioned him towards the door.

"Here's your car key. I took the liberty of driving it over. If you could drive me to the airport, I need to make a quick trip to Washington, DC to talk with my boss.

Got to keep up the ruse, as it were. At some point in the next few months, maybe even years, I will see you again in Pasadena with further plans. Meanwhile, Francine and Vern, you are true patriots. Thank you for your service."

The Lattimore's were beaming as they got up and shook Belmont's and Teddy's hands. Francine went a bit further by grazing Teddy's crotch with her fingers ever so slightly while she gave him a sly smile and a peck on the cheek as he and Belmont exited the house.

CHAPTER 45

August 2019

Tijuana, Mexico

The more he thought of it, the more Roy Vasquez realized that the Range Rover was the best choice. The last few days driving from Mazatlán had been uneventful and smooth. The Range Rover was a wonderfully engineered vehicle. This one, the HSE was customized with James Bond like accessories including bullet proof glass and non-puncture tires. The doors were eight inches thick with five inch windows. Its metal was a combination of steel, aluminum and ceramic armors just like Trump's car, The Beast. Roy openly detested the President of the USA but deep down envied him. He yearned for the same power.

In any case, flying had been out of the question. Roy was on too many people's radar. If it wasn't competing cartels it was the FBI, the police or even a son of a man he had tortured and killed. He had cut down on the cocaine. Well, in his world he was cutting down. Kind of like Keith Richard claiming he was sober because he got off heroin but was doing a fifth of Yukon Jack a day. Everything was relative, Roy thought. The last few days with Alvina had been a disaster. Roy knew that she hated him but could not accept it. In his drug addled mind, he was a good father who was looking out for his daughter's safety.

This trip was a part of that. He had been chastised by his upper echelon of commanders to have someone else make this trip. He was, after all, the head of the Venganza cartel. If he was killed or captured, the rest would fall like dominoes.

"Senor, we are almost there. Are you ready?"

Antonio, his loyal driver, was guiding the vehicle towards the Tijuana checkpoint. The entry to San Diego. From here they would go to Las Cruces and then back to Los Angeles. But first the hard part. Crossing the border.

Roy mused how he was surprised that when he was much younger he had assumed the head of an international drug trafficking cartel would have a difficult time getting into the United States unnoticed. He was wrong and quite frankly amazed that the cartels were already here in the United States and operating with impunity, using homegrown gangs like MS-13, originally a group set up to protect Salvadoran immigrants, now a lethal, murderous organization equivalent to the Italian Mafia in its early days.

No, he thought, this would not be difficult, but still he must be careful.

"Vamos."

The one word order was all Antonio needed to turn the Range Rover towards the line of cars waiting to cross the checkpoint. It was just after 5 AM this Tuesday in August. It was the least travelled time of day to cross the border. Roy watched the booth as the car in front of them was given the go ahead to pass through. Antonio slowly guided the Range Rover forward to the checkpoint. The border person in the booth was a young Mexican-American female. Her name tag said "Rosa". As Roy felt a slight pang in his chest, he wondered if this was a good sign or bad, this guard having the same name as his dearly departed Rose. The wife he hated in life but now loved in death. No matter. The fact that she was Mexican would mean that she was more likely to bust their balls. She had to prove herself of course. Prove that she was an American first. A white woman would be much easier. The luck of the draw.

"Good Morning. May I ask who else is in the vehicle?"

Antonio began to answer just as Roy leaned forward, full beard and contacts, and waved.

"Why are you visiting the United States?'

"My boss and I are here for a day of business in Chula Vista."

"I see. Where will you be staying?"

Antonio handed her the fake but beautifully crafted documents indicating that he and Roy represented the Mazatlán chapter of the Chamber of Commerce. Roy smiled and then sat back again. Rosa checked the documents carefully, looked at Antonio and leaned in to get one last glance at Roy. Satisfied, she waved them through.

"Enjoy your time in America."

Antonio guided the Range Rover to the freeway. Once entering the 5 North ramp he maintained the speed limit although there was not much chance of being stopped for speeding with the traffic.

Antonio had known Roy since they were kids. He was an orphan. His mother had been collateral damage in the war between the Juarez and Venganza factions. Frank, Roy's father, made sure he had a place to live and enough schooling to be able to read and write. After Frank's death, Antonio became Roy's trusted bodyguard, driver and jack of all trades. Antonio was the perfect foil for Roy. He didn't drink or do any drugs, and he seemed to have no interest in woman. Roy knew that he wasn't gay. If he was, he would have been buried in the desert a long time ago. He was the opposite of Roy and he could trust him. A perfect partner for what most people would see as a suicidal mission of retribution. Roy saw it as just another part of the game. The game he had played since his father died, from the time he saw Rose, to his consolidation of his cartel empire, to the betrayal of Rose and her death, to this day which found him heading to Las Cruces.

Roy was tempted to stop in Pasadena. Antonio talked him out of it. Priorities. It was necessary to pay a visit to the home of the girl, now dead, that Alvina had met in Juarez. Tie up some loose ends. Visit the couple who had met with the FBI scum and that gringo Teddy, the man who had soiled his beloved daughter, and in Roy's crazed mind caused the death of the love of his life, Rose. Dear Rose. He missed her so much. The dreams now almost every night. Even the OxyContin would not dim them. Each one the same.

The stage. It seemed endless. But it wasn't inside a theatre. Somehow it was inside a hospital. Roy knew it was a hospital because there were men and women in scrubs and then there were the children. Multitudes of children. They were singing, "Uno, dos, tres... Chocalate".

Roy knew the song from when Alvina was a baby. She and her friends would sing it in school. Alvina had driven her car into a wall and then had disappeared. She had gone to Juarez. Met that American whore and then that gringo. Roy had seen his picture. Yes. Alvina came back though. Sometime later there was a baby. Yes, the baby. It was lost though. A woman also, and there was a priest. Too many drugs. *What happened to the baby? What was her name?* He hadn't thought of the child in years.

But who was this now? The dream again.

A multitude of children on the stage. They began to rise. Rising as if they are going to the heavens themselves and then they seemed to part. There was the priest and a small child now. Only those two. The priest was crying and the little child was consoling him. Roy came closer. The girl turned to him and she was a gargoyle. A monster. Red eyes and a serpent's tongue. She opened her mouth and locusts flew out. Roy began to run but he couldn't get away. He heard her/its voice. "I am Lexy and you will not hurt my mother. You will not hurt my mother, you will not..."

"Oh, Jesu Cristo!!! Mama! Mama!"

Antonio slowed the car and pulled to the shoulder. Roy was in a cold sweat.

"Boss, it's just that dream again. Boss, it's okay. You're okay."

Roy stared straight ahead for a moment and then took a long drink from the water bottle on the console.

"Thank you, yes, thank you, my friend. I'm okay now. Where are we?"

"On our way to Las Cruces. We just got off the 8 East and are on the 10 freeway."

"How much longer?"

"About 600 miles. If we drive all night as planned, we should be there in about nine hours."

"Too bad you don't like the cacao leaf my friend. We could get there even sooner."

Antonio laughed and picked up his thermos.

"This is my 'cocaine,' boss, Black Rifle Coffee. I won't sleep for days."

They both shared a laugh and then Antonio guided the car back onto the freeway.

There would be one stop before Las Cruces. A diner off of the 10. To the unseeing public, just a broken down rest stop. It was actually an armory belonging to the MS-13, now an ally of Venganza cartel. Antonio and Roy would pick up the necessary armaments and then move on to Las Cruces for a short stop. That was the plan in any case.

Roy looked at Antonio now. They had been driving for six hours.

"You look wide awake. I don't understand. How do you do it, my friend?"

"I think about my mama and my papa."

"You remember them?"

"I was about five when they died. There are good memories. I try to think of those only."

"But you were there when they died?"

"Boss, here is the exit for the guns."

Roy took the hint and got into business mode. There could be no show of weakness with these MS-13 punks. None at all. Unfortunately, aside from a Glock that Antonio had hidden in a custom compartment, they had no protection. The armory was going to be their source of weaponry. Roy thought they may have trusted in MS-13 too much. In any case, it was too late now.

"Very good. Turn your lights off as soon as we get to the gate."

Antonio saw the movement near the gate first. He dove across Roy's body and covered him as the shot rang out, whizzing past the side mirror. Then silence.

"You okay, boss?"

Antonio saw that Roy was moving. He grabbed the Glock and jumped over the seat and into the back. Roy for a brief moment thought Antonio was abandoning him as he realized this was a trap. A double-cross. Roy thought about the Salvadorans that his father Frank had executed years ago over what now seemed like a petty dispute.

Was this payback?

"Reitirarse por! Stand down! Bajate del carro!"

The gunmen wanted them out of the car. Roy knew that would be a death sentence.

Out of the corner of his eye, Roy glimpsed Antonio holding something. Not the Glock now. Much bigger.

"Tell them you are coming. Go to the driver's side first, and when I count three, turn on the brights."

"We are coming."

"One, two, three..."

The high beams revealed four men with heavy weapons. Something flashed past Roy and then...white light, flames, heat. Unbearable heat. All emanating from the flamethrower that Antonio had unleashed. Where there had been four human beings there were now just burning, screaming husks.

After a moment, silence, then whimpering. Antonio climbed out of the car and walked towards the simmering mass, took out his pistol and put multiple rounds into the burnt flesh.

"A flame thrower! Where the fuck...?"

"I got it from an old Gulf War buddy. He has a stockpile just off the freeway. You were asleep. I didn't want to bother you."

The block house was about 30 yards away. Nobody there. Stockpiles of munitions. These MS-13 gangsters were not very smart. It appeared it was only the four. Antonio and Roy took what they had come for and then Antonio set charges around the block house. Booby traps if you will. Roy was sure there would be other members of the gang paying a visit soon. Just to get restocked. Well, they would be in for a very sad surprise.

Time to go now. Get back on the highway after first burying the flamethrower.

A fucking flamethrower. Jesu Cristo.

Roy had to hand it to Antonio.

They would be in Las Cruces in a couple of hours. A few quick stops. Meetings with some old "friends." It's always good to meet with old friends, thought Roy. He had been so exhilarated that he hadn't even missed the cocaine. It was still there. The urge. Waiting to pounce. Maybe in Las Cruces. Just one fix. He deserved it.

CHAPTER 46

Detective Sam Jackson's Funeral

Detective Samuel Jackson's funeral was a real cop's send-off. Amazing Grace played by police bagpipers. Hundreds of cops marching down Colorado Blvd. Police car sirens wailing. Sam's wife was the last thing I expected. A low key, obviously intelligent woman who spoke only when she actually had something to say. No kids. Sad. We spoke for a bit. I offered my condolences, which unlike other funerals I had been to, were genuinely heartfelt.

The reception was held at the Women's Club in South Pasadena. Larue Belmont was still recuperating so he couldn't be there. The "Reverend's" bullet had just missed his femur. Lucky guy. He would probably not be returning to active duty anytime soon however.

Lots of cops at the reception. The booze was flowing at the open bar for Sam's cop friends. Starbucks baristas were on the other side of the room serving coffee to the Monks and Drunks A.A. guys. Sam would have liked that.

Speaking of the bar, there was a guy stationed in front of the bartender with a scraggly beard pouring them down like no tomorrow. He looked oddly familiar. Like when you know somebody but you can't place him because it's out of context in some way.

I made my way closer, and then I heard it. That voice. Fucking Teddy Dabrowski?!

Just like that, like he's reading my mind he turns around and looks me right in the eye.

"Is the beard that bad?"

His look tells me that we should move the conversation to a more secluded area or at the very least not acknowledge his actual identity. He stuck out his hand.

"Do I know you buddy. I'm Alan, Alan Smithee."

Any doubts I had evaporated. Teddy would be the only one I knew privy to the fact that we had discussed "Alan Smithee," the name that used to be inserted at the beginning of films when the real director wanted no part of the production. Maybe the editing or the cuts by the money people or countless other issues that popped up in the crazy industry I was a part of. So I had told Teddy in one of our Bard Café talks, "If you see a movie directed by 'Alan Smithee,' it's probably a good idea to watch something else or read a book."

I coughed and leaned into him.

"Rest room."

A few minutes later, after scouting the stalls for any potential "shitter spies" and securely locking the door, the Teddy Dabrowski- Ben Rooker reunion took place in the Women's Club rest room.

I pulled on his beard. It was real and then we hugged followed by tears.

"I don't understand. How are you alive? I mean, I am happy, beyond happy that you are, but what the fuck!?"

Teddy released me after a bit. I could see that he had been holding back the emotion as per usual. Yes, this was definitely my best friend in the world, Teddy Dabrowski, back from the dead.

"Okay, Ben, okay. First, you can't be calling me 'Teddy.' I'm still dead as far as the rest of the world is concerned. Until... anyway, not important now, you bald fuck you."

"Until what? What the fuck is going on? This is connected to the bombing, right? Sure! Damn, of course."

Teddy grabbed me and shoved me against the sink.

"God damn, Ben! Look I know this is a shock. More will be revealed . Just not now. You have to trust me on this."

No, I don't think so.

I kneed Teddy in the balls and the next thing I knew we were rolling around in the urine covered bathroom floor. He wasn't happy, but neither was I. I mean, I had just got past the acceptance step in the grief process for Christ's sake. Now what was I supposed to do?!

"You crazy bastard! What the fuck did I do to deserve a shot in the nuts. Not fair!"

"Bar fight rules, Teddy. You taught me that."

Out of breath I let him go and started to get up. Bad move. He stepped on my hand.

"You south side prick! I'm a god damn cancer survivor!"

Damn that hurt. I was holding my hand while he was still grabbing his balls. What a sight. And then Teddy started laughing. A low kind of laugh that built until the old Teddy maniacal guffaw that I had grown to know and love was in full voice. I forgot about my hand and helped him up. I kissed him on the cheek just as I heard the rest room door lock turning. Too late. The door opened and in stepped a rather bemused old guy in Dickeys. He walked past us acting like two guys kissing in the venerable Women's Club bathroom was just part of a normal work day for him. Teddy slipped me a card and walked out. I figured I'd wash my hands, one of which was swollen but probably not broken, just to keep up appearances. When I returned to the reception, Teddy was nowhere to be found. My cell rang. It was Paula.

I had another funeral to attend.

CHAPTER 47

Forest Lawn Cemetery
Lexy's Funeral
Glendale, CA
Two days later

The doll casket was lowered into the ground moistened by a light morning rain, and I lost it. For the first time in months—the Bard Café bombing, Teddy's "death" and then "resurrection," my cancer diagnosis, the chemo, my death sentence and then my cancer "acquittal"—all of these life changing moments I had experienced without much or any emotion. But now it was all coming out. For the first time since the bombing, I was remembering everything in 4K HD detail. Images of the carnage at the Bard Café.

Rose had been there several times before the fateful day of the bombing. It dawned on me that there was a guy who always had sat with her. Teddy and I never paid much attention to him.

Now I'm seeing him clearly in my mind's eye as if he were seated right next to me. A stunned look on his face as he watched a steady stream of red fluid shooting from his stump where an arm had just been. Dave Baxter. That's what they said his name was on the news. Looking at the stump and the blood as if he were studying a colony of ants on a summer's day or admiring a babbling brook. Then just like that, his expression turned to one of horror. I could have sworn that he had looked at me and then he collapsed, falling in a heap like a pile of laundry before settling next to Rose Vasquez' headless torso.

I guess all this shit had to come out sometime. Lexy Perez' funeral was just as good a time as ever.

I knew she had cancer. A terminal cancer. I knew that she was only here for a short time. Paula had told me that on numerous occasions. I was not a naïve person.

Still, I never believed she would die. I mean this little angel being mourned here now told me that I was not going to die. Those beautiful brown eyes, child-like yet all-knowing told me that my cancer would go away... and it did! Why couldn't she save herself? Did she want to save herself?

Did she actually tell me in the sense of speaking to me? I had always just assumed that. Now, though, as she was being laid to rest, was she still "speaking" to me. Had she joined Father Jim in a celestial reunion? Were they together on stage with a throng of angelic Children's Hospital patients?

"Are you okay, Ben?"

Paula took me out of my trance. I guess that's what it was.

"Oh yes, yes. Sorry. Lots of stuff to process all of a sudden."

""Process"...you may have a future in therapy."

She leaned over and kissed me on the cheek. Just a peck but it unleashed a swarm of butterflies. Shit, what was a swarm of butterflies called? I knew I had read it somewhere.

A kaleidoscope. They're called a kaleidoscope, you big dummy. Even I know that.

"That's right, Lexy You are a smart little..."

"What did you say, Ben?"

Paula knew that I was talking to Lexy, of course. Probably not a good idea to inform the rest of the mourners, mostly doctors and nurses who had grown to love this precious little girl who had "crossed over." I was wondering if she'd introduced herself to Sam Jackson just about a hundred yards across the knoll. Near the Michael Jackson mausoleum. The one nobody was supposed to know about. I began thinking again about the irony of Sam Jackson being in the same vicinity, and then I saw the guy with the beard get up from his folding chair in the back and start to walk in that direction. Of course, Teddy would want to be here. Things to do even for a guy who is supposed to be dead and anonymous. But that was Teddy. Not a big one when it came to taking directions. Even if they did involve keeping his stubborn ass alive. Anyway, I silently forgave him. This was for Lexy and for Sam. Two people that had affected us both. Not to mention Paula. No need to dwell on that right now. Getting hard to get used to my new found discovery of our mutual connections.

Paula was looking over as well. Did she know that Teddy was alive?

"Beautiful service. Too bad Teddy didn't get anything like this. I mean, for some reason he was incinerated, and they put his ashes in a god damn urn and sent them off to Chicago."

Paula tightened her grip on my arm and leaned in again. Her look was calm yet not without meaning. She spoke softly.

"We both know that's bullshit, Ben. He does look good with the beard though, don't you think?"

CHAPTER 48

Larue Belmont's leg hurt like the blazes. No pain killers for him, though. Ever since that day when he was seven years old and he went flying over the sting ray handle bars of his brand new bike and landed on the roof of a parked car, breaking his arm. His father had laughed at him when he cried in the hospital. The arm had been broken in two places. Luckily, clean breaks but painful as hell. The hospital, of course, gave him pain killers. Unfortunately, they were administered just as his father walked in.

"Look at the little baby. That's no son of mine. Wimp! You're just a little wimp."

Dear old Dad was drunk, of course. Again. Escorted out of the room and the hospital as Larue cried his eyes out. Once the tears went away, he vowed that no one, not his father, or anyone would make him cry again. He had kept that promise. Not without cost though. When one puts walls up, one does not love. One cannot love. Love, as his first love, Ambrose, had told him, was all about vulnerability. Well, what did Ambrose know, anyway? He had cheated on Larue. Then he got the Sickness. Died a year later.

Enough about all that. Most of it was euphoric recall, anyway. Another wonderful idea that his father had left him. Remembering the past with a positive bias became Larue's life mantra.

Larue needed to get out of here. Time to head to Las Cruces. There were rumblings that some bad things might be happening there very soon. He needed to get to Vern and Francine before certain elements from south of the border got there first.

The truth of the matter was that Larue Belmont felt responsible for the death of Detective Sam Jackson, late of the Pasadena Police Department. Larue had grown to like Sam. He even thought he sensed a marked lessening, if you will, of Jackson's homophobia, corresponding interestingly enough with Larue's realization that he himself was a racist. Larue had been working on this character defect. The first step was awareness as that ex-drunk, Ben Rooker, had once told him. Well Larue was aware now.

The thing was, he should have been aware of how crazy the Reverend Steve Radcliffe was. He had seen all the makings of a mad man in Radcliffe from the first time he had laid eyes on him in of all places the Gold Coast Bar on Santa Monica Blvd. Radcliffe had been easy to spot on "Roleplay Night" despite the competition of a normal crowd on a West Hollywood Friday Night. Radcliffe, "The Reverend," dressed in pumps with black fishnet stockings, a black shirt and a clerical collar but that wasn't the entire ensemble. No, what made the Reverend stand out was the leash he held which was attached to a Paper Mache replica of an altar boy with posterior raised in the air. It seemed that Larue had had a few too many that night as did Radcliffe, otherwise Belmont would never have given him the time of day. The Catholic upbringing he had still making him a bit wary when it came to scandalizing the church even if the priests themselves had already done a good enough job of it.

One drink had led to another and Larue ended up in Radcliffe's bed in a tiny room in the back of his warehouse. The next morning Larue was all set to make a mad dash to the door, vowing to never drink again after waking up to the ugliest queen he had ever seen in the cold light of day when something happened. A twist of fate. In scampering around, desperately seeking a way out, he tripped over something which he could have sworn was a human being. Had he been in a god damn orgy? *Oh Jesus god no,* he prayed. Upon further investigation what had first seemed to be part of a cruel menage et trois was indeed a brilliant facsimile of a human being. He was to find out later it was the part corpse and part Da Vinci like artwork created by his grotesque one-night stand.

The plan did not begin to develop until a few days later after Belmont, through some clandestine inquiries, had discovered that Radcliffe's day job was plant manager at Huntington Hospital. This, coupled with new information from his friends in Las Cruces and Washington D. C. that a certain cartel might be planning an assassination right here in the United States, got Belmont's heretofore absent creative juices flowing. In a show of courage befitting Audie Murphy (World War

II hero and movie star of the 50s for you millennials), Larue went back to the Reverend's warehouse and professed to be genuinely interested in the man in the biblical sense. Three more sleepovers involving copious amounts of alcohol gained Radcliffe's trust to the point where Larue could share information with him without worry of compromise.

The plan was simple enough. Larue needed to have Teddy Dabrowski dead. Well, dead as far as the public and certain cartel bosses were concerned. For this he needed the Reverend Radcliffe. After several meetings with the purveyor of Cadavers Inc., the FBI Special Agent convinced the Jesus freak deluxe that he would be doing the will of God by faking Teddy's death. Of course, it helped to inform the racist Radcliffe that the target of their scam was a cartel made up of Mexicans. The final nail, as it were, was Larue's not-so-subtle insinuation that if the Reverend did not go along, his "alternative" lifestyle would be leaked to certain staff at Huntington Hospital.

Radcliffe told Belmont that the best place for a body to be dropped was off the roof above the visitors' entrance. He quelled any concern Belmont had about having a "Teddy" cadaver dropped on somebody's unsuspecting Aunt Harriet or Grandma Lois on their way in to visit their dear nephew or grandson.

"I'll drop 'em before morning visiting hours. I got a good view from the roof. There won't be any accidents."

"You're sure?"

"Course I'm sure. We're doin' God's will now, ain't we? Jesus will be watching."

"Yes, well I'll be watching as well, and if there are any accidents, as you say, you will be joining your cadaver collection post haste my dear Jimmy Swaggart wannabee."

"Damn, damn, damn! I told you not to compare me to that evil man. I do not have the temptation of the flesh. I lash myself every night and I..."

"Okay, okay, enough! I do not want to hear what you do to that poor pecker of yours. I didn't piss right for days after hearing the last story. Just no mistakes. That's all I ask."

It all went down on that morning Teddy was to be released from Huntington Hospital. Larue was not counting on Ben being there. They let Teddy know about it the day before when Larue and Sam Jackson visited him, ostensibly to question him about the Bard Café bombing. In reality, this meeting consisted of, aside from briefing Teddy on his escape, a dissecting of everything Teddy remembered about Rose Vasquez. Teddy was not as cooperative as one would guess.

"You're going to sneak me out of here in a maintenance cart while that Jim Jones fucker throws a body?"

"A cadaver," Belmont interjected.

"A cadaver that looks just like me off the roof of the hospital?"

"That would be the plan, yes."

Teddy had glared at Jackson.

"And you, Detective, are all in on this?"

"Well, I guess..."

"Completely. This is a joint federal and police operation."

Jackson had shaken his head like a man who really hadn't any choice.

Teddy's mouth was agape.

"What the fuck in the world of *Car 54 Where Are You?* is going on? This is no such fucking thing. I bet you this is nothing but a joint Belmont-Jackson operation. Where's my cell? I need to call somebody before you clowns get all of us killed!"

Jackson had looked at Belmont with a "what the fuck are we doing" look and had started to leave.

"Look, Belmont knows what he's doing. I mean, I wouldn't risk my career on this if I didn't think so. There is some bad shit going on with Roy Vasquez, I mean I'm the last person to be mourning rich white folks, but bombing a fucking coffee shop in Pasadena is not cool. I mean what's next?! Torching a Roscoe's Chicken and Waffles in Compton? That was a joke. Anyway, this shit needs to stop now. It's the only way to lure Vasquez here so he can be killed or captured. Think of all the lives you'll be saving, including your buddy Ben. He doesn't know anything about this. He'll be much safer if it continues that way. I'll just keep him close by acting like I'm interrogating him. He might even know some things that you might have overlooked. Okay, I'm out, I'll catch you tomorrow at that War Memorial place in South Pasadena."

Jackson got to the door and turned to Belmont.

"Special Agent, now that I'm putting my ass on the line, you best keep me informed of everything. Are we clear?"

Jackson waited for Belmont's nod and left.

So then it had been just Belmont and Teddy in the room. The only sound was the muffled voices coming from the nurse's station down the hall. Teddy broke the silence.

"So, Mr. Special Agent Larue Belmont of the FBI and phony Cajun, you could at least buy me dinner before you screw me."

Larue looked to the door and leaned over before giving Teddy a kiss on the cheek.

"You always had a way of calming me down, you son of a bitch. Now, what's the real reason for this shitshow you are proposing?"

CHAPTER 49

Paula's Condo
Glendale, CA
August 2019

It was Wednesday evening and right on schedule, at precisely 10:45 PM, Paula Garcia had opened her Mac Book Air. It would be 11:45 PM in Mazatlán now. She searched Safari for a few minutes just in case there was any monitoring going on, though she knew this was most improbable. The cartel had grown along with Silicon Valley. Even though Roy Vasquez in his drug deluded state had not, his daughter Alvina was an expert. Ironically, Alvina was the one who had instructed Paula in the intricacies of the so called "Dark Web." It was how Paula was able to coordinate the procurement of the infant so many years ago. Everything had gone without a hitch until that priest, O'Brian, had interfered. He had threatened to expose the whole plan. Well, of course, he had been taken care of. Just a few calls to the right people. The clergy pedophile reputation was just as prevalent eight years ago as it was now. The good Father had fallen right into the trap with the little boy, "Joey." The parents were drug addicts, easy to blackmail. More than willing to make the right statements on the record. Everything had been going smoothly. The Teddy Dabrowski situation would have to be dealt with. The amateur staging of his death had not fooled Paula. In any case, Teddy had told her himself. She knew everything and had dutifully passed it on to Alvina who would deal with Teddy soon. Very soon. Meanwhile, the cocaine riddled husk of what was once the calculating head of the Venganza Cartel was making his way to Los Angeles.

Paula was using "Tor" to access the "Dark Web" as it was called. It was the way she had kept in communication with Alvina over the last several years. Paula's handle "Topo Gigio." A name her widowed mother had given her as a child in Mexico. *Topo Gigio* had been a popular children's cartoon from Italy shown on TV in most Latin America countries as well as on the old *Ed Sullivan Show* in the United States which her grandmother had watched as a child.

Paula's brother, Jorge, had died in a hunting "accident" when she was very young. Her mother had smuggled her out of the country fearing for her life. Little Paula had been hidden in the back of a banana truck and shepherded to the United States. Adopted by her cousins, the Garcia's, she had relinquished the surname of Valdez.

Of course the "accident" was nothing like that. Paula had learned the details of her brother's death while watching an expose of Roy Vasquez on *60 Minutes* at a college bar.

Paula had been a good girl, raised by a wonderful surrogate family in National City, a suburb of San Diego. She achieved top grades in science throughout her elementary and high school education, eventually becoming a registered nurse and then named head of the Literally Healing program here at Children's Hospital, Los Angeles. Biding her time. No men for her. No time for relationships. Retribution was her primary purpose. Revenge for the loss of her family. Nothing less than the killing of Roy Vasquez and anyone who tried to stop her was her goal. She would do anything to achieve it. Even to the point of manipulating someone who cared for her. She genuinely liked Ben Rooker, maybe even felt more. In a different world, a world that did not include the massacre of her brother a world that did call for, indeed insist on, her making things right, well, maybe... No reason to obsess on this. "It is what it is" borrowing a phrase from that loco gringo, Trump. Anyway, Ben seemed to like that "Choco." Reason enough to play with his emotions. Anything that would rationalize her conduct, if the truth be told. The end indeed justifying the means.

Teddy Dabrowski was a different story. Teddy had gotten close to Lexy. Much closer than what was called for in Paula's plan. The relationship had transcended that of a volunteer and a client. (The term Paula insisted on instead of "Patient.") No, Teddy and Lexy had a spiritual connection. Teddy "saw" what Lexy saw. Paula tried to downplay this in her interactions with Teddy, but she knew in her heart that it was true.

It was Paula that had first noticed the fact that Lexy was not like the other children. She had a connection to a power, there was no doubt about that. The only question that Paula had was whether this power was of good or evil. One could not be sure. When Paula gazed upon this beautiful, angelic child she had to fight the horrific images that would try to take over her entire being. The memory of the terrible story Alvina had recounted to her. A terrified Alvina, maybe 27 years old, being wrestled to the floor of her bedroom in the house in Mazatlán. Moments earlier she had been laughing with her father and then she had taken a drink. An innocent sip of diet coke. Her father had been drinking heavily again. Alvina wanted to be in control. Thus, the seemingly innocent soda. She would only learn later that Roy had spiked her drink. A "date rape" drug. This one called GHB. She had temporarily blacked out, waking to smell her own father's putrid breath, panting as his enlarged member entered her. He had no idea who she was. It didn't matter. He was a monster, and she was his prey. Nothing she could do except close her eyes and hum the lullaby, the *canciones de cuna* her mother had sung to her years before. Duermete mi nino, duermete mi amor... Alvina awoke in her own room. Naked and alone. She saw her father that night for dinner. He remembered nothing. Alvina did though. She most definitely did. She would never forget. This had not been the first time he had violated her but it would be the last.

A baby was born. At first, Alvina did not want it. She told herself she could never love this child. She tried to have an abortion, but Roy would have none of it. He never knew the baby was his, in any case. To him, his daughter was a slut just like her mother. The baby should not be punished for the sins of the mother. And so Alvina had the baby and grew to love it. She had bided her time. As soon as she was healthy enough and the baby could travel, she devised a plan to take the child to an orphanage and then escape herself to the United States. The baby had been wrapped in newspaper and placed at the orphanage's entrance. When the nun's unwrapped her a large advertisement for the rock band *Dexy's Midnight Runners* was prominently displayed. The nun, Sister Teresa, misread the "D" as an "L" and thus the little girl who was christened "Alexandria" would forever be called *Lexy*.

Paula used Father Jim and his State Department connections to get Lexy to Children's Hospital. The poor clergyman had no idea that her motive was more retribution than kindness. Soon enough though, he began to suspect.

"I thought we brought this beautiful child here to give her a chance. A chance to live a normal life and be raised by a loving family. You forget that I have contacts. People who know things. I know about you. I know that 'Garcia' is not your real name. It's 'Valdez' isn't it? Roy Vasquez killed your family. You are the only survivor because you were spirited out of the country by your dear mother."

"Be careful, Father. Of course your story is, how do they say 'ludicrous'? I want nothing but the best for Lexy, I..."

"She was born Alexandria Vasquez. She was Alvina Vasquez daughter. Roy Vasquez, the boss of one of the biggest cartels in Mexico and your family's murderer is her grandfather."

"Grandfather! You know nothing you stupid old fool."

"It is true. As I said, I have my sources. You forgot it was me that got Lexy here."

"What do you want?"

"You need to stay away from that child. She is an innocent. I don't know what you have in mind, but it is evil. You want to use her, and I will not allow it."

Silence. Paula was clenching her fist so hard that the blood threatened to come right out of her pores. She remembered her mother's lullaby.

Duermete mi nino, duermete mi amor.

It's what she always revisited in her mind in times of confusion and stress. She had taken a breath and turned to Father Jim.

"I've been thinking, to be honest with you. This job is becoming too stressful for me. Perhaps it is time that I move on. Go back to Mexico."

"Yes, it would be best. I will keep you in my prayers."

"Thank you, father."

Paula smiled at the priest as he shut the door behind him.

She took out her iPhone and dialed. Under her breath she cursed the priest as the phone buzzed and then stopped.

"Hi, Margaret? Yes, this is Paula Garcia at Children's Hospital. How is little Joey doing today?"

CHAPTER 50

The morning of Lexy's funeral
Hi, Ben. It's me.

A voice from the coffin. The Stephen King story came to mind about the guy who buries his dead friend with his cell phone and starts to get calls from the phone. This was different though. No iPhone buried with Teddy's body. He had been cremated for fuck's sake. No. Teddy was alive. Somehow, he was walking around. He had survived that fall or... Christ no. Nobody could have walked away from that. I had been there myself. Saw the mutilated body. Saw Teddy's tattoo. Okay, it was only a glimpse but Christ, you know a guy for years, well, you know when you see his dead body that it's him. God damn it that was Teddy! I knew it because I had met him just a few days ago at Sam Jackson's memorial and then seen him again in the distance at Lexy's funeral. A beard and a little worse for wear but that was Teddy. His slight limp a testament to my kick to his balls earlier.

I had been getting ready for Lexy Perez' funeral when I noticed my voice mail. "Unknown caller." I blew it off for a while thinking it was probably one of those telemarketing calls from China. The ones that start off with, "Hello Mr. Rooker, we'd like to talk to you about your Medicare Plus card..."

The thing that pissed me off wasn't so much the telemarketing aspect. No, people got to make a buck. Even the CHICOMS, as Teddy would say. What really pissed me off was the fact that these fuckers thought I was eligible for Medicare. I was 49 for the love of God! Then I thought maybe it was that senior living spot I did a few years back. The one where I played the "Young Grandpa." Yea, that had to be it.

So, I checked the voice mail.

"Hi Ben, it's me. You know. The little polish bastard. Don't really want to say too much else. I know that you're about to hang up but just listen. Not much time. Meet me at that place in South Pasadena where you took me to that one meeting about a year ago. You know the place. Lots of memories. I know you're going to Lexy's funeral this morning. I'll meet you this afternoon at 4 PM. Go to the back entrance. Later."

So, there I was at the back entrance of the War Memorial Building in South Pasadena at five minutes before 4:00. I had stayed to speak with some of Lexy's doctors and nurses after the funeral. I also wanted to figure out what was going on with Paula, but when I brought up her not so cryptic Teddy comment, she just laughed it off and changed the subject. She even asked me if I wanted to join the Literally Healing program. Of course there was no chance of that. Not without Lexy. I still had some feelings for Paula. The problem was that it was becoming increasingly apparent that I did not know who the hell this Paula was.

Jesus, Ben, don't you know when I'm having some fun with you ? Paula's response to my look of surprise at her earlier comment about Teddy's status sticking in my brain like the residue of an overcooked fried egg on a cheap Teflon fryer. Paula was many things, but she was not a very good actress. She believed Teddy was alive.

As I had looked through the War Memorial windows, a wealth of memories had flooded back. Were those tears in my eyes? I had gone to my first A.A. meeting here. Art Horner, a guy about as different from me as could be. I mean if God or whoever is running the show had decided to create two human beings totally different, that would be me and my late sponsor, Art. Dead of cancer, almost two years now. A good man. A simple man. Devoid of ego and most importantly, the man listened. Really listened. Not the kind of listening that most of us do. You know, just waiting for the other guy to finish. No, Art really cared about what was going on with me. I had suddenly missed him.

Then I saw it. Something was moving in the shadows. Near the old piano player. No, probably just a trick of the imagination. A lot of stress lately. Residual "chemo brain" as well. One never is completely cured from cancer. The after effects of memory loss and cognitive regression, commonly called "chemo brain" stayed for a while, in some cases forever.

Then I had seen it again. A figure. Walking straight at me. Closer and closer to the glass now. Something else. Movement on the figure. Jabbing at him (If it was a "Him"). The figure diving forward. A human being with an animal attached to its face. Closer and closer to the window. Then a crash. Through the glass came the human with a cat screaming as it dislodged its claws from his face, Teddy's face, and scampered away into the woods.

"Jesus fucking Christ. I thought cats liked milk!?"

Teddy's beard was full of spittle and blood and some white specks which I assumed was milk.

I took a long look at Teddy to make sure his injuries were not life threatening.

"Are you okay?"

"Yea, yea."

"You're sure?"

"Yes, god dammit. Did you see where Claudius went?"

He was up in an instant. Walking up and down the outside area of the War Memorial. Searching for something in the woods.

"Did you actually name that feline from hell?! Jesus, Teddy, you might have rabies."

Giving up his search at least for now, he motions me into the auditorium via the shards of broken glass.

"There's no alarm system here?"

"Quiet! Don't tell anybody. There's one in the front but as far as the back here, well the system has been broken for years. You should know that, Ben, with all the meetings you've..."

"Okay, fuck this. I need some answers from you."

"No worries. Just follow me down to the basement. I'll call someone who can get the glass fixed without the South Pasadena police getting involved."

"Don't tell me. It wouldn't be a certain gay FBI Special Agent?"

"You catch on fast. Oh shit, of course, the dearly departed Detective Sam Jackson couldn't keep a secret. God bless him. I should have known."

We were heading to the back of the auditorium and down a partially hidden staircase. Teddy found a light switch as we headed towards a small conference room with a few chairs and a long cafeteria style table. There was a white board at one end of the table that had been well used but recently erased.

Teddy caught my eye as I perused the board.

"The command center. I guess you've figured that out. This was my home away from home while I was 'dearly departed' as it were."

"You don't give some answers pretty soon you will be 'really departed.'"

"I see what you did there. Nice."

Teddy went over to a Mr. Coffee with coffee cups that looked like they were used by General Patton himself and poured me a coffee.

"Ben, I know you like it 'light and sweet,' but everyone that was down here including me, well, 'Once you go black, you'll never go back.' Anyway, here you go."

He handed me the coffee and sat directly across from me. My body still ached from the debacle in the Women's Club toilet, but sitting in a folding metal chair somehow helped.

"I'm listening."

Teddy took a drink of his coffee. More like a gulp. Like he's drinking a Jack Daniels. He looks me straight in the eye.

"I'm going to tell you a story but before I do, you need to know one thing. Probably the most important thing you'll hear today. Fuck, lifesaving maybe."

"Can we dispense with the dramatics and get to the point, Ted..."

"Paula Garcia wants us both dead."

The memory of my aching hand faded into oblivion as Teddy told me a story.

CHAPTER 51

August 2019
Las Cruces, New Mexico

The ride was uneventful after the MS-13 ambush. Roy couldn't put it out of his mind, though.

How the hell could those clowns be so, what is the word, "Amateurish"?

Everything about the thing was wrong. They had no backup. The would be assassins had Roy and Antonio get out of the car when they could easily have used the element of surprise to take them out right then and there. The other thing that bothered Roy was that Antonio didn't seem to be upset. Sure he was concerned, but he was the fucking bodyguard and he drove right into a trap that they got out of only through the sheer incompetence of their attackers and blind luck. Of course, there was the flamethrower. They would have most assuredly been dead without Antonio's foresight in procuring the weapon. But why a flamethrower? Antonio had set this drop up. It was supposed to be safe and easy. A cartel armory, fully guarded by cartel people. Well, as it turned out, Antonio had hired *Americanos*. He said they were ex-military. Problem was there was no sign of any *Yanquis* at the site. Again, Antonio didn't seem that concerned about it.

"Boss, I don't know. I will talk to my contact in Barstow. Maybe there was a miscommunication."

Roy was "jonesing" now. He needed cocaine. He thought he could do this mission cold turkey. Antonio had warned him about it. He was sweating profusely. Maybe even hallucinating. A few miles back they came up on an exit sign. Just a normal sign but as they got closer it turned neon. Like one of those signs Roy remembered as a kid. Yes, now this one was bright red and yellow, and just as they came up on it this thing, a clown, lunged off the sign and spewed a stream of yellow bile at the Range Rover. Roy let out a scream that damn near caused Antonio to lose control and go over the embankment. Instead, he corrected and skidded to a stop on the shoulder,

"What the fuck, boss! Are you trying to kill us? I almost..."

Roy was bent over but his head came up with the force of an enraged bull. The top of his skull meeting the bridge of Antonio's causing blood to spray all over the god damn front seat, reminiscent of the recent "clown event." Antonio was screaming, holding his battered nose.

"If I wanted to kill you, you would be dead and in the ground right now. If you ever disrespect me again, I will stick a knife inside your nostrils and rip that fucker off and then I'll feed it to the pigs as an appetizer before I cut you up for their main course."

Roy had opened up the side compartment and taken out a first aid kit. He had tossed it onto Antonio's lap.

"Stop the god damn bleeding. This fucking car is looking like the inside of a slaughter house. I'm going out to have a smoke and think about what the fuck I'm going to do with you. When I return, I want this front seat looking like I can eat off it and I want you to say nothing but 'Yes, Boss' and 'No, Boss' for the rest of this shit trip."

Roy had stood on the shoulder watching the cars go by. Thinking. Wondering why the hell he was risking everything by coming to the U.S. He knew that Antonio would not be going back with him. He sent a few texts which guaranteed that his bodyguard would never return to Mexico. The man cleaning the Range Rover was already a dead man.

The withdrawal was what was on Roy's mind. He needed to keep it together till business was taken care of in Las Cruces. He took some deep breaths and went back to the car.

Vamanos.

"Yes, Boss."

About an hour more and they would be at the house. All preparations had been made. The one thing that as far as Roy could see, Antonio had done right. So far so good.

Roy felt for the pills in his pocket. It reassured him that they were there. The Modafinil for the withdrawal and the drowsiness and fatigue. The Topiramate would keep him from convulsing and help him be less agitated. God damn he was fucking agitated. Both drugs procured by Antonio. The thought shot through Roy's mind like a hummingbird just before the rains. Maybe he should keep Antonio on this earth for a while? Then, just as quickly the notion was discarded. He had almost gotten them both killed, and besides, the order had gone out. No turning back. Antonio would be dead before they left Las Cruces. Roy would find another bodyguard.

"How much farther before the exit?"

Antonio silent. His hands trembling on the wheel ever so slightly. Roy thinking that he still needed this man at least for a little while longer. A change of tact was in order.

"My friend, please, relax. Forget what I said back there. This fucking cocaine withdrawal is really screwing with me. Please accept my apology. You know you are my right-hand man. My brother! We go back. Ever since the sad death of your papa. Come now. It's you and me. We finish the mission, go back to Mexico and I will see that you get what you have deserved. Now, are you okay?"

Antonio had the look of a man who had just been hung with a bad rope. He almost started to cry but Roy put his hand on his shoulder and nodded gently.

"Yes, Boss. Thank you. We will be at the exit in no more than ten minutes. Everything is in place. I will do you proud, El Hefe!"

"Oh yes, I know you will. I have no doubts. No doubts at all."

Roy felt the vibration of his iPhone. He knew without looking that it was the confirmation of Antonio's death sentence. He took the packet of pills out, grabbed a bottled water from the holder, took the pills and gulped them down. A few minutes later they had turned onto the exit on their way to Vern and Francine Lattimore's adobe suburban abode.

It's going to be a good day, thought the cartel boss.

CHAPTER 52

Starbucks
Pasadena
August 2019

"Ben, you look nervous. Are you okay?

Teddy had told me to be very careful in my dealings with Paula after our meeting at the War Memorial. Of course, leaving me with "Paula wants us both dead" followed by a story both fantastic and at the same time oddly believable was probably not the way to keep me away from Paula. I had certain feelings for her, as I sensed Teddy did as well. In some crazy way I even thought that this was a ploy for Teddy to keep Paula to himself. I knew better, though.

"I'm okay, fine. Maybe it's residual effects of the chemo. Lots has been happening. Sam Jackson gone, Lexy and Teddy, of course."

"Of Christ, Ben, please stop. Teddy is alive. We both know that."

Before I could object, she made me an offer that we both knew I couldn't refuse.

"Hey, I'm sorry but I need to go back to my place. I've got the graveyard shift tonight and I forgot some paperwork I've been working on. Would you mind driving over there with me? Keep me company and we can talk a little more about our very much alive, mutual friend."

The touch of her hand on mine and the kiss on the cheek sealed the deal and 20 minutes later I was sitting in the living room of her condo in Glendale.

I heard the refrigerator door open.

"I have orange juice or Pepsi."

"Orange juice is great. I've been dehydrated lately. I guess it's from the chemo."

A minute later she handed me a glass of orange juice and ice.

"Yes, the chemo will definitely cause a thirst. I hope you don't mind the ice."

She walked away not waiting for my answer. I took a sip just to make sure there was no booze in there. Old habit. There was none. I gulped it down. Damn, I was thirsty.

"I'll just be a minute. I want to freshen up, get the papers and we'll go. I really appreciate this."

Another peck on the cheek. The bathroom door was halfway open as the shower started.

"Turn on the TV if you want to watch something."

I had no interest in TV. The truth be told my mind was more on the bathroom than on Fox News. On cue the shower stopped. I heard the patter of her feet as they touched the floor. The smell of perfume to my right grabbed my attention but before I could turn, Paula wearing nothing but a Victoria's Secret silk robe was seated on the couch next to me. Any chance of a romantic interlude however was dashed by the pink handled .45 now being pointed at my chest.

"I do like you, Ben. That part wasn't fake. I just love Alvina and Lexy more, oh so much more. I need you, Ben. I need to get to Teddy."

"Hey, hey, look do you know how to use that thing? Be careful, for the love of God. Teddy's dead and..."

Her manner which was decidedly calm just a few seconds earlier had turned to rage and as if to confirm this, the gun was now pointing at my groin (see 'Balls').

"Ben, cut the fucking bullshit now. I need to talk to Teddy. Just talk."

Her words said "Talk" but her look said "Kill."

I took a deep breath, thought about a life without testicles for a nanosecond and then ventured forth.

"What do you want from me?"

"Dear Ben, please cut the bullshit. Now you and I are going to call Teddy and tell him to..."

As she said this, she stroked my bald dome which caused her to have what you might call a "wardrobe malfunction." Her left boob peeked out of her robe. We noticed it simultaneously. Paula reflexively moved her hand to adjust her robe thereby turning the gun away from me ever so slightly. I pounced. I knocked the gun from her hand just as she head butted me right on the bridge of my nose. There was no blood this time. I was actually happy about this fact but only for a moment.

In place of the crimson tide was a galaxy of stars floating in front of my eyes followed by intense pain.

Paula dived for the gun and lost her robe completely for her trouble. At that moment I actually turned away to respect her modesty, albeit only for a moment but that was all the time my luscious, loco Latina needed to gather up the.45 with one hand and regain her propriety with the other.

"Such a gentleman! Oh, my dear Ben, in another time, another universe maybe... Tell him you want to meet him wherever he is hiding. I know there must be a safehouse of some sort. That *maricon* FBI agent wasn't here just for the West Hollywood bars. Yes, I know all about him."

"What are you going to do when you meet Teddy?"

"Talk, Ben. Just talk."

The pouty lips. The almond eyes. The perfume. I almost forgot that the .45 was once again pointed at "Mr. Happy" and that to tell her where Teddy was might mean his death sentence.

I picked up the phone and dialed Teddy's number. After a moment...

"Hey, Ben here. Yea, listen I can't take you to the meeting tonight but I'd like to come over. Yea, I can be there in about a half hour. Okay. Later."

I hung up.

"Where are you going to meet him, Ben? No games now."

Suddenly I felt kind of weak. Probably the chemo effect. Drowsy. No qualms about telling her. Strange.

"We're going to the War Memorial in South Pasadena. Teddy's in the basement."

The thought (too late) of how wrong it was to give this information to Paula, a woman with a gun who wants to kill my friend envelopes me as I collapse onto the plush carpet.

CHAPTER 53

Las Cruces, New Mexico
Francine and Vern Lattimore Residence
August 2019

It was a beautiful summer evening in Las Cruces. Unseasonably cool. Francine and Vern were having dinner. Vern was treating them to his classic culinary delight, "Armadillo Surprise." In all their years of marriage, Francine was yet to discover what the "surprise" was. She had stopped searching in any case. It was absolutely heavenly. She knew that Vern used brown mustard and corn starch, rosemary and thyme, of course, but there was something else. The mystery ingredient that made it "pop" as she had heard someone on the The Food Channel say a few years back.

"You've done it again, dear heart."

Francine reached across the table to touch Vern's hand. The memories of their first meeting came dancing through her mind. No particular reason. This was not unusual. Vern and Francine's love was more whore house than Harlequin but still no less a love of a life filled with hard knocks.

It seemed like yesterday sometimes but Francine knew better. A seedy movie house in Times Square, NY. A peep show/porn house to be clear. Her mind now wandering. A bit of euphoric recall.

Francine Hogan had stumbled in. A day of drinking alone at an Irish bar on 34th Street. She had taken the train in from Long Island. Seventeen years old. Not a beauty by any means but a nice bod, as the sailors would say. Francine had known a lot of sailors since she ran away from her suburban home in Hicksville, Long Island. Yes, "Hicksville," a real name of a real town. Gerry Cooney, the last great white hope was from there. Francine dated him. Well, if you call a date a few drinks at Fitz's Place followed by a blow job in the alley a date, well, there you have it.

The truth be told, Francine was one of those girls who was easy to judge. Just call her a whore and be done with it. Made it easier to gloss over the incest, rape, and beatings she incurred in her split level suburban house in Hicksville. Much easier.

Francine met Theresa Palestrena at the Woolworths a few blocks from Penn Station when she was 15. Teri was 19 and working as a cashier there. She spotted Francine stealing some nylons and toilet paper. It was July, and she had a natty old winter coat on and was stuffing the contraband in the big pockets with the skill of a modern day artful dodger. Unfortunately, this was not 19th century London and there were cameras and a security guard who was just coming back from lunch. Teri could do one of two things. She could let this young waif get caught or she could save her.

Teri was a champion of the underdog. Sick babies, puppies, old people, any of these and more. If one went into Teri's room at the place she rented on Amsterdam Ave you would be greeted by "Billy" a two legged turtle, two goldfish named "Sam" and "Esther" with no obvious handicaps, her cat "Princess," seventeen years old and blind in one eye and "Liz," a chameleon that did not change color. She was a believer in the dignity of all of God's creatures. Here was one right in front of her to be added to her menagerie.

"Lenny, you're back already. Just in time. Can you check the sign in the front? It looks like one of the bulbs might be out?"

Lenny, the sixty something security guard was mentally recounting how much he just lost at the OTB on a nag that was probably still running at Belmont named Charmed Life, a misnomer if there ever was one, sighed and headed back outside. As a result, he missed the low-level felony taking place right in front of him. Probably a good thing as the last thing Lenny needed was more paper work. For the love of Christ, he was making four dollars an hour.

Teri watched him leave and then turned her attention back to the would-be shoplifter.

"Miss, can I help you? I can get you a bag for those items so it will be easier to carry after you pay for them."

Francine started to run but Teri had effectively blocked her way. For a moment they were staring awkwardly at each other. Teri broke the silence.

"Why don't we go in the back for a minute. There's some really nice bargains back there."

She had her by the arm now.

"Hey, Teri, all the bulbs are good."

The rent-a-cop had returned way ahead of schedule.

"Okay, thanks, Lenny. Must have been the way the sun was hitting the sign this morning. Hey, would you mind watching the front? I got to take this young lady in the back for an interview."

"Yea, yea, sure thing."

"Sit. Now!"

"You can't tell me..."

"Okay, you want me to have Lenny hold you here while I call the cops. You got like a half a dozen rolls of toilet paper and the same amount of nylons in the pockets of that rat infested overcoat you're wearing in the middle of July."

"I have a cold. Anyway, I was going to pay for this."

"Yes, and I'm Mayor Lindsay. Let's cut to the chase. You're what, fifteen? Sixteen? Where do you live? Why do you need to steal? Where are your parents?"

Francine, overwhelmed, stared at her. A deer in the headlights. Then the tears had started accompanied by her short life story.

In between the blowing of her nose and stopping to catch her breath, Francine told her new savior Teri about life in the Hogan family.

Her father was at first, a genial, loving man. Then shortly after Francine's thirteenth birthday things changed. Visits to her bed in the wee hours of the morning. Francine waking to her father touching himself while staring at her. Pleas to her mother met with the strap. A mother who herself had been a victim of abuse but dealing with it with the only weapon she had—denial.

Finally, she signaled she was done by blowing her nose again and placing her head in her hands.

Francine ended up staying with Teri. She slept on a cot in her room until she could get a job of her own then ended up working at Woolworth's for a year. Then one day Teri's boyfriend asked her to come to New Mexico with him. He had just gotten a job at New Mexico State University in the Geology Department. Francine, having nothing better to do, followed her out there.

Teri didn't see Francine as a slut or a whore even though she hung out at a dive bar in Las Cruces called the No Way Out and would go home with a different guy every night. She just saw her friend's promiscuity as collateral damage from her lecherous father. In any case it all worked out for Francine the day Vern Lattimore walked into the No Way Out and sat in the stool right next to her.

"So, you know where I can get lucky tonight?"

"You talking to me?"

"Listen, Ms. Bickel, I meant no offense. A good steak. You know where I can get a good steak?"

The *Taxi Driver* reference had been completely lost on Francine, but she liked his eyes. He was a few years older than her. Later she told Teri that he was just so "damned sure of himself."

Francine and Vern had dinner that night. A guy at the next table kept looking over at Francine. She felt awkward at first but then realized Vern was getting into it. The strangest thing. Francine followed the guy into the rest room. Vern followed shortly thereafter. Francine gave the guy a hand job while Vern listened in the next stall. They left their half-eaten steak and sped straight to Vern's place where Francine had "the best god damn sex of my life."

Francine and Vern got married a month later. They never looked back.

"Are you okay, Francine?"

Vern was shaking her hand just enough to bring her back to reality. A nice trip down memory lane, though.

"Yes, baby. Just thinking some nice thoughts. Getting a little wet."

"I love you, butter titties"

"I love you, dear heart."

A noise. Could have been the neighbor kids. Then there it was again. The front door. Turning. Opening. Vern reached for his Glock as Cujo began to growl.

CHAPTER 54

War Memorial
South Pasadena
August 2019

Paula knew that Ben would be out for a few more hours. Working at a hospital had its benefits. She was able to slip the chloral hydrate into her purse and sneak it out of the hospital without any problem. Just a few drops in Ben's drink doing the trick.

Parked now in front of the Starbucks directly across from the War Memorial. Twilight. Paula had thought about parking on the street but the cops were such Nazis as far as parking tickets were concerned. If you didn't have your wheel turned away from the curb at exactly the right angle, you were going to get a ticket. Paula thought that god damn South Pasadena must really be short on money, or the cops were just assholes. She was leaning towards the latter when she saw the guy with the beard appear from around the corner of the War Memorial. He was looking around like he was waiting for someone. Only for a moment though. Just as quickly as he had appeared, he disappeared. Paula cursed under her breath. Why the hell didn't she get more details from Ben. Was there a password?

No matter. She would figure it out. She sensed that this operation was something engineered by the FBI agent, the dear departed Detective Jackson and Teddy himself on their own. There would not be any official police or FBI honchos to worry about.

Paula got out of her car and made her way to the traffic light crossing at Fair Oaks Blvd. The exit ramp for the 110 freeway was a few feet away so it was very busy. A light could be a long wait if you caught it wrong. She had. She checked the .45 in her pocket as she waited for the WALK sign. Teddy had told her once that it didn't matter whether you pushed the button for a WALK sign or not. It would flash at a pre-ordained time no matter what you did or didn't do. Teddy said the pushing of a button was all psychological. An innate need that human beings had to control a result, whether it be a WALK sign or the firing of a gun that propelled a bullet into human flesh. Something that Paula had been contemplating as she fondled the pink handled .45 safely ensconced in her blazer pocket.

WALK.

The white sign took her back to the moment at hand as she made her way across Fair Oaks.

Teddy had seen Paula the moment she had walked out in front of the War Memorial. He had seen her car to be more to the point. Ben's reference to "a meeting tonight" had been the tipoff. They never went to a meeting on Wednesdays. This was the night off. A time to read. Take a break from A.A. meetings. Ben had told Teddy that almost three years ago when he first started talking to him about how he got sober and the A.A. meetings. There was something going on and seeing Paula's car in the sparsely inhabited strip mall parking lot had put him on alert. Now as he watched through the basement window and saw Paula approaching on foot, her hand intermittently checking something in her jacket pocket, his fears were confirmed.

Teddy opened the piano chair and took out the Mossberg 500 Shotgun. It was actually one of Sam Jackson's personal weapons. He had left it for Teddy.

Damn reliable weapon, my friend. Just aim it at the ground if need be. If you're dealing with one perp then aim for center mass. Either way, damn effective.

Teddy pushed the safety forward and opened the action checking that it was unloaded. He then placed a round in the chamber and two more in the magazine after which he released the safety. He didn't want to hurt Paula but judging from what Ben has said and seeing her demeanor as she walked towards the War Memorial, unannounced, well, let's just say that Teddy didn't want to die either.

The light indicating that someone had entered the upstairs auditorium began to flash. A recent jerry rig that had been installed by Teddy on the advice of an ex-cop working part time at the Home Depot, the place where Teddy got the window replacements after the collateral damage from the incident with Claudius the cat.

Teddy heard footsteps from above going across the auditorium floor. They stopped and then started again. Closer.

"Teddy, my dear, it's Paula. I know you're alive. I know you're here. I'm so happy. Let me see you. I want to give you a big hug. We have so much to talk about."

Teddy cocked the shotgun and headed for the stairs.

CHAPTER 55

Las Cruces New Mexico
Francine and Vern Lattimore Residence
August 2019

Antonio had no problem finding the house. The Waze GPS had done the trick. He parked a block away. The house was at the end of a cul-de-sac. Roy checked his Glock and put it in his windbreaker. Antonio did the same with his weapon.

They arrived at the front door and heard the sound of laughing. Roy knew that they had a dog, a very large one. Alvina had told him his name, "Cujo." He was anxious to meet him. He checked his pockets for the treats. A sigh of relief as he felt the bag. Antonio started to press the ringer but Roy stopped him. He knew from extensive reading and also from drunken conversations with his daughter that these yanquis in these parts had a sense of security, in many cases, false. He tried the door knob. It turned without resistance but made an ever so slight noise which was met with a low level yet vicious growl. Antonio went for his gun. Roy gave him a look which at once stopped him cold and reminded him of his boss's intense love for animals. He took his hand away from the gun and slowly opened the door. Roy pushed it the rest of the way and walked in.

A blur to Antonio's right and then he was on his back. A 200 hundred pound English mastiff pinned him to the ground. A long string of saliva hung precariously from the animal's mouth. It swung for a moment and then dropped down Antonio's throat cutting off what was to be a scream.

"Now, now, it's okay, Cujo. We love you. Here's a nice treat. I heard you love these. Yes, dried salami bits. Your favorite. Isn't it, Vern?"

Vern and Francine had entered the front parlor. Vern had his weapon pointed directly at Roy's head. Francine was standing next to Antonio who was power puking vigorously as Cujo stood over him with a bemused look.

"I heard you were an animal lover, Senor Vasquez. Never believed it though. Takes all kinds, I guess."

A look towards Cujo who was now eating the last of the dried salami off Antonio's shirt.

"It's okay, boy. Follow Mama out back. You can chase the birds. C'mon now."

The beast forgot about what happened just a few moments ago and playfully followed Francine through the kitchen and out the back door.

"Beautiful animal. A certain spirituality about him. Please excuse my associate, Antonio. He will clean up the mess he has made."

Vern a bit miffed at all of this, "You couldn't have rung the god damn bell?!"

Francine had returned having transported Cujo to a respite with the birds and squirrels.

"My dear Mrs...."

"What the fuck are doing here, Senor Vasquez? You got a tire hidden someplace to put over our heads? Well, that ain't happening tonight. You took one gamble too many coming here to the greatest country in the world. We are go..."

Antonio bent over to vomit and "boom" the report of his Glock crashed through the air. The sound of Cujo colliding with the back door as he tried to come to the aid of his master and mistress dampened Vern's screams as he grabbed his leg, now streaming blood. Before Francine could react, Roy pulled his gun and motioned for her to sit as Vern fell to the ground in pain and shock. Antonio was cured of any previous nausea and bolted to his feet, dragging Vern to the living room couch. He disappeared to the back of the house before returning with a first aid kit. Roy headed to the back door and could be heard speaking to Cujo outside in a calming voice. Roy returned as Antonio took a knife out and cut Vern's trousers. He applied a pressure tourniquet to his wound. He nodded to Roy. The cartel boss sat across from Francine. He addressed Cujo.

"Hay un hermoso perro en la casa. A beautiful dog, yes."

"You leave our Cujo alone now, you, ..."

"Senora, I would no more hurt this animal then I would my own mother. May she rest in peace."

"It's okay, Francine. He's tellin' the truth."

Francine got up to comfort Vern. Antonio tried to stop her but Roy waved him off.

"I am very sorry that we had to hurt you and especially saddened to have caused your wonderful Cujo any fear. We will only be here a short while. Just a few questions and we will be on our way."

"Well, first off, what the hell do you think you're doing?"

Francine was not acting. This was the real woman. Two men had broken into her house, scared the shit out of her dog and shot her man. She would get answers.

Roy got up and walked towards the kitchen.

"Do you have anything cold to drink? My throat is very dry. Ah, yes, orange juice. Very good. You don't mind, do you? Antonio? Anyone else?"

He waited for a moment more as a courtesy than for any actual answer. In any case, he would not be pouring orange juice for anyone. The dog was another story though. He filled Cujo's bowl with water and carried it out back to him. He returned momentarily.

"A beautiful animal. Now, to your question. I am Roy Vasquez and this is my associate, Antonio. I own a tire business in Mexico. You both know who I am. You must realize that I have sources, shall we say, in the FBI offices all throughout the Southwest United States? The beautiful Francine works in the Las Cruces office. She is listed as an accountant but we know you do much more, don't we, Francine?"

"I am a housewife and Vern is a retired Las Cruces sheriff's deputy. What kind of science fiction are you reading, hombre?"

Roy smiled and spoke to Antonio.

"Are you feeling better, my friend?"

Antonio nodded. Roy's eyes stayed on Francine though.

Roy took a drink of his juice and continued. He was toying with his gun now.

"I really wish we could just all be honest with each other. I need information before we continue our trip West. Now I am going to say a name and I want you to tell me what you know about this person. Very simple exercise. Do you understand?"

Antonio did not shift his gaze from Francine. Vern was bent over holding his wounded leg. Francine had her head down.

"Larue Belmont."

"Jesus Christmas. What the fuck is a 'Larue Belmont'?" Vern said incredulously.

In one motion, Roy's Glock came out of his pocket, and with his other hand he grabbed the nearby sofa cushion and put it over Vern's face as he fired two rounds into it. Blood shot from Vern's head and doused Francine who stared, stunned, at Vern's blood and brain particles. She began to cry like a wounded animal. Outside Cujo joined in a plaintive howl as if he knew that his master was gone.

"Make sure the back door is locked and look outside. Make sure there is no one about. Do it!"

Antonio apparently had not been let in on this part of the plan. In any case, he did not hesitate. He had seen worse during his years with Roy. Much worse. He headed to the backdoor as the dog was crying and scratching at it. It was locked. A thorough perusal of the outside of the house, back and front indicated no one was about. He came back to find Roy holding Francine in a conciliatory manner and speaking softly to her.

"He was a good man. It is okay to mourn him. Listen to that beautiful animal outside. Pure love. We humans are not capable of that unconditional love and grief. A lesson to be learned. Time will heal. Now sit and please learn from what has happened. You are a smart woman, Francine. I know that. I did not have time to, how do you say it, 'Play games with Vern.' I will ask you again what I asked him. Be aware that I will have no problem sending you to join him. But think of the loss for poor Cujo. An innocent being. Now I am going to say the name once again. Larue Belmont."

Francine had somehow gotten herself together. Antonio saw that she was still in some form of shock. A strong woman. Many other spouses would have crumbled into a babbling puddle of Jell-O. He had seen it.

"Everything you said is correct. I have worked in the FBI office in Las Cruces for ten years. Vern is, was..."

She stumbled momentarily. Roy had been listening like a local parish priest or rabbi. Full of empathy up to this point. Antonio saw the slightest change now with Francine's falter. Another few seconds and she would be joining Vern. Antonio was transfixed on the remaining throw pillow as Roy's hand edged towards it.

Francine prevailed.

"As I said, I have been with the FBI for ten years. I am technically an accountant, but I was approached by Special Agent Larue Belmont earlier this year, shortly after the café explosion in Pasadena, CA."

Francine lying about when exactly she had met Larue. A decision that could mean her life or death in the next moment.

"Brava, Brava!"

She would live. At least for now.

Roy got to his feet to applaud. As he did, Vern's head fell forward dumping grey matter on the rug. Francine in a scene reminiscent of Jackie Kennedy on that long ago day in Dallas, took her sweater off and gently wrapped it around her dead husband's head. As she did so, Antonio helped lay him down on the couch. Roy was watching her intently, ignoring the action by Antonio. He was waiting for her to continue. She cleaned her husband's head as best she could and then placed the sweater over his face. It would have to do for now.

"Agent Belmont came to visit us, Vern and I, here. Right here in this living room."

"And what was the reason for that meeting? Please answer with straight answers and to the point. You can understand the tight schedule Antonio and I are on and our desire to leave as soon as possible so we can finish our business and get back to Mexico. Please do not take this as an insult to your wonderful country and, of course, your hospitality, but as you say, 'Time Flies.'"

Antonio was watching Roy closely. He had seen this before. Roy had gone across that line between the sane into the wasteland that was complete insanity. He did not have any connection to reality anymore. Vern's corpse might as well have been a coffee table.

Francine took a slight breath and continued.

"Agent Belmont wanted to recruit Vern and I to help locate Alvina Vasquez, your daughter."

Roy was moved by this. Not anything that would have been noticed by an unbiased observer but Antonio saw it. A slight sigh. Imperceptive.

"This is interesting. Why did he want to find my Alvina?"

Francine weighed her next words but only for a moment. There was no going back.

"Belmont needed Alvina to get to you. He wants to kill you."

"Continue."

"My dear friend, is, was Eileen Palestrena's mother."

Roy looked at Antonio. It is obvious he did not know the name.

"Boss, that was the girl who was with Alvina at the jail in Juarez."

"Oh, yes, of course. The noisy bitch."

In an act of self-control that Antonio deemed equal to even the most courageous victims of Roy's torture cells, Francine remained in her chair. The only sign of any emotion was the pulsating vein on her forehead which had gone into warp drive.

"Okay, okay, continue!"

Francine bit her lip to stop from crying out.

"Eileen and Alvina met in Juarez at a bar."

"Yes, yes, of course. There was a gringo with them. This Teddy, ah…"

"Dabrowski, boss."

"Yes, the one who fell off the roof of the hospital. Dead now."

Antonio read something in Francine's look. Roy missed it. *Teddy was alive.*

Roy got up and walked to the kitchen. The door to the backyard opened. Cujo began to bark. There was the sound of speaking, inaudible yet gentle. The dog's barks died away. Roy closed the back door and returned.

"Thank you so much, Mrs. Lattimore. We are sorry for any convenience we may have caused tonight. You have a wonderful dog. Now, if you will, please get on your knees."

CHAPTER 56

War Memorial
South Pasadena
August 2019

Paula Garcia saw the two figures as soon as she reached the top of the stairs. They were in the shadows so it was difficult to make them out. One was taller than the other. He or she was dressed in black. The smaller figure was in white. Their backs were to her. That much she had also discerned. She felt for the gun in her bag. Finding it she was reassured. Not for long, however.

"Is that you, Teddy? Who is that with you? Look, I just want to talk. I'm your friend. You know that."

Silence. The figures still had their backs to her. She headed down the stairs, holding the gun inside her bag. Halfway down and the taller figure turned. He was looking directly at her.

"Oh, for the love of God!"

She dropped her bag. It rolled down the stairs and the gun inside went off. The round pierced the chest of the man looking up at her. The priest was nonplussed. He was smiling. Father Jim reached down to pick up Paula's bag.

"We are so happy to see you, dear Paula, are we not, Lexy?"

The smaller figure had picked up the gun. She turned to face Paula. It was Lexy but not the Lexy Paula remembered. This was a creature not of this earth. A grotesque figure with ravaged features and green puss oozing out of her mouth and nose. When she spoke though it was with the still angelic voice of the Children's Hospital "Lexy."

"My favorite nurse. I'm so happy to see you. But why did you take me away from my mother? I want my mother. Please, I need my mother."

Now the voice was no longer the soft, full of light Lexy. It had taken on the guttural sound of a monster.

"My father! Where is my father? He hurt my mother. He made her suffer. He must pay for his sins!"

A green substance hit Paula in the face. Before she could react, Father Jim put a hand as cold as ice on her and wiped the mire away.

"It's going to be okay, my dear one. We just need to find the father. The unspeakable act must be avenged. Retribution is the Lord's."

This was too much. Paula bolted backwards and tripped over a stair. She rolled downward and downward until there was nothing but a dingy abyss.

"Paula! Wake up! Are you okay? Paula!"

The outline of a human head. A blur and then light coming from above. Paula recognized Teddy just as a headache pulsated through her head. She instinctively reached for her bag.

"The bag is on the chair over there. The gun is in my pocket. I'll give it back to you when and if you give me an explanation that I'll believe as to why the hell you're here."

"That's my god damn gun. Give it, oh my head."

Paula laid back down and closed her eyes.

"Look, you might have a concussion. You took a pretty good fall down those stairs. Just try to stay calm and drink this water."

Paula took a sip of the water. She touched her face. No foreign matter.

"Your face is fine. Beautiful as ever."

"What have you done with Lexy? What have you done with her? I saw her. Not her! Something *Chupacabra*, a monster. What did you do with her!"

Footsteps from the top of the stairs. Paula looked up. A man in black.

"No, God help me. Father Jim! Stay away from me! What have you done to my Lexy?"

Paula passed out as the man, limping slightly, made his way to the bottom of the stairs.

"What in the name of Miles Davis' ghost spooked her?"

"I don't know, Larue. I got an idea, though. Help me get her up on this couch."

The FBI agent helped Teddy get Paula onto the couch. Teddy touched her head. It was clammy but her breathing seemed normal. Larue Belmont eyed him throughout.

"Roy Vasquez is in the United States. Probably heading here. An MS-13 outpost a couple of hours from Las Cruces that we were monitoring near Barstow was hit with four cooked, very well-done bodies left behind. A flamethrower no doubt. Trademark of Antonio Ruiz."

"Where have I heard that name before?"

"He's the bodyguard."

Paula awakened. Eyes open. Mumbling.

"What did you say, Paula?"

"Ruiz, he is the bodyguard. The bodyguard of the scum, 'Tire Boy.' What are you doing with these men? He raped her. He... I will kill you. Kill you all!"

"Settle down, girl! You don't know what the hell you're saying."

Teddy looked at Belmont. There was something there behind the cop façade. An answer to his question of what was happening with Paula. Why she was here. It was not forthcoming just yet, however.

"Look, Larue, I thought this was about Roy Vasquez. Bringing him down. What's this about his bodyguard and a rape and this other bullshit? Is this about Alvina? For Christ's sake it's just you and me now and maybe, Ben. Though I'll tell you the truth, I don't know whether I can even trust you telling me the sky is blue after everything that's happened. It seems I get a new surprise every day. Why the fuck did Paula come here with a gun? I thought she might want to kill me and Ben, but I guess I didn't really believe it or want to believe it, until I saw the gun. But why?"

Teddy had Paula's pink revolver in his hand now. He pointed it at the FBI Agent.

"I need some answers and I need them now. Talk."

"Teddy, this is crazy. I am not the bad guy here. In any case, you are not going to shoot me."

Teddy lowered the gun.

"Look, Christ, I'm sorry, I don't know what's going on. I need answers. I just need..."

And then, too late, Teddy saw the white blur from out of the corner of his eye.

CHAPTER 57

Glendale, CA
Paula's Condo

I have had headaches before. Headaches that were collateral damage from a hangover. They were excruciating, and I deserved them. I did not deserve what I was going through on that mid-August day as I woke up with carpet burns on my face and dried puke on my hands. My head was pounding just like the time I drank the bottle of Mescal in Tijuana and ate the fucking worm. The worst hangover of my life and God that was no small feat. This was just as bad, and all I had done was sniff the perfume of a gorgeous Latina and drink a glass of orange juice. Or was it Pepsi? Somewhere there was a flash of breast in the story as well. I got up slow like an old man testing his legs on his first day at assisted living.

I looked out the window. It was early morning. The sun was rising over the Verdugo Hills. With all the craziness, the traffic, the taxes, the wacko leaders, California was still a beautiful place to live. Teddy used to say that. Grudgingly, but... Teddy, Jesus Christ. Paula had been gone all night. She was after Teddy. That's why she drugged me. That was what this was. I had been slipped a "Mickey" of monumental proportions.

I had to get to my friend, fast. I just hoped I wasn't too late.

After a furious search of the place, I realized she had taken my keys with her. I called an Uber and headed to the War Memorial. As the car pulled out onto the 134 I remembered what Teddy had shared with me the last time I saw him. Just after the infamous cat attack at the War Memorial.

My headache was subsiding as Teddy's story came back to me. My mind was somewhat clear.

Teddy had known all along who Rose was. He knew that she and Alvina were in danger. He willingly let Larue Belmont use him as bait knowing that Roy Vasquez would come to Southern California to try to kill his daughter and Rose. Sadly, Roy had succeeded with Rose but Teddy was going to save Alvina. The faked death of Teddy had all been part of the plan to lure Roy in. Make him think that the FBI thought Teddy was the bomber at the café. As a result Roy believed he was safe from any scrutiny in that respect. His confused, drug crazed mind had him thinking that he could just slip in and slip out of the United States.

Of course, it wouldn't be quite accurate to say that this had been an FBI operation. Unless of course you believed that Larue Belmont represented the whole god damn bureau. No, this was Larue, Teddy, poor Sam Jackson and yes, I thought, Rose as well. All part of this insane caper to kill Roy "Tire Boy" Vasquez. The motive an age-old one – revenge; for everyone involved but one.

What the hell reason did Special Agent Larue Belmont have for going rogue and risking his career, not to mention his life to kill Vasquez?

And what about Paula Garcia? My head was starting to ache again. Teddy said she wanted to kill him and me. What the hell for? Hopefully, I would get some more answers from Paula, Larue and Teddy before they or I or all of us were dead.

"Here we are, Ben. Thanks so much for taking Uber. Hope to see you again."

"Hey, how'd 'you know my name?"

What an ass I was. Too damn paranoid. Of course, the Uber driver had known my name. It was on the damn app.

"Sorry, yea, just one of those days."

I thought about going over to the Starbucks across the street but then I caught myself. Teddy might already be in dire straits. It was a sunny day. Not a cloud in the sky. I made my way round back. When I got there, I remember being impressed that the windows that had been broken just a few weeks before were already mended.

I'm pretty sure Teddy had seen my approach. I wanted it that way. No surprises. I knew he was packing as was dear Paula and God knows where her head was at. Christ, she might have already blown Teddy's off.

"Help me!"

It's difficult to describe what I saw at this point. I'll start by saying a lovely Latina women had broken through the rear exit so recently repaired and was now running across the back lawn of the War Memorial with a white piece of fur attached to her head. Right behind her was Teddy Dabrowski screaming at the top of his lungs.

"God damn you, Claudius! Paula, he's really a nice cat. He just has to get used to you. Damn!"

"Good to see you, Teddy."

"Ben!"

He stopped running, bent over and gasped for air. Teddy needed to work out. Long overdue for some cardio. Not a priority right then.

"Hey, Teddy. I came here to warn you about Paula but it looks like you've got things under control."

Before Teddy could respond, Larue Belmont came limping out behind him.

"Oh my. Well, another repair in order for this back exit. Just use the same guy from last time, Teddy. Sorry I can't chit chat, Ben but I need to catch a flight to Las Cruces. I'm behind schedule already."

And with that, Special Agent Larue Belmont limped to his car while in the distance Paula Garcia was sprawled on the ground. Claudius the cat came prancing back towards Teddy, quite ecstatic with a patch of brown hair prominently hanging from his mouth. Teddy promptly picked him up and brought him back inside the War Memorial. A short time later, Teddy emerged, after, I assumed, he had placed Claudius in an area where he could not escape and do more damage to Ms. Garcia. Teddy motioned for me to follow him, albeit at a cautious pace, towards our mutual Crazy Ex-Girlfriend.

CHAPTER 58

Las Cruces, New Mexico
The Lattimore Residence

FBI Special Agent Larue Belmont hated flying. It all started when he was a kid, about 11 years old and his father, who was stationed at a Naval Air Station, smuggled him aboard a P-3 Orion and told the pilot to take him for a spin. Of course that meant dips and banks and all manner of vomit inducing, unauthorized, aerial acrobats. The little boy was not expecting any of this. When the plane landed, he had to be carried off. He had puked and shit his pants and was sick for the next three days. His father laughed at him the whole time.

He tried to block all this out as he stood at the Ride Share Pickup waiting for his Uber. His recently repaired leg was barking like a Louisiana coon dog who had just picked up the scent. He should still be in the hospital he knew but some things could not wait for recuperation of simple flesh. It was a beautiful New Mexico morning with the sunrise creating a peach-like color in the skies, strangely reminiscent of a Georgia O'Keefe painting Larue had seen while in college. He was praying that he would get a driver who would not talk his ear off about his hopes and dreams.

Larue knew from his contact at Baxter Security and Alarms that a Venganza Cartel "Kill Team" had entered the United States within the last few days and was headed to Las Cruces and possibly Pasadena. The only problem was that no one was sure which destination was first. Larue and his man at Baxter had a shared gut feeling it would be Las Cruces and the Lattimore residence and so here he was in the Uber with a 50 something driver wearing a hat that said *Writer* heading through airport traffic towards the Lattimore house.

"Did you have a nice flight? Yea, I'm a writer. I guess the hat gives it away. No point you sitting there the whole ride wondering what it means. Yea, I am a writer. I'm not a young guy, but I figure I got the edge on these younger guys and gals with my experience, if you know what I mean? I bet you didn't know that Cervantes, the guy who wrote *Don Quixote,* was 67 when he wrote it. Of course, talk about experience!? He was captured by pirates and spent years in prison. That's where he started writing *Quixote.* Imagine that!?

"So, what have you written?"

"What's that?"

Larue had had enough. Heartless-mode engaged.

"What have you written? A novel? Short stories? Magazines? Anything I might have seen in *The New Yorker*?"

"Well, I..."

"When did you start writing? What do you read? Do you read?"

"Well, I'm a writer. I don't have time to read."

A nervous laugh. The poor guy was done, and he knew it. Still Larue wanted to finish him. The killer instinct. The sins of the father indeed.

"So, you are a writer who doesn't read and apparently does not write."

"Well, it's all a process. I mean..."

"I see. Did you ever think that your place in this world, the thing you are supposed to do, the thing you are best at might actually be what you are doing now–driving for Uber?"

Larue thought he saw the man's soul take flight but it was only the white smoke from the Greyhound bus in front of them.

"Here's your destination, sir. Have a great day."

****

Jack Saldebar knew something was wrong, very wrong in the house. It had been about an hour since he had seen the SUV park a few blocks from the Lattimore residence. He had been surveilling the place for the last two days. The crazy, well, eccentric would be more appropriate, FBI guy, Larue Belmont, was supposed to have been with him but was recuperating from a gunshot wound gifted to him as a last gesture of fucking insanity by the guy Larue had used for what he called Operation Cadaver.

This was the first night or day for that matter where anything untoward had happened. He hadn't seen anybody get out of the SUV but he had heard the dog barking and finally did see a couple of figures come to the front door and enter. Jack knew there had to be at least one more operative coming in from the back. He thought he had detected the sound of a silencer on the parabolic sonic listening device microphone that was planted in the Lattimore house smoke detector. He wondered what Dave would do in this situation. He would have the answers. He always had. Jack had been told by Larue to stay in the van until he arrived though.

Jack Saldebar had served with Dave Baxter during Desert Storm back in the eighties. He had been a demolition expert and good with small arms. Dave had saved Jack's life one night during what was supposed to be a routine patrol on the outskirts of Mosul. There had been a number of landmines reported in the area by a SEAL Team Six operation that had been through there the week earlier. Dave's squad was tasked to clear the mines and check for anything else that might be deemed as suspicious activity in the area. Dave could have opted out of the patrol. He had what turned out to be the beginnings of gangrene on his left shin. A few weeks before he had been on patrol when an IED went off a few yards from him. Billy Pointer, 18 years old from South Bend, Indiana a FNG, "Fucking New Guy," in military parlance, had half his face blown off and died in Dave's arms. Dave himself got a piece of shrapnel in his leg which, in customary Gunnery Sergeant Dave Baxter USMC style, he did not report. The leg had begun oozing a putrid smelling liquid recently that Corporal Jack Saldebar had noticed and mentioned to his Gunnery Sergeant. For his trouble he had been verbally bitch slapped by his Gunny. Under no terms would the Corporal tell anyone about his Gunny's condition.

So, there they were, traipsing through a mine field on the other side of the world, two middle-aged guys who had already done more than enough time for their country.

Dave had tried to explain to the woman who would soon be his ex-wife why he was doing yet another tour at the age of 38 here in the hell on earth called Iraq.

"Why honey?! Why? Other guys can go. You've done your time."

Dave just shook his head, got out of the car and headed for the military airlift command terminal at LAX. Whatever he said, poor Abby would never understand. All he knew is that he needed to be there with his men.

"Did you see that, Gunny?"

Baxter was already heading towards the dune. He didn't answer but instead had motioned for the patrol to stop while he waved Saldebar forward.

Jack had crawled up to a position alongside Baxter about 50 yards from what the morning intel brief indicated was the outer boundary of the mine field.

"Do you see it?"

"See what?"

"The wire, for Christ's sake. It's as plain as the nose on your face."

Jack knew that Baxter had amazing night vision, but this was ridiculous. It was moonless without a star in the sky this night but...

"Put your god damn night vision goggles on."

"Shit! Sorry Gunny."

And there it was. A wire as clear as a ranch fence in Colorado at noon. Hanging there attached to two posts about four feet off the ground. The posts blending into the sand.

"P-25. Trip wire. Italian made. Sold to Iraq probably. Put a bunch of guys in VA hospitals. Back rooms. No public visits. Faces gone. Assorted other catastrophic injuries as they say.

"Corporal, I ever see you without your NVG after sunset I will bust you to Private so fast you'll feel like a Tijuana hooker who just woke up in a convent."

Saldebar on full alert then as he whispered back to Baxter, "Roger that, Gunny. Think there's more?"

"Could be. But we're not going to stick around and find out. We'll get rid of this one and make a report to the intel boys when we get back."

"Roger that. I'll just go up there and deactivate it."

"Sounds like a plan."

So Jack had crawled up to the P-25. He had been taking the last Explosive Ordinance (EO) tool out of his pack when he smelled it. Rancid. Like the breath of a dead man who had shoveled a case of bad anchovies down his throat before expiring. The Iraqi had a knife to Saldebar's throat before he could put it all together. It was a trap of course. A dummy mine manned by a not so dummy but most deadly and desperate Iraqi. Saldebar saw the scar on the man's face as he yelled "For my dead children! Allah be praised" in Farsi. Just as the knife was coming down and Jack was flashing images of himself on a tricycle at four years old, the high school prom, Patricia Guzman letting him fondle her boob, the Iraqi's jugular exploded, spewing red blood and mucus all over the Corporal. Gunny Baxter wiped his knife clean, checked the dead man for any explosives, reconnoitered the area in a flash and pointed to the rear area where the rest of the squad were still waiting.

"Jesus Christ, Gunny, you saved my..."

"Forget it. You can buy me a Miller in the Philippines. Let's get out of here."

Of course, it ended up being more than beer. Jack had spent the last twenty or so years helping build Baxter Alarms to what it now was. A major operator in domestic and international security. A kind of Haliburton without corrupt political influence. Oh, Baxter Alarms had their share of lobbyists but Jack Saldebar had never seen a dollar exchanged for a favor in all his time there.

Now, as he waited in the surveillance van outside the Lattimore house he missed his friend Dave. He grew impatient waiting for that FBI agent Larue Belmont. He wasn't doing any of this for Larue, the FBI or the U.S. government for that matter. He was doing this for his dear departed friend, Dave Baxter. The man who had saved his life and represented another time when loyalty and honor, not to mention courage, actually meant something.

"Senor, please give me your gun and any other weapons you are carrying."

Jack hadn't heard the door slide open. An amateur, possibly a fatal mistake. The rancid smell from so many years ago here again as the knife pressed against his throat.

CHAPTER 59

War Memorial
South Pasadena

"Stay the fuck away from me. Where is my gun? I'll kill you! I should have done it a long time ago!"

"Hey, hey, settle down? Kill me! I thought you loved me. Damn, I got to get better at reading women."

I remember stifling a laugh as I watched Teddy struggling with Paula. Poor Paula who had just been attacked by the feral cat Claudius, covered with white fur. I had to intervene.

"Look, Paula, you need to settle down. You don't want to kill Teddy. He, we are your friends."

The look she had given me brought me back to my childhood. When my first girlfriend, Patty Blandino, finished reading a short piece of mine and promptly told me that she thought my writing was "childish" and "Oh, by the way, I'm dumping you for John Bennington who is going to become a minister."

The same look and the same feeling of uselessness and a loss of hope. Like my testicles had been removed from my body without benefit of surgery.

"You really are naïve, aren't you, Ben? How long have you known the wonderful Teddy Dabrowski, anyway? Did you know what he did when he left here or even before you met him? I like you, Ben. You're a good person. That's why I can't figure out how you could be friends with a cold-blooded killer."

Teddy had glanced at me and then, "Paula, you are in shock. Something like that. In any case, you are really fucked up. I don't know where the hell you get this 'murderer' bullshit from. I...This is total horseshit. You do realize that I was sitting right there with Ben. Why would I put myself in danger of being blown to shit?"

"Because when the bomb went off you made sure you were safely inside. At least that was the plan. Unfortunately for you, those dumbasses that you and that faggot FBI agent hired, miscalculated the detonation time and instead of you being back in the toilet of the Bard, safe and sound, you had just gotten inside the store. The bomb was in the storeroom off the outside patio. The door was supposed to be open but the morons in their white van with the Kansas plates, left it closed."

This had been too much for me.

"Belmont? Look, let's get you cleaned up, Paula, and back inside," I pleaded.

"I'm not going anywhere near that loco cat and I am definitely not going anyplace alone with this murderous bastard."

"All right, look, how about we all go across the street to the Starbucks? Lots of people. Daylight. Okay?"

"Ben, you don't believe any of this shit, do you?"

"Let's get some coffee, Teddy."

"Why you god damn rat turd! You believe her, don't you? Well, you both can get fucked. Should have known not to trust a squid asshole. Go get your Starbucks. I'm done with you."

He started to walk away and then turned...

"Watch out!"

Too late. Teddy nailed me right in the jaw. Another good sucker punch. That South Side upbringing. To be fair, he had warned me about it on several occasions, "When it comes to fist fights, no such thing as fair. If you want fair, go to Pomona."

I remembered coming to and looking up at Paula in what was becoming a regular occurrence. Not that I minded looking at those beautiful brown eyes but, oh shit, I hoped my jaw wasn't broken. Then as if by telepathy, "It's okay, Ben, I don't think it's broken," as she touched my very sore face.

"Where's Teddy?"

"He went back into the building. Probably looking for that cat."

I start to laugh and pain shot through my chin like when I got hit on the elbow by Tommy Carpenter's fastball in Little League a hundred years ago. Paralyzed my arm for at least 10 minutes. Same feeling now but in my jaw.

"Shit, let's get a coffee anyway, just the two of us. I don't believe Teddy is himself. They have straws over there, right?"

****

"You don't believe me do you, Ben?'

"What do you mean? Believe that my best friend in the world is a psycho bomber who is also allied with Roy Vasquez and that he tried to kill me as well as a number of other innocent souls? I think you got lot's more 'splainin' to do, Ms. Garcia. For one, why the hell did you drug me?"

Before she could answer, Paula's phone beeped. A text. She looked down at it and then back to me.

"The office. Nothing important. Call me Paula, Ben, Christ. How's your jaw? How about the coffee? Is it okay?"

Who or what was this woman?

"The jaw will be fine. Starbucks is always fine. I live for caffeine. 'Death before decaf' and all that. If you don't mind, I'll stick with 'Ms. Garcia' until I figure out what's going on here. For starters, why the hell did you drug me? Talk. Por favor."

"Oh no. Teddy has my gun."

"The last thing you need to worry about right now. You'll get the gun back when and if you convince me that what you said earlier is true."

"Okay, okay. Where to start? All right. You do know that Teddy sleeps with Larue Belmont?"

CHAPTER 60

Union Station
Los Angeles

"Alvina Vasquez?"

"Yes, and you are 'Martin'?"

"That's me. Do you just have the one bag?"

The Lyft driver started to take Alvina's backpack. She waved him away politely.

"It's okay. I'll hold on to it, thanks."

"You got it. Any choice of music? I got everything from Ricky Martin to Kelly Clarkson."

"You're quite the eclectic Uber driver."

"Lyft, please! I am a renaissance man. Lyft is the home of creatives. Uber is the home of the dregs of society. Basically, if you have car keys you can drive for Uber. Lyft on the other hand has quite an extensive background investigation process. We are also very interesting to talk to and..."

"What if one does not want to talk? As for your background investigation process, apparently they don't screen for 'driving while masturbating' or drivers with rape convictions on their records. Both of which happened recently in Boston and San Francisco."

"Okay, well, I guess that means no chit chat desired and you can do without Kelly Clarkson?"

"Thank you."

It had been a bad trip. The flight from Mazatlán had been delayed due to weather and then was bumpy, anyway. Alvina took the train from LAX and sat next to a homeless woman who looked at her and promptly puked on her shoes. No worries though, she thought. She was here now. It would be good to see Paula. So many years. All they had been through. Alvina had texted her when she arrived. No response. She had started to text her again when the reply had come across. It was brief. Paula's address in Glendale and the time, 4 PM. Two hours' time.

"Here you are Alvina."

"Thank you."

She exited the car, opened the Lyft app and gave the driver 5 stars. The least she could do. Alvina loved to fuck with ride share drivers. A sin inherited from her mother, Rose, she thought. Rose always said "Expect the worst from everyone, Alvy, and most of the time you won't be disappointed."

A lump in her throat as she looked at the rubble now all swept up and bulldozed over. The remains of the Bard Café. You wouldn't have even known that a bookstore/café once existed here. The place where her dear mother had taken her last breath. She walked underneath the yellow police tape and knelt down to pray. She knew her mother was outside when she was blown to bits. This would be the approximate place where her table and chair stood. Alvina said a brief prayer for her mother's soul and then comforted herself with the knowledge that Rose had probably died quickly. There had been no pain. There couldn't have been. She was with the angels now. Alvina would join her dear mother someday. Not today though. Today was the day of retribution.

The second Lyft driver was less talkative. For a second, Alvina amused herself with the fantasy that she was now on a "No-Talk" list. That somehow the Lyft drivers shared information about problem passengers.

"Something funny, Ms.?"

"Oh, no. Just caught up in my thoughts. It happens to me when I travel. Have a nice day."

Alvina departed the car, opened the Lyft app and promptly gave Jamie 2 Stars. There was a Porto's right up the block from Paula's place. The bakery was a landmark in Southern California. Over 40 years old, it was a must visit place for tourists. Porto's was a big supporter of Children's Hospital and the founder was a woman named "Rosa." "Synchronicity," Paula had said while they were chatting on the dark web last month. She had also told Alvina that the product of her father's incest was alive and in a hospital bed at Children's and that Teddy Dabrowski was the child's best friend on earth.

The memories had come flooding back as she waited for 4 PM. Alvina was so anxious to see her daughter. She punished herself daily for not visiting when she found out she was at Children's Hospital but Paula had mentioned the cancer and the fear was too much. Alvina had been enslaved by the whiskey and the cocaine, the demon sisters of addiction. There was no chance of her visiting her daughter in that condition let alone even having the strength to leave Mexico. Now she was sober, though. She hadn't had a drink or drug for two months. All for her daughter. She hadn't told Paula she was coming until yesterday when she texted her from the airport. Paula responded that she would be happy to see her but curiously made no mention of Lexy. No matter. Texts could be restrictive to many people, Alvina thought.

She had looked up the type of Leukemia that Lexy had before she left and even talked to her GP in Mazatlán about it, albeit framing the discussion in the hypothetical so as not to set off any alarms with her father. In any case, he was nowhere to be found. His bodyguards and associates not giving out any information. Alvina had dismissed his absence as another binge. He had had several lately.

The internet said that the type of cancer Lexy had was in many cases of the terminal variety. Her Mexican doctor was cautious in his prognosis saying that, "I cannot really give a valid diagnosis without actually seeing the patient..."

In any case, Alvina began praying to the same God who got her sober for the safety and health of a little girl she had dropped off at an orphanage in what now seemed like a lifetime ago.

Just as she was about to order, her phone vibrated.

"Hello."

"Alvy, you're here?"

"Right around the corner from your place. The place we talked of."

"I'm on my way."

CHAPTER 61

Outside the Lattimore House
Las Cruces, New Mexico

"Just stay still. No quick movements. Everything will be *bueno*. You understand?"

"Who the fuck are you? I'm just an alarm installation guy, I..."

Antonio hit Jack Saldebar squarely on the back of his head with his free hand. The other hand grazing lightly across his Adam's Apple.

"What the fuck, man. That's assault."

"It will be murder if you don't stop playin', you gringo cocksucker. Now what other weapons do you have in this truck? I'm going to search and if I do find any that you have not pointed out I will cut your balls off and feed them to the nice dog across the street."

Jack's head was pounding. What a stupid, amateur mistake, he thought.

And what the fuck was these cartel guys' obsession with removing testicles and feeding them to dogs?

The shadow. Swift. Unnoticeable from behind his assailant but Jack saw it.

"I got nothin in here, you spic son of a whore. Why don't you put down the knife and..."

PFT PFT

The silencer had found its mark.

"Jesus Christ, Larue, I got Leaf Blower Man's brains all over this shirt."

"Yes, well, you're welcome. Damn, you Guatemalan's are extremely racist. What is up with that? Help me push this hombre to the side and out of the way. I'll ask you why the door was unlocked later. If we're both still alive that is."

After moving the dead body to the corner of the van, Larue pointed to the house.

"What's the status?"

Jack glanced at Antonio's body.

"I really need to quit this shit, pronto. Maybe start my own hardware store in South Pasadena. Shit, fuck that. Prescott, Arizona. That's the place."

"Okay, Jack. Yes, my flight was good. Even though I hate flying. I know you didn't ask because you don't give a shit, but in any case, I'm here. Just in the nick of time. Oh, yes, you're welcome, for saving your ass. Now, although I would love to hear about your midlife crisis career change options, I need to know what is going on in that house. Are Vern and Francine even alive? Not to mention Cujo. Lastly, who the fuck is in there with him?"

Before Jack could answer, Larue had done a thorough search of Antonio's body. He was looking through a passport and a wallet intently.

"His passport says he's 'Jose Luis Ayala.' Born in Tijuana. No doubt a forgery. A very good one though. This is a cartel's work. They're the only ones with passports this good. You say there are two of them?"

"Yes. They both came in the front but I heard the dog barking in the back and someone 'shushing' him... and one other thing."

Larue looked at Jack . He had only known him a short time. The connection with Dave Baxter was their introduction. Saldebar looked worried.

"What is it?"

"My sound gear picked up something. About an hour ago. I recalibrated it and was ready to play it back, but then our friend here paid a surprise visit and..."

Larue motioned Jack to the side and rewound the sound gear. Nothing discernable at first. One, two, five, six times and then he heard it.

"It's a god damn gun shot. Muffled. Not a silencer. Probably a pillow or something like that. Shit we got to get in there."

"Whoever's in there is getting worried about old 'Jose' here. Probably got eyes on us as we speak. We need to..."

"Help me! He killed my husband! Help...."

Larue recognized Francine right away. Stumbling now and covered with blood as she headed towards the van.

"What the fuck are you doing? Larue you can't..."

Belmont was already on his way towards Francine. Jack lined his Glock up with the open front door and waited.

"It's alright, Francine. I got you now. Come with me."

"The son of a bitch is in there. He killed Vern. He's in the back with Cujo. So fucked up he forgot about me."

"It's okay. We'll get him. What's all this blood? Hold on. Let me check you for a minute."

"I'm fine. It's not my blood. It's Vern's."

"Jesus Christ, I'm sorry Francine. Who was it? A cartel soldier?"

"Hell no. It's Roy Vasquez. Roy fucking 'Tire Boy' Vasquez. I know it sounds crazy but..."

"Hurry, Larue. The cops are going to be here soon with all of this screaming. Get in the god damn van!"

Belmont and Francine stumbled into the back of the van. There was still no sign of anyone at the front door.

Then the barking started.

"Oh Jesus, he's going to kill Cujo. Not my Cujo. I've already lost Vern. You got to stop him, Larue. Please, Jesus, please."

"Okay, okay Francine. Take a deep breath. You're safe with us now. No one is going to hurt you."

"Larue, if that's Vasquez we need to get him. It may be our only chance. But why the fuck would the head of the Venganza Cartel put himself in danger like this?"

"He's not in his right mind. The drugs. It's the drugs. He's completely insane. I saw it. He killed my Vern like he was putting out a cigarette. I figured I would be next so I just ran for it when Roy went to get more food for Cujo. The mother fucker does love anima..."

Larue motioned for quiet.

"Do you hear that? Police sirens. We need to move. Now!"

CHAPTER 62

Chicago
Little Jim's Tavern
2007
The Marine Meets the Special Agent

The marine hunched over the bar and promptly knocked his Jack Daniels onto a group of just washed glasses. The bartender was not happy.

"Sir, please I think you may have had enough. Would you like me to call you a cab?"

Corporal Teddy Dabrowski was home on leave. The visit to his mother at Mercy Hospital was heartbreaking. To see his mother, the only one who ever loved him in his entire life, the person who had stood up to his father when Teddy was a little boy, to see this angel lying there in ICU ravaged by cancer, this had been too much. No hope for recovery. The pain, relentless despite the morphine. Teddy cried by her bedside until there were no more tears, and after hitting every bar on Rush Street, ended up here at Little Jim's Tavern, a place that made strong drinks and, until now, had let him imbibe in peace.

"What's your name?"

"Jaime, sir."

"Have you ever been in the military, Jaime?"

"Gawd no, though I do love those sailor suits. Your uniform's not so bad either, sweety."

The right cross was launched and was headed for a direct hit on Jaime's prone jaw when it was intercepted by the man that had been sitting two stools from

Teddy for the last hour. Jaime had turned slightly to acknowledge another customer so never knew what might have been.

"What the fuck, man?"

Teddy was swept off the bar stool and escorted to an open booth by the man who had just kept him from spending a night or more in the Cook County jail.

"Please sit, Corporal. I know a bit about the military. My sainted father was in the Navy and I grew up on Navy bases. I know you are a marine and I know you are enlisted and thus despise being called, 'sir.' You know who your parents are and all that."

"Yea, you got it. Yea. But why the fuck didn't you let me knock his faggot ass on the deck."

The heavy-set man with the brush cut and the pink bowtie just smiled and shook his head.

"Oh yes, one other thing. One other bit of information. This bar, this place you have been drinking in for the last several hours happens to be one of the oldest gay bars in Chicago."

"Fuck me to tears."

"Indeed. You also might want to look around and notice that many of these men are big enough to break you in half, marine or no marine. The owner was a member of SEAL Team Six."

"May I take your order, Larue?"

"Thanks, Jason. I think we'll start with a coke for me and a black coffee for my marine friend here."

"Are you sure, Larue."

"Yes, he'll be fine. I take full responsibility."

"Okay, you know best. I'll be right back. I'll leave the menu."

After a few black coffees and proper introductions, Teddy came back to some semblance of life. He was still a bit ornery though, and it was obvious that he was suspicious of this stranger.

"So, your name is Larue, and I'm guessing that you're a cop."

"Close. Larue Belmont and I'm in the FBI."

"Nice. I'm Teddy Dabrowski. So, what may I ask is a guy who works for the FBI doing in a gay bar in the middle of the afternoon?"

"Well, it's evening now; actually about 7 PM and how does being in the FBI and drinking in a gay bar, off-duty, I may add, become mutually unacceptable?"

"Holy shit! You are a 'Benny Boy.'"

"A 'Benny Boy.' I have heard a number of homophobic slurs but never that one."

"Oh, don't get your panties in a twist, Mr. Larue Belmont, it's just what we used to call the boys in the Philippines who wanted to be women."

"I see. What's going on with you, Teddy? I'm pretty good at peeling the onion."

"Yea, well don't get any ideas of handling any of my onions."

"You're in pain, my new friend."

"Why do you give a flying fuck? Everybody is in pain. It's life, 'friend.' Why do you give a shit about me, anyway? I'm not a homo, if that's what you're thinking."

"I wasn't thinking that at all. Well, not until you found it necessary to bring it up. Can I tell you a secret?"

"You're Madonna?"

"Very funny. Good stuff. You're coming back to life. Not all gays like Madonna, but in any case, I digress. No, I am Special Agent Larue Belmont of the Federal Bureau of Investigation and I am based out of the Chicago office."

"A gay G-Man. Very cool. So why should I care about any of that?"

"Talk to me about Juarez, 2005."

Larue Belmont had interrogated his share of people since he joined the Bureau. Murderers, spies, child kidnappers. He had experienced what he perceived as pretty much the whole gamut of humanity's misery. He had never seen anything like the look that Teddy Dabrowski was now exhibiting. The coffee cup that Teddy had started to raise to his lips began to shake uncontrollably in his hand. He struggled to put it down but not before it spilled over his fingers and onto the table. The coffee was hot. The waiter had just brought a fresh cup, yet Teddy had never even looked at his scalded hand. He smiled at Larue. A smile that became a grotesque contortion as his lower lip started to move like that of a palsy victim. His eyes went dark. He lowered his head and then—he wept.

Larue did nothing. The waiter started to come over, but he motioned him away with a flick of his hand. He sat there motionless and in silence for a good five minutes as Teddy cried the tears that had been stored the last few years.

"Feel better now? I believe I can provide further absolution."

He paid the check and walked Teddy to his car. A few minutes later they were sitting at Larue's kitchen table.

"I'll ask you again...Juarez 2005. Why the interest?"

So Larue Belmont told Teddy Dabrowski about the love of his life. His one true thing. His salvation. Teddy listened and never interrupted. Not a peep. He was entranced as he listened to this chunky guy with the redneck haircut and the pink tie. A paradox.

"I believe of course that I was born gay. I mean, I know that now, but for the first decade or so of my life, I just assumed like many boys that I was heterosexual. I mean it was a given. I stayed that way through high school. I even dated a few girls. Lost my virginity to Lorraine Giancarlo. Huge rack and a five o'clock shadow to boot."

"Look, Belmont, this is all very fascinating, but how the hell do you know about Juarez? What do you know about it might be a better question. Is that why I'm here? Why you picked me up at the bar. Why you're sharing wonderful anecdotes about your tortured childhood?"

"Well, I thought I'd break the ice with a few stories. Get you comfortable so you would be easier to seduce."

"You're a regular 'homo Jay Leno' now, aren't you Belmont?"

The FBI man moved his chair closer to Teddy while pushing a manila envelope towards him.

"Open it."

Teddy did as directed. There was an 8"x11" black and white photo inside. He looked away but then somehow composed himself.

"Who's that in the picture?"

"My lover and my best friend. His name was Jim. Last name not important. We met when we went through the academy in Quantico together, we..."

"Christ, there's more than two faggots in the FBI? What is this world coming..."

Larue slid his legs under Teddy's chair and in one motion kicked it out from under him, leaving Teddy sprawling on the floor like an overturned turtle.

"First and last warning you ignorant motherfucker. Next time you utter anything close to a gay slur, you leave without your teeth. Are we clear?"

Teddy started to charge at Larue, saw the look on his face and thought better of it. He made his way back to the table, picked up his chair and took a seat.

"God damn! Shit! I didn't mean anything by that. I'm sorry about the loss of your...ah...friend. How did he die? Who killed him? Why are you showing me this shit? I mean you obviously know I was in Juarez in 2005. I always thought they were dead. Now I know. Closure, right? That's supposed to be a good thing."

"Jim was tortured and slaughtered by the Cartel under the orders of Roy 'Tire Boy' Vasquez. He was working undercover and had succeeded in getting very close to the top of the cartel. Someone gave him up though and he was killed."

"Damn, he, ah Jim looks pretty bad, they..."

"Castrated him. Yes, those are his balls in his mouth."

"Jesus fucking Christ."

There was a prolonged silence. Teddy was having a hard time processing all of this. Larue gave him a moment and then slid another picture to Teddy. It was a picture of a young woman.

"Veronica. How did she die?"

"Alvina. She may have used another name with you. She was with Eileen and you. She's alive."

"Alive? Why? How? They were together. I don't understand."

"Alvina Vasquez is Roy Vasquez daughter. We're not sure yet what happened to Eileen. We do know that Roy Vasquez wants to kill you."

" Me? What the fuck?"

Larue hands him one more picture.

"What, you got a photo lab in the back there somewhere? Now who might this be."

Roy thinks that you raped his daughter. At least that's what he is putting out to the cartel. He will bide his time with you though. For now, you are part of a bigger plan. This picture is Roy's estranged wife, Rose. He is after her now as well. She made the unpardonable sin of leaving him.

I don't believe you. I don't believe that Alvina or Eileen are alive. You just want to use me. Yea, that's what I think. Fuck this. Now if there is nothing else, I'd like to get out of here so I can start making my way to Los Angeles. I'm processing out of the Corp next week. My enlistment is up. This makes my transition to civilian life a bit more complicated. I'll need to take some steps to, you know, stay alive."

"That's why I'm here."

"I'm sorry?"

" I'd like to help you."

"What's the catch?"

"I need you to go undercover."

"Oh, that's just wonderful. I can't help looking at this picture of your boyfriend... I'm sorry. Okay, so what do you need from me?"

"Go to Los Angeles. Get a place there. Pasadena area would be fine. We'll pay you so you can tell anyone that asks that you're on disability from the military. We know you were in Iraq. It fits in nicely.

"Rose Vasquez lives in San Marino now. Her boyfriend happens to be working for us already."

"I see. And, of course, you want the big tortilla, Roy Vasquez, who will be going after both of us."

"Not quite so simple but 'good enough for government work' as they say."

"What do you mean 'not quite so simple'?"

"More will be revealed. Trust me."

"The FBI, the U S of A is behind this, right?"

"Of course it is. You will have the full protection of the Federal Bureau of Investigation."

"But you're my contact, right?"

"Roger that."

"Of course."

The two sat for a moment, staring at each other. A kind of mutual understanding had enveloped them. Teddy found this guy reassuring in some strange way. He couldn't quite put his finger on it. To Larue, Teddy, who was a few years his junior, was in some strange way the little brother he never had.

Larue looked down and saw his hand in Teddy's. It was almost an out of body experience. No idea of who initiated the touch. It was there, though. It was warm. It was real. It was true. Their lips touched. A tear. The strangest thing. Teddy thought of his first baseball glove. The smell of it. How natural it felt when he put it on his hand. All's right with the universe.

Bliss.

CHAPTER 63

Porto's Bakery
Glendale, CA

"Alvina? Oh my God, it's you!"

Paula embraced Alvina and promptly knocked over her coffee.

"Look at me, I'm such a klutz. I'll get you another."

"No, it's okay. Really. Just sit. None got on me. It's wonderful to see you! Anyway, I want to leave soon. I need to see my baby. Is Children's Hospital far?"

"You must have the cheese roll! Or the spinach feta empanada. Oh, I've put on so much weight living so close to this place, but you are so thin, you…"

"Is something wrong, mi amiga?"

"Of course there is nothing…"

"Stop with the bullshit. Look me in the eye. How is my Lexy?"

One look at Paula told Alvina the answer.

"Oh Jesus God. Oh my Jesus! What? How?"

"I hadn't heard from you. I didn't know whether you were alive or dead. We thought she could be saved with a bone marrow transplant, but before we could get a donor, her condition turned critical. It's like that with that form of cancer."

"When did she…?"

"A month ago. It was peaceful. We can go to her resting place. It is very close."

It started as a low, almost imperceptible sound. Slowly it rose to a guttural, almost inhuman plea. The cries of a mother who has lost her baby. The same throughout nature. Whether it be a mama grizzly or a frail young Mexican woman who has suffered more than any living creature should suffer. Paula got up from the table and embraced Alvina. She let her cry. A flood of tears rolled down her face and into Paula's eyes. A true sharing of the most devastating form of heartache. The loss of a child. The fact that this soul was the product of the most obscene of transgressions meant nothing. A life was gone. A beautiful, angelic soul had passed to the other side. That soul was at peace, but as is now and had been the plight of the human race since time immemorial, the living were left to suffer.

"I'm okay. Thank you."

"We can sit for a while. Let me wipe your eyes."

"I want to go to her. Now."

"But are you sure you...?"

"Now."

****

"It's a beautiful place. Thank you."

Paula held Alvina close once again. The wind had come up at Forest Lawn Cemetery in Glendale, and with the unusually cold rain, she couldn't tell whether Alvy had started crying again.

"The flowers are beautiful."

"Yes, listen why don't I let you have a moment alone with your daughter. I'll just check my emails or whatever. I'll be right over here. Take whatever time you need."

The younger woman smiled as Paula headed over to a nearby bench. There was a text which required Paula's immediate attention. The number was international. Mexico. She looked at the three words on her cell phone screen with a mixture of horror coupled with a strange relief.

RETRIBUTION IS COMING

After a moment she looked over at Alvy. She was speaking. Probably praying, Paula thought. Best to leave her alone, for a few more minutes at least. Things to do, though. Decisions to be made. She put her phone back in her coat pocket and began to plan...and then she saw it.

Alvina was still speaking but now there was a child listening to her. An angelic figure wearing what looked like hospital scrubs. Paula was only a few feet away but still had to strain her eyes to see the child through the now heavy rainfall.

"Alvy, who is that you are talking to? Are you okay? We should go soon. This rain..."

"I love you, Paula. It's okay. I'm just telling mama that everything will be okay."

Paula rushed towards Alvy.

"Who are you! What is this? I don't..."

"She couldn't stay. She has much to do on the other side. She is so beautiful, my Lexy. My lovely child."

Alvy was smiling at Paula. A smile of understanding.

"She forgives you."

CHAPTER 64

Teddy took a sip of his home brewed venti drip as he sat inside the War Memorial basement speaking to Larue on the cell, "She just left. Why the hell are you so pissed off?"

"Look, I'm on my way to the hospital. Jack Saldebar, you never met him, but anyway, he got a bump to his head which seems to be hemorrhaging. I can't talk long. Look, you need to find Paula. She's with the cartel. She's not who she seems to be. I'll explain when I see you. Roy Vasquez is here in New Mexico. Actually, he's probably on a private jet enroot to Los Angeles, as we speak."

"Christ, Larue, are you... I mean you're not hurt are..."

"I'm fine. Hey, this is not the time to get all Lifetime channel gay on me."

"I have no idea what that means. I don't really give a fuck. Just stay safe."

"Don't you watch anything but Fox news and sports? Damn. I'll explain later, like I said. I'm going to get Jack fixed up and then I'm catching the first plane back there. Find Paula. Whatever you do, don't let her see you coming. Just call me when you locate her. I'll take care of the rest."

"What about Roy? Can't you put an APB or whatever the hell you call it out on him?"

"I could if this was an official FBI operation. You and I both know that it's not. I'll probably be drummed out of the bureau for my 'cowboy' tactics after all this is over, but I don't really give a shit."

"Personal vendettas are not the way to go, Larue. Your friend is gone. You can't bring him back. Just let the bureau take care of this."

"What makes you think this is all about my boyfriend of years ago?"

"Shit, even worse if this about me. I can take care of myself. You know that."

"Yea, of course. Problem is, I'd much rather take care of you. Later."

The phone signal clicked off before Teddy could reply. He headed to his car in the Starbucks lot and was on the 134 West headed to Forest Lawn Cemetery in a matter of minutes. He almost lost control of his rental as he took the Glendale exit. A few blocks down and there was the cemetery of celebrities, Forest Lawn. He parked and headed in the direction of Lexy's grave.

"Teddy!"

He almost tripped over the parking lot curb. I guess I scared him a bit. Truth be told, I'm probably the last person he expected to see there and then. His good buddy, Ben, still struggling with a sore jaw after he had sucker punched me at the War Memorial. No time to hold a resentment. I needed to save my friend before he got in so deep that he couldn't get back to the shore.

"Fuck you, asshole. Don't come near me, or I'll turn you into Chuck Wepner."

For you millennials, Chuck Wepner was a member of the "Bum of the Month Club" in the sixties. He was actually a pretty good fighter, especially by today's standards. He took Muhammed Ali to 15 rounds; well, a few seconds short, and that was when Ali was in his prime. Legend has it that when Sylvester Stallone saw that fight it gave him the inspiration for *Rocky*. In any case, Teddy was alluding to the fact that Wepner had a mashed nose and therefore I was going to look like that if I came any closer. Great story, but alas, it did not deter me.

"Stop for a minute! You got one life already, I don't think you have another. I know why you're here. You're thinking that Lexy will tell you something - Like who killed Eileen or who wants to kill you. Well, my friend, it is not safe to go near that beautiful child's grave. Not now anyway. Just stop and fucking listen to me."

He continued on, so I slugged his dumb ass right there in Forest Lawn. We rolled around on a few graves (Never good luck) until, both out of breath, we sat huffing and puffing next to "Marilyn Walker, Loving Mother and Beloved Wife. Born 1901. Died 1929."

Shit. Well, we can guess what happened there. Couple of kids. Father working his ass off. Saving. Then good old 1929 comes along. The Great Depression. Life. It's a bitch sometimes.

The next series of events you can either believe or disbelieve. All I can tell you is I saw what I saw. I was sober and, as far as I knew, Teddy was as well.

Two figures off in the distance, more specifically to my right field of vision were heading towards Teddy and I. At first, they seemed to be walking at a normal pace. Then they increased their speed and were well, running. Running at a very

242

fast pace indeed. Teddy and I were entranced. Speechless, one might say. The closer the two bodies came the more entranced we became. You see there was someone or something else that had just entered the picture. The two people; I guess you would call them that, were getting closer. I could even begin to make them out. They were coming from the direction of where Lexy was buried. A young woman and a child. Then we heard it. I know Teddy did. His face went pale as he dropped to his knees.

"Teddy, Teddy! It wasn't your fault. Get away. Go now."

"Go away, Teddy. We love you, but it's not safe. Get away!"

Closer and closer they came.

"No, Jesus God no! Go away Eileen. My God, and you, Joey. How? Why?"

Teddy recognizing the little boy as the child that Father Jim had held at the orientation years ago.

A hand had touched Teddy on the shoulder. He turned and collapsed. The priest bent over and held his hand. He looked directly at me. He gave me a kind look. I heard him say that he was sorry for what happened to me. He didn't speak but I "heard." I was calm. I should not have been but I was. Serene even.

"Hello, Father Jim. So very nice to meet you. Teddy was right about you. I have so many questions. Lexy, my cancer, Rita, oh dear, Rita."

I looked back towards Lexy's grave. Eileen and Joey were gone and when I turned again, so was Father Jim.

"Teddy, are you alright? It's okay, Teddy. We have to get away from this place. It's not safe here."

No answer. His eyes were closed. His face felt cold and clammy. I checked his pulse just as the first shot rang out. The ground exploded an inch from Teddy's head. I instinctively covered him with my body. Another recoil, this time coinciding with a sharp pain in my thigh and the feeling of hot liquid running down my leg. A quick flashback of my 10-year-old self crying outside my house. Mom was supposed to be home, but she was at the bar trying to get Dad out. I had no key. Rather than go to the neighbors, I pissed in my pants.

No time for fond childhood memories.

There was no point in trying to run. I didn't dare look up as I covered Teddy's body with mine and waited for the end.

CHAPTER 65

A Private Airstrip
Twilight
Somewhere outside Mojave, CA

"I see it. I see the landing lights. Just there."

Javier Cortez spoke in clipped tones as he relayed the news that the jet carrying the VIP was on approach. The unmarked limousine screeched out of the airport hangar and headed for the airstrip.

"We got it. On our way."

"Sir, we are on our approach. We will be landing in 10 minutes. Please fasten your seat belt."

Roy Vasquez ignored the flight attendant. He had more important matters at hand.

"That is not a god damn word! 'Xi' what the fuck is that."

Like the true addict he was, Roy had become immersed in the "Scrabble Go" app on his iPhone XS. He had only one tile left and was about to beat "Big Time Mama" when she came up with what Roy felt was a ridiculous word and put herself in the lead with no tiles left. He had a "J" left and would lose 8 points and the game.

"Fuck your mother! God damn it to holy hell."

The online Websters had confirmed that "Xi" was indeed a word. It is the fourteenth letter of the Greek alphabet. Beto Martinez, one of the top soldiers of the Venganza Cartel knew as much as he watched his boss play. No use to dissuade him though. He would calm down with time. Hopefully no one like the cute stewardess would have to die in the process. Beto waved her away as she further courted disaster by walking towards Roy, no doubt to tell him again to buckle up for landing.

"We are fine. It's okay."

Roy was oblivious. The stewardess would live another day.

"You believe this shit?"

Beto knew he was not expected to reply. He stared straight ahead and waited for the inevitable. Minutes went by and then the shoe dropped.

"How long will it take us to get to Pasadena?"

Roy had moved on. Disaster had been averted. "Big Time Mama" was alive because the game was played in cyberspace. Saved by the Internet.

"It's about 95 miles. A little over an hour drive time."

"Make it an hour. No more. We need to do this and get the fuck out of Gringoland."

"Done, boss."

Roy buckled up just as the landing gear went down. The plane landed without incident. Roy and Beto exited the plane and got into the waiting car. The driver had not recognized the obese man with the unkempt "Grizzly Adams" beard as the head of the biggest cartel in Mexico.

"Good Evening, sir. Welcome to..."

"No further conversation unless you are spoken to. Here is our destination. We need to be there in an hour."

Beto handed the driver the address in Pasadena. The car was on the freeway in a matter of minutes. Roy had been dozing since they entered the car. He raised his head and looked at the driver in the mirror.

"What is your name?"

"Sancho Ramirez, Senor"

"And you are from Mexico?"

"Yes, Senor. I grew up in Tijuana."

"You have a wife and a family?"

"Yes, Senor, a wife and two young children. A girl and a boy."

"That is a wonderful thing. Family is everything. Sancho, if we are pulled over by the police for speeding, for anything really, Beto here will rape your wife and then burn her face off with a blow torch. Your children will not be tortured. I am a civilized man. They will be shot and dropped in an abandoned well. Do you understand me?"

The car veered across the center divider for a moment and then came back.

"Yes, Senor. I understand."

"Now, Beto, please help me with this god damn scrabble. I'm sure this Cabron who is playing me is being helped."

The car drove on as Sancho struggled to keep his composure and prayed that the VIP did not smell the piss leaking through his trousers.

CHAPTER 66

The Home of Dr. Moise Solomon
Burbank, CA

"How do you know he's here? Are you sure it's him?"

Moise Solomon has had a very long, sleepless night. A large part of the responsibility for this lack of sleep could be blamed on Moise himself. Last night, in a moment of weakness he had relayed to his nurse, Rebekah, the love of his life, that Mossad had contacted him with information of the utmost importance involving the head of the Venganza cartel. The most powerful drug and terrorism operation in Mexico and possibly the world. She had not stopped interrogating him about it for the rest of the night and into the morning.

"Moise, I thought this whole Mossad thing was just bullshit. Just another story you let out to entertain the old women in the office. Now you're telling me that it's all true. What the fuck?"

"Hey, my baby! The language, please. You are a good, orthodox Jewish woman."

"Don't make me gag. Tell me how many good, orthodox Jewish women can touch you the way I did last..."

"Okay, okay. You have made your point. Is there any coffee? What is it, six in the morning? I am not getting any sleep. This much is clear."

"I'll make the damn coffee. And after I do, I want to know everything."

Rebekah got out of bed still naked. A middle-aged woman who had kept the body of a 30-year-old. Moise Solomon watched her and only with the discipline that a Spartan, let alone a Mossad deep cover agent, would be proud of kept himself from fondling her and pulling her back into bed.

Moise Solomon had met Rebekah Leibowitz when they both were working with Doctors Without Borders in El Salvador, a little less than a decade ago. He was working with poor families in rural areas. That much was true. The other part, the part that Rebekah had never known, was that he had been recruited by Mossad shortly after arriving.

The process was very subtle yet effective. Mossad had already begun branching out back then. It was in Israel's best interests, not to mention the world's, to bring down the notorious drug cartels that had sprouted up in Mexico and all through Central and South America. It was not just a moral issue but a national security one for Moise's birthplace. It was bad enough that Israel was a country surrounded by millions of people who wanted nothing more than to erase her from the very planet. The people of Israel, particularly the youth, needed to be healthy in mind and body. Moise Solomon, Doctor of Oncology knew that better than most.

He thought of that day as Rebekah put her robe on thereby averting another few hours of passion in bed and headed to the kitchen.

****

It had been early morning in San Salvador. Moise was an ambitious doctor who had found himself treating cases of measles, rabies, typhoid and yellow fever. It made him immensely angry every time he treated a measles case. It was the 21st century, he thought. Why am I treating measles he thought? How could that be? But it was and, indeed, still was the case.

The poor, they will always be poor.

He had arrived at the free clinic on that day so many years ago at five in the morning but already there was a long line, mostly mothers and their children waiting to be seen.

"Doctor Nariz Grande! Good morning. Please help Miguel. Look at all his spots!"

In America and many other places, calling a Jewish doctor "Doctor Big Nose" might be construed as poor taste and maybe even racist. Not here though. The people who came to the Mediclinic San Salvador had grown to love their gringo doctor with the big nose and the funny jokes and always a candy or a small toy for a child. The feeling was reciprocated, as well. A hundred times over. Moise Solomon had found his niche. This was indeed what he wanted to do with his medical training. He would spend his life here. Maybe even marry the cute nurse called Rebekah with the chest like Jayne Mansfield and the heart of the Old Testament Rebekah.

"Juanita, I will take care of him just like all the others. Please wait like the rest of the mothers. We will see your Miguel. Not to worry. He will be okay thanks to modern medicine and six years of NYU medical school."

Juanita smiled, shrugged her head and went back to talking with the other women about their husbands and who was working and who was cheating and the latest Telenovela starring Erika Buenfil. This was the normal routine every Monday, Wednesday and Friday morning when Moise came to the clinic. He not only was used to it but had come to enjoy it. It was wonderful to be among real people after his internship in the Hamptons with the rich and famous (see elite and privileged). Life went on. "And so it goes", as Moise's favorite author, Kurt Vonnegut would say.

"Excuse me, Doctor?"

Moise had turned to see the man with the distinctly midwestern American accent standing before him. He was wearing Bermuda shorts and a flowered shirt along with canvas flip flops. He had the beginnings of a bad sunburn. The guy was the poster boy for *The Ugly American*.

"Yes, can I help you? I am very busy. Wednesday is our heavy day. Well, Christ, they all are busy, as I'm sure you can see. So, what do you need?"

"I'll get to the point. I'm Dick Burtner. I'm with a large company based in the states. Let's just say we are interested in working with you. A business opportunity, you might say."

"Oh Christ. Look, with respect, do I look like a guy that you really want to go into business with? I mean...oh shit of course. You're another god damn pharma company salesman. Jesus, does your HR department know you dress that way when you're trying to fleece doctors?"

"Well. I..."

"Shit! Hey look, I'm sorry. Been a rough week. Kid died on the operating table the other day. Complications from measles for the love of God! It's almost the 21st century. Nobody is supposed to die of measles. For fuck's sake...!"

Juanita had heard all this as had most of the waiting room.

"Doctor, please. Do not blame yourself."

She turned to "Dick" now, "He is a good man. A funny man. He tries so hard. We love him."

"I'm sure. I can see that."

Moise smiled at Juanita and motioned that everything was okay. He took the flower shirted American by the arm and lead him past the line and into the clinic. A moment later they were seated in his cramped office with a picture of Golda Meir and Pope John Paul II on the wall behind the doctor's desk.

"Okay, let's cut right to the fucking chase. Why is the frigging CIA visiting me, a small town doctor who does not...."

"Mossad."

"Okay, look, 'Dick' or whatever the fuck your name is, I..."

"Adam Dohan."

"But..."

"I grew up in Milwaukee. My grandfather was killed in Auschwitz. I'm 45. I went to Marquette. A part of the 'Jew Quota.' Good school actually. I met and married a nice Catholic Irish girl named Katie. I have a son and a daughter. I'm here because your country needs you."

"America is my country. I was born in Jerusalem, but we left when I was two. I grew up in America."

"You are a Jew. You know that being a Jew makes you a permanent citizen of Israel. This is more of a spiritual thing than a man-made certification, and thus it is infinitely more binding. As I said, your country needs you. If it makes you feel better, America needs you as well. We are at war."

"There are wars everywhere. Not just in the Middle East."

"I'm talking about the drug war. Hundreds of the best and brightest of Israel's youth dying every day. Overdose, suicide, car accidents, shot while stealing for drug money. I could go on and on."

"Okay, fine but how can I help. I am a medical doctor. I am interested in saving human beings, all human beings."

"You are far too humble, Moise. May I call you Moise?"

The Mossad man did not wait for an answer.

"Did you know that your name is not of Jewish origin? 'Moise' means 'Crawling Mountain' and is of Native American origin. Anyway, we know that you were an officer in the Israeli Defense Forces."

"I did not see combat. I..."

"You saved two soldiers at the risk of your own life after a Palestinian suicide bomber drove through a checkpoint near Jerusalem. You were the station doctor and just happened to be at the guard post when the truck rammed through the gate.

You ran to the truck as it came to rest. The two guards were disoriented from smoke grenades that had been tossed at them from the would be bomber's truck."

"The bomb didn't go off. I was not interested in being a hero. The truck driver was a terrified 12-year-old Palestinian child. I merely did what anyone would do."

"You tried to cut the bomb off the terrorist. Child or no child, he could have killed several people that day. You calmed the kid down somehow."

"I asked him about his mother. His name was Jaleel. His mother's name was Dalia. He told me she was very sick. I think she probably had cancer. He would kill Israelis and Allah would save his mother, he told me."

"In any case, you saved many soldiers, and you saved the kid."

"I simply told him that we were the same. We were Semites, the both of us. All of us, Arabs and Jews."

"Everyone knows that."

"Yes, but sometimes it's all about the way a fact is conveyed rather than the words alone."

"I don't understand."

"I hugged him when I said it."

"I see. Well..."

"He was killed a few days later. Trying to escape."

"Yes, well, these things happen."

"Oh, is that your answer to thousands of years of senseless war? 'These things happen'?"

"It is what it is. Now, to more pressing matters."

Dohan had handed him a picture of a young girl.

"Who is this and why are you showing me her picture?"

"Her name is Lexy. She is in an orphanage in Mexico. She will be taken to America soon. We need you to follow her."

"To America?"

"Los Angeles to be precise."

"And why should I do this?"

"Because if you don't, Lexy Perez, the incestual spawn of cartel boss, Roy 'Tire Boy' Vasquez, will die before she gets to Children's Hospital, Los Angeles. In any case, you are already a member of Mossad. You were born a Jew in Israel. We need you. Your country needs you. You are Mossad. Congratulations."

"Of course I am concerned about the welfare of a young child but why is this one so important to Mossad?"

"You will know that when it is necessary for you to know. For now you will obey orders."

And that's how it had happened. Just like that.

"Why they hell are you muttering and shaking your head? You were off in space again. I worry about you."

Rebekah was back now wearing a flower dress. Moise was "back" as well. Back in the present. He knew what he must do. The final gesture. Almost quixotic yet so real. No dream here but yes, a tilting at a windmill. This one in the form of Roy Vasquez. Mossad had told Moise that the head of the Venganza cartel was on a quixotic mission himself. That of making his own drug induced personal demons disappear. These demons were near. Their names, Alvina, Paula, Teddy and of course, Ben.

Ben Rooker, widower of dear Rita, now in the cartel crosshairs by another simple twist of fate as our bard from Minnesota, Mr. Robert Zimmerman, AKA Bob Dylan would say.

"Dear Rebekah, the love of my life from now until Armageddon, give me a hug."

CHAPTER 67

Forest Lawn Cemetery
Glendale, CA

"I'm okay, officer. Just a flesh wound, I think. We're both okay."

Alvina and Paula must have gone in the opposite direction as soon as they saw the flashing lights and heard the blaring sirens of the park police. Teddy and I needed to leave soon. Unfortunately, the cops were having none of it.

"Both of you need to come over to the station with us. Going to need to take statements from both of you."

First of all, I needed to get to Alvina. I believed that Paula would kill her as soon as she'd lost her usefulness. That is if Roy didn't get there first. I thought it out very carefully and then did the most sensible thing I could think of.

"Officer, my friend and I cannot go the station with you."

"Yea, well, you are going. Both of you. That's procedure. Now let me help you up. Mr. Dabrowski, you look okay to walk. It's just over that way. Only about a hundred yards. Among that group of brick..."

And that's when Teddy power puked on Officer Davidson. It wasn't just a standard barroom toilet power puke. No, my friends and neighbors this was of *The Exorcist* variety. The ultimate regurgitation. The Super Bowl of projectile vomiting. Are you reading? Great.

The last things I remember about the good Officer Davidson was the look of perplexity. He didn't quite know what had happened to him. Then a second later the face of pure abject horror. Damn, I wish I had had my popcorn.

In any case, since the other responding officers were at the far end of the cemetery searching fruitlessly for Paula and Alvina, Teddy and I made easy work of alluding the petrified policeman. In a matter of moments, we were in my car and on the way to my apartment.

Due to my leg wound, Teddy drove and we arrived at my Pasadena abode a few minutes and one or two near-death experiences later.

"Jesus Christ, how many 18 wheelers did you pass on the right on merge lanes? It must be a record."

"Sit down, I'll bandage you up."

It turned out that I had told the recently puked upon Forest Lawn police officer the truth when I said my wound was not serious. It was just a flesh wound.

"You missed your calling my friend. You should have been a nurse."

"Blow me."

"I'll pass. So, your friend the whack job, sorry, eccentric FBI agent is going to meet us here?"

In between my panic attacks on the *Death Race 3000* drive over here, Teddy had updated me on the current situation and the fact that Special Agent Larue Belmont had landed at Bob Hope Airport in Burbank and would be joining us shortly.

"There are a few things I need to tell you, Ben. Sit down."

"Fire away. Shit, don't take that literally."

"This is serious shit, Ben."

I hadn't seen Teddy like this since the 35er seemingly an eternity ago when he spilled his guts to me about chances not taken, and life changing, might have been, affirmations, all contained in one fateful day in Juarez with a couple of girls calling themselves Veronica and Eileen.

"I hide a lot of things, man. I think maybe you know that already. Anyway, the thing with my upbringing and everything, you know, my father, and all that shit. Well, fuck, I don't even know if that had anything to do with it."

"With what? What's going on man? We are in the middle of some shit here. I frankly don't understand how, but I got to say it's partly my fault. I should have been a better listener. I was always thinking about my own shit. In any case we may be dead by tomorrow morning."

"Now who's being overdramatic?"

"For the love of Christ, out with it."

"I'm in love with Larue Belmont. I'm gay. Or maybe Bi, oh, who cares. Why do I need a fucking label? The point is I love that fucking brush cut, pink bowtie wearing redneck. I have for a while."

"I know."

"What?"

"Paula told me. To tell you the truth, I had an inkling before then. Your body language. How you reacted when we talked about him.

"Anyway, after your first comment I think the 'I'm gay' part was probably a bit redundant. I'm happy for you."

"You're happy for me? That's all you're going to say?"

"Well, I mean your 'Right wing loon, homophobe' label is probably not going to work anymore for you, but other than that, hell yes, I'm damn happy for you. Like I said, I kind of guessed it, anyway."

"Okay, well terrific. I appreciate your understanding. Big relief and all that. There is one other thing, though."

"Yes. Go ahead, bro. What could be more... ah whatever... spill it..."

"I've known Larue for a while."

"Well, I kind of figured that. I mean you need time to fall in...wait a minute. Holy shit! He knew about this whole shit show with Vasquez. That Eileen was... and fuck... god damn it, he planned it... and you were in on it. All these fucking years. I am going to kick your ass right now. Fuck me."

Teddy had just looked at me. I believe he would have let me kick his ass. Then it hit me.

"So, you knew Eileen was dead all along. You knew that Roy had killed her. So, this whole plan was about Eileen..."

"Not entirely."

And then Teddy told me about Larue's other love. The agent who had been tortured and killed along with Eileen.

"Okay, I'm going to hug you now." We shared an embrace. It was good. It had been long overdue. Teddy broke the brief silence.

"Okay, I'm not even going to ask how the hell you knew..."

"Like I said before, I knew you were in love. It was all over your face. When I saw you at Forest Lawn, I didn't know who, of course, until you talked about Belmont. Then it became very obvious. You don't have to be Dr. Fucking Phil. You are nothing if not an easy read, my friend."

Teddy thought about this for a while. I let him run all the various scenarios that were probably going through his mind. The truth of the matter was I was happy that my friend had found someone, but things had not been going very smoothly lately. I mean, we were in deep shit. The following was just an abbreviated list of how screwed we were.

Paula, who we both loved, although it was quite clear now that our love was not the same; mine being of the "biblical sense" variety and Teddy's being, well of the girlfriend variety, wanted to kill us both. Christ was the "girlfriend" comment homophobic? At that point I didn't care. My leg was actually starting to throb a bit. We now probably had the entire Glendale, Pasadena and more than likely the LAPD joining the Park police in pursuit of us. God knew what Alvina's desires were. Who knew what Paula had told her about Teddy and me? She might have kissed Teddy or shot his nuts off.

These people were all very small fish of course. The Great Brown Burrito was coming for us, not to mention his henchmen. We knew that Roy Vásquez was not coming to Pasadena alone. He would have some highly trained, sick ass mother fucking hombres with him. Roy didn't care who he killed, really. By all accounts he had been so loaded up on his own product he would have made Hunter S. Thompson look like a Miller Lite drinker. No, we needed to get focused. Soon.

It's raining men...

Teddy's new ring tone. I'm serious. He picked it up and by the look on his face, it was Larue Belmont. Teddy actually fixed his hair before he spoke to him. I tried to give him some privacy, but shit, our lives were on the line. Belmont, the future "Mr. Dabrowski" or not was an integral part in keeping us alive. I mean he was the FBI agent in this allegory.

"Thank God, you're okay. We're here at Ben's place. You should have my text with the address. Fifteen minutes? Okay. Yea, we're good. Ben has a flesh wound. Oh, and we had to ditch a few park police. Don't get mad. Jesus. Just get here as soon as you can. Okay. Yeah, me too."

"I'm assuming that wasn't a telemarketer?"

"Larue. He'll be here in..."

"Yea, 15 minutes. When one goes gay does one lose their sense of humor? Forget I asked that. Does he have a plan?"

"He'll fill us in when he gets here."

My friend was acting kind of strange right then. I mean he was an emotional guy, subject to outbursts of violence one moment and then tears of joy another. None of that was happening at that moment. He was like one of the pod people in *Invasion of the Body Snatchers*, the original made in 1956 and starring Kevin McCarthy, not the remake with Donald Sutherland. Anyway, I told you the backstory on that earlier, about it being filmed in Sierra Madre. It's not important right now.

I went into my little kitchen to make some coffee. Starbucks Breakfast Blend. Teddy's a Chock Full of Nuts guy. I am not going anywhere with that one. At this point, though, I don't think he cares. As I was filling up the filter in my Mr. Coffee circa 2002 my iPhone vibrated.

Unknown Caller
"Hello."
"Hello, Ben."
The Voice.
"You're a zero. Not my son. A zero."

CHAPTER 68

Paula's Condo, Glendale, CA

"So, I still don't completely understand how my baby died."

Alvina had been interrogating Paula for the last half hour. Ever since they made their "escape" from Forest Lawn Cemetery. Too many questions. Well, in any case just a few more hours. He would be here soon. Then this would all be over, the head of the Literally Healing Program at Children's Hospital thought as she made some coffee and looked forward to her next decidedly different position.

Paula Garcia finished pouring the contents of the Starbuck's breakfast blend into the Mr. Coffee cone. She smiled to herself as she thought that this might be the last coffee she would ever make herself. By this time tomorrow she would be incredibly rich and powerful if all went as planned. Now if this Puta would stop asking questions all would be well.

"The coffee will be ready soon. You take Sweet and Low and creamer, right?"

"Why do you continue to ignore my questions? I thought you were my friend. To tell you the truth, I am not sure anymore."

"I told you. She was born with cancer. It was Leukemia. A rare form the doctors told us. I cared for her as best I could at the hospital."

"You are lying to me. When Father Jim took her out of that shit hole orphanage she was sick but heading for the treatment that could save her."

"Father Jim was a god damn child molester. He must not be believed. He was using Lexy and you, your entire family, don't you understand?"

Alvina was on her feet. She had gone face to face with Paula in the kitchen. There was an air of impending catastrophe. Both women felt it though they gave away nothing. Time went by without either of them noticing. Seconds? Minutes? Who knows?

Finally, "I know all about fucking child molesters. My father was one. How the fuck do you think Lexy was born!?"

"Why you bitch! How dare you insult your father, the greatest man in Mexico. The benefactor to his people. The savior of the children."

This was too much for the younger woman.

"What the fuck has happened to you? He killed your brother! Wait, you're with him now, aren't you? This was all a trick, a set-up! Holy fuck. He's coming here, isn't he? I'm getting the hell out of here. I'm going to see that you rot in prison for what..."

Alvina saw the needle a nanosecond too late. Paula caught her as she passed out and carried her to the bedroom. She laid her prostate body on top of the covers, closed the blind and turned off the light.

Paula knew that Roy Vasquez was a flawed man but she also knew that she could change him. Even when he went astray. She loved him from the very first night she consoled him after Rose had deserted him. She had looked on it as a chance to kill him but then something changed in her. It was subtle at first. His problem was the drugs and the alcohol, she told herself. He was in his heart a good man. He even loved animals, she thought. Yes, her Roy would be here soon, and she would prove how much she loved him. In medical jargon, Paula had become a victim of The Stockholm Syndrome, a psychological affliction that causes victims to embrace their captors. It had been a gradual process. Indeed she had hated Roy Vasquez at one time. That was real. No matter though, Paula's pain over the death of her brother so many years ago had been eased, in fact vanquished by her new love for the man who had killed him. Human beings are complex creatures especially when it comes to dealing with pain.

It had been a good idea to bring the heavy dose of syringe-delivered Ativan from the hospital, thought Paula as she put on make-up and began to put on her favorite black dress for his imminent arrival. Soon everything would be the way it was supposed to be. She would take her rightful place at his side. The mistake that was Lexy would be forgotten and along with it her mother, Alvina. Yes, Alvina would have to be taken care of. Out of the picture for good, thought Paula. She would have to wait for Roy. To kill Alvina herself would be a mistake. Assuming too much, she thought. Yes, she would wait for her deliverance. Only a matter of time.

Time healed all wounds.

I loved you.

"Who is that?"

Paula didn't dare turn around for fear of seeing the thing she dreaded most in all the world. She knew it couldn't be Alvina. She'd given her enough Ativan to subdue a small elephant.

Father Jim said you would protect me. You promised to protect me. Why did you let me die?

"Oh, Jesus God!"

Paula saw the shadow of the small figure out of the corner of her eye. She caught a glimpse of the light blue hospital gown. She didn't dare turn around any further. Her primeval instinct told her to flee, and she ran. Full of terror and a reckless abandonment reserved for the frightened and the guilt-ridden she headed for the living room and the door. Unbeknownst to her, Ben had left a sofa cushion lying on the floor. The always tidy Paula was startled as she took it underfoot and fell forward, landing face first on the corner of the coffee table her dear Roy had sent her last year for her birthday, her head cracking open like one of the coconuts she fantasized about savoring with him, her love, her only love, Roy Vasquez. Lounging in some idyllic resort. The squalor of her childhood a distant memory. She lay prostrate on the carpet, the rich red blood pouring from just above her eye. She swore she could see a clerical collar. It couldn't be, she thought.

"Father Jim? Is that you? I'm sorry, Father Jim. I'm sorry I lied. I had to. Don't you unders..."

Her head was pounding. The lights slowly went off. The music ceased as the darkness engulfed her.

CHAPTER 69

Parking Lot Outside Paula's Condo
Glendale, CA

Moises Solomon pulled his car up to the security shack and lowered his window to speak to the guard, "I'm looking for a dear friend of mine. She relocated here recently. She was a nurse when we worked together in South America."

The security guard would be done with his shift in a few minutes. The last thing Gino Alonso wanted to do was give this big nosed clown information on a resident. He was pretty sure he was looking for that hotty in 301, Paula Garcia. She was one stuck-up bitch, he thought. In any case he needed to get over to the Colorado for Happy Hour. That Pasadena City College chick, Lola, was bar tending tonight. He thought he just might have a chance with her. Talk to her about Richard Bach and *Jonathan Livingston Seagull*. It was amazing that she had never heard of that book. Gino was an old bastard but he knew how to read these college girls. They said they wanted to be independent, but deep down they all wanted a real man. Well, Gino was that, whatever his ex-wife Angie thought, that fucking bitch. Running off with that plumber of all people. His best god damn friend to boot. Anyway, he needed to get over there. Get rid of this Jew Boy somehow.

"Okay look, I got to go. I can't give out any info..."

Moise Solomon handed him the fifty dollar bill and was amazed how quickly it disappeared from his hand into the security guard's pocket. His feelings about the common man had taken yet another kick in the teeth. The guard now smiling in a shit-eating manner said, "Paula Garcia. Unit 301. You didn't get that info from me."

"Of course not. Thank you so..."

The guard was in his car and had already started to drive away.

Moise sighed as he parked in a guest spot.

He got out of the car and looked around in the studied way of a trained Mossad. Taking in everything while he appeared to be looking at nothing in particular. He took the safety off his .22 LRS hand gun and headed into the building but not without being spotted by one of the two occupants of a van nearby.

"We have company."

"Where?"

"12 o'clock"

"What the fuck is 12 o'clock?! Just point or say left or right. Enough with the fucking *Mission Impossible* shit!"

"Sorry, boss. Straight ahead about 100 yards."

Roy Vasquez had had a rough couple of days. Three days off the cocaine, to be exact. Off everything, truth be told. No booze, drugs, nothing. Just a shitload of Starbucks expresso to keep him going.

"Is that the Jew? Jesus he looks good. Lost some weight since San Salvador. Still got that nose though. What is it with the Jews and the noses?"

"I don't know, Senor. I mean Italians have big..."

"You are getting on my last nerve, Beto. It was a rhetorical question. It doesn't need an answer. You get me? Wait. What the fuck is he doing. He's walking straight towards us. You don't think he saw us do you?"

Before Beto could answer, the front tire of the van exploded.

"Jesu Cristo, the mother fucker is shooting at us. Run the bastard over!"

Beto started the van, released the emergency brake, put it into drive, as the Mossad/oncologist fired five more rounds. One of them took Beto's ear off. The last went through his eye leaving a gaping hole in the back of his head where blood flowed out like a broken soda fountain that Roy remembered from his youth. Beto slumped forward onto the van horn which sent a shrill monotonous blare throughout the parking lot.

Roy was just a young boy and his mother had taken him to an ice cream parlor in Central Mexico. Roy didn't remember the town, but he remembered the soft vanilla ice cream and the cherry soda that his mother poured from the machine. Just as she had filled his cup halfway something malfunctioned in the soda machine's inner mechanism spraying red liquid all over his mother's new dress. Little Roy felt so sad for his mama. He felt like it was all his fault. He knew that's what his father would say. Mama was different though. Her stunned face broke into the most beautiful laughter Roy had ever seen or heard. She laughed so much that it became contagious. Roy laughed along with her. He had the best day of his young life.

"Hands on your head, 'Tire Boy' or whatever they call scum like you these days. Up! Now!"

Back to the present. Glendale, CA. Beto's brains mixed with the "cherry soda" on the seat next to him. The Jew doctor crouched down in front of the van, his Mossad Special with silencer attachment pointed at Roy's temple. Roy looked around. A few people off in the distance. All oblivious. Life in L.A.

"You did not have to shoot Beto. He's just a driver. I am only here to visit my daughter."

The Mossad agent opened the driver's side door and kept his gun trained on Roy's torso. He glanced at Beto's body.

"Get out of the van. Your driver? Beto Martinez, on every Interpol and FBI list in the world. Responsible for at least 35 murders, including women and children. Until about two minutes ago, your personal bodyguard, after the untimely demise of your last one. I may practice oncology but I still have access to Mossad files. Now, here is what's going to happen. I am going to put my weapon under my shirt as so. You will turn the van off and leave the keys. You will then take your gun out and leave it on the floor board. I know you have at least a Glock. There you go. Now place it down under the steering wheel so it can be easily found. I am going to walk around the van and come up behind you. You will walk and I will talk. When we get to my vehicle, I'll give you further instructions. If you yell for help or make any sudden move, I will not hesitate to put one in your head. Do you have any questions? Good."

Roy thought of that crazy movie with the American actor Lloyd Bridges about 40 years ago. *Airplane* was what it was called. He had commiserated with Bridges' character. Yes, indeed.

He had picked "The wrong week to give up oven cleaner."

CHAPTER 70

Paula Garcia's Condo
Glendale, CA

The same dream again. Alvina was walking towards Lexy's hospital bed. She had heard the child's voice but couldn't make out what she was saying. Closer now. Then the smell. A putrid smell. A combination of onions and moth balls. Closer and closer. The voice was clearer now but no longer that of a child. It is that of an old woman. Yes, an old, feeble woman. There was a curtain. The scent was overwhelming. She hesitated in front of the curtain. There was a shadow showing through. It was a bent figure. Alvina was terrified. She turned to run away but a cold, bony hand grabbed her and held her back. She looked up and screamed as she saw what had once been Father Jim but was now a skeleton with a cleric's collar. She turned back again and the curtain opened. It was Lexy, but she was a hundred years old. Green foam was pouring out of her mouth. She was smiling but had no teeth. She struggled to speak just as a wretched creature emerged from her gnarled mouth. It was an aborted fetus. Alvina started to scream but nothing could be heard. A ringing, blaring sound was coming from the fetus. RING. RING. RING.

Alvina awakened. The dream was over but the ringing continued. RING. RING.

She looked around and realized that she was in Paula's bedroom. She had some recollection of an argument with Paula but couldn't remember what it was about. It was all on the fringes. She would remember soon, she thought.

RING. RING. RING.

There was someone at the door.

Why isn't Paula answering her door?

Now the handle was being turned. Jostled.

"Look let's just get security and have them let us in for Christ sake."

"And what reason are we going to give? My friend Teddy and I are here because we believe that Ms. Paula Garcia the owner of this condominium is going to kill one Alvina Vasquez or whatever her name is these days. Oh, and furthermore, Mr. Security Guard, we are expecting the head of the Venganza Cartel to drop in for coffee fairly soon, as well. We don't know why the fuck he is coming or who he wants to kill, but we got this tidbit on good authority from Larue Belmont, Rogue FBI Agent and most recently the lover of my friend here, Mr. Teddy Dabrowski."

"I am going to punch the shit out of you."

Teddy and I had been ringing the damn bell for several minutes. We were just about to take more aggressive measures which, by the look of Teddy's eyes might have involved yours truly's head being used as a battering ram, when, lo and behold the door opened.

"Hello Paula. Damn that is a nice bump you've got...Hey, how about pointing that gun someplace else?"

"Get in here. The both of you. Sit on the couch. Don't say a word."

Paula had looked a helluva a lot better. Blood-red eyes. Dried blood caked in her hair and a disposition I wanted nothing to do with right then. Neither did Teddy. We sat as directed. Someone was in another room. Trying not to make any noise. Failing. Teddy saw her first.

"Oh Jesus! Veronica? It's you. It is you. I'm so sorry."

My buddy had broken down. A pile of Jell-O on the living room rug. Paula looked like she was about to shoot him when Veronica nee Alvina ran to him.

"It's not your fault, Teddy. I know that now."

Alvina was glaring at Paula now.

"I know everything. It's not your fault. It never was. We had no chance. Me, you, Eileen. We had no chance. We were all in Juarez at the wrong time."

Ah yes. That simple twist of fate again. So here was Alvina. In the flesh. Up close. No longer the phantom figure running from us in the cemetery. I felt for her. I really did.

"Get up Alvy. Don't touch him. Go back in the kitchen and go to the first cabinet on the left. There's some duct tape and rope. Get a knife out of the utensil drawer too. Hurry up."

"Paula, what are you? What the fuck. Children's Hospital. The kids. Lexy, for the love of God."

"That's funny. Real funny, Teddy. You never were the kind of guy who could see past his own nose. The big picture. No, you self-obsessed fucker, that's why it was so easy to use you. To get close to dear Lexy, to..."

"What are you saying? Lexy? What the fuck did Lexy have to do with any of this?"

Alvina had come out of the kitchen and was holding a rope, duct tape and a rather large butcher knife. Teddy sensed an opening and pleaded with her.

"Alvy! What are you..."

"It's Alvina. Alvina Vasquez. But you know that already, don't you, you gringo bastard."

Apparently Alvina was not sure what was up and what was down. She had no idea who her friends were. She was exhibiting mood swings that would be the envy of a 13-year-old girl with an unlimited Tic Tok account. I realized then and there that if I, or Teddy, or Larue Belmont; if he ever got his dead ass over here, could not bring her around, well, we would all be wearing flame tire tiaras on our heads very soon. I had a real sense that Alvina's dear padre was in the general area. Teddy had hinted as much on the way over.

"That's my girl. Now you are coming around. Now, just tie both their hands behind their backs. Use the knife to cut a few pieces of rope. Don't worry, I have the gun on them. I'll blow off their balls if they move."

"This obsession with the destruction of testicles is unbecoming, Paula. I mean I know you..."

The glass tumbler crashed off the wall missing my head by inches. Back to plan A. No talking.

Alvina finished tying us up. She was good at it. Why was I surprised? I mean when all was said and done, she was the daughter of Roy 'Tire Boy" Vasquez.

"Very good, Alvy. Now if you both promise to speak only when spoken to, we will hold off on duct taping your mouths shut."

I hated duct tape unless it was applied voluntarily during the second or third date, and Teddy's head would have exploded if he could not physically speak for any period.

"We're good."

"Excellent. Alvy, sit behind the couch. I don't want Teddy making any phony gestures to you. You are still fragile, my baby, and he knows that. They both do."

Alvy looking a bit dazed said, "I need something. Coffee. Please. It feels like I have been drugged."

"You were tired from the emotional stress. Yes. There is coffee in the kitchen. Bring me one too, please."

"I'll have one too. Cream and a couple of...."

Paula with the agility of a desert bobcat lunged across her chair and hit Teddy square on the jaw with her Glock. Blood started to trickle from his mouth.

"Not another word. My last warning."

"Paula, why are you hitting him? I don't understand."

Paula sensed that she might be losing control of the young woman. She knew that her mood could change in an instant. A kinder, gentler approach was needed.

"Alvina, this is all for you. Whatever I have done is only for you."

Alvina nodded, albeit hesitantly and went into the kitchen. A few minutes later she returned with two cups. She handed one of them to Paula who drank it with a smile.

"Thank you, my little angel."

Teddy was about to speak when...

RING. RING.

"Say a word and you are all dead. I'll kill Alvina as well."

Paula had used her best stage whisper.

RING. RING.

"Paula, it is Roy. Please open the door. I am hurt. I need help. Please open the door. They are after me. Beto is dead. Hurry. They are coming. The gringo bastards. Please."

"Papa, I'm coming."

"No, you stupid bitch. Stay away from the door."

Alvina was having none of this. She got up and ran towards the voice of her father. Paula turned the gun on her. Just as I was expecting the report of the Glock and Alvina's body to slump on the ground something amazing happened. The gun fell from Paula's hand. She stared straight ahead for a brief moment and then fell forward in a heap. A mixture of red and yellow liquid had slowly poured from her mouth onto the carpet. Alvina stopped for a second to glance at her. She surveyed the body and then the coffee cup without emotion and continued to the door. The Dark Web that Paula had introduced her to was also a wonderful market for drugs of the deadly variety. She appreciated the irony as she pulled the door open and the bound Roy Vasquez, the head of the Venganza Cartel, came tumbling in followed by my former oncologist and part-time Mossad agent, Moise Solomon.

CHAPTER 71

The 134 Freeway
Two miles from Glendale, CA

"Look, I can't explain anymore right now. It's a condo in Glendale. Yelp says it's on..."

Larue Belmont had always hated people who texted when they drove. A horrible habit. Of course this was an exception. He believed that Teddy was in dire circumstances. He needed to get help to the scene. It no longer mattered that his career would be effectively over when it was discovered he had broken countless FBI directives while going rogue these last few years. It didn't matter that the ends justified the means. All this was a moot point though as, having just swerved into the lane of an 18 wheeler while attempting to drive and find the unit number of Paula Garcia's condo on his phone simultaneously, his rental had become airborne and was headed across two lanes of traffic and towards an embankment. He was about to die. He knew it.

He closed his eyes and waited to meet whoever was running this shit show. He had a few things to say to him, her, they, whatever.

Then everything stopped.

Caltrans is short for California Department of Transportation. They are the department that oversees road maintenance among other transportation needs. Part of this maintenance involves sprinkler systems which in this high tech age that we live in are governed by computers. These computers are housed in the stainless steel boxes that you see along the road and probably never thought twice about. They are caller "controllers" and are sophisticated timers which turn water on and off. They are wonderful inventions; when they work.

It seems that the particular controller that was responsible for turning off the sprinkler that Larue Belmont's car sat on now surrounded by two feet of mud had been vandalized two weeks ago. California maintenance priorities being what they are, Caltrans resources that normally would be used to fix this controller were deployed to cleaning up a homeless encampment at an underpass a half a mile down the freeway. This sprinkler had been running constantly for days until it got so buried with mud that it stopped but not before creating a quagmire worthy of monsoon season in the Philippines. Larue Belmont's car, which had been launched off the freeway after sideswiping that 18 wheeler just a few moments before, under normal circumstances would have been destined for a rendezvous with a rather large tree. Instead, it had come to an abrupt finish not unlike that of an F-35C fighter jet being caught by a catapult trap on a U.S. Navy aircraft carrier.

"What the fuck!? What's that? No, I'm okay. Just had a little interference. Yea, LA traffic. What was I saying? Probably not important. Look, I'll get back to you soon. Got to recharge my phone."

Larue Belmont, Special Agent, Federal Bureau of Investigation discreetly checked his shorts. Miraculously they were not soiled. He said a quiet prayer to Saint Anthony, the patron saint of lost causes. He then went back to searching for Paula Garcia's unit number for her last known address. After a call to Triple A and then an Uber, he found himself on Stockton Ave about a half hour later.

"You don't want to go right to 301, Larue? I can take you. No problem."

"No thanks. I want to surprise my cousin. Plus, I need a little exercise."

"No worries. Have a great day."

He gave the Uber driver five stars and then put his phone away.

Steve Radcliffe was a racist, a homophobe and a few other things that made him a decidedly unsavory character. All things considered, though, he was a damn good plant manager. Larue Belmont knew this. It was the main reason he put up with his shit for as long as he did. He had discovered at an early age that one could learn something constructive from anyone. Never discount a person out of hand. One of the lessons his first love had taught him. So now as he walked towards the facilities office that serviced Paula Garcia's HOA, he remembered what he had learned from old, not so dearly departed Steve Radcliffe, the plant manager at Huntington Hospital. The guy who helped fake Teddy Dabrowski's death also knew quite a lot about the inner systems of buildings. What made them work and, more importantly, what could make them stop working.

"What's up? What can I do for you? What unit are you in?"

"Oh no, I'm sorry, I'm not a resident here. I have a friend that lives here, though. I feel kind of weird about this. Okay, here goes. You see my friend, well she's really my fiancé, and I wanted to surprise her."

"Hey, buddy, you need to check with the main office."

Larue was seated in the facilities office eying the name plate behind the desk. "Oscar Shank, Facilities Supervisor." Directly behind his desk was a picture of Bin Laden with an American eagle taking a shit on his head. Oscar was about 5'5", in his mid-forties with a comb-over that would make Trump's hair look real in comparison. It wasn't just the comb-over. It was whatever the hell Oscar was using to color what was left up there. It had shades of cottony white along with a streak of blood red and even a bit of green. It reminded Larue of the peacock's hindquarters he had seen during mating season at the Los Angeles Arboretum months ago. He was entranced until the suggestion of going to the main office broke the spell.

"I'm with the FBI, Oscar. Can I call you Oscar? The friend thing is bullshit. I need to cut to the chase. I need your help and I needed it yesterday. Nothing that I say can leave this room. We are talking about global terrorism at its highest level. You got me?"

"Fucking rag heads! I knew it. I bet it's that fucking Packi couple with the snot-nosed little bastard that just moved in. She says she's a doctor. Whoever heard of a female camel fucker that was a doctor?"

"Yes, indeed. Anyway, Oscar can you help me?"

"Whatever you need, Special Agent. America first!"

Larue made a mental note that if he ever got out of this alive, he would run a computer analysis on the percentage of racist, homophobe plant managers in the United States.

"Your country thanks you. Now... what can you tell me about the plumbing system in this complex?"

CHAPTER 72

Paula Garcia's Condo
Glendale, CA

"She is quite dead, I am afraid."

This was not a real surprise to anyone in the room. Ms. Garcia had been starting to reek for lack of a better word within the last few minutes. I noted the time as 5:15 PM as I picked up my phone with my very sore hands. Alvina was way too good at tying people up. Unfortunately, she was horrible at untying people as was noted by the scrapes on my wrists and Teddy's as she cut us loose with a box cutter. Stressful moments indeed.

"What a sad and tragic day this has been. First my dear Beto and now Paula. We must all say a prayer."

Alvina had been visibly torn from the moment her father had made his entrance, but she had been holding herself together. This last comment from this despicable cur who happened to be her rapist and the father of her dead child changed all that. Moise Solomon saw the gleam of the box cutter blade first. He caught Alvina's arm with the point of the razor a millimeter from the cartel boss's jugular.

"Let me kill him. Scum! Scum of the Earth!"

"It's okay. Please calm down, senorita. He will pay. Not this way, though."

"Oh, my dear baby, what kind of swill has your dear departed mother put in your brain? I love you. I have always loved you."

"You need to keep quiet unless you want me to duct tape every fucking orifice on your body," Solomon uncharacteristically going to street mode. The hate he had for Vasquez unbridled now.

"May I use the bathroom? I have to piss like a race horse, as I believe you Americans say."

"Piss on yourself like the animal that you are."

For some ungodly reason I felt sorry for Roy Vasquez at that moment. I will never know quite why. Maybe it was because despite all he had done, he was still the father of Alvina, this damaged young woman that I had become strangely attached to.

"I'll take him to the bathroom. Just give me a gun. We don't want this place smelling any worse than it already does."

Teddy, who would have under normal circumstances, stopped me from doing such a moronic thing as escorting a sadistic murderer to take a piss was not, shall we say, emotionally available to save me at this moment. He had not taken his eyes off Paula's body since we entered the condo. With everything that had happened, Teddy still had feelings for her. Whether those feelings were platonic, involved love, or were just the product of a dysfunctional upbringing that bred guilt, codependency, and dates that ended with 911 calls, remained to be seen. Suffice it to say, Teddy Dabrowski was not himself at this moment.

I took Paula's Glock from Moise.

"It's loaded. Just press the trigger. That will disengage the three safeties. Unload all ten rounds on the scum if he even looks at you the wrong way. Keep the bathroom door open."

Great. So, there I was next to Roy as he started to pull his zipper down while standing over the toilet. One hand had been untied as there is no way in hell that I was going to be holding *It*. The door was open, but the bathroom was off to the right of the living room so we were out of view. Something I hadn't realized until it was too late. I was pointing the gun at his torso. We were two feet from each other. No way I could miss him.

Then, just as Roy was about to commence urinating, I realized that Paula's bathroom had a wonderful scent of lavender. In the nanosecond that the itch made its way from my chest, throat and then my nostrils I remembered that I was allergic to all forms of lavender.

I sneezed.

Roy's hand went from his dick to my gun hand in a flash. The gun landed in the sink and he grabbed it.

"Are you okay, Ben?"

Of course, I should have responded in the negative to Moise Solomon's question. The downside of course was that I would have been dead. There was no upside. Roy had already freed his other hand and was whispering to me while the Glock was pointed a centimeter from my head.

"I'm fine. Yes. No worries."

Roy motioned me to lie next to the toilet while he actually commenced to piss. I guess when you got to go, you got to go.

And this, my fellow travelers, as I'm sure you remember is where the journey started.

Yes, the man has a prostrate. A very good one. Amazing, given how he has treated his body over the years. I'm thinking about what an inglorious way this would be to die. Being shot in the head by a guy who has just splattered remnants of at least a gallon of his piss on me.

He finishes.

I await eternity.

Apparently, Roy was too engrossed in his piss that he didn't hear the hissing. It started like a low whisper and then built to a cacophony of cobra-like sounds. I instinctively put my hands over my face, turned away and curled up in a fetal position.

"What the fuck are you..."

BOOM.

I dare not look up as I feel a brief yet intense heat emanating from the toilet directly above my head. After a moment though, Roy's screams make it impossible to avoid a quick gaze to my right.

I don't actually trust what I am seeing. I brush pieces of ceramic and paint chips away from my eyes and stare. What I see is something that every inch of my being wants to turn away from, yet I continue to stare, fixated.

Roy has two stumps where his hands use to be.

Something not unlike burnt underbrush has replaced what was once his manhood. He collapses headfirst into what was a few seconds ago a toilet and is now a firepit which effectively burns most of Roy's face off.

The condo door shatters as Larue Belmont and some weird looking guy with a "Live Free or Die" ball cap and chewing tobacco drool come barging in. Larue hesitates for a moment and he and "Tobacco Drool Guy" go straight to the area where the bathroom used to be. I am ignored.

"How much fucking gas did you re-direct here? It was supposed to be a diversionary tactic. You almost blew the whole god damn place up."

"Tobacco Drool Guy" is a bit frazzled, and it doesn't seem to be helping that a 6'3" southern boy is right in his face.

"Look, Mr....."

"Special Agent to you!"

"Okay, yea, Special Agent, you didn't give me any time. I mean, I thought we were supposed to be saving the country. I did the best I could considering ..."

"Yea, yea, considering... considering you are a fucking moron!"

"Hey, okay, let's keep it down here. Is everybody okay. Aside, of course, for Mr. Vasquez here."

Teddy is trying to calm the situation. The explosion brought him out of his stupor. Alvina joins the rest of them at the entrance to what was the bathroom. She begins spitting on her father's body and tries to punch him. I hold her back. I hug her. I can feel the beat of her heart. Her tears on my cheek now. I might just love this woman.

Fire engines with sirens blaring are entering the parking lot below.

"Don't say a word. I will take care of everything. Everyone leave. Now."

We did, and Moise Solomon, oncologist/Mossad agent, good as his word, took care of everything.

EPILOGUE

February, 2020
Huntington Hospital,
Pasadena, CA

I got away with some minor cuts and scrapes. The gas leak that Oscar the Plant Manager had jerry-rigged into the plumbing system was isolated to the toilet the late Roy Vasquez had been standing over. The flames shot straight up out of the toilet, thus having the effect of a point blank blow torch on Roy while limiting my injuries. It was fate that Roy happened to be standing there when he was. It could have been anyone. I thought it was also pure luck that I had been knocked to the bathroom floor a few feet from the toilet by Roy when he had grabbed my gun and I had instinctively gone into "turtle mode", thus protecting myself from the ensuing vertical firestorm.

You really think so, Ben?

"No, I guess I don't Lexy. Probably not fate at all"

Right now, I'm visiting Teddy in the hospital. Nothing serious like being blown up in a café bombing. No, this time just a bit of fatigue and upper respiratory problems. Probably a touch of the flu or bronchitis from overwork. Larue Belmont, no longer a member of the FBI, by mutual consent, but most definitely Teddy Dabrowski's husband, was worried enough to have Teddy admitted yesterday. Teddy, who still had an ear out for any and all global conspiracies, had heard some talk of biological lab mishaps in China or some such place.

"Fucking CHICOMS," some of the colorful dialogue we experienced as we drove him to the hospital.

We are still awaiting tests. Come to think of it, I'm feeling a bit run down myself. I'm alone, though, so nobody is forcing me into any hospital. Not yet, anyway.

I dated Alvina for a while after the incident at Paula Garcia's condo. Try as I could to win her heart, it was clear that it was meant for someone else and seeing as that person happened be Teddy, we both would share the misery of unrequited love. On the positive side, I've had coffee with Francine Lattimore a few times and find her quite alluring in a sick kind of way. Oh well. We'll have time to get to know each other as she is transferring to the FBI office in Los Angeles.

As I said, Larue Belmont left the FBI but not before receiving a medal and a nice pension. All completely private. All despite the fact that Joe McManus, his boss, wanted to put him in a super max and throw away the key.

Larue's cohort that fateful day at Paula Garcia's condo got a nice stipend as well. The last we heard, Oscar Shank is in Costa Rica running a bait shop and publishing an ultra-right wing newsletter. I don't expect the poor guy to be around much longer.

The only proviso for Larue Belmont was that he could not talk about his part in the toppling of Roy Vasquez and the Venganza Cartel. Larue was fine with that. He built a bookstore/café at the site of the Bard. Teddy became the manager. They called it The Second Act.

I will never have to pay for coffee there for the rest of my life.

When I'm sad, I visit Lexy. I don't even have to go to her grave. It seems that if I just think of her, she is with me. She still "speaks" to me. Her voice is as clear as if I was talking to Teddy at the old Bard Café. She still can be quite playful and a bit mysterious.

The other day she told me to buy a mask and lots of toilet paper.

END

ACKNOWLEDGEMENTS

SILVER OR LEAD was written during the Pandemic of 2020. That is a very important fact. To understand the tone of the novel one must know that during that period my Mom died, my cat Claudius passed suddenly, and my marriage went south. I escaped to my man cave and poured out all of my anger, pain and hatred towards my God via the conduit of my Mac Air. In the end I came out, well, redeemed. I don't recommend this process to all novelists. It was mine though and it informed my story. I came to the end a better person... and I stayed sober. An incredibly good result for a recovering alcoholic with almost 19 years off the "booze and the one-night stands." None of this would have been possible without my best friend, Ron Scibilia. He was the model for Teddy and he kept me going with his words of encouragement during our weekly zoom calls and later our coffees at Vroman's bookstore in Pasadena. Thank you, Ron.

I'm eternally grateful to my late mother Lucille, who's positive outlook even in the darkest of times has influenced my life and the lives of my brothers and sister to this day. She was the strongest of women. I love you, Mom.

To Bien Cox, who read my early drafts and was not afraid to give me a "tough love" critique, and pushed me back to my lap top when I wanted to quit, thank you from the bottom of my heart. I am always here for you wherever you may be. To the original Meredith Brucker Writers Group; Meredith Brucker, Lynn Palmer and Aly Kay and John Leland, thank you for listening to my early forays into the world of fiction and telling me what worked and what didn't, always with a smile. To my father, Walter Cox, a guy who tilted at Windmills until one day the storm borne of a life of addiction engulfed him and carried him to the abyss. I found your unfinished novel behind the bar that summer day in August years ago. It was good, Dad, damn good. To my siblings, Walter, Patrick and Maryellen, we made it and we came out pretty good, all things considered. I love you all. To Bill Wilson and Doctor Bob Smith who met in Akron in 1935 and saved my life and the lives of millions of others, my eternal gratitude and the promise that I will always be there whenever another alcoholic asks for help. To my current and past life muses, some here, some gone, Steve Beilman, Jimmy Thomas, Gino and Jeanne Ardito, Harris Shore, Shae Popovich, Mike Davis, Mike Horner, Kevin Coleman, Mary Jarrett, Victoria Patterson, Susan Taylor Chehak, Art Chamberlain, Mac McKenna, Ed Franks, Mark Michelson, Judy O'Keefe and Mrs. Biggs, my 7th grade English teacher who taught me how to diagram a sentence and to always be a gentleman, God Bless you all. Last but certainly not least, to my wonderful creative team at Black Rose Writing who took a chance on a first time novelist; Reagan Rothe, David King, Justin Weeks, Christopher Miller and Minna Rothe, thank you!

Onward

James Cox

August 27th, 2021

ABOUT THE AUTHOR

James Cox is a writer, an actor and a twenty-year veteran of the U.S. Navy.

Silver or Lead is his first novel. James has written several plays which have been presented at various Los Angeles area theaters. *Love, Madness and Somewhere in Between*, a solo show that James wrote and performed in at the Hudson Theatre, won the Ovation Award at the 2019 Hollywood Fringe Festival.

He is currently working on his second novel, a thriller set in Japan. He dedicates *Silver or Lead* to his late mother, Lucille.

He lives in Pasadena, CA.

NOTE FROM THE AUTHOR

Word-of-mouth is crucial for any author to succeed. If you enjoyed *Silver or Lead*, please leave a review online—anywhere you are able. Even if it's just a sentence or two. It would make all the difference and would be very much appreciated.

Thanks!
James Cox

We hope you enjoyed reading this title from:

BLACK ROSE
writing™

www.blackrosewriting.com

Subscribe to our mailing list – *The Rosevine* – and receive **FREE** books, daily deals, and stay current with news about upcoming releases and our hottest authors.
Scan the QR code below to sign up.

Already a subscriber? Please accept a sincere thank you for being a fan of Black Rose Writing authors.

View other Black Rose Writing titles at
www.blackrosewriting.com/books and use promo code
PRINT to receive a **20% discount** when purchasing.

CPSIA information can be obtained
at www.ICGtesting.com
Printed in the USA
LVHW040502300122
709511LV00003B/14

9 781684 339211